SYLVIA GARLAND'S BROKEN HEART

SYLVIA GARLAND'S BROKEN HEART

HELEN HARRIS

HALBAN
LONDON

First published in Great Britain by
Halban Publishers Ltd.
22 Golden Square
London W1F 9JW
2014

www.halbanpublishers.com

A CIP catalogue record for this book is available from the
British Library.

ISBN 978-1-905559-70-1

Typeset by Spectra Titles, Norfolk
Printed in Great Britain by
Berforts Information Press, Stevenage

For Nina and Becky

PART ONE

2004

AFTER MANY YEARS, Sylvia Garland returned to England. She had never intended to stay away so long. But one thing had led to another somehow and what had originally been meant as a short refreshing absence had turned, unimaginably, into thirty-five years.

Thirty-five years; it was half a lifetime and yet, when she thought about it, Sylvia really could not say how it had come about. All she knew was that at some moment there must have come a tipping point, unnoticed at the time, after which returning no longer made any sense and so they had decided to stay put until Roger retired.

But wasn't it extraordinary that she could not account for how she had lived more than half her life? Or was that maybe the way more often than one imagined; that when people looked back at their lives, they were forced to acknowledge that they had actually not been in control at all? Everything had happened willy-nilly, they had simply blundered along, making the most of unpredictable circumstances and the lives which they ended up living bore little resemblance to what they had originally intended. Of one thing Sylvia was certain; she no longer bore any resemblance to the well-intentioned blonde young woman who had set out so bravely from England, newly married, in 1969.

Her flight landed at Heathrow at half past seven on an overcast April morning. Neither the time nor the season was of her choosing but she was looking forward to one thing: the feel of cool damp air on her face as she stepped out of the plane. She had hoped, during the last part of the flight, that the pilot would use some lovely English expression to describe the weather in London as they began their descent – "drizzly" or "nippy" – or that he might advise his passengers arriving from desert heat to get their "macs" out before they disembarked. But no such luck; the pilot was, wouldn't you know it, Australian and he simply remarked that it was "a grey old day" in London which was perfectly obvious to everyone.

Sylvia looked down at the small tidy country appearing beneath the clouds, all neat little rows of identical houses and orderly cars driving obediently along narrow roads like a toy town laid out in a good boy's bedroom. She felt excitement and apprehension in equal measure; her son, whom she had not seen since shortly after the funeral, would be waiting to meet her at the Arrivals gate but beyond that lay the unknown. Well, not absolutely the unknown of course since she had spent the first twenty-five years of her life in this country but, as everyone overseas was always telling her, it wasn't the same anymore.

When the cabin doors were finally opened after a

tedious and uncomfortable wait, during which the ridiculously overweight passenger sitting next to her made three utterly unnecessary calls on his mobile phone, Sylvia made her cumbersome way to the exit, nearly beside herself with excitement. But instead of emerging into cool damp air, as she had happily anticipated, a tubular passageway had been attached to the side of the plane and she emerged into another indoors. She was so disconcerted, she did not watch her footing and nearly stumbled as she stepped over the threshold. Determined to be brave at all costs, she exclaimed audibly "Oops-a-daisy!" and quickly regained her equilibrium without any help from anyone. But it was under the banner of "Oops-a-daisy!" that her return to England began.

She traipsed a remarkably long way on her swollen feet along anonymous corridors to what was now called Border Control. Ahead of her in the plastic booth she saw a dark-skinned young woman wearing the Muslim veil low on her stern brow. Sylvia could barely believe her eyes and, for a few disorientated moments, she imagined that she had got out at the wrong airport or that her flight had somehow come full circle and carried her back to where she had come from. She was roused from her fantasy by the passport officer calling her sharply to come forward in a broad Yorkshire accent.

Startled, Sylvia stepped forward, forgetting her hand luggage which she had parked on the floor beside her. The fat family who was standing behind her in the queue all four called out bossily, "Your bag, your bag" and, it seemed to Sylvia, everyone for several hundred yards around turned to stare at her. Blushing, apologetic, she retrieved her bag, dropped her passport which she had been holding ready in her hand, bent to pick it up and came forward again to the passport booth, flustered and flushed.

The young woman sitting inside looked at her severely. Sylvia smiled at her ingratiatingly – although why she should feel the need to ingratiate herself on this unprepossessing young woman, she had frankly no idea. The young woman tapped the counter impatiently. "Passport?" and Sylvia realised with embarrassment that she was still clutching her passport in a moist hand. Hastily, she handed it over. She was considering whether or not to tell the young woman that this was a big moment for her when she scornfully returned the passport to Sylvia, without even looking at her and called, "Next."

Sylvia left the counter feeling hurt. Of course, the passport officer had no idea that Sylvia was coming back to live in England after thirty-five years away and in tragic circumstances too. But still, she could see from the passport that Sylvia had every right to be here, this was her home, wasn't it and besides didn't the young woman come from a culture which traditionally treated older people with more respect?

Clearly, Sylvia thought indignantly as she made her weary way towards the baggage hall, clearly that young woman had chosen to adopt the worst of Western ways. In her off duty hours, she probably loitered in shopping malls, frequented discos and afterwards gorged on fast food. Still smarting, Sylvia spent some time trying to identify which carousel was receiving the baggage from her flight. The hall was crowded with milling multitudes, all unslept, unwashed, unshaven and all calling to one another in a bewildering assortment of languages. Sylvia might as well have been anywhere. To make matters worse, the passport woman had made her feel as if she was as much a foreigner here as any of them; a time traveller who had returned from a distant, more polite past.

It took Sylvia an age to find the right carousel. To make matters worse, she could not exactly remember her flight number anymore either – was it 106 or 160? – and she had lost the stub of her boarding card which would have helped. She was so tired too, she could only dimly remember where she had come from. She had hardly slept; all night an irritating small child with apparently disproportionately large feet had kept kicking her seat back and snivelling. Sylvia had nearly given its useless parents a piece of her mind.

Finally she spotted the preposterous overweight passenger who had overlapped indelicately into her seat for much of the flight. He was standing beside a rotating carousel which did not yet have any suitcases on it, still talking volubly with extravagant hand gestures on his mobile. Sylvia went to occupy a vacant spot at a safe distance away from him, confident that she must at last be in the right place. Sure enough, within a few minutes, suitcases began to tumble forth and, remarkably quickly, she spotted her own which she had made easier to identify some years earlier with a number of eye-catching transfers of exotic birds.

As her case came towards her, she turned instinctively

to point it out to the person who should have been standing next to her and to step considerately out of his way as he lifted it off. But an icy wave flooded through her because she remembered instantly that she was alone, alone and bereaved and she had not hauled a heavy case off one of these contraptions herself for a long time. Still, icy wave or no icy wave, there was nothing for it but to step bravely forward, to seize the case with both hands and to hope for the best. Heavy lifting could have unspeakable consequences. Before she knew what was happening, a short but tremendously broad-shouldered man in a black leather jacket had pushed unceremoniously in front of her, grunted brusquely "No!" and lifted her case off the carousel and placed it politely at her feet with as little visible effort as if it had been a pill box.

Sylvia was so overcome, she staggered slightly. She was overwhelmed by the icy wave turning to a warm wash of embarrassment and by a sneaking feeling that wasn't betrayal exactly but possibly disloyalty. She had just been the recipient of gallantry from a strange man. She stood there, blushing and battling with her fluctuating body temperature and afterwards she was not even sure if she had remembered to stammer "Thank you." She felt quite ashamed of herself too for the man who had come to her aid so promptly, so perfectly was one of those Russian Mafia types whom they had always made such fun of in Dubai. He had vanished into the crowd already, with his leather jacket and his puff of powerful cologne, leaving Sylvia looking after him helplessly, awash with her swirling emotions.

She took a grip on herself and simultaneously on her suitcase and went in search of a trolley. Feeling needlessly guilty as always, she made her way through the "Nothing to Declare" channel towards the Arrivals door. Halfway along she came upon her Russian rescuer being intently questioned by two customs officers who had opened both his expensive suitcases. Sylvia faltered, she was on the verge of dashing over to put the customs people straight, to tell them what a perfect gentleman the Russian was. But memories of the stories she had been told in Dubai about rich Russians and the kind of things they were said to carry in their suitcases made her walk on towards the Arrivals door, feeling even guiltier still. In any case, Jeremy was waiting for her and she didn't want to keep him waiting any longer than necessary, poor dear.

An African woman walking slightly ahead of Sylvia, pushing a trolley piled high with her vivid luggage, reached the frosted glass double doors first and they slid apart. Beyond them, a crowd was waving and roaring. There were people from all four corners of the earth gathered here: every possible colour, every possible race, every conceivable style of dress and headgear. Sylvia knew she was in London but, frankly, looking around her, she might as well have been anywhere. Jeremy was nowhere to be seen.

Sylvia came forward between the slung ropes which formed a passageway through the crowd. 'How absolutely typical,' she thought to herself, 'of Jeremy not to be here, today of all days.' She wondered what mistake he might have made: the wrong flight, the wrong terminal, still stuck somewhere in heavy traffic due to having set out too late? She knew her displeasure must already have been visible on her face when she finally spotted him, right at the back of the crowd – did he not have the gumption to come forward? – and, simultaneously catching sight of his mother, Jeremy lifted his arm in a stiff little gesture of greeting.

He extricated himself with evident difficulty from the thicket of people where he was waiting and made his way forward towards Sylvia, she noticed with affection and irritation in equal measure, carefully apologising to everyone he brushed against on his way.

Finally, they stood in front of each other and for a moment neither of them seemed to know quite what to do. Jeremy seemed fearful of patronising his mother with a consoling hug and Sylvia hesitated to embarrass him with a display of affection in front of all the gawking people. So they just stood there for a few seconds and neither of them did anything at all. But, when all was said and done, Jeremy was still her boy, even if he was thirty years old now and unwisely married and it was the most obvious thing in the world for Sylvia to scoop him into her arms and draw comfort from his warmth and strength and youth. As she did so, she felt Jeremy's hand reach around and tap her awkwardly but well-meaningly on the back.

They let each other go quite quickly and began to talk, covering their embarrassment with a brisk exchange of questions: "How was the flight?" "Where's the car?" "Have you been waiting long?" Jeremy took his mother's trolley and, rather too obviously slowing his pace to hers, began to lead her towards the car park. It was only then, as Sylvia recovered a little from the ordeal of her arrival and took pleasure in the sight of Jeremy's slim, strong silhouette pushing the trolley – was he not maybe getting a little round-shouldered? – that it occurred to her belatedly that her daughter-in-law had not come to meet her and, immediately offended, she wondered why.

"Jeremy," she asked cautiously, doing her utmost to sound concerned rather than reproachful, "where is Smita?"

The strangest expression crossed Jeremy's face. To Sylvia, it looked like a child who has been caught out in naughtiness, a booby trap, a stink bomb; guilt and delight in his own ingenuity in equal measure.

"She's awfully sorry," Jeremy volunteered quickly. "She was fully intending to come of course. But she wasn't feeling at all well when she woke up this morning and we both decided it would be better if she stayed at home."

Sylvia saw him sneak a furtive look at her face and she knew her expression was one of dignified offence.

Jeremy added placatingly, "I think maybe she felt you and I might like to have a little time together on our own, in the circumstances."

Red-faced, Sylvia thought but refrained from saying, 'What a load of tosh Jeremy. Since when have you and I *ever* wanted to spend time on our own? Well, *I* might have, I suppose, on occasion but I don't think you ever have and if your wife doesn't know that, then she doesn't know you very well, I'm afraid.'

Of course, she said no such thing. She followed Jeremy across the ugly vastness of the terminal, still no sign anywhere one could see that she was in England. She added to herself, 'Besides, Smita doesn't think like that, as far as I'm aware. Smita thinks about Smita, my boy and not very much about either you or me.'

She brought herself to the point where she always began to feel sorry for Jeremy, saddled with his self-centred ice maiden of a wife. This time she felt guilty too for hadn't she just added to his burden by deciding to come back to England? Although where else was she supposed to go, for heaven's sake?

She looked fondly at Jeremy's slightly stooping figure as he pushed the trolley. His shoulders were definitely rounder than they used to be. She resolved that, come what may, she would not be a burden to him. At that moment, Jeremy stopped without warning and Sylvia trod heavily onto his heel. Jeremy winced and Sylvia said sorry and everything was immediately back to normal; chafing along together, friction generated by the simple fact of being in the same place at the same time, unintentionally hurting each other by everything they said and did.

They were nearly at the doors which led out to the taxi rank and the walkway to the car park when, in the nick of time, Sylvia realised that she was making a terrible mistake; she didn't want to live in the same city as Jeremy and Smita. She grabbed Jeremy by the arm. "Darling, stop."

Jeremy stopped, frowning. There were people ahead of them and people behind them and their sudden halt would inconvenience everyone. "What is it?" he asked irritably.

"Darling," Sylvia said, reddening at her audacity. "I'm afraid I've changed my mind. I'm not sure I want to come and live here after all."

Jeremy let out an exasperated exhalation and wrenched the trolley out of the line of people. "For Christ's sake."

"Please don't take it personally," Sylvia continued hastily. "I started to wonder about what I was doing on the plane actually and I just think I may have rushed into this rather too soon."

Jeremy glared at her. "Is this to do with Smita?"

"Goodness!" Sylvia lied, "no, not at all. It's to do with me getting cold feet, can't you see? I'm not sure I actually *want* to live in England again."

"So what exactly are you intending to do?" Jeremy demanded. He was getting red in the face too. "You're not telling me you're turning round and getting straight back on a plane to somewhere else, are you? Because that's frankly ridiculous."

Sylvia wondered where she might catch a plane to; there must surely be some attractive destinations on the departure boards. She smiled placatingly at her son. "Please don't get angry, dear," she told him. "I think it's probably for the best."

Jeremy looked as if he might lose his temper completely. But instead he reached out his hand and laid it on her arm. Soothingly, he said, "I don't think you're quite yourself at the moment, you know. You've been

13

through a lot, you've been up all night. I think the right thing for you to do at this point would be to have a little break here in London. You don't need to commit yourself to anything, you can think of it as a short-term thing for the moment. But please, just stay here for a while."

Sylvia looked at him gratefully. Contrary to her expectations, he had risen to the occasion and she decided she would express her gratitude by staying for a while. It would be as Jeremy said, a short-term move which would give her a chance to pull herself together a bit and work out where she really wanted to live.

Outside the terminal building, they were shockingly engulfed in a squall of cold wind and rain which felt to Sylvia like an assault. She had temporarily forgotten that it could be so cold and she was astounded to see everyone around her stoically plodding ahead instead of running for cover. Jeremy did likewise so, when Sylvia stopped to find her jacket in her holdall, he left her behind. It was difficult to fight her way into the jacket in the wind and, as she was struggling, Jeremy turned round to see where she was and she realised from the look of alarm on his face that he feared she might have had second thoughts again and fled back into the terminal.

She called, "Coming, coming" and started after him, the sleeves of her peach jacket which had looked cheerful when she bought it in Dubai but now looked, she feared, simply garish flapping brightly about her.

Jeremy did not say much in the car park. She knew he was displeased with her and she thought it best to keep quiet.

But as they were driving to the exit, Jeremy asked, too casually, "So what do you think of the new car?" And she exclaimed eagerly, "Oh my goodness, yes, it's silver, isn't it? And your old one was black."

Jeremy smiled wryly and Sylvia understood straight away that she had said the wrong thing; the new car must be much more modern and expensive than the old one but she had failed to notice. She thought with a pang that Jeremy's father would certainly have noticed and complimented him on it right away. They would have discussed engines animatedly. She sat in disconsolate silence as they left the airport.

Jeremy drove out onto the motorway, his expensive car accelerating impressively amid the morning traffic. Sylvia leaned back and sighed. She watched the ugly urban sprawl going by and tried to pretend their silence was companionable.

Why was it, she wondered, that the approaches to London were so relentlessly dreary? She had driven into other cities – New Delhi, Riyadh – along wide avenues, past imposing monuments but London seemed simply not to care what newcomers thought of it.

As Sylvia watched and struggled with her fatigue, the motorway rose up onto an elevated section and she remembered blearily that soon on the left-hand side she would see the familiar Lucozade advertisement which she had enjoyed seeing on her return for years. It was high up on the side of a tall building; it showed a brilliantly illuminated bottle of Lucozade pouring bright electric bubbles into a glass, filling it up again and again, perpetually. "Lucozade replaces lost energy" the slogan alongside it read. Sylvia, arriving back on home leave from Hong Kong or Delhi or Riyadh, would smile fondly at the Lucozade ad as if greeting a long-lost friend. But Jeremy's expensive car sped past the place where the Lucozade ad should have been and Sylvia realised with a pang that it had gone, probably swept away because it was too simplistically old-fashioned in its message for today. Besides, she wondered, does anyone even drink Lucozade anymore? According to what she had heard from younger expats, nowadays something called Red Bull was all the rage. She turned to show Roger that the Lucozade ad had gone but of course Roger wasn't there anymore either.

꙳

Jeremy checked his watch for the hundredth time and tried to control his anger. Why on earth had he bothered to get to the airport on time, rushing away from Smita, leaving without breakfast? He could have predicted that his mother would be the last passenger off the flight from Dubai. They had been traipsing out for at least half an hour now, he recognised the airport security stickers on the bags but there was still no sign of his mother. What was she doing?

Irritably, he imagined her plodding off the plane with her familiar flat-footed step, probably stopping for lengthy goodbyes to some member of the cabin crew whom she had befriended overnight while the poor wretch, at the end of an eight-hour flight, smiled through gritted teeth and longed to be off for a shower and some much-needed rest. Maybe the person delaying her was a fellow passenger, some extraordinary new bosom friend to whom she had poured out her woes over a night's succession of gin and tonics. She would doubtless be in a pretty rough state when she emerged.

Eventually Jeremy began to worry. Her flight had landed almost an hour ago. Surely she should be out by now? He left his prime spot by the railing at the front of the crowd and went to check the arrivals screen again. There was nothing about delays to baggage. Oh Christ, what had happened to her?

He knew that friends had seen her off last night, waited with her at the check-in and only waved her off as she went through security. They had texted him to say she was on her way. But what if she hadn't actually got on the flight? She might still be sitting in some sort of traumatised state in the international departure lounge in Dubai. How long would it take before someone noticed her?

His father's death had completely overwhelmed her. Jeremy had actually been taken aback by the intensity of her grief; the prolonged and public weeping, the howling, the constant prop of gin and tonics, the staggering. He had never given it much thought, he supposed, but he had expected a bit of a stiff upper lip. When had he ever seen any interaction between his parents to suggest otherwise?

It was true he had been shocked himself by how profoundly his father's death had shaken him. Considering they had never been close, considering Jeremy's feelings about his father.

He wondered if he should go and speak to someone from the airline. Or should he maybe call Smita and see if by any chance she had heard anything? No, if she had she would have called him and besides she mustn't be worried. She was worked up enough already about his mother coming; he mustn't add to her stress levels.

As he ran through a checklist of gruesome possibilities, it dawned on him sickeningly just what he had let himself and Smita in for.

Really, it made no sense that he should be standing here, waiting to welcome his mother and presumably to take responsibility for her. He had done his best to avoid her his entire adult life. But now, here he was waiting dutifully to meet her as if everything which had gone before, his childhood, her track record as his mother, had been completely different.

He looked around him. Some of the other people standing waiting were holding balloons and handmade banners and big bunches of flowers. They were craning forward, excitement and anticipation all over their faces. Every few minutes delighted cries would go up, small children would burrow forward under the railings and throw themselves onto some emerging passenger. Around him people were embracing and weeping. He wondered whether he was the only one waiting there who felt sick with apprehension. There was an East European guy standing alone a little way off who looked pretty edgy.

Jeremy was distracted by the arrival of a large African family group, he couldn't identify where they came from, tall, stately robed figures who proceeded to greet their waiting relatives by inclining their heads and solemnly touching foreheads. The waiting crowd fell silent as they watched the ritual. If only Jeremy's reunion with his mother could be as low-key and dignified. But no, she would squawk and fumble and drop things, he would squirm like an adolescent and then later there would be Smita's reaction to deal with too. It would all be horrible.

Grimly, Jeremy went to the back of the crowd to check the arrivals screen one last time and when he turned round, his mother had finally appeared, lurching towards him looking desperate, pushing a trolley with a wonky, loudly squeaking wheel.

As he made his way forward laboriously through the crowd, the weirdest thing happened. Suddenly, all the reunions with his mother from his childhood came back to him and he wasn't thirty anymore but three or five or seven, running eagerly towards his lovely blonde mother and, however thrilled she acted to see him, he remembered how somehow she never seemed pleased enough.

Smita looked down from her front window a dozen times but there was still no sign of the car. She supposed that at this point some women might have started to worry about motorway pile-ups but Smita immediately started to wonder what her mother-in-law might have done to delay them. The possibilities were of course endless; she might have lost something, started something, might have got herself into some sort of situation at passport control, with a porter, with another passenger. Whatever it was, no way would she have given a thought to all the delay and trouble she was causing them.

Caught up in her own drama, she wouldn't stop to think about Smita preparing a welcome lunch for her, however awful she was feeling, nor Jeremy standing waiting patiently for her while the price of the car park went up and up.

Smita could have texted Jeremy of course to ask what the matter was but she didn't like the idea of her mother-in-law getting involved in any form of communication between herself and Jeremy. His phone would beep and Jeremy would say innocently, "We'd better get a move on. Smita's wondering where we are."

Sylvia would get all indignant and reply something like, "Well, we simply have to sort this out first, dear", whatever it was, "Smita will simply have to wait."

Jeremy would go all red but of course he wouldn't *say* anything. So, instead of understanding that Smita's question had been prompted by concern, anxiety, Sylvia would straightaway assume that Smita was being bossy and demanding and she would deliberately do everything even more slowly than usual. Whereas, in actual fact, Smita had gone to a lot of trouble for her. She had taken the day off work, got up much earlier than she wanted to do the shopping and now she was settling down to prepare a full-scale Indian lunch because that was what Sylvia liked best even though she, Smita, couldn't stand Indian cooking because it was so time-consuming and so unhealthy. The renewed realisation that her mother-in-law was coming to London to *live* made Smita suddenly feel even sicker than she already did. She laid down the sharp knife with which she was chopping herbs and made herself a cup of peppermint tea. She carried it across the big open-plan front room, sat down carefully on the new cream couch and stared miserably out of the window.

She was so proud of their beautiful minimalist penthouse in one of the best parts of Belsize Park. Their builders had worked on it for a year before they moved in to transform it from the top half of a tall Victorian house into the striking ultra-modern space it was now. She and Jeremy had spent the best part of another year working to finish it off and furnish it. It was intolerably cruel that just when everything was finally almost ready and they were about to embark on a brand new phase of their life, her mother-in-law should come along to spoil it. Because Smita had no doubt at all that was what Sylvia was going to do. Not intentionally, of course; Sylvia was, God damn her, a good woman who just couldn't help doing the wrong thing at every step. She would blunder into their beautifully organized lives and, with the best will in the world, she would wreak havoc. She always did.

Whatever the circumstances, she had the capacity somehow always to put her foot in it. When she first saw Smita's new kitchen for example, with its clean lines and post-industrial look, she had giggled and said it reminded her of her school science lab. Now that was obviously a totally trivial, insignificant thing but it had rankled and, ever since, Smita had rarely entered her kitchen without remembering it.

Then there were the wretched flowers; every year, for

the past three years since they had got married, Sylvia had sent Smita a bouquet on her birthday. "How *sweet*," her friends said. "How lucky you are to have such a lovely mother-in-law." But what they didn't seem to grasp was that the flowers always came on the wrong day somehow or they were flowers which Smita didn't like or to which she was allergic. Of course she knew that Sylvia hadn't done it on purpose; the flowers were ordered online from Dubai. Jeremy told her she was being unreasonable; his mother meant well and how could she be expected to know Smita's taste in flowers? Smita had to display the bouquets prominently or Jeremy would have taken offence but every year she would glare as she passed the vase, a heavily scented reminder of her mother-in-law in her front room.

Now it was going to be her mother-in-law herself and, for the zillionth time, Smita felt it was more than she could bear. Especially with the other change that was on the way. How could she be expected to cope with the extra responsibility of having her recently widowed mother-in-law living around the corner?

If it had only happened the other way round; if it had been Sylvia who had gone first and not Roger, how much easier that would have been. Well, for Smita of course, not for poor Jeremy, whose relations with his father had always been even worse.

Although frankly his relations with both his parents had always been something of a puzzle to Smita. Her relations with her own parents, her mother, Naisha, and her father, Prem, were so much more straightforward somehow; she loved them, they drove her mad, they loved her, she drove them mad but, at the end of the day, they all took it completely for granted that they were a non-negotiable part of one another's lives and they would no more try to distance themselves from one another than they would try to do without food or clothes or shelter. Jeremy called Smita's family "claustrophobic". But Smita had trouble recognizing Jeremy's relations with his parents as family relationships at all.

For a start, they had lived on different continents most of the time since Jeremy had been sent away to boarding school at the age of eleven. When they met, they were cold and distant and formal with one another. Jeremy and his father shook hands, never hugged. In some respects they didn't even know one another all that well. If Smita asked Jeremy before a visit, "Does your Dad like fish?" or "Would your mother prefer tickets to the theatre or the ballet, do you think?" he would look blank. Smita knew exactly how much coriander her father liked in his favourite dish. Jeremy only spoke to his parents every few weeks, if that, and when they were all together, they always seemed strained and awkward.

But at least Roger could be good fun, when he was in the right mood, with a drink in his hand and he definitely had a soft spot for his feisty daughter-in-law. Smita wouldn't have minded nearly as much if it had been Roger, recently widowed, coming back to live out his days close to his only son. Except that would never have happened because, if it had been Roger coming back, he would have gone to live in the country somewhere, in a village with a nice pub. He would have bought a large and shambling dog to keep him company and he would hardly have bothered them at all. Who knows, he might even have taken up with some merry widow in the village and started out on a whole new chapter of life. Whereas Sylvia –

Smita heaved a huge sigh and abandoned her peppermint tea. She stood up and went over to the big window again and there were Jeremy and Sylvia down in the street below, busy unloading Sylvia's luggage from the boot of the car and apparently already in the middle of some fractious disagreement. Why on earth had they brought the luggage here instead of leaving it at the hotel first? Had there been some awful last-minute change of plan? Smita panicked; she wasn't having Sylvia staying here. *No way*.

As she watched Jeremy and Sylvia, wondering what on earth was going on, Sylvia suddenly looked up and saw Smita's face at the window and gave a great, enthusiastic wide wave with both arms as if they were dear long-lost friends or as if she were signalling to a taxiing aircraft. Smita waved back, just a little, with one hand and, straight away, Sylvia plunged back into the boot again as if she had been rebuffed.

Smita retreated from the window. Now she felt sicker than she had all day. She simply could not face what was about to happen. But there was nothing at all she could do about it either, now that her final wicked prayer for a plane crash had gone unanswered.

The intercom buzzed. Smita walked over and lifted the

receiver and when she exclaimed, "Hell*o*!" Jeremy's voice answered rather shortly, "Hi, we're here."

Smita dashed to the bathroom and splashed cold water on her face. Never let Sylvia see her looking less than her best. She gave a last quick look around her apartment, saw that it was looking beautiful and went downstairs to hold the front door open welcomingly.

After a moment, she could hear voices in the stairwell; Sylvia's carrying tones and someone else who, oddly, wasn't Jeremy. Smita craned to listen; it was the downstairs neighbour, cranky old Mrs Castellini; Sylvia and Mrs Castellini apparently engaged in an animated conversation about the unusually cold spring weather. Not a squeak out of Jeremy; what was he doing, why didn't he hurry her up? And how come Mrs Castellini was being so matey with Sylvia when she was always so hostile to them?

Smita could imagine Jeremy standing on the stairs, doubtless seething, red in the face, probably carrying all his mother's luggage too but still not managing to open his mouth and tell her to get a move on. Smita waited; oh, this was so typical. She could hear Mrs Castellini recalling the long hard winter of 1963 – snow lying in London for two months, the Thames freezing over – and Sylvia outdoing her with 1947; she had only been a small child but she could still remember it quite clearly, the snow that had fallen in January and stayed on the ground until Easter. In sheer exasperation, Smita closed the door quietly and went back upstairs. She may as well carry on with making the lunch until Sylvia finally deigned to make her way up and greet her.

A few moments later, she heard Jeremy push against

the front door, assuming it would be open, exclaim and unlock it before coming into the flat calling loudly "Smi? Smi? Where are you? Are you okay?"

"I'm fine," she called back. Now her hands were covered with green flecks of chopped coriander. Too bad; she came out into the high glass atrium, holding her hands up so Sylvia could see how hard she was working on her behalf and greeted her, she thought very warmly, "Hello Sylvia, how *are* you? How was the *flight*?"

Sylvia was out of breath from all the stairs – and all the talking – and instead of answering, she barged forward and seized Smita in a smotheringly close embrace. As if, Smita thought resentfully, she was trying to make up with the scale of the hug for the slightness of her feelings.

Afterwards in the kitchen, Jeremy whispered to her – Sylvia was paying a lengthy visit to the bathroom to freshen up – "Couldn't you at least have come down and opened the door to her?"

Smita was indignant. "But I *did*," she whispered back. "I *did*. I stood there for *ages* waiting for you both to come up. But she was taking so long, nattering away to Mrs Castellini, that I gave up and came back up here to get on with the *lunch*." She glared at her husband. "Why did you bring all her luggage here instead of dropping it off at the hotel first?"

"It took forever to get here," Jeremy whispered back, "and anyway *she* wanted it this way round."

"Oh," Smita said nastily. "Of *course*." Then, relenting, she asked, "Apart from the weather, what on earth was she talking to Mrs Castellini *about*?"

"Mrs Castellini was offering her condolences," Jeremy whispered. "Actually she was rather nice."

"How did she *know*?" Smita whispered.

Jeremy looked a little uncomfortable. "I happened to have a chat with her a few weeks back. I told her that my father had died."

Smita was amazed and rather put out. She whispered, "I thought we weren't talking to them until they agreed to redecorate the common parts."

Jeremy shrugged. Before he could continue, they were both alarmed by a sudden squawk and a loud thud from the bathroom. They exchanged glances. Jeremy ran over to the bathroom door and called loudly, "Mum? Are you ok?"

The door opened and Sylvia hobbled bravely out. "My, your tiles are slippery!" she exclaimed, rubbing her hip. "I nearly fell, you know. Thank goodness, I managed to grab onto the towel rail and save myself."

Smita made a mental note to check the towel rail for damage and, sure enough, when she slipped discreetly into the bathroom a little while later, the towel rail was visibly lopsided and there were cracks running across two of the tiles to which it was fastened. Smita was livid. Sylvia couldn't care less of course. Why, she hadn't even noticed. She hadn't been in the house for five minutes and already she was wreaking havoc. There was naturally no point in complaining to Jeremy. He would just say it was an accident and thank God his mother hadn't been badly hurt. So Smita contented herself with writing "Call tiler" in large legible handwriting on the To Do board in the kitchen and she hoped that Jeremy would notice it pretty soon.

He settled his mother comfortably on the cream couch and brought her a drink. Smita would rather he had seated her anywhere else for she would surely spill her drink but at least to start with Sylvia opted for tonic water only so Smita was grateful for that.

She carried on preparing the lunch, resentful that she should be working away in the kitchen when she felt so terrible while Jeremy sat across the room with his feet up, talking to his mother. If she was honest with herself, she would *rather* be in the kitchen than talking to his mother, but still.

Lunch seemed to be an ordeal for all three of them. Smita could only manage some rice and, while Sylvia made a great display of appreciation, in actual fact she only picked at her food which made Smita feel even more resentful, considering all the effort she had gone to. The only one who ate heartily was Jeremy, taking big demonstrative second helpings of lamb and rice and dal. Smita knew he was doing it partly to placate her and partly because, with his mouth permanently full, there was no way he could be expected to take part in the conversation.

Nobody seemed to have a great deal to say. Sylvia whose chatter normally drove them both to distraction was distinctly subdued; her bereavement and the overnight flight, Smita supposed. She herself was feeling so dreadful – and depressed now too – that it was an effort simply to keep up appearances and Jeremy who might have been expected to jolly things along seemed to have decided to opt out and eat himself into an early grave.

In order to fill a particularly long silence, Sylvia told them for the second time the not terribly interesting story of the Russian gentleman who, it turned out, was no gentleman at all who had helped her with her case. Even though Jeremy and Smita had agreed many times before that if an old person started to repeat herself, it was a kindness to point it out to her, there was no response from Jeremy beyond a non-committal noise and leaning across to take a couple more spoonfuls of raita.

Smita would have made the effort, would have contributed *something* if only she hadn't been feeling so unwell and, of course, if the only topic worth talking about was not totally taboo. She stuck to doing the hostess thing, offering food and afterwards tea and pretending to listen politely to whatever her mother-in-law had to say.

The meal was, all in all, a ghastly strain and Smita was glad when Sylvia said to Jeremy, soon afterwards, "When it's convenient, would you run me over to the hotel please dear? I simply have to have my forty winks, I'm afraid."

To Smita, she said brightly in the hall, "Thank you for a lovely lunch, dear. I'm sorry you went to so much trouble when you weren't feeling well. I hope you get over your bug quickly. And maybe in a couple of days, when we're both more ourselves, I can invite myself over for a cup of tea?"

"Of course," Smita answered through gritted teeth, "of course you can."

When the door had closed behind Sylvia and Jeremy,

Smita went wearily back into the front room and started to clear up. Jeremy had told her to leave it all for him but she preferred to have a job done to her liking. She wondered whether Sylvia really had no idea what the matter was with her daughter-in-law or whether, not having been let in on the secret, she was just being coy. She decided that Sylvia really had no idea; she was so self-centred and so obtuse, it was hardly surprising that she hadn't worked it out. Well, if Smita had anything to do with it, she wasn't going to find out in a hurry either because Sylvia simply couldn't help herself; she would immediately tell the news to every single person she met. At the realisation that her mother-in-law was now part of this too, Smita allowed herself a few hot angry tears.

☙

In the car on the way to the hotel, Sylvia apologized to Jeremy. "I'm sorry I wasn't the life and soul of the party. All this has rather knocked the stuffing out of me, you know."

"It's OK," Jeremy answered, without looking at her. "No one expects you to be bubbly at a time like this."

He negotiated an apparently nonsensical junction in silence. Outside the window, a blurred city slipped past.

After another pause, Sylvia added, "I'm sorry Smita's not feeling well. I hope she gets over it quickly."

Jeremy seemed to be giving her a strange look.

"It's not anything serious, is it?" she asked in alarm.

Jeremy appeared to be having difficulty controlling his

emotions. He was sweating profusely – although maybe it was just all the curry he had stowed away at lunch.

"Honestly," he said, apparently indignantly, "have you really not got a clue what's the matter with Smi?"

"No," Sylvia replied in genuine bewilderment. "No, I haven't."

Jeremy went extremely red in the face and Sylvia wondered how on earth she had angered him this time. She was so tired, her mind was in so many different places that at first she didn't really take it in when Jeremy exclaimed, "Can't you guess? She's *pregnant!*"

"Ah," said Sylvia. A moment later, she jolted wide awake and cried, "Jeremy! That's marvellous news. Congratulations!"

If Jeremy hadn't been driving, of course Sylvia could have hugged him or at least given his arm a good squeeze. As it was, she had to limit herself to a cascade of exclamations and questions. But it was too late; however much she exclaimed and however many eager questions she fired at him, she already knew that Jeremy would never ever forgive her for that first pause when she hadn't been listening properly. He wouldn't accept that it was due to fatigue and distraction; he would believe that it was because deep down she didn't like Smita. She didn't like Smita and consequently she wasn't really all that thrilled that they were having a baby because it would surely cement their marriage.

So Sylvia jabbered away, being as overjoyed and effusive as she could manage in her exhausted state, while sneaking sideways looks at Jeremy's quizzical expression and finally she said the one thing which must surely make Jeremy feel sorry for her, "Oh, isn't it such a shame that your father isn't here to hear the news? He would have been so thrilled."

To which Jeremy responded, turning deftly onto the forecourt of an immense hotel, "It's a great shame. He would have made such a wonderful grandfather."

Did Sylvia hear a reproach? She busied herself gathering her belongings and decided, if it was a reproach, that she would not hear it. How could Jeremy possibly know what sort of a grandmother *she* would make? Goodness, a grandmother; she had not really thought about that before.

She hobbled into the hotel lobby behind Jeremy, feeling suddenly indescribably old. Her feet and ankles were still swollen from the flight and her shoes hurt. While Jeremy dealt with the details of her booking, she sat down in a deep leather armchair, her head reeling. It was all too much, frankly; first, she had without any warning become a widow and now, equally suddenly, she had been told she was going to become a grandmother. She felt she was losing all sense of who she actually was. She was sitting in an anonymous hotel whose name she didn't even know in a city where she had no wish to be and outside the floor-to-ceiling windows of the lobby, instead of the English spring which she had happily anticipated, it seemed to be the bleak midwinter.

"Are you ok?" Jeremy asked, stooping over her.

She must have closed her eyes for a moment. "I'm fine," she replied resolutely, "just tired."

She struggled to get to her feet out of the enveloping depths of the armchair and Jeremy had to offer her a hand and help haul her up.

They did not speak in the lift because they had to share it with a tremendously fat Middle Eastern-looking man in a white towelling bathrobe. He filled the lift with the potent reek of chlorine and Sylvia drew a little passing comfort from this sign that somewhere in the hotel there was a swimming pool – and maybe a sauna too – warmth and another element into which she could escape. All her life, she had used swimming as an escape from all sorts of things.

Jeremy unlocked the door to her room and instructed her how everything worked – the curtains, the television, the minibar – as if she had become completely incapable. Then he said rather awkwardly, "Ok, well I'd better be getting back. I don't want Smi to have to do all the washing up. Now you have a good rest, won't you. I'll give you a ring in the morning and we'll take things from there."

Only then, as he was on the point of leaving, did it occur to Sylvia to ask, "How far along is she Jeremy? When is the baby due?"

And, pink and pleased in spite of himself, Jeremy answered proudly, "Nearly ten weeks. The baby's due in October."

Sylvia started. "Ten weeks?" she repeated. "But that's exactly when – " her voice broke off.

Jeremy looked uncomfortable. "I know. Dad. The timing was really weird. Quite hard on Smi actually. We found out the day after the funeral."

Sylvia dabbed at her eyes with a handy hotel tissue. "Well it's marvellous news anyway," she mumbled, "Marvellous. I'm so pleased for both of you. Please make sure to tell Smita I said so." She was frankly sobbing now and she knew she was due another wooden embrace from her son and another staccato little pat on the back. When it came, she responded by squeezing his other hand energetically. Then she pulled herself together and said bravely, "Now run along Jeremy. Smita needs you."

The hotel room was silent and still. It was on the cold side too but Jeremy hadn't shown her how to turn up the heating. Bed was the place to be. Why in Dubai it would be nearly bedtime. She would feel a lot better tucked up in bed; she would shut her eyes and shut out London. Sleep would do her the world of good.

It was in Hong Kong that Sylvia had first discovered the secret pleasures of the siesta although of course in those early years of married life sleep had nothing to do with it. Sometimes, on the steamiest days, Roger would nip home from the office on the pretext of a business meeting or a long lunch with a client. In broad daylight and with the thermometer showing simply unbelievable temperatures, they would sneak into their huge bedroom with the rotating fans, away from their snooping maid and close the blinds. In the sultry half-darkness, they would get up to things they would never have dreamt of in London. Most days of course, Roger couldn't get away from work; he really did have business meetings or long lunches with clients. Or so he told Sylvia.

How odd it felt to be having a siesta with cold rain

lashing at the window. As soon as Sylvia lay down, she felt wretched; the hotel bed seemed huge and she felt unutterably alone in it. She could almost feel a howl beginning deep within her. She did hope that she wasn't going to start that frightful wailing again as she had when they first brought her the news in Dubai. She had no idea she could make a noise like that. It was a noise straight off the television; the sound of Arab women mourning their lost loved ones at a funeral. Sylvia had not even realised straight away that the noise was coming from her. How mortifying it would be if, in spite of herself, she started to make that noise again here. People would come running down the hotel corridor, they would bang on her door. If she didn't answer, they might let themselves in with a skeleton key and, seeing the state she was in, they would doubtless summon Jeremy. She would be in trouble again.

She wrenched her mind away from Roger and firmly she thought of her grandchild. Conceived in January, revealed in February, he would be born in October. There was not even a shadow of doubt in Sylvia's mind that he would be a boy. The extraordinary timing, that he should first make his presence known in the same week in which his grandfather was laid to rest, could not be mere coincidence. Not that Sylvia was the least bit believing. While she might have had mindless inclinations towards church when she was young, all those years she had lived in India and in the Middle East, seeing the ravages of religion close-up had thoroughly put her off it. You simply could not witness everything which she had witnessed during her sixty-two years and still go on believing in a

God. But the timing of her grandson's conception seemed to send a signal; one way or another, the little boy was coming to take his grandfather's place. Here she was, on the verge of howling one minute and counting on her fingers to calculate the time of his arrival the next. Sylvia shivered with excitement – and a little bit with cold from the chilly sheets.

So not everything was over. Until now, when she tried to look ahead, she could only foresee lessening, withering. She had imagined this next, last stage of her life would be terribly bleak and would require great bravery. Yet here was something completely unexpected which had already – ten weeks after Roger's death – filled her with a great rush of excitement and anticipation.

Sylvia had never given much thought to being a grandmother, never having been – if the truth were told – all that motherly. But now that it was going to happen, she understood what a marvellous thing it would be. All the thoughts which she knew she would have later – about how English the little boy might look and how Indian and about Smita's suitability as a mother – she pushed to one side and focused only on the imagined child. She could not see him at all clearly but she could see herself taking him to the zoo in Regent's Park and to the dinosaurs at the Natural History Museum in South Kensington, all the same things in fact which she had found such a crashing bore when she had first done them years ago while home on leave with Jeremy. What was striking – and baffling – was that, this time round, she felt thrilled at the prospect of doing them. She would need to keep a close eye on

36

Smita and Jeremy of course; they would neither of them make ideal parents. Their flat was nightmarishly unsuitable for a small child too with all those sheer drops and all that glass. Sylvia thought her way around it, making a painstaking inventory of all the things she would have to tell Smita to change. It was a long list and it grew rather boring after a while.

When she woke up, it was night time. For the first few seconds, she had no idea where in the world she was or what sort of time it might be. The luminous digital alarm clock showed 20:20. But Sylvia felt wide awake and adventurous as if it were already morning. She knew that Roger was dead but, for a moment, the disorientation distracted her from her grief. She looked out at all the little lonely lights of the city twinkling in the dark – she hadn't drawn the curtains – and she wondered what on earth she was going to do here. Then she remembered she was going to have a grandson.

Feeling remarkably business-like, she got up. She drew the curtains, competently, as Jeremy had shown her. Then she began to rummage in her suitcase for her costume and rubber flip-flops which she never travelled without. Of course, they were buried right at the bottom; she had not foreseen that she would want to go swimming her first cold evening in London. But she did urgently, knowing that as soon as she pushed away from the side and began to propel herself slowly and steadily through the water, everything would immediately seem a lot less dreadful.

The hotel corridors and the lift were empty. She supposed that everyone was having dinner. She hadn't thought yet what she would do about dinner; she certainly wasn't going to sit alone in the restaurant. But first she would have her swim; she would think about dinner afterwards. There was a small plaque next to the ground floor button in the lift which said "Leisure Complex" and Sylvia headed there.

She supposed she had expected a Dubai-style pool, vast and lavish and she was rather shocked by what she found. A somnolent Polish teenager in a less than fresh tracksuit was lounging at the reception desk of the "leisure complex". He greeted her by reciting sleepily a welcome obviously memorized from a training manual and handed her a towel and a token to use a locker. She descended a narrow flight of stairs into a basement region which stank of chlorine and rubber. She changed in a distinctly disagreeable changing room, reproaching herself for not having thought of getting changed upstairs in her room. Then she plodded back up the basement stairs and pushed open the door to the pool.

Why, it was minuscule and made even smaller by a sloping shelf at the shallow end so that the first few feet were not even deep enough to swim in. For a moment, Sylvia wondered whether it was worth getting in at all. But she longed for the buoyancy of the water, the release which swimming always granted her and so she waded in down the sloping tiled shelf holding firmly onto the handrail. Jeremy and Smita would never forgive her a broken limb at this stage.

As soon as the water was deep enough, she kicked her legs out behind her and she was off. The water was warm but not too warm and chlorinated but not excessively so. Once she adjusted to the short lanes – twelve strokes and back, twelve strokes and back – the swimming gave her the same pleasure which it always did. She was no longer Sylvia Garland, newly widowed and alone in a city which she had not lived in for thirty-five years. Her mind emptied of all her preoccupations and focused narrowly, repetitively on twelve strokes and back, twelve strokes and back, her fingers held together, scooping the water, her shoulders obedient and synchronised, her hips and knees flexing, no longer perfectly these days but in unison.

She was an aged sea turtle, swimming steadily to and fro in her tank at the aquarium. Like Sylvia, the turtle had memories of former lives in other oceans which streamed behind her as she swam: the Pacific Ocean and islands, cherished eggs laid on remote beaches, other turtles. Sylvia might be swimming in a laughable little pool in a London hotel but she had swum in her time off Lantau Island, at Kovalam Beach, in the turquoise waters of the Gulf. Now, like the turtle in her tank, she ploughed to and fro, her face set in an expressionless mask, her neck saggy and wrinkled, her flippers scaly and scarred. But, like the turtle, she swam trailing memories of distant seas.

Ten, fifteen, twenty minutes passed as a turtle and then Sylvia was tired and wanted to get out. She had had the pool to herself the whole time but as she emerged from the water, two small Indian boys in bright trunks which were too baggy for their scrawny legs burst noisily into the room followed by their small slight father whose spectacles immediately steamed up in the heat. Both excited, maybe new to London, just released after a long flight from somewhere, the little boys scampered and screamed alongside the pool. One of them skidded and nearly fell and was reprimanded by his father. Just as Sylvia, wrapped in a towel, withdrew to the sauna, the little boys plunged into the water splashing and shouting. Their thin brown limbs flailed, their glossy black heads bobbed in the water. The scene reminded Sylvia of so many swimming scenes in the East: swarms of little brown boys cavorting for tourists, diving for pennies. It occurred to her with a shock that her grandson might well look like one of those little boys. It depended, of course, whose looks would predominate, Jeremy's or Smita's, and it had to be said, so far in that marriage, it was Smita who had predominated at every turn.

Sylvia relaxed in the sauna for ten minutes, relishing the heat. Then she showered and went back downstairs to change. As she walked past the pool, she noticed, which she had not seen while she was swimming, the night-time street scene outside, only partly screened by the foliage in the hotel garden. Buses and taxis were lumbering past, lit up inside and offering glimpses of a hectic city life from which she was excluded. She stood for a few moments, observing the nocturnal cavalcade until one of the little boys jumped in right behind her and splashed her. She gave him a generously indulgent smile and she retreated from the poolside, thinking that she was perfectly happy not to be part of the whirl of the city and, as far as she was concerned, things could stay like that for a good while yet.

She ordered tomato soup and a toasted sandwich on

room service and settled to eat them in front of a documentary about Emperor penguins in the Antarctic. The soup was Heinz, which gave her no end of pleasure, although she supposed that a four-star hotel might have done better. The documentary was marvellous and without Roger's withering running commentary – he hated wildlife programmes – she could really enjoy it. She had no idea that penguins led such an orderly, civilised life or tended their young with such selfless devotion. She wondered how the young penguins took care of their parents when they grew old. Nothing to take comfort from there, she supposed; there were no granny flats, no carers in Nature. She imagined the elderly penguins abandoned amid the screaming blizzards, stiffly, stoically freezing to death. She ticked herself off; by no stretch of the imagination had Jeremy and Smita abandoned her. Jeremy had met her at the airport, Smita had made her lunch. But then they had dumped her. They had their own lives to lead, of course, they were both busy, working, expecting. Still it was Sylvia's first evening back in England, newly widowed and she was sitting alone in a hotel room, drinking tinned soup. She had every right to feel sorry for herself.

Crossly, she reminded herself that she didn't want to be Jeremy and Smita's house guest. Perish the thought; Smita's house beautiful would suffocate her within the week. Why, earlier on today, hadn't she been on the verge of turning round and leaving at the prospect of having lunch with them, let alone living with them? It was only the howling of the icy blizzards in Antarctica and a predator circling over the penguin colony with outstretched wings which had made her briefly backtrack. She thought about ringing her sister Cynthia – if she could master the hotel phone – but quickly thought better of it. Sylvia knew she was not yet up to speaking to Cynthia. The penguin programme finished in a crescendo of uplifting orchestral music – as if the penguins might miraculously take celestial flight – and was followed by the evening news. No longer so baby-faced Tony Blair was holding forth against a backdrop of more bloodshed in Iraq. Sylvia turned the television off smartly. Things were bad enough without watching the bloody news.

In the morning, Jeremy phoned her, as promised, on the dot of nine, as if she were a business call. His manner was business-like too. He told her he had drawn up a list of local estate agents who let service apartments and he proposed driving her round a selection of them so she could choose where she was going to stay until she had made up her mind what to do next.

Sylvia said, "But I like it here."

She heard Jeremy exhale.

"You can't possibly stay there for a month," he said reprovingly. "The cost would be astronomical."

"Who's talking about a month?" Sylvia exclaimed. "I meant just for a few days until – until – "

"Until what?" Jeremy asked. "I'm sure, judging by the state of you, you'll need much more than a few days to decide where you're going to live, what you're going to do.

Smi and I have talked it over and a service apartment is definitely the best option. It'll have everything provided, you can pay for it a week at a time and meanwhile you can look around and make up your mind what you want to do longer term."

It was no good telling herself he meant well; his tone made her immediately contrary.

She asked, "Will it have a pool?"

"A pool?" Jeremy repeated wonderingly.

"Yes." Sylvia answered briskly. "A pool. I need one nowadays for my health. In fact, I went for a swim here in the hotel just last night."

Jeremy retorted, "You've spent too long in Dubai, you know."

Then he relented. "I'm sure Smi can get you into her gym on a guest membership. You can swim there."

Belatedly, Sylvia thought to ask, "How is she feeling this morning?"

Evidently recognizing a red herring, Jeremy answered briefly, "Much the same. If I come to pick you up at ten, will you be ready?"

"I seem to recall it gets better after the first three months," Sylvia went on. "So she should start to feel a bit more cheerful in a couple of weeks in fact."

"I'll see you at ten then," Jeremy replied and he rang off.

Sylvia made a point of being ready in the lobby at the right time; she knew she was on thin ice where those two were concerned. While she waited for Jeremy because *he* was, typically, late, she sensed a resolve taking shape. It was

43

too early to call it a decision but it was a dimly outlined resolve.

When Jeremy drove onto the forecourt, she didn't recognize him because of course she was watching out for the old black car, rather than the new silver one. Jeremy had to get out and gesticulate foolishly to attract her attention. She leapt to her feet, having wisely avoided the deep leather armchairs and waited perched on a little gilt chair instead. She hurried out, pursued ignominiously by an off-duty Japanese air hostess waving her handbag, which she had in her haste left behind on the floor. Jeremy settled her into the front passenger seat, unsuccessfully trying to conceal his impatience. Sylvia noticed that his posture was no better than the day before but she refrained from comment. It was obvious from the way he slammed his door and twisted the key in the ignition that he was finding this morning a strain.

Sylvia considered asking after Smita some more but thought better of it. Smita would no doubt be using her pregnancy to lead Jeremy a merry dance and really she ought not to get any more attention than she deserved. In silence, Sylvia looked out of the window and wondered how on earth she would ever live here again.

An unimaginably long time ago, a well-intentioned young woman called Sylvia had got married, amid great hilarity, to a fun-loving young man called Roger. 1964. They had bought the most minute house off the King's Road in Chelsea and moved in there to live happily ever after. Of course they hadn't lived there happily ever after because a few years later they had gone off to Hong Kong.

Their married life had been far from plain sailing anyway. But it was the certainty that she could never again return to that cosy little house which had made her turn against London. Even though the house had been incredibly inconvenient in a number of ways; so tiny that some days Roger seemed to fill it up entirely and its internal walls so paper thin that you could hear absolutely everything. Still, after forty years of marriage, how on earth was she supposed to choose somewhere to live on her own?

Jeremy drove a short distance to the office of an estate agent with a silly name something like "Dullard and Square" where they were joined by a swarthy young man who climbed into the back of the car, mid-sentence on his mobile, bringing with him an overwhelming scent of cheap cologne and, when he had finished his phone call, he introduced himself, implausibly, as Gid.

Sylvia recoiled from his brashness. With Gid in the car, forget the choking cologne, it felt as if the volume had suddenly been turned up far too high.

"Got some ace properties for yer," he yelled at Sylvia from the back, as if she were deaf, she thought irritably. "Nothin' *like* what yer used to in Dubai, er-hah, er-hah, but *really* nice places yer'll see."

His phone rang again, his ringtone a raucous blast of rock music and he promptly launched into a furious, expletive-laden argument with someone, apparently a colleague who had failed to arrange their first appointment. He rang off, having ended the exchange by calling his colleague a "fucking tosser", shouted jokily at Sylvia, "'Scuse my French" and told Jeremy to "throw a U-ey" and to set off again in the opposite direction.

Sylvia cast an indignant sideways look at Jeremy; what on earth was he thinking of, inflicting Gid on her? But either Jeremy was too preoccupied with the perils of trying to do a U-turn in a rather busy road or he did not find Gid's behaviour nearly as outrageous as she did. Sylvia looked balefully at her son. She resolved there and then that, however suitable they might be, she would not move into any apartment provided by Gid.

Of course Jeremy knew that his mother would be difficult; how could it be otherwise? But to describe all six flats which the agent showed them in the course of a very long morning as "uniformly ghastly" seemed to him unfair.

It was true, the first two, in big 1930s blocks in St John's Wood, were a bit grim: labyrinthine corridors, stale cooking smells. But to call them "tombs", to refer to the blocks afterwards as the "Valley of the Dead" seemed to Jeremy pure provocation. Did his mother not realise he had taken time off work at his own initiative to do this for her? Did she not understand the extra stress she was causing him?

She claimed to have seen a very old lady creeping along one of the corridors, stooping, dressed in a black coat, a black hat and black shoes, clutching a black handbag as if it might at any moment be torn from her clutches. The old lady had thrown his mother a warning look, she claimed; abandon hope all ye who enter here. Well, Jeremy had been walking along right next to her and he had not seen any such thing.

She was a little less harsh about the next two places, in a flashy, horrifically expensive block next to Regent's Park. The agent was just trying it on; they were way over budget. She also infuriated Jeremy by sharing a nasty little racist exchange with the agent about the furnishings.

"What kind of people live here?" she asked fastidiously as they viewed the third flat.

Jeremy already suspected that his mother had no intention of living in any of these apartments; she was simply on the lookout for reasons to reject them.

The agent laughed nastily and answered, "Yer would feel right at home here, Mrs Garland, coming from Dubai. It's full of Arabs, this block." He added gleefully, "Can't yer tell from the taps?"

His mother laughed heartily for the first time since she had arrived.

Afterwards, while Gid was returning the keys to the porter, Jeremy told her that it was not acceptable nowadays to make that kind of casual racist comment and she should be more careful. But she retorted, "Oh don't be such a prig, Jeremy. Everyone knows that Arabs like showy bathrooms." Oh, she was insufferable.

Jeremy had high hopes of the last two flats because they were just around the corner in Belsize Park; it would be so convenient. As a temporary measure, they both seemed perfectly acceptable to him but, in the first one, his mother objected to the repeating mauve pattern on the bathroom tiles, saying it was enough to give you a migraine. The final one, which was decorated a bit frostily throughout in pale blue, she said would be like living in an igloo.

In the car afterwards, she raised the subject of the baby and managed to get on Jeremy's nerves even more. She raised the subject in such a way that instead of feeling straight away cheered, as he usually did, Jeremy felt furious. She told him patronisingly why none of the flats which they had seen were the least bit suitable for a visiting grandchild. She was surprised he couldn't see it. While she was about it, she added that their penthouse – on which they had just spent everything they had – was utterly unsuitable for a small child too.

Feeling rancorous and headachey, Jeremy drove his mother back to the hotel. He had intended to take her to lunch in a Japanese restaurant he liked to toast her new apartment. But there was nothing to celebrate and he couldn't wait to get rid of her.

In the hotel car park, he asked sullenly, "D'you want me to join you for lunch?"

His mother stared bleakly ahead. "I don't have anyone else to have lunch with."

Of course Jeremy felt guilty then; he ought to make allowances. He went round to the passenger side and helped his mother out. She did look a sorry sight crossing the hotel forecourt with her jacket buttoned up wrong and her make up smudged. He should be more understanding.

As soon as they sat down in the hotel coffee shop, Jeremy regretted the Japanese restaurant. The coffee shop was awful – full of piped music and off duty aircrew – and his mother would probably have found the Japanese restaurant soothing with its paper lanterns and swooping calligraphy. Although she might have annoyed him there too with one of her put-downs: "Oh, I can see this is just your sort of place, Jeremy," something like that.

They both looked morosely at the laminated menu: tuna burger, BLT. His mother ordered a cappuccino and a piece of cake and Jeremy a reproachful small salad and a mineral water. Smita was very keen that he watched what he ate and didn't put on weight in sympathy with her like some men did.

His mother leant forward and said, "Listen dear, I expect you mean well but you really must understand that I can't be rushed. I'm sorry if I'm inconveniencing you and Smita. But I need to do this at my own pace." She sat back and sighed demonstratively.

Jeremy heard the "dear" and relaxed a fraction. "I'm only trying to be helpful," he said plaintively. "I could be sitting in my office working right now. I *should* be sitting working in fact. But I've taken time off to help you get settled. I know this is a bloody awful time for you. But you won't make it any better by digging your heels in and getting all stubborn and refusing to do the simplest thing." He glared at his mother and felt himself flush.

Their food came. Jeremy's salad looked strikingly unhealthy with quantities of bright pink dressing and croutons and his mother's cake looked like a Japanese plastic display model of a piece of cake.

Jeremy persisted. "Exactly how long are you planning to stay here? It's not even all that nice."

His mother said deftly, "*You* chose it."

Jeremy felt himself flush again. "We chose it because it was nearby – obviously. We imagined you would stay here two or three nights max and then move into a service apartment – as we'd *discussed* – and take your time to work out your next move." He puffed in exasperation. "I don't see why it's such a big deal suddenly."

His mother laid down her cake fork and clasped her hands. She looked away from Jeremy at some distant vista. "I don't think I want to live in North London," she said.

Jeremy was outraged. "Where *do* you want to live?" he demanded and, without waiting for an answer, he exclaimed, "Yesterday you wanted to get back on a plane without even leaving the airport. Today you tell me you don't want to live near your own son and daughter-in-law. How am I supposed to take *that*? In a few months time you'll have a grandchild here too, your first grandchild – "

"About the grandchild," his mother interrupted, suddenly veering off on a tangent as she always did, "there's something I need to ask about him."

"Or *her*," Jeremy said reproachfully.

His mother gave a knowing smile. "Of course you're right dear, so long as he's healthy, that's all that matters." She paused. "There's something that's bothering me though."

Jeremy was alarmed. "A health issue?"

"No," his mother said hastily. "No, not a health issue." She hesitated.

Jeremy asked, "So what is it then? So long as this isn't just a ploy to change the subject."

"It isn't," his mother answered huffily. "Rest assured. Afterwards we can go straight back to discussing how many nights you think I ought to stay at the hotel and where you think I ought to live."

They glared at each other.

"Well?" Jeremy asked.

His mother picked a glace cherry from her synthetic-looking cake and rolled it dubiously around her plate with a fork. "I hope," she began hesitantly, "I hope that Smita will let me be involved with the baby."

"You what?" Jeremy asked.

"I hope," his mother repeated uncertainly, "that Smita will let me have a role in my grandchild's life, you know what I mean, that she won't keep me at arm's length."

Jeremy was outraged. Furiously, he replied, "I don't understand you. What has Smita ever done to make you say such a thing?"

"I'm not really *saying* it," his mother ploughed on. "I'm asking it. You know perfectly well Smita doesn't have a very high opinion of me. I've never been a high flier like she is, more of a plodder. I'm worried she won't think I'm up to scratch. I need to know. Will I be involved in the baby's life or won't I?"

Jeremy didn't care anymore if he sounded exasperated. "Of course you will be. You'll be the baby's grandmother."

"Ah, but the baby will have two grandmothers, remember," his mother said. "And it's perfectly natural for a woman to turn to her own mother first. I realise that. So I'm asking: do you think Smita will allow *me* to do things with the baby too?"

With a sinking heart, Jeremy understood that a whole

new avenue of trouble was opening up ahead of him. "What sort of thing," he asked cautiously, "did you have in mind?"

His mother volunteered eagerly, "Babysitting. Taking him for walks and outings. Maybe having him to stay when you two want a weekend away. After all, I'll be much closer here in London than Naisha up in Leicester."

Uneasily, Jeremy said, "You know, it's awfully early days yet."

"Of course it is," his mother agreed. "Of course. But I need to know. If I'm expected to make plans."

She went back to rolling the toxic-looking cherry around her plate.

Jeremy sighed. He checked his watch. "Listen," he said impatiently, "I really have to run. I don't know why you have to go looking for trouble before it's even happened. I'm sure – if you don't scare Smi by coming on too strong way too soon – she'll be perfectly OK about all this kind of thing."

He stood up. "Please, whatever you do, just don't say anything to her about this whole issue yet. She's feeling very fragile at the moment."

His mother grinned. "Pregnant women can be terribly touchy."

Jeremy ignored the remark. Before he left, he said, "You'll have to tell me on the phone tonight where it is you actually plan to live. I'm curious."

As he drove out of the hotel, his phone rang and it was Smita complaining that he had forgotten to telephone her father to wish him a happy birthday, as he had promised.

Jeremy had never understood why, in Smita's family, a phone call was always expected as well as a card. For a moment, he had the disagreeable sensation that he was surrounded by demanding women. But it only lasted for a second or two and afterwards of course he was ashamed of it.

ॐ

Sylvia watched her son leave and reflected, for the umpteenth time, how very foolish he was. It was only when he was out of sight that she realised how very foolish she was too. She was starting out on the wrong foot entirely. She had only been back in England for twenty-four hours and already she and Jeremy were rubbing each other up the wrong way. Her only son. Why did it have to be like this? And the baby, her only grandson; why was she already getting into an argument about him before he was even born?

She leapt up from the table, in as much as someone of her age and build could leap, and charged out of the restaurant after Jeremy. Behind her, she was dimly aware of someone calling and a commotion but she carried on. She reached the revolving front door of the hotel in time to see Jeremy's car turning out of the forecourt into the street. Too late. Dispiritedly, she turned away to be confronted by two waitresses from the coffee shop, one holding out her bill and the other her handbag.

She retreated to her room; sleep, what other consolation was there? As she lay in bed, curiously untired the moment her head touched the pillow, she reflected for the umpteenth time on Jeremy and Smita's marriage and what a very ill-conceived pairing it was.

Jeremy had first brought Smita out to meet them about five years ago. They were still living in Riyadh then, Riyadh the dusty, Riyadh the drab, Riyadh the insufferable. They had known he was seeing a girl for some time but he had never told them anything about her. Silly boy; did he imagine they would be shocked that she was Indian? When they had lived all those years in Delhi and absolutely loved it? In any case, as soon as he announced that he was bringing a girl and that her name was Smita, of course the penny dropped. Sylvia and Roger were absolutely thrilled; firstly, because it laid to rest certain unspoken concerns which they had long had about Jeremy and, secondly, because they imagined that having a young Indian woman in the house would be such fun. Quite what they had imagined, she really couldn't say now – doe eyes and ankle bracelets? – but it certainly hadn't been Smita.

Of course what they didn't know then was that Smita Mehta had been born and brought up in Leicester and was, as far as she was concerned, not really Indian at all. Her parents, who had arrived in Britain when they were young children, might still be Indian, especially her father, Prem. But she was utterly one hundred per cent British Asian, a new generation which had never previously existed, cutting swathes. She had never even been to India and she had no wish to go there either.

She listened with an expression of polite amusement as Sylvia and Roger reminisced about their years in Delhi. They had moved there from Hong Kong in the early

Seventies when Sylvia was expecting Jeremy and they had ended up staying for nearly ten years. It was true they had loved it although Sylvia was conscious as she described it to Smita – the lovely big house in Lodhi Colony, the amusing servants, the drinks on the veranda in the sudden Indian dusk – that it did all sound awfully days of the Raj. So she was keen to stress that it was the *place* they had loved; the myriad sights and sounds and smells of India which first startled and then captivated you, the flowers, the birds and chipmunks in the garden, the markets and, oh, everywhere, the colours, the glorious colours.

Smita listened politely but eventually she said, rather primly Sylvia thought, that it sounded nothing like the country which her parents described. Well, that felt like a slap on the wrist.

Sylvia protested to Roger afterwards, "Of *course* there's poverty and ghastliness in India, we all know that, but there's no point pretending you can't have a perfectly marvellous life there too. Where in India did her parents come from anyway?"

Roger had replied "Gujarat" and Sylvia had been surprised by a pang of jealousy because, obviously, Roger had been having private personal conversations with Smita on his own.

Sylvia had to admit, guiltily, that there was something a little disagreeable about having an attractive young woman around the house. Ever since her marriage, Sylvia had been the woman of the house. Smita was very attractive. She would lie beside the pool in her scrap of a bikini, slim and flawless, and Sylvia would come out for a dip in her capacious floral one-piece and she felt like a whale, sploshing up and down the pool.

Everyone thought Smita was wonderful, partly because she was so very pretty and partly because it made their ex-pat friends in Riyadh feel good that here was an Indian person with whom they could actually make friends.

Apparently only Sylvia could see clearly, by the end of that first visit, what was wrong; Jeremy had been caught up in Smita's chariot wheels, as she put it to Roger after the young couple had left. They said goodbye at the airport, Jeremy all stiff and awkward as usual and Smita utterly charming but chilly. That was it, Sylvia complained to Roger; the girl was cold. She had set her sights on Jeremy for reasons of her own – maybe she liked the glamour of his career in broadcasting – and poor Jeremy was helpless, like a rabbit caught in the headlights.

Roger replied thoughtfully, "It's unlike you to be so uncharitable, Syl. I must say, I found her a lovely young woman. A bit reserved maybe, yes, but I suppose she was on her best behaviour, wasn't she?"

Sylvia tried hard to see things from Roger's point of view. It would make the whole situation so much better if Roger were right. But, in her woman's heart, Sylvia knew what was what and, besides, it went against Roger's nature to think badly of any pretty young woman.

When Jeremy and Smita announced their engagement, about six months later, Sylvia sent an enormous bouquet, hoping to make up with an excess of flowers for her shortage of happy feelings. It was arranged that she and Roger would have dinner with Smita's parents when they were next home on leave.

Sylvia preferred to gloss over that acutely awful evening in a showy restaurant in St John's Wood. Smita's mother, Naisha, an optician – as she managed to mention in most sentences – talked nineteen to the dozen. Her father, Prem, barely spoke. Jeremy and Smita both looked exquisitely embarrassed throughout and Roger, in his hale and hearty way, was so determined that everyone should get on and have a jolly evening that he had far too much to drink and ended up making a number of distinctly risqué jokes. Oh, it had been dreadful and afterwards Sylvia had felt terrible for Jeremy who was walking so innocently into the clutches of those two predatory women, Smita and Naisha, who would both perch on him and peck him to bits. She had never really had the closeness with her son which would have permitted her to say something. If she attempted to say anything, it would certainly be a disaster and it was a pity that knowing that hadn't stopped her from doing it.

It was only three weeks before the wedding, she had left it far too late and when she caught Jeremy on his own one evening – Smita was at her book group – she should have stuck to discussing the wedding arrangements and not suddenly burst out, clutching her G and T for dear life, "Oh Jem, are you absolutely sure about this?"

Jeremy looked appalled. His mother hadn't called him "Jem" since he was about ten years old. "What on earth are you talking about?" he snapped, as usual reddening immediately.

Sylvia couldn't contain herself any more. "You and Smita," she asked desperately. "Are you really absolutely sure you're right for one another?"

Jeremy laughed. It was a harsh sarcastic laugh. "You're unbelievable," he replied, shaking his head. "How long have Smi and I been together? Two years? And the wedding's been planned for the last six months? And you're asking me now, with just three weeks to go, whether I'm sure we're right for one another? For Christ's sake!"

He walked out of the room with Sylvia calling beseechingly after him, "I wasn't implying anything. It's just, it's a big step you're taking and, you know, your backgrounds are very different."

Jeremy reappeared in the doorway. Icily, he said, "*You* may have misgivings about Smi and her 'different' background but I don't." He paused menacingly. "And I don't want to hear anything more about it ever again."

The wedding passed off as well as could be expected. There were two weddings actually: first the registry office and then a ceremony in a Hindu temple in Leicester which Prem and Naisha had apparently insisted on. Sylvia was entranced by the ceremony: all the chanting of prayers and the fire and the smearing of auspicious dabs of colour on the young couple's foreheads. It took her back years to the myriad sensations of Delhi and she thought rather badly of Smita for looking so obviously bored and sulky throughout. Jeremy looked frankly ridiculous, with his groom's garland and his loose coloured shirt. But Roger said good for him for agreeing to go along with it and putting on such a brave face. Even when he was decades younger, there was no way that Roger would ever have agreed to sit cross-legged on the floor like that, draped in flowers, and let himself be daubed with coloured splodges. Sylvia snorted with laughter at the very idea of it.

The reception was held in a lavish country house hotel some way outside Leicester. For all her misgivings about the marriage and about her son being pecked to bits, Sylvia had to admit that it was a beautiful setting. Smita looked lovely and Jeremy, apart from grinning foolishly far too much, looked very dashing too. The large number of ill-assorted guests mingled good-humouredly and the sun shone. When Jeremy and Smita were driven away in a dark grey pre-war Bentley, Sylvia felt a predictable pang. She cheered herself with another glass of champagne and the hope that things might not turn out as badly as she anticipated after all.

Three years had gone by since then and Roger, poor dear Roger, had been starting to wonder aloud about grandchildren. Sylvia had reminded him hypocritically that young women nowadays had careers as well as children and it was only natural that Smita, having done so well, should want to make the most of it before having to deal with babies and nappies. Sylvia felt rather virtuous for appearing to speak in Smita's defence when in actual fact – although nothing terrible had happened in these last three years – everything had reinforced her conviction that Smita was a cold calculating person. For all Sylvia knew, Smita didn't even want children. Well, she had been proved wrong about that.

But look at the way Smita had welcomed her yesterday,

not even bothering to come down to open the door to their absurd loft-style apartment. Smita had a pernicious influence on Jeremy too. The poor silly boy was so easily led. It was certainly Smita's idea, not Jeremy's, that Sylvia should stay for a mere two or three nights in the comfort of the hotel before being packed off to a service apartment to save money. Once there, conveniently stowed away, they would manage her life as they saw fit. She was a nuisance obviously and they had decided to deal with the nuisance as best suited them.

Sylvia's dimly glimpsed resolve of the morning swam into view, now large and solid and unavoidable as an iceberg. Jeremy and Smita would no doubt kick up a fuss, they would reproach her for playing havoc with their tidily laid plans. But she was not going to live in their pocket. It was silly to run back to the airport, she acknowledged that now. She would have to live in London; she really had nowhere else to go. But she was not going to live round the corner from Jeremy and Smita, no thank you.

She would go back to a part of London which she knew, somewhere she had once belonged and she would make the best of things there on her own terms. Not Chelsea; that would be far too painful and besides those little postage stamp houses were exorbitantly expensive nowadays. But it would have to be an area she was familiar with and one which was a long ride away from Belsize Park. She felt sad at the thought of being a long ride away from her grandson. But maybe he would be allowed to stay for longer with her on each visit if it took some time to get there. In her mind, she revisited the haunts of her youth as drowsiness slowly began to get the better of her. She remembered all the places where she had been young and happy and, just before sleep blotted out her thoughts, she set her sights on Kensington.

స్

Smita was horrified to discover, one morning towards the middle of May, that she could not do up the waistband of her favourite black trousers. She could pull and strain but the two sides wouldn't meet, however hard she tried. For a few moments, she felt something close to panic. Of course she knew, in the abstract, that when you were pregnant your tummy swelled up. Now it was actually happening to her, she felt suddenly desperate, trapped almost. It was as if she was losing control of herself, of her body; she, who had always prided herself on her supreme self-control. Now her body was doing something she didn't like, didn't approve of and there was absolutely nothing she could do about it. Angrily, she forced the zip closed and left the two buttons undone, to be concealed under a long top. It was uncomfortable but it worked. She was nearly halfway to the Tube before it occurred to her that cramming her expanding belly into tight trousers might harm the baby and, terrified, she had to rush back home to change. Thank God, Jeremy had already left for an early meeting so she didn't have to explain her sudden return to him. He would have been really angry with her and accused her of putting vanity before their child's welfare.

Smita felt annoyed, not for the first time, that Jeremy

seemed to be adjusting to prospective parenthood so much more quickly and easily than she was. It was all very well for him, she thought rancorously, as she changed into a loose grey tunic dress with a sober black top underneath; he had so much less to lose.

She had noticed the reactions at work when she broke the news of her pregnancy – and they hadn't all been congratulatory by any means. There had been some quickly concealed irritation from her boss at the inconvenience but also perceptible glee from certain of her colleagues as if, with her announcement, Smita the front runner had voluntarily sidelined herself. Of course Smita intended to return to work at the first possible opportunity. There was no way she would ever be a stay-at-home mother. But still she realised that, from now on, her single-minded dedication to the Gravington Babcock consultancy would be forever in doubt.

So losing her figure was the last straw really. The thought of buying maternity clothes filled her with gloom. She had imagined that she would manage somehow by leaving her jackets unbuttoned and wearing things that were stretchy and loose. But she understood now how ridiculously unrealistic that was. She was only sixteen weeks and already her trousers wouldn't do up. There were still five months of this humiliating experience to go and it was obvious that by October, even if she starved herself, she would be as big as a bus. She stood sullenly on the crowded Tube, feeling sorry for herself and resentful. At least she didn't show yet; if some slightly younger and much slimmer girl stood up to offer Smita her seat, she would simply die.

By the time she got to her desk, she was in such a black mood she could barely concentrate. Of course, in all the to-do over changing clothes, she had not had time to get any breakfast and now she felt guilty about that too. She was too disciplined normally to succumb to the ten thirty round of muffins and croissants but today when one of the secretaries called, "I'm going over to Starby's. Does anyone fancy anything?" Smita answered "Me please" and of course the stupid girl seized on it and joked loudly, "Ooh, eating for two, are we?"

Smita replied stonily, "A skinny decaf latte and a low-fat muffin please." She was pleased to see the girl looking embarrassed as she collected Smita's money.

Smita ate the muffin and drank the coffee without enjoyment. How was it that so much seemed to be slipping out of her control suddenly? Over the past few months, there was an endless succession of things which hadn't gone the way she wanted.

It had all started of course with Roger's sudden death and then her mother-in-law's return to the UK. The timing had been simply gruesome. Smita had already suspected she might be pregnant for about ten days. But the awful shock of Roger's completely unexpected death – while inspecting a building site in terrible heat – and then the gathering of the family for the funeral had made Smita put off a pregnancy test. She didn't want her proud announcement to be overshadowed by everyone else's sadness. She felt a secret last minute reluctance too. She had gone ahead with "trying for a baby" because it was what one did after a couple of years of marriage and everyone else – Jeremy, her parents – seemed so keen. But privately she was hoping it would take much longer than this to happen. So in a way it was good to have an excuse to put off finding out.

But, the morning after the funeral, she could bear to wait no longer and she used the testing kit which had been lying ready in a drawer. It came up positive so quickly that she had no time to get nervous. She stared at the two inky blue lines in the little window and felt horrified. What had she *done*? She hadn't even made up her mind yet if she wanted children.

Hurriedly, she went to find Jeremy, knowing that his excitement and enthusiasm would be contagious. He was sitting at his desk, looking down at a great confusion of papers. "It's amazing," he said, without looking up, "how much there is to do when someone dies."

Smita said, "Turn around and look at me and, please, for a moment, don't think about your father."

Jeremy spun his chair round and looked at Smita in disbelief. "Hang on a minute Smi, we only buried him yesterday. What's that you're holding?"

Smita clasped her hands, one of which was still holding the pregnancy test wand, behind her back. "Concentrate," she instructed him. "Promise me you're not thinking about your father or the funeral or the cemetery or anything sad."

Jeremy raised his eyebrows. "This had better be good."

Smita produced the pregnancy test wand from behind her back and leapt into the air, flourishing it and crying, "Ta-dah! I'm pregnant!"

She came to a standstill and waited for Jeremy's reaction. But, for a few moments, he simply didn't react; he sat motionless in his chair and stared at her with no perceptible emotion on his face at all.

"Well?" Smita prompted him, hurt and uncomprehending. "Aren't you going to say anything? Aren't you *pleased*?"

Jeremy stood up with a major effort as if he were ill or exhausted and came over to her without saying anything. He put his arms around her and held her silently until she pushed him away impatiently to look up into his face and ordered him, "Say *something*." Then she saw he was crying.

She was devastated; Jeremy never cried. He hadn't even cried at his father's funeral when she felt he really should have. It took only a second for Smita's shock to turn to anger. "What's the matter?" she demanded. "I thought you wanted me to have a baby?"

Jeremy took her hands tenderly in both of his. "Smi, Smi, I'm incredibly happy," he sobbed. "It's just I'm incredibly sad too."

In that instant, Smita understood that nothing was going to turn out how she had intended. From the moment of her conception, her baby daughter was part of Jeremy's and Sylvia's and Roger's story too and not, as she had fondly imagined for the past couple of years, exclusively her own. Later, when she had a chance to think the whole messy situation over, it made her feel – slightly – as if the minute being inside her was partly an alien; not totally her own flesh and blood but all sorts of other people's relative too. She didn't like this feeling which she suspected was unnatural and she worried that actually she was not cut out to be a mother at all.

For the days before and after the funeral, Sylvia had stayed with her friend Heather Bailey in Knightsbridge. Thank goodness she wasn't staying with them because, forgetting Sylvia's grief-stricken state, Smita would have found it intolerable to have to share the first days of her pregnancy with her mother-in-law. Besides she wanted to be – quietly, tactfully – happy and how would that have been possible with Sylvia sobbing and hiccuping all over the place? To Smita's dismay, Jeremy was pretty miserable himself which she hadn't really anticipated – he and Roger had always had so little to do with each other, frankly – and even though he had risen to the occasion superbly after her announcement – once he had stopped crying – with flowers and a gift, he was still much more subdued than she would have wanted after such amazing news.

So it had gone on; in due course, Sylvia had returned to Dubai, clutching her ninety-fourth gin and tonic, to pack up her life there and sort out her affairs. She hadn't been back for a month when Jeremy told Smita, grim-faced, that his mother had decided to move back to London. Smita had been so outraged that for a few moments she could barely speak. How could this happen? How could *he* let this happen? Then she had started raging and crying and she had worked herself up into such a state that Jeremy had told her to calm down; it was bad for the baby.

"Bad for the baby?" she had shouted indignantly. "It's bad for the baby to have your mother announcing she's coming to live here." And she had run upstairs and flung herself face-down on their beautiful huge bed and wept.

Jeremy had followed her, wretchedly unhappy, red in the face and perspiring. "Smi, listen to me, Smi" he pleaded. "*I'll* deal with her. She'll be *my* responsibility. And we'll *contain* her; we'll make sure she does everything on our terms."

Smita rolled over and threw her husband a scornful look. "Contain her?" She had repeated sarcastically. "What are you talking about? You can no more contain your mother than the Niagara Falls."

She had been rather pleased with this pronouncement which had effectively silenced Jeremy.

But it gave her no pleasure of course when she was proved utterly right the minute Sylvia stepped off the plane some six weeks later. They had everything worked out, they had talked about it for weeks; she would stay for two or three days in the hotel down the road, they would find her a convenient service apartment, make sure she didn't rush into the purchase of some crackpot property for at least three months and then they would aim to have her settled somewhere within easy reach but off their backs before the baby arrived in October. But Sylvia, of course, had insisted on going her own sweet way and she had ridden roughshod over all their thoughtful plans.

Looking back over the last few weeks as she sat at her desk, unable to concentrate on her work, Smita shuddered at the sheer chaotic unpredictability of it all. She had complained to her own mother on the phone that it was like having a rampaging rhino let loose in your life and her mother had giggled and then chided her for being uncharitable. Her own parents' uncomplicated joy at her good news, accompanied in her father's case by a great deal of praying, went a long way towards making up for all the death-related complications on Jeremy's side. But nothing could really compensate for the massive black cloud of Sylvia's presence in London.

Smita could forgive Sylvia a number of things. After all, she was newly widowed and Smita would have to be pretty unfeeling not to make allowances. But even so, she found herself outraged by Sylvia's doings every single day.

Even though he had sworn he wouldn't, Jeremy had gone and told his mother about the baby the day she arrived. Three days later, Sylvia had come round to have tea with Smita and, after hugging her uncomfortably close, she had spent the whole time telling her how simply marvellous it was for *her*, Sylvia, that this should have happened at this tragic juncture of her life.

"Forget about *me*," Smita had raged later at Jeremy, "and how awful it might be for *me* to have my pregnancy linked like that to someone's death. Honestly, she went on as if the baby was just a replacement, a substitute for Roger." She stopped when she saw Jeremy wince.

What she didn't tell him, because she wasn't at all sure how he would react, was that the very *worst* part of the visit had come towards the end when Sylvia had taken it upon herself to tell Smita what a wonderful grandmother she would be and all the wonderful things she would do with the baby. 'Well,' Smita had thought to herself viciously, 'forget it.' There was no way, no *way* she was ever letting Sylvia go off anywhere with *her* baby. If Sylvia was lucky, if she behaved, she could sit the baby on her knee for a short while – but only if Smita or Jeremy were close at hand – and she could buy her presents. That was *it*. It made Smita quite angry in fact, recalling Jeremy's stories of his own childhood and what a distant, uninvolved mother Sylvia had been. Now here she was, trying to make up for it by becoming much *too* involved with her granddaughter.

Then there had been all that awful business with the hotel and Sylvia's refusal to move into any of the perfectly nice flats which Jeremy had found for her. She had stayed at the hotel for three weeks, three *weeks*, running up enormous bills as if money were no object. And then she had virtually turned her back on them.

When Smita remembered Sylvia's offhand phone call, announcing that she had moved to Kensington, she still felt furious. Of all the thoughtless and hurtful things Sylvia had ever done, that was the worst. No, it wasn't. Even back in Saudi, the first time Jeremy had taken Smita to visit his parents, the signs had been there. Of course, Smita had taken no notice then, she had given Sylvia the benefit of the doubt. Because, even though she had been privately pretty sure that she and Jeremy were going to get married, she had assumed that she would never have very much to do with her blundering rhinoceros of a mother-in-law. She lived in Riyadh after all.

There had been that excursion to the old ruined city in the desert: she and Jeremy, Sylvia and Roger and those ghastly friends of theirs, Nikki and Nigel Palmer who had treated Smita as if she were someone really exotic, newly arrived from the Amazon rainforest. She was from *Leicester*, for Christ's sake.

Just as they were all getting ready to leave, in two cars, Sylvia had suggested, "Let's do girls and boys, shall we?" And Nikki had exclaimed, "Ooh yes, let's" and even though Smita had looked desperately at him, Jeremy had blushed but said nothing and, as a result, Smita had been stuck in one car with Sylvia and Nikki while Jeremy suffered separately with his father and Nigel. Of course it was petty, it was insignificant and it was not a long drive. But it showed Sylvia's game so clearly; right from the start, she had weighed her own wishes against Smita's and she had made sure that, thanks to Jeremy's weakness, she won every time.

Then there had been that horrible incident right before the wedding when Sylvia had suddenly taken it into her head to warn Jeremy off Smita, belatedly to raise the subject of 'cultural differences'. Jeremy had only told Smita about it long afterwards, as if he had been worried that it might scare her off. It didn't scare her but it did harden her heart against Sylvia and it also made her wonder apprehensively what Sylvia might have in store for her, having failed on that all-important issue to make Jeremy do what she wanted.

What she turned out to have in store were insincere good deeds, Girl Guidey English doing her duty by her daughter-in-law and, even though Smita should probably have been grateful – it could have been so very much worse – she resented every insincere good deed, every dutiful charade. While in time she had grown quite fond of boozy old Roger, as far as she was concerned, Sylvia could never ever make good.

So really Smita should not have been at all surprised by Sylvia's move. It was utterly in character; high-handed, inconsiderate, impervious to other people's feelings. But still it had shocked her. After all that they had done for her, after all the time poor Jeremy had spent traipsing around apartments with her, without a word to either of them, she had suddenly gone off on her own and signed a year's lease on a flat off Kensington High Street. It was so *mean*. Now Jeremy was going to have to waste hours and days travelling to and fro across London to visit her. If he went at the weekend, then their weekends would be spoilt; if he went in the week, he would be worn out. There was no way *she* was going to go; if Sylvia wanted to see her, let *her* make the effort.

And what were they supposed to do when the baby came? Put her in her little car seat and drive, doubtless with the baby screaming her head off, halfway across London and back? When Smita's own mother had already said, several times, that she would come down from Leicester every single weekend that she could to help out with the baby? No *way*. By her selfish move, Sylvia had simply reduced her likely involvement in her granddaughter's life. And, who knew, maybe she had actually done it on purpose? She had never been that interested in her own son when he was small, had she? What if all this fuss about the marvellous timing of her first grandchild's arrival was just another goody-goody charade?

When they had asked her, in bewilderment, why on earth she had moved so far away from them, she had replied that it was because she had been young and happy in Kensington and she wanted to live there again. But, according to Jeremy, his parents had lived in *Chelsea* when they were first married, not in Kensington, so what sense did that make? And, besides, given that Roger was now *dead* and that Sylvia was grieving, wouldn't it have been better to try and make a fresh start somewhere completely new?

In any case, Smita was not sure she bought Sylvia's version of their happily ever after marriage. From what she had observed over the past five years or so, Sylvia and Roger's marriage fell far short of the dream ticket in several respects. Sylvia had only been twenty-two when they got married; what kind of a choice could she have made? It would have been a choice born of convention; getting married young was what nice girls did back then. They didn't go to university or get high-powered jobs in management consultancy – which must explain Sylvia's jealousy of Smita, of course. Smita was young and attractive, successful and smart, she was slim too; no wonder Sylvia had it in for her. Sylvia hadn't had any of Smita's opportunities. She had gone straight from school to a secretarial course, she had done a couple of lowly typing and coffee-making jobs; while doing the second or third one, she had met Roger, her boss and that had been that.

A few years later, Roger's career had taken them off to Hong Kong and then, for the rest of her adult life, Sylvia had been an ex-pat wife, a jolly good ex-pat wife who kept a lovely home and threw great parties and did her bit of voluntary work. But that was it; she had never properly worked again, she had moved from country to country, wherever Roger's work had taken them and, apart from swimming and tennis and coffee mornings, she had had no life of her own at all. How could she have been happy with that?

True, Roger must have been good-looking when he was young – before he put on weight – and fun too. In the beginning, they probably loved each other. But Roger was a ladies' man. How long had he been content with his young, goody-goody wife? Smita had often observed him chatting up attractive women. She had been on the receiving end of his charms once or twice herself. Even in later life, when he had grown heavy and red-faced, Roger was still a handsome man. There must have been other women, *must* have; on business trips, when Sylvia was back in England on her long home leaves, visiting Jeremy at boarding school. Maybe Sylvia, with her English stiff upper lip, had chosen to turn a blind eye, told herself that all men were basically beasts, what could you expect? But had she been *happy*? That Smita found hard to believe.

For that matter, had Roger been happy? As the years went by and Sylvia, with her horizons limited by her circumstances, grew more and more boring, prattling on about the house and the servants, her bizarre obsession with wildlife and, in spite of the swimming and the tennis, growing heavier and heavier? Poor Roger.

And why had they waited *ten years* to have a baby? So

that Sylvia was in her mid-thirties when Jeremy was born and afterwards it was too late to have any more. Or at least that was what she had told Jeremy. Had she really had fertility problems? If so, she had certainly never said anything about it to Jeremy although, in that family, communication was virtually non-existent. Smita was always puzzled that Jeremy had never bothered to ask. Wasn't it pretty odd to wait ten years to have children? Say there had been some sort of medical problem, not infertility, wasn't it her right to know? What if for instance there had been a baby born with something terribly wrong with it who had died and it had all been hushed up, as people used to do in those days? Shouldn't she be told?

Her anxiety brought her sharply back to the present. The morning was more than half gone and she had achieved nothing. My God, what was happening to her? Irritably, she pulled her mouse towards her and, with a brisk dip of her finger, brought her screen back to life. Seventeen new e-mails; her heart sank. She had a report to finish by the end of the week, meetings with clients that afternoon and the next morning and her in-tray was literally overflowing. She was losing her grip; that was what was happening.

At that moment, the strangest thing happened. Smita felt a faint flutter deep in her stomach. What was *that*? She sat back in her chair and placed her hand on her swelling stomach. She waited for a moment: nothing. She had imagined it. But, as she leant forward to take the contents of her in-tray in both hands and empty them on to her desk, she felt the fluttering sensation again, more strongly this time and she sat back sharply, wondering what on earth it was. Was something wrong? As she sat there, perfectly still, hoping that by not moving too much she could stop whatever inner upset was under way, it occurred to her that it might be the baby moving. No, surely not, wasn't it too early? As if in response, she felt a third faint movement and this time because her hand was resting on her stomach she felt a subtle ripple pass under her hand. Smita was dumbstruck; oh my God, the baby was *real*.

She snatched for her mobile to call Jeremy but there was no answer. She checked her watch; of course, he was in his meeting, he would be in there until twelve. She had to tell someone but there was no way she could call her mother and tell her something like that in the middle of the office. Her mother would scream with delight, people would overhear, she would never hear the end of it. She looked around the room to see if there was anyone else she could confide in. Gemma? Sweet gay Mikey? What would she say? What might they say? And would they want to put their hands on her tummy to feel for themselves? Yuck. No, it would be wrong to tell anyone else something like that before Jeremy. She would just have to wait until noon. She should go outside and call him on the landing so no-one would overhear her being mumsy. She looked around the room again at all her colleagues working away, staring rapt at their screens, chattering excitedly into their phones and she felt a bit depressed that she didn't really want to tell any of them what had just happened. She sat there for a while, feeling rather isolated and lonely, because of course the truth was she knew that none of them would really care.

Flat 3, 27 Overmore Gardens was not exactly Kensington. But then London in the early summer of 2004 – as Sylvia was fast discovering – was not exactly London either. Or at least not any version of London which Sylvia recognized.

Her move to Overmore Gardens had, predictably, triggered a frightful depression. As long as she stayed at the hotel, she could, to a certain extent, keep reality at bay. She could plough up and down the little swimming pool every day, greet the tremendously fat Middle Eastern man in his dressing gown in the lift, eat cardboard and ketchup sandwiches and pretend she was nowhere at all. She could pretend that Roger was still in Dubai rather than dead. Other than when she got into bed in the evenings and Roger was not there beside her and she knew he never would be again, she could pretend his absence was a perfectly benign, normal absence; he was away on a business trip, she was here on home leave on her own. It had been that way so often over the years. It was the easiest thing to create a cocoon of sweet illusion from which she was jolted several times a day, true but inside which she could cope.

Moving to a flat on her own destroyed that illusion brutally. It wasn't true, as Jeremy and Smita had accused her shrilly, that she had rushed into it. She had thought it over sensibly for at least a week before making her move.

And anyway, once you found a flat that you liked the look of, you couldn't dither, you had to make up your mind quickly or someone else would take it. Her new estate agent, a girl called Freddy who was incidentally a much nicer person than Gid, told her so repeatedly. It wasn't that she had fallen for Overmore Gardens. To tell the truth, she didn't particularly want to live anywhere. But she could just about imagine herself living there – something about the solid dark red brick facades and the way the filtered city light fell through the tall windows – and if Jeremy and Smita couldn't understand that, well that was simply too bad.

It was all their fault that she had felt obliged to move out of the hotel so quickly anyway. They kept reminding her how expensive it was. Although why that should be any concern of theirs, she couldn't honestly see. If she wanted to spend her money on comfort and anonymity, why shouldn't she? Jeremy and Smita were both earning good salaries, they didn't need her to count the pennies, did they, even with the baby coming. And the fact they were both so ready to interfere, to bully her – in her sorry state! – into doing what suited them had made her run a mile frankly. If this was how they were starting out then, when the novelty wore off, heaven help her.

She endured a series of sorry lunches and suppers at their flat. Since Smita's pregnancy had been made public, she was acting like the queen bee and even though she was coldly polite to her mother-in-law, she managed to make it quite clear that she found her the most colossal nuisance. As for poor Jeremy, caught between the demands of his selfish wife and his duty to his newly widowed mother, you could see him squirm and suffer through every meal. It put Sylvia off her food frankly.

One night, shortly before she made her move, Jeremy and Smita had come close to having a row in front of her. Fortunately, it was nothing to do with her. But it alarmed her to see how tense and snappish they both were. She felt uncomfortable sitting with them and she knew that her clumsy attempt to change the subject by talking for far too long about the chick-rearing habits of the Emperor penguins had got on both their nerves.

"You *said*," Smita had started it. "You *said* you would talk to the Castellinis about the bikes the *last* time they left them in the hall and you didn't and now they're there again, did you notice?"

Jeremy nodded wearily. "I know but I don't think we can realistically complain about it now, do you?"

"Whatever do you mean?" Smita snapped.

"Well Smi," Jeremy replied, grinning, a mistake Sylvia thought, "in six months' time we're going to have a pram standing in the hall round the clock, aren't we?"

Smita looked aghast. "I'm not leaving my baby's pram down in that hall, thank you very much," she said quickly, though Sylvia could have sworn she looked so horrified because this perfectly obvious fact had not occurred to her. "It would get all dusty. Anyone could drop anything into it; it would be unhygienic."

"So you're planning to lug the pram up and down four flights of stairs every time you go in or out, are you?" Jeremy asked.

Smita looked uneasy but answered, "If need be."

"You mean, if I'm not there to do it for you?" Jeremy asked. Sylvia was pleased to note he could be combative if need be.

"Maybe we could build a cupboard for it in the hall?" Smita suggested. "You know, like a small shed thing we could just push it in and out of. With a lock."

Jeremy laughed. "You've been bitching about the Castellinis' grandchildren's bikes ever since we moved in here and now you expect them to let us build a whacking great cupboard in the front hall? Come *on*."

"Firstly," Smita said icily, "I don't think I've been 'bitching' and secondly, I can't imagine your poor mother wants to sit here listening to this."

She got up huffily and went over to the open-plan kitchen to make coffee and, while she was busy making it, Sylvia valiantly tried to overcome the awkwardness by launching into her tirade about the Emperor penguins.

No wonder she had decided to move away from them. It was best for everybody, she was sure. Well, it was certainly the best thing for her and she felt it was only fair that she put her own needs first at a time like this. The distance she was putting between herself and her coming grandson did trouble her. Of course it did. But she kept telling herself that the further away she was, the longer each visit would last when he came to her. Look at Smita's mother up in Leicester; she would doubtless have him for whole weekends and for every holiday.

Certainly, she had taken the little boy into account when she chose her flat. Overmore Gardens was a garden square and even though, within two minutes of leaving it, you were on the Earls Court Road which was crowded and squalid, the square itself looked respectable and safe. If she took the flat there, Freddy the estate agent explained to her excitedly, she would be given the key to the garden in the square and on a sunny afternoon she could sit out there and meet her neighbours and it would be lovely. Sylvia peered through the railings at the garden: a well-mown lawn, gravel paths, lilac. Deep in the greenery she spotted a flash of colour and, after craning awkwardly through the gate, she saw that it was a little children's playground with swings and a see-saw and a climbing frame.

"Oh," she exclaimed to Freddy. "Perfect."

Freddy flashed a ready smile. "Lovely, innit?"

"No," Sylvia explained. "No, I mean the little playground. I'm expecting my first grandchild, you see."

Freddy squealed, "Oo-ooh!" She clutched Sylvia's arm, half sharing her excitement and half steering her over the road to Number 27. "Well, he'll *love* it here."

The houses around the square were red brick Victorian mansion blocks. They looked like houses but actually they were all divided up into flats with six or eight brass bells at each front door. Each front door had a stained glass pane over it and each entrance had a porch with two great big pillars on either side, grand but grimy.

These were the sort of London homes which Sylvia remembered and, even though she still had trouble imagining herself living anywhere without Roger, she could just about imagine herself living here. Before going up the front steps, Sylvia already knew what the layout of the flat would probably be and what the stairwell would smell of – and she was right. She felt considerably cheered by this. Overmore Gardens could never be more than a staging post; it could never be home because, having moved around so much, Roger had long ago become her home. But she felt she could survive here. Unlike the pastel nonsense of Belsize Park with its transient population of generations of refugees, in Overmore Gardens Sylvia imagined she might eventually settle down – after a fashion. She might really get to know her neighbours and sit chatting with them in the square garden in the sunshine.

The flat was pretty much as she expected with a view of the garden square from the sitting room at the front and a view of other people's back gardens from the two bedrooms at the back. It was on the first floor, which would be nice and easy with a baby or a toddler. The front hall was more than wide enough for a pram. Sylvia looked around carefully inside for dangers to a small child but couldn't see any.

She walked around the flat for quite a while longer, trying hard to imagine living there, while Freddy fidgeted impatiently behind her. It was not too far for her friend Heather Bailey to come over occasionally from Knightsbridge. But when all was said and done, she knew she was going to be dreadfully lonely here. She went over to the front window, trying to ignore Freddy's fidgeting and looked down at the garden in the square again.

At just that moment, a woman of about Sylvia's age, she assumed a grandmother, was unlocking the gate to let a little boy in red trousers and a green hooded top into the garden. She locked the gate carefully behind her – well done, Sylvia thought – and followed the child hastily as he ran full tilt towards the playground. When they reached the swings, he turned to his grandmother pleadingly, his arms extended, and she bent and lifted him tenderly into a swing. First gently and then more vigorously, she began to push him. The little boy held on tight with both hands, threw his head back and laughed and laughed.

Sylvia turned to Freddy and, surprising herself by how firm and decisive she sounded, she said, "I'll take it."

Freddy squealed with delight. "Ooh Mrs Garland, you've made my week! My *month* in fact. Yay!" She rang someone on her mobile and started screeching excitedly about deals and contests and bonuses and someone being neck and neck with someone else. When she had finished, she turned to Sylvia and said, "Let's dash back to the office and you can sign on it right away. Yay!"

Sylvia asked faintly, "Do I need to do it straight away? Is there any rush?"

"Well, you wouldn't want someone else to get it, would you?" Freddy asked menacingly. "Not now you've fallen for it."

"I wouldn't say," Sylvia answered slowly, "that I've exactly fallen for it. And I'm wondering if maybe I should let my son see it after all?"

"No *way*!" Freddy exclaimed. "You're the one who's going to be living here, Mrs Garland, not him! And after everything you've told me while we've been driving round these past two days, why *would* you? He'll make you move into one of those crap places in Belsize Park, you know he will."

"You're right," Sylvia agreed reluctantly. "Very well then, lead on Macduff. I suppose I'll sign."

She did wonder, after she'd signed the papers at the agency and Freddy had whooped and called out something about champagne to a couple of her colleagues, whether she should have given more thought to the issue of furniture. Her own furniture, all her worldly goods in fact, were on a container ship on their way from Dubai. They were not due to arrive in London for another couple of weeks. She had supposed she would simply put them into storage when they arrived care of the removal company because there was no way she could squeeze the contents of a large company villa into a small London flat. It would take time and thought to work out what she should keep and what she should get rid of. She had been in no fit state to even think about that when she was packing up and leaving Dubai. If it hadn't been for their friends, Nigel and Nikki Palmer, if they had not come round and held her hand and supervised the removal men, she would never have got through it. Dear Nigel and Nikki whom they had first met years ago in India and who had somehow turned up years later in Saudi and then again in Dubai, always following them around, Roger joked.

To tell the truth, Sylvia was frightened of the arrival of the furniture too; she was frightened of what might happen to her when she saw Roger's empty armchair, when she smelt Roger's soap and aftershave and Roger's sweat still haunting his possessions. She supposed the sea voyage might have blown it away but that would be even worse. So she was in no hurry to have her own things around her again. But she hadn't really given much thought either to what it would feel like suddenly, at the age of sixty-two, to be back living in rented furnished accommodation again like a young thing of twenty.

She was sure it was that which had triggered her collapse. She had arrived at eleven o'clock on a sunny morning, as Freddy had promised, with her luggage from the hotel and her new set of house keys jangling in her bag. There were so many of them; she wondered how on earth she would get it straight. There was one for the street door, two for the flat door and a fourth grotesquely large one which she supposed must be the key to the square garden. A pity it looked like something out of the chamber of horrors.

Sylvia had a respite of a few over-excited hours after she let herself in when she still thought she might be alright. She opened all the windows, sat down looking out over the garden and determinedly made herself a little shopping list. There was nothing at all in the kitchen: not a single teabag, not a sugar lump. She went boldly out to the Earls Court Road and bought herself tea, sugar, milk and, for some reason she couldn't rightly explain, a packet of brightly iced zoo biscuits. She made herself a strong cup of tea and called Jeremy to break the news. It was not an easy phone call – Jeremy was outraged at what she had done – and afterwards she decided to go down into the garden to recover. It was lovely but empty on a Monday morning and as soon as the sun went in, Sylvia felt cold.

During the long afternoon, she unpacked her single suitcase, flinching at hanging her clothes in someone else's wardrobe and debated again whether or not to telephone her sister Cynthia whom she hadn't yet spoken to but she couldn't make up her mind. She needed to be up to it to talk to Cynthia and, as the afternoon wore on, she felt less and less that she was.

When it began to get dark, Sylvia sensed herself disintegrating; her lacquer-hard self-control cracking into millions of tiny pieces. She was sitting in someone else's armchair in someone else's living room and she herself had disappeared entirely. She stayed like that, non-existent, all evening and all night, not drawing the curtains nor turning on the lights. She simply could not bear the thought of sleeping in someone else's bed. Once or twice, she dimly remembered afterwards, she had got up to use someone else's toilet but she had come back automatically to the armchair and lapsed into nothingness again. Strangely, throughout the interminable night, illuminated only by the sickly light of the street lamps in the square, she had not moaned or cried or wailed. It was not reticence, an awareness that she now had upstairs and downstairs neighbours. Crying or wailing would have been a protest; they would have meant she was resisting her fate. Whereas, instead, she had – briefly – succumbed to it. First, she had lost her husband of nearly forty years, she had lost her house and the warm climate and the far away sky she had grown used to. She had lost the familiar, forlorn sound of the plover's cry from the lagoons and the secret rustle of the garden irrigation system springing into life at night. Against her better judgement, she had come to this cold, grey city and she had promptly cut herself off from her son, the only link to life she had left here. She had cast herself adrift and, that night, she went under.

At some point, the sky lightened and the traffic noise started up again outside but still Sylvia didn't move. If during that lost time she thought at all, she thought that if she stayed perfectly still, didn't move, didn't eat, didn't drink, she might actually fade away and that would be the best thing for everybody.

But as the morning crept along, she became increasingly conscious of two things which contradicted her non-existence; she had pins and needles in her legs and she was really dreadfully thirsty. Eventually, the twin discomforts got the better of her and she hauled herself up out of the armchair and staggered to the bathroom. She was shocked when she saw herself in the bathroom mirror; she looked an absolute fright. But she also still looked pretty substantial despite her haggard expression and her wild hair. It would take forever for her actually to fade away.

She plodded to the kitchen feeling light-headed and slightly giddy. What she needed desperately was a cup of tea.

While the kettle was boiling, she caught sight of the packet of zoo biscuits, lying unopened on the kitchen table. She remembered her grandson and she felt most awfully guilty; how could she have forgotten all about him and been planning to fade away? He would need her; he would need a good, solid, reliable *local* grandmother to take him to the zoo and to the Natural History Museum, to matinees and maybe, when he was old enough, for bucket and spade holidays at the seaside. If Smita and Jeremy caught the slightest suggestion of fragility, of instability, they would never let her near him. She had to drink her tea, pull herself together and go out and buy some proper food. Never mind if she felt hollow, if it seemed that she was a perfectly empty Sylvia-shaped vessel going about her business. She could keep that feeling to herself; no one need know. What she ought to do was not sit slumped for hours and hours in the armchair but get washed and dressed and go out and grapple with London.

About an hour later she opened the flat door, still feeling distinctly shaky and found an extremely small Filipino woman wearing a lime green top and fuchsia pink trousers standing outside on the landing apparently about to ring the bell. They both looked at each other in frank astonishment and then the Filipino woman recited the following improbable announcement. "Mrs Rosenkranz downstairs would like to meet you. When would you be free to come and have tea with her?"

Sylvia hoped she still had a voice to reply. She cleared her throat and croaked, "Well, I couldn't manage today."

"Tomorrow?" asked the Filipino woman.

Sylvia said, "Um."

"Next day?" shot back the small figure who had obviously been instructed not to return without Sylvia's acceptance.

"What time?" Sylvia asked vaguely, playing for time.

"Tea," the woman snapped. "Four pm."

Sylvia looked down at her, marvelling through her wooziness that someone so small and delicate-looking could be so forceful and weakly she murmured, "Fine. Thank you."

"So," the woman repeated firmly, "day after tomorrow. Four pm. Mrs Rosenkranz. Flat one."

"Yes," Sylvia agreed faintly. "The day after tomorrow. I understand. Thank you so much."

The woman turned and stamped back downstairs, not bothering with any niceties and Sylvia locked the apartment, fumbling dreadfully with the keys and followed her downstairs.

As the big front door fell shut behind her, it occurred to her to read the names beside the brass bells. In her deluded sleepless state, she half expected to find a Guildenstern there too. But of course there wasn't; the other residents of 27 Overmore Gardens were: Martinez, Ho, Irani, Rosenkranz and Smith. Her own name plate was of course blank which was as it should be since she didn't exist anymore. Mentally, she slapped herself on the wrist and, swaying slightly, set off for the Earls Court Road.

Two minutes later, leaving the relative peace and quiet of Overmore Gardens, Sylvia could not have said which city in the world she was in if it had not been for the double-decker buses and the Underground signs. Earls Court Road swarmed with people of every colour and kind and all of them going about their business at the top of their voices. The road was choked with traffic: buses, taxis, vans, all inching forward bad-temperedly, hooting and abusing one another as uninhibitedly as in any Third World city. Sylvia stopped on the crowded pavement, teetering slightly and tried to make sense of the vivid, raucous maelstrom. How on earth could this be London?

Over the past couple of weeks, she had watched a muted grey city from her hotel room and through the windows of a succession of cars and taxis. Now she found herself plunged into an Eastern bazaar. The day before she had not gone far; she had found a little Indian corner shop the minute she turned out of Overmore Gardens but today, mysteriously, the shop had disappeared. Had she maybe left the square in a different direction without noticing?

She blundered along for a little while past poisonous-smelling take-away food outlets, mobile phone shops and coffee bars, until she came to a rather run-down-looking food store called the Bazak International Food Centre. It would have to do. She went inside and helped herself to a warped wire basket. She breathed in a smell of spices, cigarettes and sickly sweet perfume and immediately she was back in the Middle East. In a fuddled trance, she went around the shop. She had been intending to buy sliced bread for toast, Cheddar cheese and Marmite, scones maybe and a big bag of toffees for consolation. She was completely taken aback when she arrived at the till with a basket of pitta bread, olives, a plastic tub of hummus, stuffed vine leaves and a tray of sticky pastries wrapped in cling film. As far as she was aware, she hadn't even seen any sliced bread or Cheddar or Marmite. For a confused moment, Sylvia worried whether she could pay in pounds.

She made her shaky way back to Overmore Gardens with her two carrier bags emblazoned with the slogan of a Middle Eastern airline. The Indian shop had somehow reappeared at the corner. Sylvia remembered that he sold sliced bread and cheese. Well, it was too bad; she couldn't carry any more now. She managed the front door of Number 27 and took a good look at the front door of Flat 1 as she went past. It looked much more solid than the front door of her own flat; panelled wood with a brass knocker and a brass peephole and a substantial well trodden doormat. Mrs Rosenkranz must have lived here for a long time.

After she had put her shopping away and made another cup of tea, Sylvia saw that it was only half past eleven. She still had the rest of the day, all of the next day and most of the day after before her tea with Mrs Rosenkranz. During that time, she supposed that she would not speak to a soul. Jeremy was in a sulk and would not ring until the weekend. Again, she thought about ringing Cynthia. But now she most definitely wasn't up to it; her ears were ringing and in the silence of the flat, she could hear the magnified beat of her own heart thumping erratically away. She was worn out. Ignoring the dubious pink bed cover, she lay down on the bed in the bigger of the two bedrooms and fell into an exhausted sleep.

When she woke, it was half past four. She was not sure where she was nor what day it was. As she lay there, painfully reassembling her new reality, a most extraordinary thing happened; in the room next door, she heard Roger clear his throat. She didn't move a fraction and waited for him to do it again. But he didn't and all the rest of that day she waited in anguish for some sign of him. Late in the evening, when she was in the kitchen putting some pitta bread and olives on a plate to nibble in front of the television, she heard from the sitting room one of the deep, excessive grunts of exertion which Roger made as he levered himself out of a deep arm chair. But of course when she dashed to the living room doorway, scattering olives, there was no one there.

All the emotions which she had managed to keep at bay in the hotel rose up and overwhelmed her. Roger had been part of her life, an immense and intrinsic part of her life, for close on forty years and his absence was as ghastly and palpable as a missing limb. He was gone but Sylvia could still feel his presence all the time.

In the empty flat in Overmore Gardens, she now began disconcertingly to hear him too, even though she knew perfectly well he wasn't there. In the silence Roger started to make all those shockingly loud, manly noises which used to startle her when he was still alive; the grunts as he rose from his armchair, the resounding groans of exasperation as he read his newspaper or tried to open a recalcitrant tin or jar, the enormous sneezes and throat-clearings which exploded without warning, the unashamed bass farts. Although they usually turned out to be something else – a noise from the street or the pipes or wishful thinking – they still shocked Sylvia because, like the amputated limb, after all Roger wasn't actually there.

Four o'clock on Thursday afternoon came round at last. The ghost of Sylvia Garland crept down the stairs to the ground floor, clutching a small bunch of sorry flowers purchased that morning on the Earls Court Road. If asked, Sylvia would not have been able to give an account of how she had spent the past two days. She knew she had slept more than once during the day and had been up a good deal at night. She had, to her brief but intense delight, observed urban foxes playing in the square garden in the small hours. She had made more lists: lists of everything and everyone she would need to create the semblance of a life for herself here. But the lists lay discarded around the sitting room. Some of the items on them might be straightforward enough to acquire. Others might take years or prove simply impossible: a circle of like-minded female friends, a birdwatching companion.

She had done her level best not to go off the deep end again. She had washed, dressed and forced down small regular meals. Although she could not find the consoling food she craved on Earls Court Road – Heinz tomato soup, Ambrosia creamed rice, Bourbon biscuits – it seemed easier to find okra there than frozen peas, pomegranates more likely than prunes.

She tried not to be led astray by Roger's noises. It was perfectly obvious that they were an illusion of some sort, produced by either her hearing or the plumbing. She resisted the attractive but nonsensical notion that Roger's presence was somehow haunting Flat 3, 27 Overmore Gardens. If Roger was going to haunt anywhere, she thought, surprising herself by her sudden rancour, it would probably be a certain flat in Pimlico, once inhabited by a Miss PeeJay Clarke.

Sylvia had not given much thought to Mrs Rosenkranz. She was too preoccupied by her own troubles and by the looming prospect of Sunday lunch in Belsize Park with a very angry Jeremy and Smita. It was only when the time came to spruce herself up and venture downstairs that she began to wonder who her downstairs neighbour actually was.

The door to Flat 1 was answered promptly by the little Filipino woman who didn't look particularly friendly or welcoming. She led Sylvia briskly down a narrow hallway into a sitting room which bore a close resemblance to Sylvia's except this one was excessively furnished and over-filled with so much clutter that Sylvia was straightaway worried she would bump into something or knock something over.

In the midst of all the furniture sat a very old white-haired lady in a high-backed sage green chair. She greeted Sylvia with a sweet smile of welcome and said to her "Come in my dear, come in. Welcome to Overmore Gardens!" and it seemed to Sylvia she could detect just the trace of a German accent.

Sylvia fumbled her way forward through the furniture, thinking about bulls and china shops. She took the old lady gingerly by the hand and shook it delicately for, close-up, she looked very frail.

"Lovely to meet you," Sylvia said loudly and clearly. "I'm Sylvia Garland, I'm your new upstairs neighbour."

"I know my dear," Mrs Rosenkranz replied brightly. "I

know. Your estate agent told Imelda and Imelda told me. And I was absolutely tickled because, do you realise, we share the same name?" She giggled naughtily and Sylvia looked at her blankly, unable to work out the joke.

"Rosenkranz means a garland of roses," the old lady explained, beaming. "You know as in 'ring-a-ring of roses'" – she sang it – "so when I heard a Mrs *Garland* was moving in upstairs, I laughed and laughed. What next, I thought, a Guirlande or a Girlanda on the top floor?"

"Goodness," Sylvia said faintly. "You do speak a lot of languages, don't you?"

"Yes," Mrs Rosenkranz said simply. "I do." She moved on quickly. "So tell me, my dear, where are you *from*?"

Sylvia was rather taken aback by the question since that was precisely what she was about to ask Mrs Rosenkranz.

Before she could answer, the Filipino maid, whom she now understood to be Imelda, came back in and asked bluntly, "Tea?"

It seemed to Sylvia a pained expression passed briefly across Mrs Rosenkranz's face but she answered courteously, "Yes please Imelda, that would be very nice." She turned back to Sylvia and asked her eagerly, "So tell me."

Sylvia had not for a moment intended to pour all her troubles into Mrs Rosenkranz's aged lap. It was quite the wrong way round when Mrs Rosenkranz was visibly a very old person living on her own who had probably invited Sylvia down at least partly for company and maybe in the hope of future neighbourly acts. But the combination of

Sylvia's grief and the previous days spent without talking to anyone was too much for her and as she opened her mouth to answer, her eyes filled with tears.

"This is rather a difficult time for me, I'm afraid," she began bravely, scrabbling urgently for a hanky in her bag. "I mean, this seems a very nice building in a very nice street. But, you see, I'm not really *meant* to be here."

She wiped her tears and blew her nose thoroughly. She hoped she hadn't perturbed old Mrs Rosenkranz. But Mrs Rosenkranz looked if anything pleased. "Nor am I," she answered enigmatically.

Sylvia, naturally, had no idea what she meant. She even wondered, for a moment, if Mrs Rosenkranz was alright in the head. She pulled herself together and explained shakily, "I haven't lived in England for thirty-five years, you see. My husband and I lived overseas; first in Hong Kong, then for a long time in India, then more recently in Saudi Arabia and in Dubai."

Mrs Rosenkranz clasped her papery old hands and exclaimed, "How marvellous! India! Hong Kong! What stories you must have."

Sylvia knew that it would be polite, at this point, to oblige with an anecdote or two: a little local colour, some camels and junks. But something seemed to be taking place over which she had no control; something prompted by the gentle, cushioned atmosphere of Mrs Rosenkranz's living room and by old Mrs Rosenkranz herself, sitting so small and wizened in the depths of her great green armchair. Sylvia couldn't stop herself.

"My husband died in January," she blurted out.

"Suddenly. I had to move back here on my own. My son –
and his wife – live in Belsize Park. They wanted me to live
near them but I – we – " she faltered again, fearing more
tears and as she did battle with her emotions, Imelda
returned pushing a laden tea trolley and scowling.

Mrs Rosenkranz leant forward and whispered, "I am
so sorry, my dear." She instructed Imelda where to park
the trolley but let her pour the tea and hand out the cups.
On the trolley were a Battenberg cake, iced biscuits and
cucumber sandwiches with the crusts cut off.

After Imelda had done her duty, she left the room
again and Sylvia gamely tried to make up for her outburst
by enthusing about the cucumber sandwiches.

Mrs Rosenkranz took no notice. "I gave up believing
in a higher power a long time ago," she said firmly. "But it
is hard not to imagine that you and I have been brought
together."

Sylvia shifted uncomfortably in her seat. Again, she
wondered whether the old lady was quite right in the head.
She waited for an explanation but none was forthcoming.

Instead Mrs Rosenkranz leant forward and said
consolingly, "At least you are fortunate to have a son living
in the same city. Any grandchildren?"

Sylvia brightened. "Well, none yet," she said eagerly,
"but there's one on the way."

"Wonderful!" exclaimed Mrs Rosenkranz, clasping her
hands again. "Wonderful. So, if all goes well, you will soon
have a little family here. That will be marvellous for you."

Sylvia asked, rather clumsily, she feared, "Do you have
any family close by?"

Mrs Rosenkranz's face fell. "Alas no," she answered. "That is why I have to rely on Imelda. I have a son and a daughter. But they both live a long way away; my son lives in New York and my daughter lives – somewhere else. I have five grandchildren but I only see them very rarely I'm afraid."

Sylvia felt a complicated pang of guilt and fear. She could always move back to North London when the lease on this flat expired.

"Do they come and stay with you sometimes?" she asked.

"Only very occasionally," Mrs Rosenkranz replied sadly. "My son and my daughter-in-law are both very busy and they only get very short holidays in America, you know. My daughter has a fear of flying and she cannot bear to put her children on a plane. I used to go and visit them but with time it gets more and more difficult." She sighed.

Sylvia tried desperately to think of something cheering to say. "Do you have any photos?" she asked brightly

"Oh, photos," Mrs Rosenkranz said dismissively. "I have hundreds and hundreds of photos. And even videos. They send them on the computer nowadays. Imelda helps me to watch them. But you can't talk to a photo, can you?" She shrugged. "Luckily, I still have my little brother who comes to see me from time to time. Little, I call him little, he's almost seventy now, my baby brother. But he lives in Northwood. It's a whole expedition to get here. Still, enough of me. Tell me, my dear, how you are planning to get settled here. Do you have a plan?"

"No," Sylvia said weakly. "No, I don't. And I think that may be the problem."

Much later, back on her own in her silent flat, Sylvia was still aware of old Mrs Rosenkranz downstairs as if she were a light source, radiating through the floorboards. Sylvia had ended up staying for nearly two hours, far longer than she had intended to and by the end Imelda was standing in the corner chafing. Sylvia had somehow or other told Mrs Rosenkranz all sorts of things: about her garden in Delhi and how Smita was nothing like a real Indian; about the endless sunny tedium of ex-pat life in Dubai, from which her bird-watching forays to the lagoon with Nigel Palmer were her only escape and how hard it was to adjust to London's low grey sky when, for years, you had been used to a faraway, clear blue one. She had learnt remarkably little about Mrs Rosenkranz, probably because she had spent so long blathering away about herself.

Trying to put together the few fragments of information which Mrs Rosenkranz had revealed, Sylvia wondered if the old lady had not been deliberately evasive. Was it normal to spend two hours talking to someone and leave, knowing so little about them? She had told Sylvia virtually nothing about her life before she moved to Overmore Gardens in 1972 even though Sylvia had been so forthcoming herself. Sylvia could recall all sorts of gaps and unspoken elements in their conversation which, if she had been in less of a state, she would have puzzled over. She wondered whether maybe something absolutely awful had once happened to Mrs Rosenkranz, something which you would not want to divulge on first acquaintance and which might make Sylvia's ordinary everyday woes seem frankly rather humdrum.

A couple of days later, she met Mrs Rosenkranz and Imelda in the street and discovered one thing which the old lady had concealed from her. Imelda was pushing Mrs Rosenkranz along in a wheelchair; she couldn't walk. Sylvia remembered that Imelda had done everything for her; handed round the tea things and cleared everything away. Mrs Rosenkranz hadn't stood up when Sylvia arrived or when she left. But she had somehow managed to avoid spelling out that her legs didn't actually work anymore.

Sylvia greeted them cheerily. She exclaimed, "Isn't it a beautiful day again?" She saw Mrs Rosenkranz looking at her shrewdly to gauge how forced her cheerfulness really was.

"Where are you off to, my dear?" asked the old lady. She and Imelda were on their way back home from the doctor's.

Sylvia answered untruthfully that she was off to Kensington High Street to join the library but, having told the lie, she did then feel obliged to make it come true a few days later. In actual fact, she was off on a wild goose chase to Hamleys, an utterly outrageous thing to do when her daughter-in-law was not yet even six months pregnant. But thinking about her grandson was the only thing which gave her any pleasure and planning for him seemed to be the only appealing activity. She had been seized by a sudden urge to see Dinky toys again and Hornby trains and Meccano. She had no idea if they were even manufactured anymore but she knew that if they were to be found anywhere, it would be at Hamleys. So she had abandoned a long, dithery, apologetic letter she was writing to Cynthia, trying to explain to her why she had taken so long to get in touch, seized her peach jacket which needed the cleaners badly and her bag and rushed headlong out of the flat.

There was an extraordinarily convenient bus, she had discovered, the number 9, still an old Routemaster, which went everywhere she had so far wanted to go: to Heather Bailey on Knightsbridge, to Fortnum's for old times' sake and, once, to Trafalgar Square.

That had been a mistake of course; on a rainy day, she had decided precipitously – after hearing Roger strain to empty his bowels in the bathroom in the early morning – to get out of the house and go and take a look at Trafalgar Square again.

She had imagined that it would somehow anchor her here, to stand at the very heart of London and remind herself of the national monuments and their grandeur. Instead, she had endured a particularly unpleasant bus journey; damp, overcrowded and fuggy. Fortunately a noble-looking robed gentleman had got up to offer her his seat or she would have had to stand, swaying and stumbling along with everybody else, for the best part of an hour.

She found herself sitting beside a young pregnant Asian woman whose stomach was bare and elaborately tattooed. Sylvia did her best not to stare but her eyes kept sneaking down to the ink-blackened belly. Whatever was the young woman thinking of? For a start it was too damp to be going around undressed like that; she would catch her death. Her short citric green top ended where her stomach began and someone had, with an ink-filled needle, scored a complicated design of flowers and Oriental characters around her inverted navel. Which had come first, Sylvia wondered, the pregnancy or the tattoo? It must have been the tattoo surely for who would score ink deep into the skin inches away from a developing life? Yet the tattoo did not look at all distended or distorted as it surely would have if it had stretched along with the skin. So the young woman must in fact have gone along of her own free will and proffered her belly to the tattoo artist, asking him to brand it with his lurid design. Inwardly, Sylvia shook her head; really, it seemed there was no accounting for anything any more.

When she got to Trafalgar Square, there was of course no sensation of homecoming; the immense slope of the square was crowded with tourists, all photographing the pigeons in dozens of different languages and Sylvia felt quite out of place and almost foreign herself. She went to have a cup of coffee near Charing Cross before catching the bus all the way home again. She was given a waxed cardboard bucket of coffee, crushed ice and piled whipped cream in response to her request for an iced coffee and she barely managed a couple of inches before setting out wearily on the long and clammy ride back to Overmore Gardens.

On the bus to Hamleys, she thought about Smita and the way she was cloaking, disguising her pregnancy in sombre workaday shades of black and grey. Was that right, was that normal? In Sylvia's day of course, it had been all flowery smocks and polka dots. She didn't expect Smita to take to wearing smocks – she would look absurd – but shouldn't she be just a bit *jollier* about her pregnancy? Sylvia acknowledged she would be horrified if Smita were to go around flaunting a bare tattooed belly like the young woman she had just seen. But couldn't she be a bit *gayer* somehow? It occurred to Sylvia that it would be a good idea for her to buy a gift of some brightly coloured maternity wear for Smita.

Her trip to Hamleys turned out to be no more successful than her visit to Trafalgar Square. The entrance to the store was jammed with huge crowds of customers pushing their way in. Nobody spoke English. A line of cycle rickshaws was pulled up at the kerb waiting for customers and, astounded, Sylvia was reminded of Delhi long years ago.

As she struggled towards the doors of the shop, she watched a young woman dressed in a pink ballgown and pink bedroom slippers who was standing on a box at the entrance. On her head she was wearing a small crown made of padded pink and gold satin. In her hands she held incongruously two orange guns from which she was firing a continuous stream of bubbles at the crowd. Her facial expression was one of docile resignation to the indignity and she also appeared to be suffering from a heavy cold.

When Sylvia was finally jostled across the threshold into the shop, she was assailed by a great gust of heat and noise. The ground floor was a gaudy emporium of mass-produced identical teddy bears, all lined up in rows, an army of bears. The young people who worked there, dressed in a uniform of red tops and black trousers, seemed to have been instructed to caper about as much as possible and to shout at the top of their voices like touts in a bazaar.

The boys' department was, wouldn't you know it, up on the fifth floor and Sylvia travelled up one escalator after another, past shouting shop assistants, toys with flashing lights, toys which made strident noises and, on every floor, families locked in dispute, children crying. Sylvia arrived at the fifth floor, tired out and horrified; was this what modern childhood was like?

She was greeted by a big green sign advertising something called "Alien Force". She stood for a moment looking around uncertainly; she didn't even know what the toys were. A young male shop assistant with his long hair done up in an elaborate chignon came over and offered to help her. But Sylvia dismissed him, rather brusquely she feared; she didn't need help to choose a present for her own grandson. Trying to look more in control than she felt, she strolled around the floor, looking in bafflement at an endless array of incomprehensible toys. What were Transformers? White helmets labelled "Clone Trooper Voice Changer" and "Cyber Leader Voice Changer"? A weapon called an "Electron Phaser"? In one corner, there were a few toy cars but none which Sylvia knew or recognised.

After a few minutes, she left, seriously worried for her grandson's future. On her way down, she noticed on the floor below a display of toy cars and red London buses which she had somehow missed on the way up. She stopped to look them over; nothing familiar, no Dinky toys. The cars all looked far larger and more garish than need be but still, feeling the need to buy something, now she had come all this way, Sylvia almost furtively bought a modest-sized double-decker bus. She knew it would be years before her grandson was old enough to play with it. She also worried that it was tempting fate to buy anything at all before the baby was safely born, although she was not normally superstitious. But she knew it would help her to have it in the cupboard. When things got too much, she could take it out and hold it and look at it and remind herself that life still held something good for her after all.

The shock of the boys' floor remained undiminished. On the long bus ride back to Kensington, she fretted over it. With the birth of her grandson, she was about to enter a new alien territory in which she would be again a complete foreigner. And what about her little grandson? What sort of a world was *he* coming into? What on earth would *his* childhood be like?

The horror of the visit to Hamleys remained with her all the way back to Kensington High Street and she felt it was a punishment for the foolishness of the whole venture and the prematurity of her purchase that when she got back at last to Overmore Gardens, she discovered that she had left the carrier bag with the toy bus on the number 9.

❧

Smita felt possessed. It was as if the little bean-shaped thing which she had studied in the pregnancy book Jeremy had rushed to buy had blown up massively and taken over her body. Her stomach was already incredibly distended and she simply could not understand how, between now and the beginning of October, it could get much bigger. Worse, the baby was pushing all her other organs out of the way so her bladder was squashed, she needed to go to the loo constantly and she couldn't eat anything more than the smallest snack without getting terrible heartburn. It really got on her nerves that Jeremy was so delighted by her swelling, changing shape. He had, on one occasion, called her a "fertility goddess" although the savagery of her reaction guaranteed he wouldn't do it again. It was actually becoming a bit of a problem that he seemed to find her even more than usually attractive because pregnancy was having quite the opposite effect on her. How could she be expected to have sex when she felt like such a great big unattractive blob? It worried her because she knew it was turning into yet another issue between them; like the pram in the hall, like his mother.

As well as feeling possessed, Smita felt she was being turned against her will into a different person. As far as she was concerned, there was no reason at all why she couldn't have a baby and go on being Smita, the highly successful, incredibly focused, *together* professional person. She had observed enough other slightly older women apparently pulling it off; forging ahead in the workplace, determined, effective and apparently having their kids almost on the side. You might catch them occasionally slinking off shamefacedly to a school play or a sports day. But there was no doubt, it seemed to Smita, what came first for them; it was work and career and the children, the children were a sort of lovely extra which proved that they were complete rounded people. That was how she imagined herself in years to come; still highly successful, with a beautiful little girl who would be a credit to her but having risen right to the top at Gravington Babcock – or maybe having moved on somewhere else – but at any rate earning miles more than Jeremy and everyone around her marvelling at how brilliantly she juggled her roles.

Unhappily, most of the people around her seemed to have different ideas. The worst culprits were her parents who with one voice advocated stopping work at least until the child started school.

"But, mummy, *you* worked when I was little," Smita protested.

Her mother replied, "I had no choice, did I? I *needed* to work full time. We couldn't have managed all we did on your father's salary alone. Do you think I wouldn't *rather* have stayed at home with my child?" Smita wondered. And then the killer argument: "Besides, we had Dadeema and Dadajee to look after you while we were at work. If you hadn't moved so far away, I could do the same for you."

That infuriated Smita; it was such a blatant guilt trip. She knew her mother had no intention at all of stopping work to look after her grandchild. She had only had one child herself and she lived and breathed glasses. There was no way she would ever give up the optician's even if Smita and Jeremy lived next door. She just wanted Smita to feel bad.

Jeremy in his own way was nearly as aggravating. One evening over dinner, which he had made, he asked Smita quite casually, as if the whole thing were a foregone conclusion, how good Gravington Babcock was about part-time working. Smita nearly choked.

"What on earth makes you think I'll be going part time?" she exclaimed. This was intolerable; first her parents, now Jeremy.

"Well, I suppose I assumed you might want to once the baby was here," Jeremy answered still perfectly casually, forking up food as if there were nothing at all infuriating about what he was saying.

Smita breathed deeply. Jeremy meant well. That was the trouble; Jeremy always *meant* well. But he was also an idiot if he didn't realise that, after everything Smita had achieved, she was not going to abandon it all just because of a baby.

She pushed her plate away, not having eaten very much. She did appreciate the efforts Jeremy had been making lately to cook dinner when he was the first one home. But he wasn't the greatest of cooks frankly and her heartburn was always much worse after his dinners. Now the imminent confrontation added to her discomfort.

As mildly as she could, given that she felt like screaming at him, she answered, "Well no, after my maternity leave, I intend to go back to work full-time and hire a nanny. I'm amazed you should imagine anything different."

Jeremy flushed. "You must do what's right for you, of course Smi. It's just, it's only, I've read, isn't it actually better for the child to have its mother there for the first two or three years?"

Smita glared at him. "Whoever wrote that was certainly a man: one. Two: it's not really an option in my line of work, as you perfectly well know, to drop out for two or three years and then expect to get your job back when you choose to show up. Maybe the Beeb has some sort of super-enlightened policy on paternity leave; you should check it out."

"I have," Jeremy answered evenly. "In fact, I was wondering about some sort of flexible part-time arrangement myself."

Smita looked at him, aghast. "You're not serious?"

Jeremy nodded. "I'm perfectly serious. I've been thinking about it quite a lot; I want our child to be brought up as much as possible by her parents and not by a string of nannies."

Smita was momentarily speechless. Since when had she become public property; her body, her baby, her choices suddenly everyone else's business? It was intolerable. She scowled at Jeremy. "Fine," she snapped. "Fine. But you'll have to become a house husband then. *If* we can still manage financially. Because there's no way, *no way* I'm going to be cutting down at all."

That night, again, they hardly spoke when they went to bed. Jeremy made to caress Smita's monstrous tummy; she endured it briefly and then quickly rolled away. It felt all wrong.

Jeremy seemed to fall asleep quite quickly but Smita lay awake for hours with all her furies and frustrations churning round in her head. Well, being pregnant suited some women and didn't suit others; it wasn't her fault if she happened to be one of those whom it didn't. In fact, it was quite wrong of Jeremy to insist and make her feel inadequate. She hated being pregnant. She counted on her fingers how many weeks she still had left; over two and a half months, it seemed forever. Two and a half months of being immense, of feeling fat and unattractive and suffering a string of embarrassing, slightly revolting ailments. The child inside her squirmed as though she too were cross and uncomfortable. Smita laid her hand on the small squirming body under her skin in an attempt at pre-natal discipline. What was that she could feel inside; a head, a bottom, an angrily arched little back? She wondered if her developing daughter was having a foetal tantrum and she held her hand down firmly, hoping to show her right away who was in charge here. The baby only wriggled harder. It occurred to Smita that there was something really scary, horror movie scary about not knowing anything about the person inside her; whom she would look like, what her personality might be, even exactly what colour her skin would be.

Her father Prem had announced recently, in an ill-judged attempt at broad-mindedness, "We will welcome this baby into our hearts even if he is as white as milk." Smita grinned ruefully; poor Dad, he was another one who always meant well.

Next to her, Jeremy stirred and muttered and returned

her to the present. A flexible part-time arrangement? What was he thinking of? It couldn't be that he was deliberately trying to make her feel like a bad mother, before the baby was even born. But that was the effect; how come *he* was all ready to make dramatic sacrifices and change his lifestyle and she wasn't? It was something to do with his childhood, obviously. He wanted to compensate for all the absences and shortcomings of his own childhood by overdoing it with his own child. Whereas she who had had a near perfect childhood – doting parents, doting live-in grandparents, loads of cousins – had nothing to make up for.

She felt almost sorry for Jeremy. It was true, she had thought this many times before; Sylvia must have been a truly terrible mother. When you listened to Jeremy talking about his childhood, which he didn't often, it was one long list of things missing: absent parents, the loneliness of boarding school, no friends to hang out with in the holidays because his schoolfriends were half a world away, evenings spent alone in ex-pat villas while his parents partied, never any siblings. Here Smita had to pause for of course she had no siblings either. But in her case she could confidently claim that this was mainly for economic reasons; her immigrant parents had wanted to concentrate all their resources on doing their very best for just one child. It was true there was always something slightly murky about this topic at home which she had never got to the bottom of. But on the whole she bought her parents' story; they had wanted to do their very best for Smita.

Sylvia, on the other hand, had no such excuses. She

and Roger had never been short of money, had never had to go without for Jeremy's sake. Sylvia had lived a life of pointless pleasure while Smita's mother had worked hard every day of her life. If what Sylvia had told Jeremy was true, that after his birth she had not been able to have any more children, that accounted for why he had no younger siblings. But what about the ten years *before* his birth? Smita had often puzzled about that time lapse and now she suddenly regretted that she didn't have a better relationship with her mother-in-law so she could simply ask her about it.

Just thinking about Sylvia made her all hot and bothered and she decided to get up and have a cold drink. It was already half past one; she was going to be exhausted tomorrow. But she had resolved, when she found out that she was pregnant, never to show any weakness at work – she knew that was crucial – so she would have to go in, however tired she felt. She made herself a cold drink, piled it high with ice and went to sit in the front room in the dark.

Fuming about Sylvia was not going to induce sleep but she couldn't help it. Sylvia had made the last two months pretty much a nightmare. Since she had made her idiotic move to Kensington, there seemed to have been a non-stop series of mini-crises, all of which had meant Jeremy rushing over to the other side of London to sort things out.

The first crisis had blown up barely a week after her move; a pigeon had flown in through her open sitting-room windows – why had she left them so wide open? –

and, try as she might, she couldn't shoo it out again. The bird was panic-stricken, making a frightful mess and Sylvia was at her wit's end. Jeremy had had to take a taxi all the way from the West End where he was in a meeting, stopping on the way to buy a broom since Sylvia apparently didn't own one and then chase the wretched creature back out of the window, dressed in his office clothes. At least Sylvia had been perfectly sane on that occasion and apparently really grateful too.

Then her furniture had finally arrived from Dubai and instead of simply having it all put into storage for the time being, as they had agreed, Sylvia had taken it into her head to go trekking down to the warehouse in Wapping to have a look at it. When she had actually seen it – apparently she had insisted on having a couple of boxes opened then and there – she had had a funny turn and someone from the removals company had called Jeremy at work and told him that his mother was creating an obstruction in a loading bay.

Jeremy had found his mother in a terrible state; she was sitting on a little Chinese stool which he remembered from his parents' living room, sobbing her heart out and talking nonsense. She looked, he said, like a bag lady with her possessions strewn on the ground around her. Her hair was a mess, her make-up was smudged and he was frankly embarrassed. Could Smita maybe have a quiet word with her, he asked afterwards, and take her to the hairdresser? Smita was initially horrified; there was no way, *no way* she could conceivably take Sylvia to the smart salon she went to. But when she thought over Jeremy's request, she felt a certain mean satisfaction at the idea of telling Sylvia her roots were showing and maybe suggesting to her that at her age large quantities of blue or green eyeshadow were not advisable, especially if she was going to be breaking down and weeping all over the place.

Smita knew she was being unkind but it was only tit for tat after Sylvia's incredibly overbearing and insensitive gesture with the orange and yellow maternity clothes. A couple of weeks ago, she had arrived for Sunday lunch and, almost before she had sat down, she had given Smita a whole lecture on how pregnancy was a time of "mellow fruitfulness" – that had been her expression, "mellow fruitfulness" – and how it ought to be celebrated and made the most of "like a harvest festival". From her bag, she had produced two gaudily wrapped packages, one of which had a blue balloon attached to it, and she had given them to Smita, beaming all over her face and saying, "I hope you enjoy wearing them, dear."

When Smita opened the packages, she had been outraged; the contents seemed a strident criticism of her whole personality. One package contained a tangerine-coloured maternity dress with a pattern of bright green pineapples and the other an immense pair of yellow maternity dungarees.

Smita had given her mother-in-law a chilling look. "D'you think they're really me?"

"No," Sylvia had virtually giggled. "No I don't. But I wanted you to have a splash of colour in your wardrobe during these months. Not everything so dark and business-like."

Smita knew she had glared at Sylvia.

Jeremy had intervened. "I think they look rather fun, Smi."

"Do you?" Smita had snapped at him. She had stood up, bundling the lurid clothes together. "Well, I appreciate the thought, Sylvia. But please don't try and choose clothes for me again."

She had gone over to the kitchen, regretting the open-plan layout – not for the first time – because what she really needed was a door to slam behind her.

Sylvia quavered, "You will at least try them on dear? They *can* be exchanged."

Smita heard Jeremy murmur, "Leave it, leave it."

Of course Smita hadn't tried them on. She had acted deliberately hurt and distant throughout lunch and, as soon as Sylvia had left for her interminable double bus ride back to Kensington – well, serve her right – Smita had flipped. She had turned on Jeremy; how dare he, how *dare* he defend his mother when she had done something so unspeakably tactless and rude? It had turned into one of their worst rows ever and, just thinking about it now in the dark, Smita felt dreadfully depressed.

The worst thing was their worry that Sylvia was actually losing her mind. Jeremy said that when he arrived at the warehouse in Wapping, Sylvia had been making no sense at all. She was crying, holding on her lap a cushion which seemed to have some special significance; she kept patting it and she was sobbing that even though Roger was dead, he was still there.

"How *can* he be dead?" Jeremy said she was repeating,

over and over again. "How *can* he? I can still hear him, I can still smell him. I can *feel* he's there." Over and over: "I can hear him in the flat, you know. Even though I *know* he's not there; I can hear him."

Jeremy had persuaded her to get up, he had packed away the little stool and the cushion and all the stuff that was scattered on the ground around her: Chinese fans and Indian carved wooden animals and an ornate oriental metal bird which had suffered a bent beak in transit. He didn't think he could take her on the train in that state so he had ordered a ruinously expensive taxi and, for virtually the price of an airfare, he had taken her back to her flat and on the way he had said to her seriously that she should see a doctor.

Of course she had taken offence. She had told Jeremy bitterly that no doctor could bring his father back, that all that was wrong with her was grief and although she wasn't surprised that Jeremy didn't understand that, frankly it didn't make her think all that well of him.

After that, they hadn't spoken for several days, one of their periodic fraught stand-offs. But then, just last week, there had been the whole business with the Romanian cleaner who had turned out to be, in Sylvia's words, "light-fingered" and Sylvia had phoned Jeremy again because she needed him to help sort out another fine mess of her own making.

Smita sipped her drink and sighed. Sylvia was losing it, she was definitely losing it. They would have to be incredibly careful around her when the baby came.

Suddenly, from their bedroom, Smita heard Jeremy

call: "Smita?" It was an anguished, high-pitched, rather unmanly cry.

She answered. "I'm here. What is it?" She heard Jeremy, half-asleep, mumbling something.

She called, "I can't hear you."

For a moment, she stayed sitting on the sofa waiting, then, impatiently, she stood up and made her way back upstairs. She supposed she ought to get back to bed anyway. As she climbed the stairs heavily, the glass steps were refreshingly cool under her bare feet. She stood at the foot of the big bed and repeated bossily, "What is it?"

Jeremy moaned theatrically. "I had the most awful nightmare. I dreamt you'd left me."

Smita laughed. "In this condition?"

Jeremy reached out to her with both hands. "Come here, let me feel you."

Gingerly, Smita lowered herself onto the bed. "Honestly, Jeremy, it's past two."

"Where *were* you?" Jeremy asked beseechingly. "Where *were* you? I woke up and you weren't there." He enfolded her in his arms; he was warm, sleep-smelling and he snuggled against her tenderly, cautiously.

Smita answered. "I couldn't sleep. I've got a lot on my mind."

"I know," Jeremy said drowsily. "I understand. It must be hard for you adjusting; scary. But just promise me you won't ever – "

"Ever what?"

"Ever leave me. *Ever*."

Smita laughed. "Ever's a long time."

In the dark, Jeremy's hand reached down between her legs, reminding her of what she was denying him. Smita stiffened slightly but all Jeremy did was grip her thigh teasingly, squeezing the flesh tighter and tighter. "Go on. Say it."

"Ever," Smita repeated. "I won't *ever* leave you. If that's what you want. Now let go of my leg and let's try and get some sleep."

Jeremy appeared to fall back asleep immediately as if he hadn't actually been fully awake.

Smita lay there a little longer, feeling calmer.

It occurred to her that maybe what they needed was a last baby-free holiday together. There was still just time; she could fly for another few weeks, she thought. Work would be a problem. A week's leave at short notice; no one would be pleased. But she had just finished a massive report for them and surely they would understand? Well, too bad; they would have to and if need be, dear obliging Dr Levy would write her a note saying she needed a week's rest. Which she did.

She imagined where they might go; somewhere luxurious and sunny of course, somewhere Mediterranean maybe, not too far away but far enough to sound attractive. Somewhere with good doctors and hospitals, just in case. She thought her way pleasurably around different destinations and she imagined herself and Jeremy enjoying a tourist brochure idyll; walks hand in hand along pristine beaches, sipping cocktails – well, at least long drinks – watching the sun set, romance restored. In her mind's eye, she was somehow slim too.

Of course Sylvia would sulk. Left on her own in London, abandoned she would doubtless say, by her selfish son and daughter-in-law, what awful calamity would she come up with to spoil their holiday? Smita set her jaw. They were going to have this holiday, Sylvia or no Sylvia. Jeremy was owed loads of leave, he had been talking about taking some to do up the baby's room. This was far more important. They would go away together somewhere beautiful and forget all about the stresses and strains of recent months. For a few days, she could hopefully try and forget all about the baby too.

꙳

London at the height of summer was a rum place, Sylvia decided. Although she had returned to England on visits every year, somehow she had failed to see all the changes. Well, the changing population; you could hardly fail to notice that. When she and Roger had left for Hong Kong in 1969, black and Indian faces were still a relative rarity, at least in the parts of London which they frequented. Over the years, of course she had noticed that there were more and more of them. But she was rather glad of it actually; given the long and intensely happy period which she and Roger had spent in India, it helped her to feel at home here when she came back on leave. Besides, they all tended to be so much jollier than English people anyway.

Little by little, with the passage of the years, Sylvia had noticed she felt less and less at home in England, as if she didn't really belong here anymore. She had always supposed it was because she had got out of the habit of England. She had become a sort of foreigner herself. She had always tried her best to fit in wherever it was she was living – "going native" they used to call it – although you weren't supposed to use words like that anymore. She had forgotten how to fit in in London. When she came home on leave, her friends would tease her for her unfamiliarity with all the latest trends. Once someone had even asked her where her accent was from. She had assumed that the change was mainly in herself and she hadn't really registered how much the country had changed too.

How *could* she have been so unobservant? Well, one obvious reason was where she had spent the bulk of her time when she was home on leave: for years, her visits had been centred on Jeremy's boarding school in the Oxfordshire countryside and that was a time warp, if ever there was one. Her trips had been timed to coincide with parent-teacher evenings, school plays, sports days (although poor Jeremy had never shone at sports days.) The school strived to present an unchanging, gilded version of England especially for all the overseas parents: the Hong Kong Chinese, the wealthy Nigerians. The boys wore blazers and straw boaters in summer, they used all the old-fashioned slang of "prep" and "tuck" and they had no contact at all with the local people in the nearby market towns. If that was all you saw, you could certainly be forgiven for thinking, like in the Rupert Brooke poem, that there was "honey still for tea".

But of course that wasn't all Sylvia had seen. She had nipped up to London regularly for shopping trips and matinees, get-togethers with old friends, check-ups at the doctors. How come she had never noticed how much the country was changing from one year to the next? She supposed she had been cushioned; she had stayed in hotels, hadn't she, travelled by taxi and she had stuck to the same old places.

After Jeremy left school, there had been a period of several rather dreadful years when her visits had centred mainly on her mother's nursing home in Bournemouth. Time had certainly stood still there as it did in her poor mother's mind where "that dreadful Harold Wilson" was still Prime Minister and Sylvia was still living in Chelsea and working as a secretary. Her mother had always disapproved of Roger; no wonder she had written Sylvia's marriage out of her memory. Jeremy had contrived to make those visits even more forlorn than need be by travelling endlessly throughout his university vacations and somehow always managing to be out of the country when his mother came. Sylvia felt a momentary pang of extreme bitterness as she remembered that period. Well, nothing had really changed, had it; it was late July, summer holiday time and Jeremy and Smita were away, doubtless having a whale of a time in Sardinia while she was on her own in sweltering London.

Take the climate for instance; how come she had never noticed that the weather in England had changed so dramatically since her youth? When had it ever been this *hot*? The truth was in recent years she had not come back nearly as often. Jeremy and Smita preferred to take their holidays in Dubai. Sylvia supposed too that if you lived in

Dubai or in Saudi, however hot it got in England, it was always going to seem relatively cool, wasn't it?

Still that was what struck her now as she grappled with her first globally warmed summer in London; how much the weather had changed and, perhaps as a consequence of that, how much people's behaviour had changed too. It was no longer anything like the country which she remembered.

One boiling afternoon towards the end of July, Sylvia sat in Holland Park and watched the virtually naked people lying on the grass in front of her. She simply could not believe how little they were wearing and what some of them were doing in full public view. She wondered if, now the weather was warmer, standards had slipped and what she was seeing was a more relaxed, easy-going sort of country. But in no hot country she had ever lived in had she witnessed scenes like those which she was now viewing in horrified disbelief on the crowded wilting lawn. This wasn't a country at ease with either the weather or itself; this was a country which had no idea how to behave in hot weather and which had collectively lost its head. Peering censoriously from the shadows, where she was sharing a bench with a negligent East European nanny chattering on a mobile phone while her small charges got sunburnt and a woman cloaked from head to foot in a black abaya, Sylvia tutted to herself.

Almost at her feet, three fat young women were sunbathing in their scanty underwear. Maybe they had been released from a nearby office; they had the round shoulders and spreading rears of office workers. Though when she was their age, Sylvia had been nowhere near as fat. After spending some time covering one another in glistening white sun cream which emphasised both their paleness and their inflated contours, they were lying side by side on their backs, visibly turning pink, talking at the top of their voices with their eyes shut – as if that afforded them some imaginary degree of privacy. They were talking about sex.

Sylvia could not believe her ears. She had brought a library book with her to the park – not that she was really up to reading yet – and she held it open on her knees and every now and then she turned the page to give the impression she was reading but she was actually simultaneously riveted and revolted by the girls' conversation.

They were comparing the attractions of various men of their acquaintance, maybe colleagues at work.

"Well, I think he's fit," said Girl One. "And he's got a lovely bum too."

"Yuk," Girl Two replied loudly. "I'd never go with him. Have you seen his *teeth*?"

"What's wrong with his teeth?" Girl One asked, indignantly.

Girl Two shuddered. "They're all in the wrong place and he don't clean them that often either."

"You mean he's got bad breath?" asked Girl One. "You been that close?"

"No-oh!" exclaimed Girl Two. "I wouldn't. I told you; kiss him and I'd be gagging. You don't need to get that close to notice."

Girl Three, who had lain quietly up to this point, piped up, "The one I fancy is Mark."

"He don't half fancy *hisself*," Girl One replied quickly.

"Yeah," added Girl Two. "He's so up himself."

After a moment, Girl Three said proudly, "He's asked me out."

Her companions both sat up and screeched. "Oh-my-God! *Shut up!* Are you going to go?"

"Why shouldn't I?"

"'Cos you know what'll happen, that's why," said Girl Two menacingly. "You remember him and Zara?"

"Zara's a slag," said Girl Three.

"Well, if you don't mind everyone hearing afterwards how rubbish you were in bed and what your boobs look like close-up," Girl One jeered. "That's what he did to Zara. That's why she left."

Girl Three was silent for a moment. Then she answered, "I'm not Zara."

"No," Girl Two told her loyally, "You're not. But still. I wouldn't go with him, no *way*."

"Ooh yes, you would," Girl Three said sharply. "If you was *asked*."

A sulky silence followed this exchange until Girl One, who seemed to be the ringleader, exclaimed, "I'm dying for an i c. Anyone come with me to get one?"

Girl Two sat up. "I'll come with you."

They both got up, put on some – but not enough – of their clothes and walked towards the cafe, leaving Girl Two alone on the grass, her legs splayed, beginning to burn.

Sylvia's gaze wandered. Nearby lay a couple of

123

indeterminate colour and origin; Sylvia supposed they were what she had recently been told to call "mixed race".

Jeremy and Smita had had a go at her one Sunday lunchtime on account of her outdated vocabulary on this topic. It was funny though; Jeremy had been far more exercised on the subject than Smita. Bossily, they had banned from Sylvia's vocabulary a number of perfectly harmless expressions which she and Roger had used unthinkingly for years: "coloured", "dusky", "swarthy", "touch of the tar brush" and so on. Instead, they instructed her prissily, there was a new set of approved terms for all the different shades of humanity and her old-fashioned vocabulary had apparently become deeply offensive. There were also new names for people who were handicapped and an absurd complicated one which she couldn't remember right now for people who were backward.

Sylvia had found the whole thing frankly ridiculous and had said so. Smita had shrugged but Jeremy had got very red in the face and told her if she wasn't careful, she would end up being called a racist. Sylvia was outraged and she had told Jeremy that in that case he had better make a "Colour by Numbers" chart for her with all the right names for the right shades since otherwise she would never be able to remember such nonsense. She hadn't meant to upset him of course but afterwards he had got into one of his states and had barely spoken to her for the rest of her visit.

The couple on the grass, whom before Jeremy and Smita's lecture Sylvia would probably have called "café au lait", shocked her even more than the plump girls. They appeared to be at an advanced stage of foreplay; lying almost on top of one another in full view of all the people including a number of small children. The man had his hand inside the young woman's blouse and, even worse, it seemed to Sylvia, the young woman had her hand inside the young man's trousers. They were undulating embarrassingly. Sylvia looked away. But all across the lawn similar scenes were being played out, indifferently interspersed with family groups, fat mothers with fat children – when had everyone put on so much weight? – and here and there a solitary oddbod like herself gawping at the spectacle. A few outsized pigeons, approximately the size of small hens, waddled here and there among the people, pecking indiscriminately at their litter.

Suddenly, Sylvia felt disgusted. Thank goodness she would have to leave soon anyway; it was nearly time for her tea with Mrs Rosenkranz. As she stood up, Cynthia's letter, which she was using as a bookmark, fell out onto the ground. She stooped to pick it up and as she stood straight again, her tiredness suddenly overwhelmed her and the letter, ridiculously, seemed to weigh a ton. She sat back down heavily. She shouldn't of course, it would only upset her, but she felt compelled to re-read the letter for the umpteenth time, making herself endure the lash of Cynthia's tongue all over again like rubbing salt into an open wound.

"Dear Syl," it read in Cynthia's furious jagged handwriting. "I don't know how you expect me to feel frankly. You move back to London without informing me or consulting me. You wait almost Three Months to deign to tell me that you are here. Then you invite me to come up to London for *Lunch*?! Yet again, your arrogance takes my breath away. Or rather, it would if I were at all surprised by it. Coming as it does, after years of such abusive behaviour, of course it doesn't surprise me one bit. But let me tell you, I won't be coming up to London, not for lunch or dinner or breakfast for that matter either and here is the reason why; I made a major effort when your husband died. You may not have noticed but I did. Putting aside my own feelings towards Roger, I dropped everything and prepared to fly out to Dubai, a place which, as you know, does not agree with me, so as to be with you in your Hour of Need. But just as I was about to leave the house – in fact I had already made arrangements for a neighbour to feed the cat – I received a curt phone call from Jeremy telling me in the coldest of terms that I was Not Wanted. You chose to interpret my absence at Roger's funeral as a slap in the face but, in fact, although a slap in the face would have been perfectly justified, the Truth of the Matter is that I was kept away by illness (a flare-up of trigeminal neuralgia) and had to stay at home on Doctor's Orders. My letter of condolences (sent 7.2.04) went unanswered. I have heard nothing from you since until I received your bizarre and wounding letter last week, informing me tersely that you are now living temporarily in Kensington, awaiting the birth of your first grandchild. Frankly, I do not know what you want of me Syl. You reject me cruelly Time and Time Again and then you expect me to come running when it suits you. Well, no, Syl, I'm not playing. If you sincerely want to see me and let Bygones be Bygones, which I doubt, then you will have to come down to Lewes and visit me. You have never been to see me here although I have been living in Lewes as a well-respected member of the Artists' Colony for more than twenty years now, exhibiting my work annually and regularly receiving favourable reviews in a number of prestigious art periodicals. I realise that Roger no doubt preferred the fleshpots of the metropolis to Lewes and that probably made it difficult for you to come. But you have no excuses now and I shall expect to see you here before the summer is out. Otherwise you may as well consider all communication between us At an End. As ever, Cyn."

Sylvia was drenched in sweat. She felt all trembly too and on the verge of tears. Why did things always seem to go wrong between her and those closest to her? It wasn't only Cynthia although Cynthia was, everyone agreed, quite uniquely troublesome. It was also Jeremy, Smita, it used to happen all the time with her own mother and her own mother-in-law. Why even with Roger there had been crossed wires and fallings-out. Never for long though and, now that Roger was gone, she preferred not to think about their bad patches but to concentrate steadfastly on the happy times. What was the matter with her that she couldn't seem to communicate smoothly with those around her? Why did life have to be like this?

Shakily, Sylvia gathered up her bits and pieces and set off again. Thank goodness for old Mrs Rosenkranz who was so easy to talk to.

As Sylvia walked towards the gates onto Kensington High Street through the lower reaches of the park, she passed a young Indian woman pushing a baby in a pram. With a vivid spurt of happiness, Sylvia remembered her grandson-to-be. She had not thought about him for at least an hour. Impetuously, she stopped and blurted out to the startled young mother: "Oh, may I take a look at him? My daughter-in-law's Indian too and she's expecting her first baby in just a few weeks."

The young woman looked taken aback. Grudgingly, she stopped and let Sylvia peer beneath the lightweight crocheted blanket which was shading the baby from the sun. "It's a girl," the young woman said sullenly. "Her name is Daisy."

"Oh," Sylvia said brightly. "Not an Indian name?"

The young woman frowned. "Why on earth would I give her an Indian name? She's going to live her life here, isn't she, not in India."

Sylvia beamed at her conciliatingly to make up for what seemed to be yet another inexplicable faux pas. "It's a very pretty name," she said gushingly. "And she's lovely."

As she carried on her way, she reflected that what she had just said was in fact not true; Daisy was a common or garden name and the baby wasn't lovely at all. She was a very hirsute baby actually with a surprising quantity of thick black hair and beetle brows. She frowned just like her sullen mother.

For the umpteenth time, Sylvia tried unsuccessfully to imagine what her grandson would look like but somehow she couldn't manage it; Jeremy's face but Smita's colour, Smita's face but Jeremy's colour, how would it work? Puzzling over this conundrum, she made her tired way back to Overmore Gardens. She thought of Smita and Jeremy lying on a beach in Sardinia, irresponsibly exposing the baby to the risks of air travel and gippy tummy. How very selfish they were. Well Smita of course only ever thought of Smita but surely Jeremy, who was in such a frightful tizz about the baby, should have known better. Smita had doubtless bullied him into going and he, spineless as he was, had given in to her. After all, it wasn't as if they needed to get away to see the sun. Really, this heat was unnatural for England; she would need to have a bath before she went to see Mrs Rosenkranz.

Thinking about baths reminded her of toilets or rather their lamentable absence. The England she had left all those years ago had been plentifully supplied with public toilets where you could, literally, spend a penny. She remembered the ubiquitous reek of disinfectant, the worry that you might not have the right coin for the little brass box on the door, the occasional kindly soul who would in a principled way hold the door open for you as they left so you wouldn't have to pay. What had happened to all the public toilets? What merciless bureaucracy had got rid of them all without a thought for those with weak bladders, especially older women who were prone to urge incontinence, for whom a dearth of toilets could have the most awful consequences? There was not a single toilet the whole length of Kensington High Street and hurrying in this heat was out of the question. She would just have to hope for the best.

Mrs Rosenkranz had invited Sylvia back to tea about a month after her first visit and then a fortnight after that and then, without anything apparently having been said, it had somehow turned into every Thursday. So Sylvia, still adrift in a bafflingly transformed country, now had two fixed points in her week: Sunday lunch with Jeremy and Smita and Thursday tea with Ruth Rosenkranz. To Sylvia's surprise, she and the old lady seemed to be in some unfathomable way kindred spirits. What was simply astonishing was that Ruth Rosenkranz, whom Sylvia found so very interesting and *different* with her Continental background, seemed, incomprehensibly, to feel exactly the same way about Sylvia.

Sylvia was not used to being considered interesting. Every week, the old lady questioned her avidly about her life abroad. She was interested in every little detail and sometimes, frankly, in the strangest things. Hong Kong: how many of the Chinese spoke English and how many of the English spoke Chinese? (Not many.) Was it true that in the colonial past the British had put up signs forbidding entry to certain places expressly to the Chinese and dogs? Were any of the signs still to be seen? Did they keep them in museums as a shameful memory or had they all been destroyed? Delhi: could Sylvia please explain the Indian caste system? (Not really.) On what was it based exactly and what symbols did they use to identify those on the bottom rung, the untouchables? Did they have to wear anything in particular to mark them out? Mrs Rosenkranz had apparently never travelled much beyond Europe and she found Sylvia's ex-pat experiences fascinating. Which was in a way a pity because Sylvia would have loved to ask her about the big unspoken gaps in her life story but she was so busy chattering away about trips to the silver market in Delhi where you bought jewellery by weight like meat or fish and the scandalous antics of the younger expats in Dubai that there was never any time. Sometimes Sylvia wondered if the old lady was doing it on purpose.

Sylvia had managed to establish that Mrs Rosenkranz had been born in Berlin which of course explained the trace of an accent. She had come to England in somewhat unclear circumstances in the late Thirties and then there was a long silent gap until the early Fifties when she was newly married to Mr Rosenkranz who, despite his name, came from Sheffield and they were living in Maida Vale. From this time on, she spoke relatively freely about her life until another blank period in the early Eighties when her daughter had got married and something to do with the marriage had upset her so deeply that she could not speak about it. Well, Sylvia could certainly identify with that.

Whatever topic they lighted on, they always had plenty to say. In fact, Imelda had taken to going out on Thursday afternoons and leaving Sylvia in charge of the tea which made it easier to let their hair down. Although of course the truth was that Sylvia was letting her hair down much more than Mrs Rosenkranz.

Lying in the bath before her visit, Sylvia recalled that last time they had talked a lot about her years in India. She had described her house in Lodhi Colony and her beautiful garden and a particularly happy excursion to Naini Tal. Mrs Rosenkranz had listened, apparently enchanted.

Next door, Roger began to hum tunelessly: tum-pom-

pom, pom-teedee-pom. After three months in the flat, Sylvia no longer started when she heard him. She lay in the bath and listened wistfully as the water cooled refreshingly about her and she went downstairs on the dot of four, feeling curiously comforted.

Mrs Rosenkranz seemed in good spirits too, despite the heat which was oppressive in her stuffy flat. It struck Sylvia as she made the tea in the airless kitchen that she could perhaps wheel the old lady up to the park one day; it would be a slog but there was that ramp for the front steps and you could certainly get a wheelchair into the new black cabs. Maybe she should experiment with somewhere nearer at hand first? A vision came to mind of the two of them sitting in the roof gardens of Derry and Tom on a sunny day, listening to the sound of the fountains gently splashing and both enjoying a strawberry ice cream. Goodness, Sylvia hadn't thought of the roof gardens for years but she could still see them ever so clearly; colonnades, flower beds and palm trees and that startling illusion of a Spanish summer holiday. She wondered if they were even still there. Well, she would have to find out and, if they were and not turned in the meantime into something monstrous, she would invite her new friend to come along with her to visit them. Excited by her idea, Sylvia added the teapot to Imelda's perfectly prepared trolley and wheeled it into the sitting room.

Mrs Rosenkranz looked up at her brightly. "I have an invitation for you," she said, smiling.

Sylvia giggled. "Great minds think alike."

"Meaning?" asked Mrs Rosenkranz.

Sylvia beamed. "I have an invitation for *you*."

"For *me*?" exclaimed Mrs Rosenkranz. "An invitation for me? But I can't get up the stairs to your apartment, my dear, not unless you and Imelda carry me there."

"It's not to my *flat*," Sylvia said quickly. "I've thought of somewhere *much* nicer. And with a lift too."

Unfortunately, Mrs Rosenkranz had no idea whether the roof gardens were still there either but that didn't stop the two of them reminiscing about the gardens at some length as they drank their tea and Mrs Rosenkranz said that if the gardens still existed, she would accept Sylvia's invitation with the greatest pleasure.

Almost as an afterthought, towards the end of the afternoon, she said coyly to Sylvia, "I haven't yet told you about *my* invitation for you."

Sylvia smiled politely. What could an eighty-something year old offer to rival Derry and Tom?

The old lady announced, "Siggy, my little brother, is coming from Northwood to visit me. Not this coming Sunday, but the one after. Would you care to join us for lunch?"

Sylvia felt a bump of disappointment. "Oh," she said. "I can't."

The old lady frowned. "Why not?"

"I have lunch with Jeremy and Smita every Sunday," Sylvia said forlornly. "They'd never forgive me if I didn't come."

"Really?" exclaimed Mrs Rosenkranz. "Are you sure? Maybe they might enjoy a Sunday on their own for a

133

change? Maybe your daughter-in-law might be glad not to have to cook for once in her condition?"

Sylvia thought over what Mrs Rosenkranz had said, meanwhile helping herself pensively to a third little sliver of ginger cake. It was true, it was only a sense of obligation which kept the Sunday lunches going; neither she nor Jeremy and Smita really enjoyed them. In fact, it would serve them right, having left her on her own for two Sundays in a row while they were away on holiday, if on the third Sundays she was unavailable. She finished the last of her cake.

"Maybe you're right," she said slowly.

"Good!" exclaimed Mrs Rosenkranz. "That's the spirit. You will see; you will all appreciate each other much more if you see each other when you choose, not just according to the calendar."

Sylvia thought miserably that if Smita could choose, she would most probably never see her mother-in-law at all. Jeremy's feelings she preferred not to probe. "I expect I'll get into trouble though," she said dubiously.

"Never mind!" declared Mrs Rosenkranz. "So you'll go along with flowers for your daughter-in-law the Sunday after. I have told Siggy so much about you when we speak on the phone; he is longing to meet you."

Sylvia wondered afterwards if she hadn't made another dreadful mistake. Of course Jeremy and Smita would be cross with her and, as for the seventy-year-old little brother, how entertaining would he be?

∂

Smita's maternity leave began in the second week of September, a month before the baby was due. Her colleagues at Gravington Babcock took her out to lunch and presented her jokily with a very large Mothercare voucher which annoyed her as she intended to shop in much more upmarket baby shops than that.

It felt strange waking up in the morning and not having work to go to. Jeremy told her to make the most of these last lazy days as he headed out to work. Apart from their short break in Sardinia, which had not worked out quite as well as Smita had hoped, this was the last rest she would get before the baby came. But Smita had the longest list of things she wanted to get through and so she carried on getting up bright and early and working her way through her tasks. She had only managed two or three of them – selecting and reserving a pretty Moses basket and a pram and booking appointments for the following week for a hair cut, a manicure and a pedicure – when she woke early on the third or fourth day with a low backache which kept coming and going and feeling generally so unwell that she didn't think she could manage anything. She felt incredibly frustrated. It was awful to waste even a moment when time was so short. It was also not like her at all to have to take things easy or to lie around in bed. Once the morning sickness had passed, she had sailed through the whole pregnancy without major problems and without a single day off work. She had pretty much hated it – lumbering around like an elephant – but she had got on with it. Now, as she lay waiting for the alarm clock to go off and for Jeremy to wake up and make her a cup of tea, she seethed at the thought of a wasted day. She had been planning to go to her anti-natal yoga class, to shop for baby clothes and then to research waiting lists for nursery schools. Maybe if she rested for an hour or two, her back would improve. She must have overdone it, rearranging furniture yesterday. She was completely unprepared for Jeremy's reaction when he woke up and she told him how she felt.

"Christ!" he exclaimed, scrambling urgently out of bed. "Maybe the baby's coming." He caught his foot in the sheet and stubbed his toe. "Ow, shit, ow."

"For God's sake, calm down," Smita told him sternly. "It can't possibly be the baby; it's nearly a month too early."

"It *can*!" Jeremy insisted, hopping around, holding his foot. "It absolutely *can*! Don't you remember what they said at the class: up to a month beforehand is perfectly ok."

Smita started to feel a bit scared. She was also irritated that Jeremy seemed to have been a better student at the ante-natal classes than she had. "For Pete's sake stop hopping around like that," she told him sharply. "I'm sure it's *not* the baby. You couldn't get me a cup of tea, could you?"

To her dismay, instead of going red in the face but controlling himself and doing her bidding, Jeremy ignored her. "You're in denial," he said forcefully. "It said in one of the books that at the beginning women often don't recognize that they're in labour."

"I'm not in labour!" Smita nearly shouted. "I've got backache." She sat up. "If you won't make me a cup of tea, I'll have to go and make one myself."

She swung her legs over the side of the bed, stood up and had to catch hold of the wall. Her back really hurt terribly. "Look," she snapped, "could you please just stop lecturing me and bring me a cup of tea?"

Jeremy came round to her side of the bed. He stooped over her and there was an expression on his face which silenced her; he was scared.

"I'll make you a cup of tea," he said firmly, "quickly. And then we're going straight to the hospital."

"That's ridiculous!" Smita protested. "It's a waste of everybody's time. You're just panicking. That's what *men* do."

Jeremy did not answer. He pulled on some random clothes, without showering, brought her a cup of not very nice tea and then stood resolutely waiting in silence while she got herself ready.

Smita could barely make it down the stairs. She kept having to stop and pant, she was not sure why, and although Jeremy was doing his best to hide his alarm, she could see it in his eyes and it infuriated her. Luckily, they made it out of the front door without meeting the Castellinis.

In the car, despite her pain, Smita kept up a resentful running commentary on Jeremy's panic, his fussiness, his foolishness and Jeremy, bloody typically, kept his eyes on the road and said nothing.

They got to the hospital soon after eight. Smita, still subjecting Jeremy to a series of angry glances and pursed lips, was examined by a midwife who confirmed, to her horror, that she was in the early stages of labour.

"But don't worry," the midwife reassured Smita. "Your baby's quite big enough already even if he's decided to come a little bit early. He'll be ok."

"Forget the baby!" Smita felt like shouting. "What about *me*?"

She could hardly bear to look Jeremy in the face as she was taken away to the labour ward in a wheelchair. The midwife had told them that it would still be several hours, "a long way to go", before the baby was born and Jeremy had plenty of time to go home and get Smita's ready-packed suitcase which she had adamantly refused to bring with her. As Jeremy hurried towards the way out, a slightly stooping, unkempt figure, trying not to run until he had left the building, Smita had a last absurd image of herself running for the exit.

Her baby was born finally – but still nearly a month too early – just before midnight. The intervening day was an abyss of pain, terror and total humiliation which Smita knew already she would never repeat. She sent Jeremy out of the room at some point after the pethidine but before the epidural because his anxious reassurance and his sweaty stroking were getting on her nerves. Besides she wanted to punish him for having been right and excluding him from this all-important event was the cruellest thing she could think of.

But even that didn't begin to repay him for the agony and the embarrassment, the horrible humiliation of the whole experience. The midwives persuaded her to let Jeremy back in for the actual birth, cautioning her that it might have a bad effect on his bonding with the baby if he was excluded. They didn't know how besotted Jeremy was with the whole idea of the baby, much more than she was to tell the truth.

He came back in sheepishly, grinning at her and saying, "Hi Smi," as if nothing at all out of the ordinary were happening. Smita tried to act cold and distant towards him but, under the circumstances, it wasn't really possible. In any case, when the climactic moment at last arrived, when the baby emerged fully, was dabbed down and laid in Smita's apprehensive arms, of course she forgot about everything else. She and Jeremy were united as never before in the miraculous stunned moment of beholding their child.

A perceptible amount of time went by before Smita had another shock. Maybe the midwife had said something but she had missed it. Adjusting the white towel around the baby a fraction, she saw in utter disbelief, as if a cosmic mistake had been made, that her daughter was a boy.

If Roger had lived long enough to find out that he had a grandson the colour of an acorn, Sylvia could only too well imagine what he might have said. For a start, Roger would certainly not have described the little boy as the colour of an acorn or even nut brown which sounded healthy and ruddy and sporty. He would most probably have said that the baby was swarthy, one of the words which Jeremy and Smita had banned and in any case an absurd manly word to use about a tiny infant. If he was struggling not to offend, which was always a struggle for Roger, he might self-consciously have called him "café au lait" which Sylvia thought was probably even worse; it suggested something diluted and watered down.

As she tried to imagine Roger's reaction to the arrival of his half-Indian grandson, something she did a great deal in the first weeks of the little boy's life, she had a thought which felt at the time like a dreadful betrayal; maybe it was not such a sad thing after all that Roger was no longer with them. She didn't mean it of course. She dismissed the thought as just another of those nonsensical notions which kept disturbingly crossing her mind these days. Such as: what might the baby have looked like if Jeremy had ended up getting married to Martha, his Chinese girlfriend at university? Or: if Jeremy and Smita had another child, would it be the same colour as this one or might they have different shades of children?

She missed Roger, sometimes desperately; on days when she didn't hear him humming in the bathroom or clearing his throat. She missed having him there to discuss the baby with too; whether his ears were Jeremy's or Smita's and whether his baby behaviour reminded one at all of his father's, the kind of detail one could really only discuss properly with a close family member. Sylvia did not have many of those left.

But, at the same time, there was no denying that Roger's absence liberated her from his considerations of lineage, the rupture of family tradition, mixed and muddled heritage and yes, regrettably, skin colour. For Roger cared about all those things, cared deeply and Sylvia was sure he would be raising an eyebrow on high. Not that Sylvia herself never thought about those things; she was not that modern. Before her grandson was born, she had worried about them a good deal in fact, as well as whether her daughter-in-law would make a worthy mother. But now that the little boy was so astonishingly here, not having Roger there did make it much easier for Sylvia to forget all about those things. There was no one to mention them, no one to care about such suddenly irrelevant issues.

The instant Sylvia saw the baby in the hospital, all those worries remarkably dissipated and she thought with delight, "Why, he's just the colour of an acorn!" The image, with its accompanying suggestion of ancient woodland, made him seem immediately utterly English. It was something to do with the little crocheted skullcap he was wearing and his dear little nut brown face peeping out snugly from underneath it which reminded Sylvia straightaway of an acorn in its cup.

That magical September morning, when she cradled him in her arms for the first time, a wonderful, warm, snuffling, frankly brown miracle, she wanted so terribly to hold him out to Roger and show him that, look, their grandchild was a wonder beyond all comprehension and whatever *dear* shade he was, he was self-evidently a Garland through and through.

Smita had insisted on a private hospital. Sylvia had mixed feelings about private hospitals. Despite her years abroad, during which she had been treated for various run-of-the-mill ailments by a succession of private doctors whom she had paid with fistfuls of local cash, she had kept a nostalgic fondness for the NHS. But the birth of her first grandchild was an entirely different matter and, on this unique occasion, she was prepared to defer quietly to Smita's wishes.

Still, when she arrived at the hospital at nine o'clock in the morning, as soon as she could get there after Jeremy's incoherent phone call, she found it frankly extravagant. In fact, she was not sure at first that it was the hospital at all because, although it seemed to be the right address, the liveried flunky on the front steps, the immense and tasteless flower arrangements in the front hall and the theatrically made up receptionist all seemed more like a grand hotel than a hospital. There were no nurses in evidence, no doctors, no medical equipment, even no hospital smell, just some cloyingly scented air freshener which doubtless went under the name of "Spring Meadow" or "Summer Pasture" and which made Sylvia sneeze far too loudly in the stillness.

She took the upholstered lift up to the third floor as directed, without passing anyone who looked in the least medical or anyone who looked remotely ill either. At the third floor reception desk, she was greeted by a buxom young East European nurse whose heavy Slav accent and plait of ash blonde hair wound round her head made her seem as if she too was playing a part.

"Well khello," she greeted Sylvia after she had given Smita's name. She smiled excessively. "You must be the grandmother."

"Yes," Sylvia answered eagerly. "I am."

She wondered briefly about the other grandmother, the dreaded Naisha, who must even now be on the motorway on her way down from Leicester. If the baby hadn't taken them all unawares by coming nearly a month early, Naisha would already have been here of course, staying with Smita and Jeremy, taking charge of everything. Smita had it all planned, she had informed Sylvia firmly a few weeks back and there had been no place for Sylvia in her plans.

As she walked down the immaculate corridor, Sylvia could not help briefly imagining the baby she was about to meet as a little accomplice. Smugly, she thought of Naisha and Prem racing to get here; Prem probably driving and Naisha next to him in the front passenger seat urging him to drive faster and better. She would be dressed, doubtless, in one of her smart polyester pant suits and clutching in Sylvia's imagination a little attaché case of cut-price spectacles. But Sylvia quickly scolded herself for snobbery and malice. What nonsense; Naisha's heart would be beating just as fast as hers was this morning and she would be bringing not her latest line in diamanté reading glasses but baby clothes and flowers and cries of joy and tears of pride.

As she reached the door of Smita's room, Sylvia suddenly worried that Naisha had beaten her to it and was already sitting there, enthroned beside her fruitful daughter's bed, in gloating charge of the proceedings. It was only just nine o'clock; surely Naisha could not have got there already? Outside the door of the room, Sylvia paused and listened; if Naisha were inside, she would be audible outside, effusing, exclaiming and issuing orders to the lot of them, especially to her husband, the downtrodden Prem. Sylvia could not hear a thing. She breathed a discreet sigh of relief and after one last unendurable moment of anticipation, she knocked and opened the door a chink.

The room was suffused with a peach light. For a moment, Sylvia thought that all the lights must have peach-coloured bulbs. But then she realized that the whole room and everything in it – the walls, the floor, the curtains, the sheets and blankets and the washbasin – were all peach-coloured and it looked simply frightful.

In the middle of all that peach colour lay Smita, propped up on at least three pillows, looking miraculously groomed, with her glossy dark hair brushed and her make up flawless. To one side, at a disadvantage in the peach light, stood Jeremy, looking exhausted and somewhat seedy. In the furthest corner, almost incidental – another small entity in Smita's retinue rather than the new centre of the world – stood a see-through plastic cot and in the cot Sylvia could see a small shape, breathing and present.

"Darlings!" she exclaimed, stopping at the foot of Smita's bed, not sure how to proceed and not wanting, at this highly-charged peach moment, to do the wrong thing. "Show him to me."

Smita smiled graciously. She beckoned imperiously to Jeremy. "So show him to your mother" and Jeremy, grinning foolishly and fumbling, carefully lifted the little shape up from the plastic cot and held him out to Sylvia.

She took his slight warm weight into her arms, not much, a couple of bags of sugar, no more and yet the entire world. She looked down at her grandson in breathless wonder.

To tell the truth, she had not known exactly what to expect of this moment. Would a partly Indian baby still feel completely like her grandchild? She had been secretly apprehensive that she might not feel what she ought to. Although she had shared her apprehension with Ruth Rosenkranz who had simply laughed.

Sylvia remembered still, thirty years ago, the disappointment she had felt when Jeremy had been laid in her arms; who *was* this, was this what all the fuss had been about? That feeling had eventually passed of course, to be replaced by a degree of maternal fondness and pride. But the feelings which she had experienced back then were nothing, she realised incredulously, compared to the rush of sheer elation which she felt now. For a start, today she was not exhausted by labour as she had been back then. This baby had landed in her arms weighing no more than his own small body weight, not with the leaden burden, the ball and chain of motherhood attached to him. Because of his visible difference, there was in the first instance none of that possessive petty cataloguing which she remembered so tediously with her own son; Roger's eyes, Grandpa Neville's nose, someone else's hands, the baby ultimately only the sum of its parts, a descendant. This baby was a brand new adventure and Sylvia, confronted with his reality, his exquisite wriggling reality, was so excited she could barely breathe.

She took in the baby's wavering unfocused brown eyes, newly arrived from another dimension, his puffy little cheeks and his shrewd mouth. The few strands of hair which emerged from under the skullcap were glossy black like Smita's and his black brows seemed unusually well defined for a newborn. He looked to Sylvia like a diminutive Eastern sage and as she gazed down at him, lovestruck, she imagined that in the years to come this little boy would teach her far more than he would ever learn from her.

She remembered to look up at Smita and Jeremy and murmured, "He's adorable. Oh well *done*, darlings."

They beamed back, in unison Sylvia saw as they rarely were. Jeremy was already all gentle, soppy, caring gestures, as he usually was in fact only more so – and sweaty, she noticed, too – and Smita, even Smita seemed somewhat softened by the experience she had just been through; beneath her perfect make up she was less sharp, less diamond hard. For a rare moment, Sylvia could actually imagine that they might make each other happy after all. The baby would bring life to their unconvincing marriage and they would flourish as a family the way they had never really appeared to as a couple.

But this idea flashed through Sylvia's mind in seconds and she did not want to let it distract her from her grandson for even a moment. She looked down at him again, relishing him, drawing out the moment until Smita asked her expectantly, "Well, Sylvia, who do *you* think he looks like?"

Sylvia answered cautiously. "It's hard to say when

they're so small, isn't it? Who do you two think he takes after?"

Jeremy looked hesitatingly at Smita who answered promptly, "Oh, I think my side, definitely. Jeremy's not sure."

"I couldn't say," Sylvia said, she hoped diplomatically. "But whoever he takes after, he is absolutely beautiful." Again, not wanting to say the wrong thing and not sure either how a brown-skinned baby could, frankly, take after Jeremy's side, Sylvia changed the subject. "Tell me, have you thought about names?"

"No," said Jeremy.

"Yes," said Smita.

They all three laughed and Sylvia said hastily, "None of my business, I know."

Maybe disturbed by the sudden laughter in the quiet room, the baby stirred in Sylvia's arms and let out the beginning of a small wail. Sylvia made to hand him over to Smita but she waved him away.

"Put him back in the cot please Sylvia," she said languidly. "I'm *far* too exhausted to be holding him constantly. And I want to begin as I mean to go on; not picking him up and cuddling him and fussing over him all the time so he just cries out for more." She glanced warningly at Jeremy who looked ready to reach out and take his small son and fuss over him for all he was worth.

Obediently but regretfully, Sylvia returned the baby to his cot, surreptitiously caressing him as she covered him up. Wasn't it funny; thirty years ago she was sure she would have acted exactly like Smita but today she yearned to hold onto the baby and to be his warm source of comfort and reassurance.

Abandoned between the cold hospital sheets, the baby's small wail rose to a frank scream. Jeremy hung over the side of the cot, looking thwarted but apparently not daring to pick him up.

Deliberately turning her face away from the cot, Smita said to Sylvia, "We have discussed names, obviously. But it's difficult to reach a decision when there are *two* traditions to be taken into account."

"Plus," Jeremy interrupted, grinning, "up until last night we were convinced we were having a girl."

"*Were* you?" Sylvia exclaimed. "*Really*? Why, I was absolutely sure – " she caught sight of Smita's frown and broke off. "Who cares my dears, so long as he's healthy."

"Absolutely," Jeremy agreed. Sylvia noticed he was sneakily stroking the baby with a single finger.

"Anyway, about the name," Smita went on. "We'll have to wait until my mother gets here; she's been taking advice."

Sylvia didn't like to ask from whom. She assumed it must be a priest at Prem and Naisha's temple and she felt that in any case the topic was probably best left alone. Besides, she tested herself; how much did she actually care what they called the baby? To her surprise, she cared very little. She didn't seem to have any sentimental wish for him to be called after Roger or to bear any of the traditional family names. In fact she realized she was actually hoping the baby would have a brand-new name, a name which no-one in their family had ever had before, just to underline what an exciting brand-new person he was. So long as she could pronounce it of course. She thought briefly of Heather Bailey with her far away Amharic-speaking grandchildren with whom she could barely communicate. It was true; you never knew how your children would take their revenge.

Benevolently, and raising her voice slightly above the baby's crying, Sylvia said, "Honestly dears, whatever you come up with is fine by me. I won't be sticking my oar in."

Smita shifted uncomfortably in bed, whether at the implied comparison with her own mother or whether because she really was uncomfortable, Sylvia couldn't tell.

"Now tell me Smita dear," she asked kindly. "How are you?"

Smita shot Sylvia a dark warning look. Sylvia supposed she wanted to ward off any overly intimate questions about the birth; private parts made public, stitches, tears, that sort of thing. But, goodness, Sylvia would never have dreamt of asking about all that. She ploughed on, "You must take it easy as much as you can until you have got your strength back."

"Jeremy and my mother will take good care of me." Smita smiled frostily. "Don't you worry Sylvia." She turned to Jeremy and said, "Maybe someone could bring your mother a cup of tea?"

Sylvia sat with her tea, relegated to the status of visitor, drank and tried not to feel excluded. It was only natural that Smita should want to have her own mother to help. Sylvia was careful not to outstay her welcome especially when the baby's screaming grew so anguished that Jeremy had to lift him out of the cot and pass him to Smita and they began to bicker over whether or not he needed to be fed.

As she left, Sylvia reminded herself how secondary her concerns were. The little boy, *her* grandson, had come to rescue her from drowning. She had – as of this morning – a new and important role, whatever Smita said or did. From now on, she must drink less gin and take more healthy exercise. She had a vital task ahead of her; to be a superlative grandmother, to make up for the parents' shortcomings and she was going to do it her own way and nobody else's. Her world was so much more infinitely interesting with this little boy in it that she sailed beaming down in the upholstered lift, sailed out into the street, sailed onto the bus and sailed beaming all the way back to Overmore Gardens where she rang Ruth Rosenkranz's bell to share her marvellous news.

"That is your mother all over," Smita complained to Jeremy later. She was feeling tired to the point of tears and, as usual, Sylvia's visit had been the last straw. "Either knock and wait or come in without knocking. Why do both? It's so typical. She knocks so you think she's being considerate but then she comes in anyway. She is so aggravating. What if I had been breastfeeding?"

Jeremy, looking haggard and apparently distracted by the perfection of his baby son's fingernails, answered vaguely as he had so many times before, "She means no harm, Smi."

"Marvellous!" Smita snapped. "She *means* no harm but she just does it anyway; barges in, tra-la-la, and causes trouble left, right and centre. At least my mother, whatever nonsense she inflicts on us, you know she has thought about it beforehand, planned it, worked it all out and she *believes* what she is doing is right even if it's nothing of the sort. *Your* mother – " she broke off and gestured in exasperation at a large cardboard box in the corner. "I mean, what about her present? What sort of a weird outlandish thing is *that*?"

Jeremy considered his mother's gift for a moment: a large, very brightly painted mobile of Indian figures twirling amid moons and stars and elephants and tigers. Sylvia had explained proudly that the two largest figures were the Indian deities, Rama and Sita. "I think it's rather quaint," he said carefully.

"Quaint!" Smita exclaimed crossly. "It may well be quaint but is it *safe*? Is it hygienic? Where was it made exactly? For all we know, there is lead paint on those figures. And look at the feathers on the elephants' headdresses – where did *they* come from? I mean, doesn't she *think*? It's enough to give our little boy an allergy just *looking* at it."

❧

That evening, Sylvia's phone rang particularly shrilly and it was Naisha.

"I *had* to ring and celebrate with you, Sylvia dear," she exclaimed. "Congratulations to both of us, don't you think? He's gorgeous, isn't he?"

Sylvia felt conscience-stricken that she hadn't thought of ringing Naisha. She had always assumed that where other people had a heart, Naisha had a splendid gleaming calculator which worked out her every move. Her daughter had inherited the same calculator. Everything Naisha did or said was decided by a profit motive, either material profit or some other sort of tangible gain. Any altruistic motives in that household Sylvia attributed only to Prem, poor, grey, hen-pecked Prem with his never-ending devotions, his prayer corner and his long drawn-out visits to the temple.

But here was Naisha proving her culpably wrong. Why hadn't *she* thought of lifting the phone and congratulating Naisha? She knew why (apart from her antipathy towards Naisha); it was because she was not sure what to say and in a stupidly English way, she had said nothing at all. Which was undoubtedly the wrong thing.

Naisha went on boldly. "He has the best features of both parents, don't you think? The mouth and the chin are definitely Jeremy's, wouldn't you say, but the eyes, the eyes are Smita's. For sure. Of course it's probably far too early to tell anything, isn't it? They change so much in the first few weeks. But the temperament; I think you can see the temperament already quite clearly in the first few hours, don't you? And our little darling has the temperament of his maternal grandfather, of that I am sure. He lies there so calmly and sweetly, such a serene expression on his dear little face. Prem is beside himself with happiness. He has gone off to the temple just now."

An unpleasant thought crossed Sylvia's mind to the

effect that Prem would doubtless have gone off to the temple if he had been beside himself with sorrow too. She tuttingly suppressed it and tried her best to focus on Naisha's deluge of presumptive pronouncements about the baby. In fact, their images of him were not that far apart; where Sylvia had seen the epitome of an Eastern sage, Naisha had seen her own local version, saintly Prem. In the distance, Sylvia thought she heard for a moment a bellow of indignation from Roger. But it faded. Besides, Naisha was continuing: "So lovely to be linked in this way, Sylvia dear," she was saying graciously. "I hope you share my feelings."

At this, Sylvia's shame was complete for hadn't Naisha behaved impeccably, said and done exactly the right thing while she, Sylvia, was still debating whether or not to send a card?

She responded to Naisha's question rather more firmly than she actually felt. "Absolutely," she agreed. "Absolutely."

Naisha clucked. "We are truly blessed," she sighed happily. "I am only so sorry that poor Roger did not live to see this day." Then, disconcertingly briskly, she added, "Well, must rush. Lots of phone calls to make. Bye Sylvia dear. Looking forward to seeing you at the naming ceremony."

Sylvia sat perfectly still in her sitting room for about an hour after Naisha's phone call. Outside in the square, the sun was starting to set and the dark red brick mansions of Overmore Gardens seemed to be glowing. So many powerful emotions were surging through her, she feared that if she moved too suddenly, they might overflow and she might start to weep or howl or laugh hysterically like a mad woman. She needed to pull herself together if she was not to have another slip-up.

Her first act of responsibility towards her grandson was to eat a sensible supper. She went into the kitchen which, she noticed, was getting into rather a state. The truth was that, all those years abroad, she had always had someone to help her keep the kitchen tidy. But now, since that frightful business with the Romanian cleaner whom she had accused of stealing things, she had nobody. The thing was that, later on, she had found all the different things which she had thought were stolen. She had managed in her muddledom to misplace them but she had never confessed to Jeremy and Smita. Now she felt too guilty to hire another cleaner.

But there was one cupboard which was beautifully tidy: at the end of the kitchen there was an empty unit which she had been filling up over the past few weeks with supplies of baby formula, bottles, a sterilizing machine and jars and jars of baby food. She opened the cupboard and gloated over her prudent supplies. Straight away, she began to feel much better.

For days after the birth, Sylvia stayed in a state of elation, as if some parallel hormonal event were happening in her own body. She rang Jeremy so many times on his mobile the first two days that he ended up snapping at her. Of course, Naisha had now arrived and taken over; he had his mother-in-law to deal with too. But Sylvia still could not resist ringing; she had to know every development, every last little detail. She could think of nothing but the baby. When Smita went home from hospital – far too early in Sylvia's opinion, after barely two days – Sylvia could ring their home number freely since the only person who answered was Naisha and she loved to broadcast the latest details from her privileged position.

"He is feeding well," she reported excitedly. "Sleeping so-so. He cries a lot; he obviously needs to exercise his lungs." She chuckled. "And he has such *strong* lungs, Sylvia dear."

At night, Sylvia woke every two or three hours as if she herself had a newborn baby to feed. She imagined the night-time scene in Jeremy and Smita's apartment on the other side of London; the high-pitched cry rising in the darkness, Smita climbing wearily out of bed, taking the baby out of the bedroom so as not to disturb Jeremy and settling with him at her breast in the big front room, Naisha bringing her daughter tea and snacks.

Sylvia was outraged when she discovered, on her first visit to their flat, that Smita was not breastfeeding the baby at all. It wasn't that she couldn't (like Nikki Palmer, say, who had no milk.) She was flatly refusing to; she said she found it disgusting and degrading and, to Sylvia's chagrin, Naisha took her side, saying the baby got a much more nutritious feed from the bottle anyway. The only one who seemed upset by this development was Jeremy but it was already clear that nobody was listening to him.

Sylvia sat with the little boy on her lap – he still had no name, they were still arguing – and she wished she could hire a wet nurse for him like in the olden days. It was only on her way home that a huge advantage occurred to her; if the baby was bottle-fed, he wasn't dependent on his mother, was he? He could be anywhere, with anyone competent to feed him. As soon as she got home, she washed her hands and got out the sterilizer. All evening, she practised sterilizing bottles and making up the formula until she had it to a T. It came back to her surprisingly quickly.

Naisha was staying down in London for ten days. Sylvia knew she would not get a look in until Naisha had gone. But once she was, she would prevail on Smita, who was naturally exhausted, to let her take the baby for a night or two so Smita could sleep through. She knew it was a long shot but she was determined.

In the meantime, she tried to keep her feet on the ground in her giddy sleepless state by being a good neighbour to Ruth Rosenkranz, wheeling her out into the garden square and sitting there with her through the lovely Indian summer afternoons with a flask of iced tea and generations of baby stories.

Ruth kept promising that her baby brother would come to Sunday lunch again, after he had cancelled so suddenly the last time. Although Sylvia was, frankly, not that interested in the baby brother, she had found his excuse intriguing; he was marooned on the Isle of Wight. Sylvia wondered how on earth anyone could manage to be marooned on the Isle of Wight when there were ferries steaming to and fro to Southampton so regularly. She wondered why Ruth didn't seem to realize that the excuse must be a smokescreen. Was there some sibling difficulty between them; Ruth much keener on keeping things going than Siggy? But she spoke of him so dotingly, her adored baby brother whom, given their age difference and other circumstances, she had virtually brought up herself. Surely he must appreciate and adore his big sister too? Or maybe he found her bossy, intrusive, perhaps judgemental about the life he led?

One afternoon, she wrote a card to her sister Cynthia, informing her of the baby's safe arrival and explaining that, now he had arrived, so much earlier than expected, she would unfortunately have to postpone her planned September visit to Lewes. "PS," she added, "no name as yet!"

Then Jeremy called her, the first time he had done so since the day of the birth, and told her that they had finally chosen a name. "We're calling him Anand," he announced proudly. "It means happiness."

❧

The birth of his son caused Jeremy to relive his childhood in an unexpectedly vivid way. For years he had systematically avoided thinking about it. But now all sorts of memories came crowding back, unwelcome, unhappy, forcing him to experience all over again as an adult episodes which he had already suffered through uncomprehendingly as a child.

He had anticipated nothing but joy from Anand's arrival – ok, hard work and broken nights – but basically a life-changing happiness, like everyone said. He felt fortunate to become a father at a time when fathers were encouraged to take part in their children's upbringing;

when they were expected to change nappies and push prams and show emotion. Jeremy intended to do all those things and he was looking forward to it no end. He was utterly unprepared for the crush of distressing memories which sometimes threatened to overwhelm him in the first few months of his little boy's life. He knew that new mothers could get post-natal depression (and Smita seemed to for a while). But there was nothing comparable mentioned in the books about new fathers. Jeremy wasn't depressed exactly; most of the time he was perfectly happy. Yet as he sat cradling Anand in his arms, frequently, instead of gazing down at him, he found himself contemplating long-forgotten scenes of misery from his own childhood which seemed to have returned to haunt him. He would hold his baby closer as if it were himself he was trying to protect.

He hated having to go to work and being separated from Anand five days a week. He was jealous of Smita for having him to herself all day and disapproving that she didn't seem to enjoy it more. At the weekend, he would do everything he could to have Anand to himself. He would take him out early on Saturday and Sunday mornings to let Smita sleep in. As he pushed him in his pram through the deserted misty streets, Jeremy would gaze down at the little chap, snug in his hat and hood and covers; he would imagine Anand's future childhood and compare it inevitably with his own. If there was one thing he wanted for Anand at this stage, it was that he should look back on his childhood with greater happiness than Jeremy looked back on his.

If Jeremy had to pick a single adjective to describe his parents, it would be half-hearted. They had had their only child in an offhand sort of way and then they had pretty much ignored him for the next eighteen years; that was how it seemed to him. Of course, as a young child, he had taken it all for granted, the solitary, rather anachronistic ex-pat childhood. But once he was sent away to boarding school in England aged just eleven, part and parcel of that upbringing, he had a chance to compare his childhood with other boys' and to realise how deprived he had been.

During half term holidays, he would sometimes be invited to other boys' houses as the holiday was too short to fly back to India or later to Saudi Arabia. In the home of his friend Alastair Woodward, he discovered childhood with siblings, a gentle diffident father who didn't think his son was weedy and a jolly dishevelled mother who evidently didn't find her children a bore. At Olly Glockner's house, he met an astonishingly fat and hilariously funny father who didn't care at all about success on the sports field, who was proud of Olly's singing voice and his role as Lady Bracknell in the school play. Olly's mother, also a character, who dressed incredibly strangely, served dinner late because she was lost in a book and the book was the faintly scandalous *The Women's Room*. Eaten up with envy, Jeremy would sit at his friends' crowded tables and learn about teasing, squabbling and family catchphrases. He observed how having brothers and sisters gave you a degree of freedom from your parents' expectations; one sibling could be the sporty one, one the brainy one and one was allowed to be a freak.

Every long holiday, he would fly back to India, later to Saudi, feeling a notch more resentful each year, to a house which never really felt like his and to parents who scarcely paused in their round of socialising to acknowledge his return. By the time he reached sixteen, Jeremy understood, with rock-solid teenage certainty, that he had been cheated.

What he thought was his earliest memory was of his mother going out to a party. He was in the garden of their Delhi house, probably playing some solitary game in the benignly negligent care of his ayah. He would have been three or four. It was about to get dark any minute. In India, night fell very quickly and Jeremy was always scared of being caught in the wrong place when it got dark. He was playing close to the house and keeping a watchful eye on the encroaching shadows.

Suddenly a brilliant light came on upstairs in his parents' bedroom and his mother stepped out onto the balcony. She was wearing a shimmering multi-coloured cocktail frock and as she called out "Good Night" and spread and folded her arms to mimic a hug, she looked like a wonderful exotic bird perched up on the balcony, calling into the dusk.

Jeremy must have cried out, stretched up his arms; he wanted a real hug, not a pretend one. His ayah scooped him up quickly before he ran inside and delayed his parents' departure. Jeremy struggled. He didn't want her bony arms around him; he wanted his mother's plump, freckled, scented ones. So in desperation – because his ayah's arms although bony were very strong – he bit her, as hard as he could, in her sinewy upper arm. His ayah screamed and dropped him and he ran into the house as fast as his legs could carry him.

But when he got upstairs to his parents' bedroom, he didn't get a motherly hug; he got a furious scolding – and a mighty spanking from his father who was up there too, struggling with his cufflinks, when Jeremy came running in. It was all right to speak peremptorily to servants; biting them was not.

With hindsight and listening to Smita complaining about the drudgery of caring for a small baby unaided, Jeremy could understand the appeal of his parents' ex-pat lifestyle. If they had stayed in England, they would never have lived as well. His father, a civil engineer and his mother, his father's former secretary, would have lived comfortable but never luxurious lives. They might have moved out of London to somewhere like Surrey, to the commuter belt, achieved a bigger house with a bigger garden which his mother would have fussed over. But they would never have experienced the elegance of their villa on the Peak in Hong Kong which his mother had gone on and on about for years after they left. They would never in their wildest dreams have had a house full of servants and while his mother might have done just as little with her life in Surrey, she would have had a lot less fun doing it.

'Ah, fun,' Jeremy thought bitterly. Fun had always been his parents' guiding principle. They had had years and years of it: parties, picnics, trips, games. They had always been off somewhere having fun while Jeremy was growing up. Had anyone else had as absent parents as he had? For Jeremy had understood at a young age that he was not part of the fun, that his presence was in fact incompatible with fun.

Another bad memory came back to him; he was a little older this time, maybe five or six and he was woken one warm night by the sounds of one of his parents' endless succession of parties. He could hear a lady's high-pitched shrieks of laughter and, as he woke up completely, he recognised that they were his mother's. He got up and went out onto the long landing, looking for her. To his surprise, the hoots of laughter weren't coming from downstairs where the party was going on but from the guest bedroom next door to his. That was why they had woken him up. He went running in, gladly calling, "Mummy, Mummy!" and he found his mother inside sharing a joke with a man who was laughing so much he had fallen flat on his back on the bed. Jeremy couldn't see who the man was because the light was off. His mother was furious. She leapt up off the bed and shouted at Jeremy – very red in the face – to go back to bed. She shouted at him, "You're spoiling my party!"

Jeremy was a teenager before he understood what that was all about. By then, he had spied enough other instances of his parents' private fun to work out what was going on. Along with the lavish lifestyle and the warmer climate, his parents had embraced the swinging ex-pat scene. Free and easy, far from home, you could get away with things there you would never have dreamt of in Surrey.

Even all these years later, sitting holding his little Anand, Jeremy still felt hurt by that memory. What sort of mother would shout at her child that he was spoiling her party? He worried for a minute that Smita might. But of course there was no comparison between his mother and Smita. Smita was suffering from the inevitable difficulties of adjustment; from pursuing a full-time and highly successful career to having to deal with nappies and bottles and endless piles of washing. Whereas, before Jeremy was born, his mother had done simply nothing. That must have been the trouble really; she had enjoyed years and years of utter idleness before little Jeremy had come along to spoil it. She had grown used to the heavenly selfishness of the unemployed ex-pat wife: coffee mornings, tennis, swimming, a bit of voluntary work maybe but not much. She had never forgiven Jeremy, the little pain, for threatening to put a stop to it.

He hadn't managed to though, had he? The fun had carried on uninterruptedly over his head throughout his childhood and, not knowing any better, he had adored his lovely blonde mother from afar. If anyone had been the villain when he was young, it was his father; his father who bellowed and spanked and always wanted him to be bigger and stronger than he was, his father whom he had caught out in extra-marital fun and games far more explicitly than his mother.

Jeremy must have been no more than five or six when he took it into his head to hide under the dining table on a night when his parents had guests for dinner. Everyone must have assumed he was tucked up in bed; no one came looking for him. It was a great game to start off with; matching the legs and feet to the voices overhead. His parents were of course the easiest to identify. Besides they sat in their usual places: his father, in heavy lace ups even at dinner, at the head of the table and his mother, in strappy silver sandals with crimson nail polish on her toes, at the foot. So why had his father somehow undone the laces on his big right shoe and stuck his foot in its great lozenge-patterned sock up the tight skirt of the woman sitting to his left? Jeremy had observed the manoeuvrings of his father's foot for some time, mystified and repelled. His mother's feet were squarely planted on the parquet floor, nowhere near her neighbours'. His father's foot was burrowing up and up between the lady's legs. It must have been horribly ticklish for her; why didn't she make him stop? Jeremy slid on his bottom to the far end of the table, as far away from the burrowing foot as possible and as close as he could get to the familiarity of his mother's silver sandals. He must have scooted a bit too far or maybe his mother had shifted her feet because he collided with them and overhead his mother let out a startled squawk.

He was discovered amid much laughter. His mother kept repeating, "I thought it was a stray cat who'd sneaked in."

It seemed at first that Jeremy wasn't going to be told off all that seriously because everyone thought it was so screamingly funny. But once the fuss had died down, his father stood up with a face like thunder. He must have spent those first few minutes struggling back into his shoe.

"Excuse us for a moment," he said, far too seriously

and he led Jeremy out of the room by the hand, holding him not fondly but too tightly like a victorious soldier leading a captive.

Upstairs in Jeremy's bedroom, there was the usual telling off, the usual spanking, even more furious than usual. In the middle of it, Jeremy shouted out, "I saw. You had your foot up a lady's skirt."

His father stopped spanking to scoff. "What nonsense. I did no such thing."

"Oh yes you did," Jeremy cried. "I *saw*."

His father laughed. "How could you possibly tell whose foot was whose, you little silly? If anyone was playing footsie under the table, it would have been Nigel Palmer."

"*Your* foot," Jeremy insisted. "*Your* socks."

"Didn't you notice?" his father retorted. "Nigel and I are wearing *the same socks*."

Jeremy had forgotten all about that incident, gladly, buried it deep along with all the other upsetting memories until Anand was born. Then it had swum disconcertingly back to the surface like the murky remnants of a crime from the bottom of a pond.

He tried to tell Smita what was troubling him but she didn't really get it. Maybe it was because the baby was a boy; nothing similar seemed to be happening to her. Or maybe it was because her childhood had been so straightforwardly happy; she had been the adored, spoilt princess of the all-providing Indian household. Her doting grandparents had substituted for her parents when they were out at work. She had never been without at least two close relatives waiting on her hand and foot. It still showed, Jeremy thought resentfully. Smita simply couldn't understand how Anand's arrival had triggered all this maudlin soul-searching.

"For goodness *sake*," she snapped at Jeremy. "Why are you digging that up all over again? It's *finished*, done with. Our little boy is a brand new chapter, aren't you sweetie?" And she bounced the baby on her lap, his short towelling-clad legs splayed out stiff and straight: "A *brand new chapter*!"

But Jeremy knew that wasn't true. He sensed that everything about himself as a father had been formed by those unhappy childhood years. Even if his main motivation was to escape from them, above all not to repeat them, they were still *there*, they were part of who he was and he was terrified that he would somehow, in spite of himself, transmit all that misery, that inadequacy to Anand. It troubled him so much that some nights he couldn't sleep. He worried that he didn't have it in him to be a really great father. He would get up to give Anand his bottle to Smita's amazed gratitude. Smita had no such worries. For her, motherhood was just another job. She never doubted her competence – and she was very competent – although Jeremy kept wishing she would enjoy it a little more. Already, when Anand was barely two months old, she was talking eagerly about hiring a nanny and going back to work.

That broke Jeremy's heart; he couldn't stand the thought of some uninterested Polish nanny caring for his son. It would surely be history repeating itself; a child, whose parents were too busy leading their own lives to bring him up, being raised by servants. Most days, he would have dearly liked to give up his job to care for Anand full-time himself but obviously that wasn't financially practical. He felt angry with Smita for refusing even to consider going part-time as so many women did.

Having his mother around didn't help of course. The birth of her grandson seemed to have had a peculiar effect on her too. Having practically turned her back on them with her eccentric move to Kensington, since Anand's arrival they had trouble keeping her away. She was always ringing up, asking to come over and sometimes even turning up unannounced – all the way from Kensington – which drove Smita up the wall.

It made Jeremy feel rather cynical frankly. Here was a woman who had been a virtually useless mother, who had never shown the slightest interest in her own son's doings, becoming so sentimentally maternal towards her grandson. He wondered how genuine it was; if it wasn't some sort of complicated, competitive attempt to show Smita up. Smita certainly resented her mother-in-law's continual busybodying visits no end and she complained to Jeremy about it constantly.

"Can't you *do* something about her?" she begged. "Can't you *stop* her coming round all the time? Can't we go back to just Sunday lunches?"

One weekend in early November, Jeremy experimented with having sole charge of Anand for an entire day. Smita was desperate to go out with her girlfriends who had organised a day of shopping, lunch and a visit to a beauty salon, so desperate that she was prepared to leave Anand with Jeremy all day and even for him to drive Anand all the way to Overmore Gardens to spend some time with Sylvia. The truth was that Smita's own mother had not lived up to her word; having assured them countless times before Anand was born that she would be down from Leicester every weekend if she was needed, she had only managed to make it once, blaming the demands of her business which seemed to be particularly pressing. Sylvia, with her unexpected excess of grandmotherly feelings, had stepped gladly into the gap left by Naisha.

Jeremy hadn't been to his mother's flat for nearly three months and he was completely taken aback by what he found there. The drive from Belsize Park went smoothly, Anand slept obligingly all the way, Jeremy found a parking spot relatively easily and he pressed the intercom and climbed the stairs to the first floor, feeling almost jaunty, swinging Anand in his car seat in one hand and a holdall crammed full of baby supplies in the other. He was looking forward to hearing his mother crow over how much Anand had grown in the five days since she had last seen him, over how increasingly wonderful he was in every way.

His mother greeted them ecstatically. She cooed so noisily over Anand that she woke him up and then she could hardly wait to snatch him up from the car seat and parade him in her arms around her big front room. "This is where Grandma Sylvia lives," she trilled, "yes it is, yes it is."

Jeremy followed his mother in and he could barely believe his eyes. The living room was as full of baby things as if there were really a baby living there: one of those bouncy baby seats which Smita thought were so dangerous, an Early Learning Centre play mat with mirrors and bells and a whole spread of brightly coloured baby toys. In the kitchen there was a steriliser and a row of prepared baby bottles in the fridge which his mother proudly showed him and in the second bedroom a brand new cot complete with a suffocating frilly cot bumper. The room had been transformed into a picture perfect nursery, better than anything Anand had at home where Smita tried to keep clutter to a minimum. There were nursery rhyme stencils all around the walls, a baby changing table and an extraordinary quantity of cuddly toys. Again, Smita would have freaked out because of all the fluff and Jeremy was grateful that she wasn't there.

"Isn't this rather over the top?" he asked coldly. "Just for a visit?"

"Oh Jem," Sylvia exclaimed. "I'm hoping this will be the first of *many* visits." She carried Anand into the spare bedroom turned nursery and crowed, "This will be *your* room, Anand, yes it will."

"But still," Jeremy persisted severely. "Haven't you got an awful lot of stuff? Realistically, he's never going to be here for more than a few hours, is he?"

"Why ever not?" Sylvia retorted. "I'm hoping that when you and Smita get a little more used to things, you'll agree to leave him with me overnight sometimes, for the odd weekend maybe. I mean, it's obvious we're not going to be seeing as much of Naisha as Smita was hoping. In any case, Anand will be *much* better off here with me than left with some babysitter, you know. Plus it'll be a lot cheaper." She nuzzled Anand's tummy with the trunk of a small peppermint green elephant. "Besides, we'll have such fun together, won't we, Anand, yes, we will!"

Seeing her doting on the baby, Jeremy didn't have the heart to tell her that there was no way that Smita would ever agree to her having him overnight. A weekend would be out of the question.

But as the day went on, Jeremy caught himself wondering more than once if his mother would really be as disastrous with Anand as Smita claimed. Surely, for all her eccentricities, she would be better than a hired babysitter, wouldn't she? At least she really loved Anand, didn't she?

He observed her deftly changing the baby's nappy, laughing in delight at the modern convenience of sticky tapes and scented wipes. She tickled the soles of Anand's feet and he gurgled with pleasure. She warmed his midday bottle to just the right temperature in the microwave and shook it heartily to avoid hot spots. It was true she spouted a load of nonsense while she was about it but on basic care he couldn't fault her. Besides, no Polish nanny would ever call Anand "sweet pea" nor bounce him so lovingly on her knee, warbling, "Ride a cock hoss, To Banbury *Crorss*, To see a fine lady upon a white hoss."

After lunch, they went down into the garden square and, while Anand napped, they wheeled him in his pram up and down the garden paths. In the weak winter sunshine, Jeremy noticed that his mother had lost her year round tan. She looked rather pale and weary and Jeremy felt a passing pang of guilt that he had been so taken up with Smita and the baby in recent months that he had not paid her much attention. It was less than a year since his father had died; he should have given her more support.

"How are *you*?" he asked, perhaps a bit abruptly and he saw his mother immediately look wary, as if it might be a trick question.

"I'm fine thank you Jeremy," she answered briskly, increasing her pace a little, as if her fitness might be under scrutiny.

Jeremy persisted: "I mean in yourself. How are you – adjusting?"

His mother's face fell. He saw a shadow pass across it. But she replied bravely, "I'm ever so much better now this little chap has come along to keep me company."

Jeremy winced inwardly. He understood how impossibly difficult it was going to be to keep his mother and Anand apart, the way Smita wanted, the way he had thought *he* wanted too, although today suddenly he was no longer so sure.

Over tea, for the first time, his mother raised the subject of Anand's colour. She did it in her characteristically insensitive way; Anand was lying on the play mat, waving his arms and legs vaguely like a sea anemone and, gesturing at him, Sylvia asked Jeremy point blank, "What colour would you say he was?"

Jeremy answered reprovingly, "He's mixed race."

"Oh don't be such a prig, Jeremy," his mother laughed.

"Mixed race isn't a colour. I mean, what exact shade would you say he was: beige, coffee?"

"I haven't really thought about it," Jeremy lied. He had thought about it a good deal actually; how his little boy could look so apparently totally Indian and yet be so utterly *his* son. Smita insisted the baby had Jeremy's mouth and chin but he couldn't really see it yet.

"But you *must* have," Sylvia insisted. "Don't pretend you can't *see* he's a different colour."

"Smita's a different colour too," Jeremy replied coldly. "I don't think about that on a daily basis either."

"It's not rose-coloured glasses you're wearing Jeremy but blinkers," his mother told him briskly. "Honestly, I really don't see what's wrong with talking about his colour. It's not as if I've got anything against it, is it? I think he's the most gorgeous colour. I would call it fudge."

"You make him sound like something edible," Jeremy replied irritably.

Sylvia giggled. "Oh but he *is*!"

She got down onto her knees beside the playmat and Jeremy noticed how stiffly she moved these days. Of course she had nowhere to go swimming anymore. He felt another pang; Smita could so easily have taken her to her sports club where there was a beautiful pool.

Conciliatingly he said, as his mother pretended to nibble Anand's toes, "I suppose you could say he was golden."

His mother let out a cry of delight. "My golden boy! How *priceless*. Do you know your father once won £500 on a horse called My Golden Boy at Happy Valley? For ages after that, people kept calling him 'My Golden Boy' because of his winnings."

Anand suddenly flinched and Jeremy realised that tears were falling onto him from Sylvia's bowed face.

"Hey," he said, half-jokingly, "don't get him all wet."

Sylvia scrabbled for a hanky in her sleeve. "No, no, that wouldn't do at all."

She shook a lurid rattle energetically over the baby to distract him. For a few moments, they sat in silence, watching Anand's reactions to the toy. Then, in an unsubtle attempt to deflect Jeremy's attention away from herself, Sylvia asked, "Have you and Smita discussed at all how you're going to include both bits of his background in his upbringing?"

She meant well, Jeremy knew that, but still he felt the familiar surge of anger even though her face was still tear-stained, she was still sniffing. Why did she have to be so clumsy, so heavy-handed? Her attitudes were laughably old-fashioned – and why did she have to create problems where nowadays none existed?

"What exactly do you mean?" he asked sullenly, a teenage boy all over again.

"Well, for example, will you take him to church at Christmas or to the temple at Diwali?" Sylvia asked, "and will Smita make sure he learns some Gujerati so he can be in touch with his roots?"

"Why on earth should we take him to church *or* to the temple," Jeremy exclaimed, "when we never go to either ourselves? It would be complete hypocrisy. And Smita can't even speak Gujerati herself; she can just about understand it but that's pretty much it. What would be the *point*?"

Sylvia sighed. "It just seems such a pity for it all to be lost. You've given him an Indian name, haven't you? Shouldn't you give him some Indian culture too? Otherwise he'll be – cut adrift."

"You're making him out to be far more *different* than he actually is," Jeremy said impatiently. "Haven't you noticed? London is full of kids who look just like Anand, who are called Dev or Sunil or Ramesh but they're all more or less completely English. You're doing just what you always do with Smita, you know and it drives her mad; making her out to be so terribly different and exotic when she was actually born and brought up in Leicester. I *wish* you wouldn't do it."

Sylvia looked strangely stubborn. "I just want what's best for Anand," she said quaveringly and Jeremy couldn't be sure whether she was still feeling emotional because of talking about his father or whether she really felt so strongly about preserving her grandson's tenuous links with India.

He remembered her arrival at the hospital on the day Anand was born, clutching that huge gaudy Indian mobile which Smita had refused point-blank to hang over the baby's cot. He hadn't given the gift much thought at the time – too much else to think about – but now he understood what his mother had been driving at. Oh, Smita was so right; she was preposterous. She was just trying to reconnect with her own long-lost halcyon days in India, regardless of the passage of time, regardless of what Smita's own family might want.

"I'm sure you do," he said coldly. "We all do." He looked at his watch. "I really should be getting going, you know or he'll get hungry and start screaming on the way home."

"You can give him his next bottle here," Sylvia said eagerly. "I've got one made."

"No," Jeremy said firmly. "No. I promised Smita I'd give him his bath and put him to bed at the normal time. She's very keen on establishing a good routine right from the start."

"Well, she's right of course," Sylvia agreed. "But you could make a little exception just once, couldn't you?"

She tickled Anand lovingly under the chin and he gave her an ecstatic smile.

"Oh!" Sylvia gasped. "Did you see that?"

Jeremy couldn't help smiling too. Anand had only started to smile a couple of weeks earlier and, every time he did, there still seemed something extraordinary about it like a double rainbow or a shooting star.

He said a little more kindly, "No, no, we really have to go now otherwise we'll get stuck in traffic and Anand will give me hell."

Together, they packed up the baby's considerable collection of stuff.

"Now I've seen how straightforward it is to come over here with him, maybe we can do it more often," he added conciliatingly.

Sylvia clasped her hands. "Oh please!"

On the way downstairs – his mother came with him to help with all the stuff – she asked whether Jeremy had time to stop for five minutes to show Anand to her downstairs neighbour. Of course he couldn't say yes; the five minutes would surely turn into thirty and he would have to crawl all the way back in Saturday night traffic. But he couldn't help feeling a passing curiosity about this neighbour who seemed to be playing an increasingly important part in his mother's newly widowed life.

As he fixed the car seat into place and arranged Anand's stuff in the back, his mother stood forlornly on the pavement and cooed at Anand. "Bye bye sweetpea. You're gorgeous, whatever colour they'd call you in the paint box."

Jeremy felt himself flush with annoyance all over again. "You simply must stop saying things like that before you seriously upset someone," he told her crossly.

They ended up parting rather coldly, despite the happier interludes of the visit. The minute Jeremy closed the car door and drove off, the strangest thing happened; Anand stiffened in anger and straight away began to scream. It was as if he was protesting at their departure. It took Jeremy over an hour to drive home with Anand screaming nerve-janglingly all the way until, somewhere past Paddington, he irritatingly fell fast asleep which would of course play havoc with his routine.

Jeremy felt exhausted by the time he got home and completely conflicted too. On the answering machine, he found a message which was his mother warbling a bedtime lullaby for Anand. Jeremy felt entrapped in contradictions; she was appalling, she was insufferable but she adored his son with a selfless, spectacular love, comparable only to his own and Smita's.

When Smita came home, thrilled by her day out, he was not as receptive as he should have been. She had had her hair done, it fell stiff and glossy to her shoulders, so deeply black it was almost blue, and she had had some sort of treatment to her face too; it looked artificially uniform and smooth, her eyebrows shaped into unnaturally perfect peaks.

Jeremy noticed that she didn't seem that upset that Anand was already fast asleep whereas he was sure that he would have felt disappointed and cheated if he had come in from work to find he had missed out on his evening with Anand.

Smita put on her new clothes to show him. She twirled in front of him, showing off her regained figure. At one point, she paused to slap the small pout of baby tummy that was still visible and declared, "I've just got to get rid of this and then I'll be good to go."

Jeremy admired her new clothes absent-mindedly. An inadmissable thought formed in his mind to do with his mother's substantial frame. Wasn't a mother *meant* to be a rounded, nurturing figure? And wasn't Smita's fierce insistence on returning as quickly as possible to her pre-pregnancy shape slightly unnatural?

He couldn't sleep again that night. He was troubled by the day's revelations about his mother and by the sheer impossibility of reconciling his lifelong image of her with this new kneeling, kissing, besotted grandmother. And how on earth would he ever convince Smita of the transformation?

He thought back to the sleepless nights of his

childhood during which it had seemed that neither the night nor his childhood would ever come to an end. His mother had always taken his insomnia personally as if he was staying awake deliberately to vex her. For years and years, Jeremy had read at night inside his mosquito net instead of sleeping. Outside, in the lantern-lit garden, his parents' cocktail guests cackled and brayed. Jeremy was not allowed to spoil their party. So inside, in his bedroom, entirely enclosed by the secrecy of his mosquito net, he escaped into his reading.

He escaped to a country called England although it bore almost no resemblance to the place where he and his parents went on holiday nor to the country he discovered when he was sent away to boarding school a few years later. It was an England which existed only between the covers of old-fashioned children's books, the sort of books which, amazingly, they still had in the early Eighties on the shelves of the Delhi Children's Library. His mother thought it was a hoot that he came home with all her old favourites: Enid Nesbitt and Gillian Avery. His father wanted him to choose more manly reading; he recommended Biggles and Arthur Ransome. He was indignant that Jeremy preferred women writers.

Jeremy was fascinated by the relations between siblings – in most of the books, there were at least four – the rivalry, the traditional roles allotted to each one, from the eldest through to the youngest and the recurring misfit whose only role was that of odd one out. Jeremy wished desperately that he had brothers and sisters, at least just one. He hated his parents for not giving him any. As far as he was concerned, it was just meanness on their part. They found him boring and a nuisance; why on earth would they want to have two or three boring nuisances? But for other children, he invented the story of a sister, born long before him, who had died when she was little. Her name was Arabella. He told his friends that mentioning her upset his parents so badly that they must never ever do so.

When Anand woke at three, Jeremy got up to feed and change him. Smita mumbled in the dark, "God, you're amazing." Jeremy relished her praise but he couldn't help thinking that Smita hadn't spent time with Anand since early yesterday morning; didn't she *want* to get up and be with him?

As he settled Anand back to sleep, he heard himself humming his mother's lullaby. How ironic it was that, hardly ever having been the least bit motherly towards her own son, his mother now seemed to be metamorphosing into an exemplary grandmother. Smita of course would be deeply suspicious and, for all he knew, she was right to be. He thought with sudden rancour that he would take Smita's opinions a lot more seriously if she showed signs of being a more committed mother herself. Instead, all she talked about, all she thought about apparently, was going back to work. Her Pilates and her draconian diet were so that she would look her best when she returned to Gravington Babcock. She loved Anand to bits of course; that wasn't in doubt. But Anand had his place in her scheme of things and there was no way she was going to let him turn her world upside down. She spoke pityingly of the women in her mother and baby group who intended to stay at home with their children. Many of them, she said witheringly, were still in their maternity clothes three and six months after giving birth.

Jeremy worried. He worried that he and Smita had quite different visions of Anand's childhood. With a lurch of panic, he wondered whether he would ever manage to persuade Smita to have a second child.

Some time in mid-November, Smita announced that she wanted to go up to Leicester for Christmas. She wanted to show Anand off to all the aunties and uncles and cousins who hadn't yet seen him. It would be restful to stay at her parents where she wouldn't have to lift a finger.

Jeremy was horrified. "But we can't do that Smi," he said. "How can we leave my mother alone in London her first Christmas on her own?"

Smita scowled. "Why can't she go and spend Christmas with her dotty sister whom she never sees? Or get plastered with Heather Bailey? Or she could spend it with her downstairs neighbour she's suddenly so obsessed with."

Jeremy felt himself reddening ridiculously. "Christmas is meant to be a time you spend with your family," he said lamely.

"Exactly," Smita said smartly. "Exactly. And that is why *I* want to spend Anand's first Christmas with *my* family. Besides," she added resentfully, "your mother gets to see Anand all the time. We can hardly keep her away. My parents haven't seen him for weeks."

She ended the argument by switching on the television and Jeremy made a fool of himself by leaping up and switching it off again. He hardly ever shouted at Smita but he shouted at her now: "Why do you always have to treat her so horribly, Smi? Tell me, what has she ever done to you?"

శ

When Smita began to interview nannies, it felt to Jeremy like a continuation of their argument even though he knew it wasn't. Of course Smita had every right to resume her career, not to throw away everything she had worked so hard for. But did she always have to get her own way?

As he heard her on the phone to agencies, busily discussing her requirements – Monday to Friday, 8 am to 6:30 pm – he felt wretched. He started to worry about ghastly accidents, about neglect and abuse; Anand lying in his cot, unstimulated, hour after hour, Anand harmed in undefined, unspeakable ways, Anand hurt.

None of the first applicants were anywhere near suitable. Smita agreed with him. But a second round of interviews yielded a capable young Bulgarian woman whom Smita thought would do. The young woman, her name was Galina, looked curiously like Smita, a slightly shorter, broader version of Smita, with utterly black hair parted in the middle and a business-like manner. She stated very plainly in the interview that being a nanny was not her long-term goal. She was studying to become an accountant in the evenings, at weekends and the nanny job would just be to fund her studies.

"I like that," Smita said to Jeremy afterwards. "I like the fact she's an intelligent person, with goals of her own. I wouldn't want Anand to be cared for by a moron."

Jeremy imagined Galina's capable but uncaring hands handling Anand and he felt utterly miserable. But he knew there was absolutely nothing he could do about it. It was like the first vaccination which had marked Anand's perfect body. This was the first flaw to mar his vision of Anand's perfect childhood.

Jeremy supposed that he must have talked about his concerns to his mother. But he was sure that he had not said anything which might have encouraged her to do what she did next.

Three days after Galina's interview, while Smita was checking up on her references and debating how long before her own return to work Galina should start, their doorbell rang, relatively early on a Saturday morning and Sylvia's voice trilled through the intercom, "Yoo-hoo! It's Mary Poppins!"

She seemed to take forever coming up the four flights of stairs, they could hear her huffing and puffing – and thank goodness Mrs Castellini hadn't chosen that moment to stick her head out of her front door or they would doubtless have been waiting all morning. They were totally shocked when Sylvia finally made it to their front door, out of breath but grinning, unbuttoned her heavy winter coat to reveal a frilly white apron and launched into a breathless but jaunty version of "Just a spoonful of sugar helps the medicine go down." She even produced a little silver spoon from her pocket which she waved about theatrically. She then kissed them both resoundingly and announced excitedly, "I've come about the job."

Jeremy's first thought was that she must be drunk. To

turn up like that, unannounced, in fancy dress and singing; surely it was the only explanation. But she didn't seem drunk. She seemed in fact particularly focused. She took off her coat and handed it to Jeremy. "Hang it up dear," she instructed him. "It's a bit wet." She then turned purposefully to Smita who was glaring at her, outraged but speechless and said kindly, "Let's sit down dear and I'll explain to you what I have in mind."

Jeremy waited for Smita's certain sharp response: "I was just on my way out actually" or "Sylvia, I'm really busy right now." But Smita must have been too shocked to say anything because she followed Sylvia slowly up their glass stairs, a furious but silent figure.

As they entered the big front room, Anand, who was lying on the new sheepskin rug pumping his legs, made a sudden experimental sideways flip, almost a roll and at the sight of his mother and grandmother side by side in the doorway, he beamed with delight and gave a strangled little yelp of sheer happiness.

Smita and Sylvia couldn't help turning to one another to exclaim over what he had just done.

Grudgingly, Smita offered her mother-in-law a cup of tea or coffee. But Sylvia turned down the offer and gestured determinedly towards the armchairs. "No, no, my dear," she said, "Let's get down to business straight away. There's no time to be wasted."

Jeremy hovered uncertainly in the open plan kitchen, making tea and coffee anyway and listened to his mother's proposal in total disbelief.

"I've been thinking," she began, the moment she was

seated, "and what you two are about to do doesn't make any sense at all to me." She jiggled Anand, whom she had picked up, with Smita's permission, on her knees. "You are about to hand this little chap over to a total stranger five days a week. You are going to pay that stranger a considerable sum of money to look after him. While, down the road, you have his grandmother, one of his grandmothers – "

"Kensington is *not* down the road," Smita snapped.

Sylvia ploughed on: "One of his grandmothers, who is willing and able, who would *love* to do the job, who would not need to be *paid*. Maybe I couldn't manage it five days a week, it's true, but one or two – of course I could! Think how good it would be for Anand to be cared for by a close relative rather than a complete stranger. I would do all sorts of things with him which a nanny would never dream of. He'd have so much more *fun* with me, wouldn't you sweetpea, wouldn't you? Yes, of course you would! And if *your* mother should be able to come down from time to time, Smita, of course I would gladly, gladly let her have my days with Anand. They could be Anand's 'grandma days', we could take it in turns, if Naisha wanted, if she was able. And think of all the money you would save. Thousands and thousands of pounds, I dare say. Please say yes, my dears, please; it makes such perfect sense."

As if to show how well she would do the job, she propped Anand cosily onto her left shoulder and stood up and walked around the room, patting him lightly on the back and humming a nursery rhyme. She overdid it, accompanying her jolly "Tom-pom-pom" with a high-spirited little jig and as she came back towards the armchairs, she caught her foot on the edge of the sheepskin rug and nearly fell. Smita exclaimed and made a grab for Anand but luckily Sylvia managed to regain her balance enough to land very heavily sideways in the nearest armchair with Anand still safe in her arms.

"How on *earth*," Smita hissed at her, "do you expect me to leave Anand with you *all day*? Look, you can't manage to be with him for five minutes without something happening. How could you possibly have sole charge of him from morning till night? It's a job for a fit active *young* person, not someone in their sixties. I don't mean to be unkind. Maybe you could just about cope now while he's a small baby but how would you manage in a year or so's time when he's an energetic toddler racing around? You haven't thought this through at all. I mean, I understand you love him and you want to spend time with him and that's sweet. But it doesn't mean you can be his nanny. In fact, the whole thing's completely *silly*, surely you can see that? I need someone as a nanny whom I can tell what to do and go off to work knowing that they'll get on with it. Whereas, I'm sorry Sylvia, but you and I haven't seen eye to eye on a number of issues to do with Anand and how do I know that, as soon as my back was turned, you wouldn't just do your own thing and take no notice of what *I* want?"

Sylvia flushed. "Fashions change in childcare," she answered evasively. "It doesn't mean that the old ways are necessarily no good." She added coyly, "*My* son turned out alright, didn't he?"

Jeremy and Smita exchanged glances across the room. Smita's was one of scarcely contained fury, Jeremy's was pleading.

"Let's not go there," Smita said crisply. "There's really no point us discussing it anymore, Sylvia. I appreciate you mean well, really I do. But there's no way, *no way* you can be Anand's nanny. I'm sorry."

Jeremy, watching from the kitchen, feared his mother might cry again, showering Anand with her tears. He had winced repeatedly while Smita was speaking; he thought she was being unnecessarily hard on his mother. Was there really no room for compromise here; couldn't she be granted a regular afternoon or two, if not a whole day? Smita hadn't seen his mother taking care of Anand during his visits to her flat. She had no idea how competent Sylvia could be.

Sylvia didn't cry. She looked down fixedly at Anand on her lap and there was something in what Jeremy could see of her expression which scared him inexplicably; sadness but also an unbudgeable resolve. Anand began to wriggle, looking up into his grandmother's face and making nearly musical "Da-da-da" noises.

In response, Sylvia began to jiggle her knees – perfectly nimbly – and sang to him, "Ride a cock *hoss*, to Banbury *Crorss*" while Anand gurgled with pleasure.

Jeremy stole a look at Smita. Surely she would melt a little in response to this tableau; the devoted grandmother and the blissfully happy grandchild. But Smita had a wry curdled expression on her face and her mind, Jeremy knew, was made up.

He asked his mother, "Would you like to have brunch with us?" But before she could answer, Smita stood up and intervened. "But we were going shopping. Have you forgotten or are you trying to get out of it?"

Sylvia stood up too. She kissed Anand lingeringly on the top of his downy head and she replied, "No, no, I can't stay anyway, thank you, Jeremy dear. I'm invited to lunch with Ruth Rosenkranz. She has a special guest coming."

"Who?" asked Smita.

Sylvia seemed not to hear her. She deposited Anand carefully back onto the sheepskin rug, where he at once began to wail and asked for her coat.

While Smita was getting it, Jeremy asked his mother quietly, "Are you alright?"

She nodded bravely. With Smita's help, she got her heavy coat back on, over the frilly white apron which she was still wearing. As an afterthought, she tried to take the apron off inside her coat and became distressingly entangled. After some stilted goodbyes, half covered by Anand's crying, she left and, the minute she had gone, Smita rounded on Jeremy.

"You set her up to this," she shouted. "Didn't you?"

Jeremy was holding Anand by now, trying unsuccessfully to soothe him and he answered unnaturally softly, "Of course not. Why on earth would I do that?"

Smita burst into tears of fury. "I can't believe you did this," she sobbed. It's like a betrayal. How *could* you? How *could* you?"

Jeremy still spoke incongruously softly, jiggling Anand and patting his back. "But I'm telling you Smi: I *didn't*. It's all her idea. Why would I set her up to suggest something you were clearly going to veto?"

"Because," Smita shrieked, "because ever since Anand was born, you've been ganging up with her against me. Don't pretend you don't know what I'm talking about; all those long visits to her flat, all her tips and tricks for dealing with babies you keep passing on to me, the steady drip-drip message that a baby should be cared for by its mother, that going back to work is a selfish, harmful thing to do. D'you think I'm deaf and blind to what's going on here?"

"Smita," Jeremy interjected desperately. "You're wrong. Nothing like that is going on, nothing."

Smita ignored him. "For years, for *years* you've been telling me what a disastrous mother she was, how remote, how uninvolved. And now I'm expected to believe that, overnight, she's somehow turned into this perfect caring figure? Don't be ridiculous!"

"She has changed," Jeremy said, still in the same low controlled voice. "She's not a perfect caring figure – by any means – but she has changed and I think you could give her a chance. If you didn't have such a closed mind about her."

Smita yelled back at him. "She was a disastrous mother and I've got no doubt she'll turn out to be a disastrous grandmother too. Look at what nearly happened just now; she nearly fell headlong with Anand in her arms. It could have been *awful*. Don't you dare, don't you *dare* leave her alone with Anand or something terrible will happen, you wait and see. Now give him to me since you obviously can't manage to get him quiet."

She snatched Anand who immediately stopped crying as if a switch had been flicked and strode out of the room.

One floor down, their doorbell rang. "You get it," Smita called. "He needs changing."

Sylvia stood at the front door, looking apologetic. "I'm awfully sorry," she whispered, as if she had heard their raised voices on the way up. "I seem to have left my handbag."

"How did you get into the building?" Jeremy asked. "You didn't ring downstairs, did you?"

Sylvia reddened. "I do hope it wasn't me; someone hadn't properly closed the front door behind them. I just pushed it open."

Jeremy was grateful that Smita, changing Anand two floors up, hadn't heard this exchange; yet further evidence of his mother's unreliability.

"Come in," he said, more impatiently than he meant to. "You're sure you don't want a cup of tea or anything now you've had to traipse all the way back? When did you realise you didn't have your bag with you?"

Sylvia snorted in exasperation. "Only when I got on the bus, would you believe? I needed my Oyster card to pay the fare and of course I realised I didn't have it. I had to get off again. The driver wasn't very nice about it either."

Jeremy registered with surprise that his mother now had an Oyster card. She had managed that all on her own too. Six months ago, she was calling him every day to ask how to do the simplest things. So she *had* changed, she was making progress; she wasn't, as Smita endlessly told him, utterly hopeless.

"Run up and get it for me, would you dear?" his mother chivvied him. "I don't have time for tea or anything like that now. I'm running late for my lunch."

As Jeremy ran upstairs, he caught sight of Smita looking down. As their eyes met, she ducked away and disappeared and he heard her crooning to Anand.

When he brought the bag – extraordinarily heavy, what on earth did she have in it? – back down, he said to his mother quietly, "Don't give up hope. Smi and I are talking things over."

His mother raised her eyebrows. "So I heard," and she turned away abruptly and set off again down the stairs.

This time Jeremy and Smita's argument raged for weeks. It carried on over Christmas in Leicester and into January when Smita went back to work. Galina turned out to be an excellent nanny; she arrived for work on time, she followed Smita's instructions precisely and, after a few weeks, Anand stopped crying when she arrived in the morning.

In February, Jeremy had a few days' leave to use up and, after some rather tense discussions with Smita, who didn't want to disrupt Galina and Anand's newly established routine, they told Galina to take time off and, for three intense days, Jeremy had his little boy all to himself.

He fed him, changed him, washed him, pleased that he could perform all these tasks just as skilfully as Smita. He spent long hours contemplating Anand's every minute act: every wriggle, every smile, every small noise. He observed what seemed to him the beginnings of a distinct personality; a shrewd, rather serious little boy who would in due course prefer Lego to fire engines and police cars.

After two days, he had to admit privately that he was feeling a bit cooped up. He had a whole list of things he had intended to do but the weather was foul and most of his ideas turned out to be impractical with a six-month-old baby in tow. On the third day, he decided to drive over to Kensington, despite the midweek congestion charge and spend the day with his mother.

He found her rather subdued. Her friend Ruth had had to go into hospital for an operation and she was fretting about her, it seemed to Jeremy, disproportionately.

"She's well into her eighties, you know," she told Jeremy as she stirred Anand's freshly pureed vegetables, "and surgery at that age can be very dangerous."

Jeremy worried that his mother couldn't seem to remember exactly what vegetables she had cooked for Anand so he wouldn't be able to give an accurate account of what he had eaten to Smita. Smita was keeping a diary of new foods as she introduced them so that she could straightaway identify any allergies. He decided he wouldn't say anything; his mother had always been unimaginative about food, especially vegetables and he was sure she wouldn't have included anything exotic.

After lunch, he had to nip out to move the car; it was parked in a bay with a two-hour time limit. His mother told him to move into a residents' space and she gave him a Kensington and Chelsea visitor's voucher, another sign of her new competence. The only trouble was that all the residents' spaces seemed to be taken. Did no one in

Overmore Gardens go out to work, Jeremy thought irritably, as he drove twice slowly round the square.

It was only on the third time round that it struck him with horror that he had just done exactly what he had promised Smita he would never do; he had left Anand alone with his mother. Not only that; he was now stuck in the car with nowhere to park and no way of immediately dashing back up to correct his mistake. He began to sweat. Surely nothing could go wrong while he moved the car? Did Smita actually expect him to bring Anand down in his car seat – just when he was getting ready for his nap – and strap him in only to drive a few times round the block? That would be madness. Still he began to feel more and more worried especially when a woman driving a mammoth SUV stopped right in front of him and began to manoeuvre laboriously into a loading bay. When she finally managed it, Jeremy drew alongside her, put his window down and called, "What the hell d'you think you're doing? That's not even a parking place."

The woman looked down at him and, without a word, made an obscene gesture with one expensively gloved finger.

Jeremy drove forward, fuming and probably not paying enough attention because on the corner of the Earls Court Road he crashed into a van coming far too fast around the corner and he realised that he had driven out of the square down a side street which was one way in the opposite direction. Both he and the van driver jumped out and began shouting, the van driver angrily and abusively and Jeremy desperately. "My little boy's on his own with my mother, she's not reliable, he shouldn't be left, this is an emergency!"

Luckily the damage was fairly minor: lights and bumpers. The van driver gave him the name and address of a company which Jeremy was pretty sure were false. He claimed not to know anything about insurance: "You'll have to ask the boss about that." Jeremy was so desperate by now – his heart was pounding, he was pouring sweat – he didn't really care. He scrawled down his own details for the van driver and got frantically back into the car. The van driver made him reverse all the way back, impatiently hooting and gesturing. As he drove past Jeremy at the end of the narrow street, he yelled tauntingly "Wanker!"

Shaking, Jeremy drove round the square one more time and finally, when he was close to tears, he spotted a place in a side street. As he pulled into it, his phone beeped with a text message; it was his mother. For the second it took to open the message, Jeremy felt faint. But it read: "Where are you?! Don't ring bell. He's asleep. I'll watch from window."

Jeremy read and reread the message in disbelief; since when did his mother send text messages? He had had the greatest difficulty persuading her to accept a mobile phone when she moved to Kensington back in May. She had protested that she didn't want a phone, didn't need one, wouldn't know how to use it, anyway had no one to call. Yet here she was, nine months later, competently texting.

As he hurried back up the south side of the square, he could see her at her living room window, waving cheerily; semaphoring extravagantly with her arms across the square. As he crossed the road, she left the window and, by the time he reached the street door, she was already buzzing him in energetically via the entryphone.

He bounded up the stairs. His mother was standing at her open front door with her finger to her lips. "Ssh. He's fast asleep. Whatever took you so long? You've been an age."

For the first time in over twenty years, Jeremy felt the urge to fall on his mother and hug her. He resisted it of course but, briefly, the urge had been there.

"Trouble finding a place," he mumbled. He barged past her, averting his face and through the small hallway into the spare bedroom where he found Anand sound asleep, hugging the small peppermint green elephant.

His mother followed him in and stood behind him, proudly contemplating the sleeping infant. "Bless him," she murmured. "Now come and have a cup of tea, won't you?"

In the evening, of course Jeremy had to tell Smita about the accident; there was no way he could get the car repaired without her finding out and anyway she noticed the broken light and the dented bumper as she passed the parked car on her way in. She came up screaming, "Oh my God, what happened? Is Anand ok?"

"We're *both* fine thank you," Jeremy answered frostily. "Don't worry, it was nothing really; just a small bump while I was getting a parking place."

"You broke a light while you were *parking*?" Smita asked incredulously. "But that must have been an awful bump. Did Anand cry?"

Suddenly Jeremy felt furious; why should he have to lie, why should he have to go along with Smita's absurd neurotic rules? "Luckily he wasn't in the car," he said, glaring at her, "because, fortunately, I left him upstairs with my mother while I moved the car."

"You *what*?" Smita exclaimed.

"You *heard*," Jeremy said, flushing. "And thank God I did because otherwise he *would* have been in the car when I had my little smash. Would you have preferred that?"

Smita threw her work bag down in the nearest armchair and faced him, her fists on her hips. "That's not the point," she yelled.

Jeremy didn't answer. He turned away. He had been through enough already today. As Smita's voice rose behind him, he wondered when arguing had become their usual form of communication.

In the morning, Anand's nappies were bright green and Smita asked indignantly what Sylvia had given him for lunch. When Jeremy said he couldn't remember, Smita rang Sylvia, waking her at seven thirty am, and demanded to know.

Jeremy could hear Smita shouting from the bathroom where he had taken Anand to clean him up. "Okra!" She shouted. "What were you *thinking*? How could you give him *okra*? Babies shouldn't have okra before at least a year. Why did you do it, Sylvia? It's absolutely *crazy*! Why?"

Jeremy dabbed Anand gently clean. Anand pumped his legs in the water and gurgled. "Grandma meant no harm," Jeremy murmured softly. "Did she? Did she?"

It struck him how easy and natural it felt to call his mother "Grandma" even though he had not been able to call her "Mum" for years.

≈

PART TWO

2009

Sylvia and Anand stood perfectly still in front of the giant aquarium and waited for the biggest of the sea turtles to swim past again. It seemed to spend its days steadily circling the huge tank as if on a purposeful private mission. Despite its bulk, it swooped gracefully through the water, regally ignoring the other sea creatures and its expression, although morose, seemed to be both dignified and determined.

Anand exclaimed, "Here she comes!" and Sylvia watched the turtle swoop towards them again, its flippers extended backwards like a pair of wings, its scaly face looking weary and wise. Sylvia was pleased that Anand was not the sort of child who waved or pulled faces at a passing sea turtle – there were plenty of them about – or, even worse, shouted out names or banged on the glass. He stood perfectly quietly, only clutching excitedly at Sylvia's hand each time the turtle reappeared. How she loved the feel of his small hand in hers.

It was only when the turtle had swum out of view

again, powering up towards the top of the tank, that it occurred to Sylvia to ask Anand, "Why do you think it's a 'she', dear?"

Anand looked puzzled. "Isn't it?"

"Well," Sylvia answered thoughtfully. "Of course it *may* be but it's hard to tell with a turtle, isn't it? Why do *you* think it's a 'she'?"

Anand paused. "She *looks* like a lady turtle."

"*Does* she?" Sylvia asked dubiously. "I'll have to take a closer look the next time she comes past."

They waited again in companionable silence.

"There!" Anand exclaimed, turning triumphantly to his grandmother as the turtle reappeared. "You can see *now*, can't you?"

"Well," Sylvia said slowly, "to be honest, I can't really dear but if you say so, then I dare say she is."

"She *is*," Anand insisted. He looked up at his grandmother somewhat coyly. "She looks like you."

Sylvia scrutinised the turtle's small greenish head as it swam past for the umpteenth time. The comparison wasn't flattering but better, she supposed, than a galumphing farmyard animal.

"Well," she ventured, "it's true, I used to love swimming."

Anand exclaimed, "Why don't you ever come swimming with *me*?"

Sylvia briefly imagined Smita's horror at this suggestion. "That's an idea," she answered vaguely. "Who do you go swimming with, darling?"

"My swimming teacher," Anand answered glumly.

"He's called Kev. He's not very nice. I'd far rather go with you, Grandma."

"We'll have to think about it," Sylvia said evasively. "See what Mummy and Daddy have to say. Now tell me, do any of the other creatures in the aquarium or the fish look like anyone else you know?"

This game kept them both happy for a remarkably long time. Anand found a splodgy fish which looked like his art teacher and a creeping snail which reminded him of his friend Jonathan. Of course, Sylvia could not share with him her discovery that a pink sea anemone waving its fleshy legs in the air reminded her no end of a certain Miss PeeJay Clarke.

Afterwards, they had a quick look in the gift shop but Anand said he didn't like plastic turtles and fish, only real ones. Sylvia had a chuckle over a furry stingray; whatever next? They went and sat on a bench beside the river for a little while and talked about this and that while both enjoying ice creams. The weather, in May, was barely warm enough for ice cream but they felt like it anyway. Anand was not actually supposed to have ice cream but Sylvia frequently flouted Smita's ridiculous petty rules; what was childhood, for heaven's sake, without ice cream? Anand had chocolate and Sylvia had strawberry.

Sylvia recalled that it was she who had given Anand his first taste of ice cream on a spring day just like this, it must have been three years ago, sitting in the cafe in Regents Park. She could still remember the look of shock on his little face when she fed him that first spoonful of Cornish vanilla. He had recoiled from the cold but then, almost immediately, a look of dawning delight had come over his face and he had opened his mouth eagerly for more. Sylvia had been breaking Smita's rules then too but, really, what did Smita's rules matter? When Smita had shown herself, over the past four years, to be such a hard-hearted person?

When Sylvia looked at her watch, it was half past four and she couldn't believe how the time had flown.

"I'm afraid we need to be on our way," she said sadly to Anand. "Daddy is expecting you home for supper by six."

Anand scowled. "I don't want to go to Daddy's," he protested. "I don't *like* staying at Daddy's. I want to go home to Mummy's. Why don't you ever collect me from Mummy's? Then, *afterwards*, I could go back *there*."

Sylvia looked down helplessly into Anand's scowling face. How could she begin to explain to him the complications which surrounded their afternoons together?

Ever since the Separation, it had become terribly difficult for Sylvia to spend time with her grandson, let alone speak to him on the phone and it seemed to her that in recent months it had got even harder. Smita's disapproval of Sylvia had hardened since the Separation into frank animosity. She didn't want her little boy to have anything to do with her ex-mother-in-law now, as she saw it, he didn't have to. Except that Sylvia wasn't yet her ex-mother-in-law because Jeremy and Smita hadn't yet managed to get divorced and, even if she were, nothing could conceivably stop Sylvia from seeing Anand anyway.

Whatever obstacles Smita put in her way, Sylvia knew she would ride roughshod over them. She would not even hesitate to resort to illegality if need be. She had never felt this strongly about anything. She had always been rather a conventional, law-abiding person. But she had never before confronted a situation which was so patently nonsensical; a benevolent grandmother being denied access to her grandchild, her only grandchild, by his wicked mother. The word "wicked" wasn't too strong either for wasn't Smita the one responsible for the break-up, the one who, through her actions, had made poor little Anand the child of a broken home?

Jeremy was blameless – except in so far as being a doormat and a pushover, he had let Smita get away with everything. It was Smita who had gone back to work the minute she could, abandoning Anand to a series of nannies. Jeremy and Sylvia had both been desperately unhappy about that but Smita, apparently, couldn't care less. She had coldly rejected Sylvia's offer to look after Anand instead.

Six months after returning to work, Smita had taken on a new role which involved regular trips to the US. She had been away for Anand's first birthday; she had sung "Happy Birthday" to him over the phone from New York. When Sylvia had happened to mention what a pity it was to miss one's child's first birthday, Smita had practically bitten her head off, retorting that Anand was too little even to know it was his birthday, he wouldn't be able to remember it when he was older and, anyway, they had had a big party the following weekend, hadn't they, where they had taken loads of pictures which he could look at in years to come.

When Smita was away, Jeremy was left to juggle his own important job and the baby single-handedly. To Sylvia's surprise, he didn't actually seem to mind that much. She couldn't in her wildest dreams imagine Roger putting up with that situation for more than twenty minutes.

It was at that juncture that Sylvia reluctantly decided to leave her flat in Overmore Gardens. The year's lease was already up. In late 2005, she moved with a heavy heart to Maida Vale. It was a compromise which allowed her both to be closer at hand to help look after Anand when Smita was away and not too far from Kensington to keep up her visits to dear Ruth. Wasn't Maida Vale always a compromise?

Her flat on Sutherland Avenue was frankly gloomy but it had one huge advantage, beside which the garden square paled into insignificance. It backed onto an immense triangle of unbuilt land which formed a hidden private park between three apparently undistinguished streets. For Anand, it would be paradise. For his sake, Sylvia was prepared to put up with the many drawbacks of the move: the distance from Kensington, from Ruth and Heather and all her old haunts, the pervasive gloom of Maida Vale which hung over the anonymous streets like a head cold, the bore of having to find her way around a new neighbourhood, find new shops, new nodding acquaintances and new ways of passing the days.

Roger's noises did not follow her to the new flat which

formed another break with her past. Sylvia missed Roger's noises ridiculously, considering what a nuisance they had often been; her flat on Sutherland Avenue was deathly quiet.

She made no effort to get to know her new neighbours, convinced that none of them could conceivably be a replacement for dear Ruth and they returned her indifference. It seemed for a while that she would settle into a pitiful sort of part-life: long weeks of meaningless mere existence interspersed with glorious weeks in which, with Jeremy's connivance, she saw Anand every day.

He had become the most enchanting toddler imaginable; he had walked at eleven months, taking his new skill very seriously and refusing from then on either to sit in the pushchair or to be carried.

Sylvia had naughtily upstaged Smita by buying Anand his first pair of shoes. When Smita had protested – "Honestly, Sylvia, are there no *limits*?" – Sylvia had answered innocently that, now he could walk, Anand needed shoes. But Smita had subjected her to one of her know-all speeches about the developing foot and how essential it was for the child to walk around without shoes for at least six weeks to master the mechanics of walking. Sylvia's premature purchase had most probably done untold damage to Anand's gait. The shoes which Sylvia had bought disappeared and when, two months later, Anand was finally allowed shoes, Smita claimed his feet had gone up a size and she bought him a new pair instead. Sylvia regretted the robust little navy toecaps and the sturdy buckle and straps of the original pair. In their place, Smita bought him some ungainly-looking miniature trainers with lurid flashes of colour and unattractive Velcro straps.

Anand spoke his first word, Sylvia believed, in her kitchen. He was sitting in the high chair – without that absurd restraining harness which Smita insisted on – and Sylvia was at the cooker, with her back turned, when it seemed to her she heard him say behind her, "Yum yum." She whipped round and exclaimed, "Did you say something dear?" And, looking thoroughly pleased with himself, Anand had repeated, loud and clear, "Yum yum!"

Sylvia had cried out in delight, dropping a wooden spoon in her excitement but Anand had been so thrilled by the noise which Sylvia had made and by the loud sound of the wooden spoon hitting the tiled floor that he had not said it again.

Still Sylvia knew it had happened. She did not tell Jeremy and Smita but hugged her secret to herself. She knew that Smita would not believe her in any case; for weeks she had been claiming, absurdly, that Anand was already saying, "Mum, Mum." Sylvia knew the truth.

She did feel guilty, from time to time, about the strain all these arrangements made behind Smita's back must be putting on Jeremy. It wasn't right after all, was it, that Smita had no idea about the time Anand spent with his grandmother – or all the forbidden foods he ate there – while she was away in America. Still, whose fault was it that these arrangements had to be kept secret anyway? If only Smita were more easy-going, less rigid and neurotic, above all less *spiteful*, she would no doubt acknowledge the fundamental importance for Anand of spending time with his paternal grandmother. Especially, *especially* since there was no longer a paternal grandfather.

Yet, despite these perfectly valid arguments, Sylvia still felt uncomfortable whenever she stopped to imagine all the machinations that must be involved on Jeremy's part. What, for instance, did he tell the nanny when she was repeatedly given the day off? And what did he tell the nanny to tell Smita? Sylvia preferred not to question Jeremy too closely about these delicate issues for fear of provoking one of his outbursts. But she was profoundly uncomfortable with the idea, obvious when you stopped to think about it, that she herself might be contributing to the increasingly fraught relations between Jeremy and Smita.

Yet, when all was said and done, what else was she to do? She could not tolerate even the idea of seeing less of Anand, of having her hours with him rationed even further or, worse, shared with his squabbling parents. Sylvia had realised, to her amazement, that her feelings for this little golden boy were nothing short of passion. The illicit hours which she managed to spend with him were an idyll which sustained her through all the dreary days before and after. Since Roger's death, Sylvia had coped. She had not fallen apart in public – other than in the immediate aftermath which was allowed – she had not been found wandering in a distressed state or inappropriately dressed, she had not been caught deep in conversation with someone who wasn't there. But that was, frankly, as far as it went. Her days consisted of absence and emptiness and it was only the twin talismans of "Buck up" and "Righty-ho" which kept her head above water.

Anand's arrival had transformed everything, not straight away but gradually over the weeks and months. Sylvia had identified the excitement she felt before seeing the baby, her racing heart and sweaty palms, for what it was. She had never expected to feel this way about her grandchild; she wooed him with gifts and songs and games, she was transfixed in the beam of his smile. Her feelings towards Jeremy softened too for wasn't this the first considerate thing he had done in years?

In Saudi and Dubai, Sylvia had been surrounded by couples of her generation grumbling that their inconsiderate offspring weren't having children. Even when they weren't selfish and produced children, there could still be heartache. Look at Heather Bailey's wretched daughter, a do-gooding aid worker who had gone and got married to an Ethiopian – nothing wrong with that, no doubt – but she had selfishly decided to settle in Addis Ababa and perversely to bring her children up speaking Amharic as their mother tongue. Poor Heather shed tears when she talked to Sylvia about it. Sylvia knew – on this score – she had been lucky. Moving to Maida Vale was a small price to pay for the time she got to spend with Anand. She no longer heard Roger yawning mightily in the next room or groaning in disgust at the morning paper. But she heard the sounds of Anand cooing and burbling, waking from his nap with a high pitched expectant cry.

She told herself that she had absolutely no need to feel guilty; she was perfectly civilized, she made every effort with Smita (even though she knew it wasn't true.) As for Jeremy, poor, dear Jeremy, these days she felt she could forgive him practically anything, now he had brought little Anand into her life.

It would have been towards the end of 2005 or maybe early in 2006, it was wintertime anyway; Jeremy had popped over for tea one Sunday afternoon together with Anand because Smita was busy with something or other and couldn't manage their usual lunch.

Sylvia noticed that Jeremy seemed somewhat preoccupied but as she supposed it had something to do with Smita, she studiously avoided asking him what the matter was. She entertained Anand with one of her stack of Ladybird books, holding him on her knee and showing him the brightly coloured pictures of everyday objects while naming them clearly and cheerfully. Anand could already do, after a fashion, "Dog" and "Cat" and "Car". Every time they got to "Umbrella" however, he would explode with laughter as if the name – and maybe the object too – was simply unbearably ridiculous. While this was going on, for Sylvia read through the book two or three times before Anand tired of it, she was conscious of Jeremy staring moodily out of the window. She refrained from questioning him and instead, when Anand had finally had enough of the book, she busied herself preparing an extra special tea with jelly and sponge fingers for Anand and lemon drizzle cake for the two of them.

As they drank their first cup of tea and Anand

conducted an invisible orchestra with a soggy sponge finger, Jeremy announced, "I've got trouble at work, I'm afraid."

Sylvia tutted and tried to look sympathetic but the truth was she had no idea how to react because, she reflected, Roger had never had trouble at work. Or at least, if he had, he had never confided in Sylvia about it. Having said that, he had undoubtedly got himself into trouble with certain of his female colleagues from time to time but he would hardly have come running to Sylvia for sympathy over that. She tried to put this distracting and irritating thought out of her mind and concentrate instead on what Jeremy was saying.

"They've announced cuts," he continued. "Job cuts. Lots of people's contracts aren't going to be renewed. And I'm seriously worried I'm going to be one of them."

Sylvia stared at her son in disbelief. Jeremy's professional success, his career at the BBC was a given, as far as she was concerned. Wasn't the BBC, rather like the Civil Service, a job for life? How could it be taken away from him now, nearly ten years in, when he hadn't done anything wrong? She had no idea he was just working on renewable contracts as he rather boringly explained to her. Apparently, it was a widespread practice at the BBC. Now, because of the cutbacks, when people's contracts ran out, they frequently weren't renewed.

"But not people who do their job well, surely?" Sylvia objected. "Not people who're *indispensable*?"

"No one's indispensable," Jeremy said irritably. "And it can happen to anyone, even people who do their job well, even people who're blameless, if they just happen to be in the wrong place at the wrong time."

"Well, I never heard of such a thing," Sylvia exclaimed indignantly. "Isn't there something you can do? Someone you can speak to?"

Jeremy sighed. "It doesn't work like that."

Sylvia grew frustrated. Why was Jeremy taking this lying down? Why was he so *spineless*?

She stood up to go and freshen the teapot. "Honestly Jeremy," she said impatiently. "There must be *something* you can do."

She swept out of the room with the teapot and came back a few minutes later to find Jeremy looking hot under the collar.

"I'm not surprised you don't understand," he began. "This is way out of your experience obviously. But you could *not* begin by assuming I'm at fault in some way."

Sylvia sat down and turned her back to spoon some jelly into Anand's wide open mouth. "It's probably true I don't understand," she answered. "There are lots of things I don't understand nowadays. But I know *you* Jeremy and I know you don't ever fight back."

"What are you talking about?" Jeremy asked sharply.

"Your job of course," Sylvia lied. "I mean, surely, you need to fight back, don't you? You have a son to support now."

Jeremy snapped, "I know I have a son to support."

After a moment, he added. "Though actually Smita is making so much these days that the financial aspect is the least of it."

Sylvia turned round, horrified. "She doesn't earn as much as you do, does she?"

Jeremy laughed. "She earns a great deal *more* than I do, especially now she's taken on these US clients. You don't imagine middle-ranking BBC salaries can compete with an outfit like GB, do you?"

"GB?" Sylvia repeated, puzzled.

Jeremy looked cross. "Gravington Babcock," he said reprovingly. "Surely you know where Smi works by now?"

"I knew it was somewhere high-powered," Sylvia said defensively. "Only the name escaped me."

Jeremy tutted. "Well, try and remember it the next time you're talking to her. She gets upset when she thinks you don't care about her work."

Sylvia huffed. "Honestly Jeremy, I try my best."

Jeremy raised his eyebrows but said nothing.

Frustrated that no one was paying him any attention, Anand pushed his plastic bowl of jelly onto the floor and, at the sight of it spilt down below, burst into a loud wail.

They busied themselves with Anand and with clearing up the mess. Neither of them said anything more about Smita. But, privately, Sylvia was beside herself. Smita already had Jeremy dancing at her beck and call. If he lost his job and she became the sole breadwinner, she would have the upper hand entirely. Jeremy would be done for.

After Jeremy and Anand had left, hurrying to get home by the time Smita wanted, Sylvia sat and brooded about this unforeseen development. It was true, it did seem awfully incompetent of Jeremy to be about to lose his job. She wondered whether he really was blameless or whether he had got on his bosses' nerves the way he always got on hers; with his endless long-suffering self-restraint, his blushes and his infuriating silences. She wondered whether there was anything that could be done and, if Jeremy was right and there really wasn't, she wondered how she should tackle the dreadful situation which was about to unfold. In the end, she decided to ask Ruth, who had such extensive experience of all sorts of suffering, for her opinion.

❧

In due course, Ruth had revealed the missing parts of her life story to Sylvia. No chance of Sylvia forgetting when she had done so either; it was on July 7, 2005, a terrible day on which, it seemed to Sylvia, London had changed into a completely unrecognisable place.

It had begun as a calm, warm day, a Thursday and, having yet another empty day ahead of her until her tea with Ruth at four, Sylvia had got up late and settled with a leisurely breakfast – two slices of liberally spread toast and marmalade and tea – in front of the television. At first, she could not make head or tail of what was happening but then neither, it seemed, could anyone else; there had apparently been three explosions in the Underground, mistaken at first for some sort of electrical fault but now revealed to be a major terrorist attack on London.

People were shown emerging from tube stations, blackened, bleeding, their clothes in tatters, their faces contorted in horror and pain. Sylvia watched, appalled; how could this be London, this lurid disaster zone, these stumbling wounded people emerging from catastrophe? If it hadn't been for the familiar red, white and blue Underground signs and the helmeted policemen herding the crowds, it might as well have been some unpronounceable faraway war zone tut-tutted over on the television.

It took Sylvia a surprisingly long time to think of Jeremy and Smita and to wonder abruptly whether they were on the Tube on their way to work. She wasn't familiar enough with all the Tube lines or with Jeremy and Smita's routes to work to have any idea whether they might have been passing through one of the stations whose names kept reappearing on the screen.

Shaking, she reached for her phone. Both Jeremy and Smita's phones switched straight to their messages which was, Sylvia thought – in the circumstances – the height of selfishness. They were doubtless chattering away to someone else – maybe even to each other – about the attacks with not a thought for her. Didn't they realise she was eaten up with anxiety about them? Maybe they were simply sitting in their high-powered meetings with their phones switched off and not a care in the world?

Sylvia left four increasingly aggrieved messages on Jeremy's phone and one comparatively restrained one on Smita's. More than half an hour must have gone by before it occurred to her, in slow motion horror, that the reason Jeremy and Smita weren't answering their phones might be that they were caught up in the middle of the disaster; hurt, injured or maybe even worse.

Tottering, Sylvia stood up and made for her front door.

The uneaten slice of toast fell marmalade side down – naturally – onto the carpet. Ruth wasn't expecting her until four but who else could she turn to? As she made her way downstairs, clinging to the banister, she fleetingly imagined Anand orphaned, sobbing heart-rendingly for his Mummy and Daddy who would never come home and she, Sylvia, swooping down and carrying him back to Overmore Gardens to bring him up herself.

Imelda answered the door crossly and Sylvia panted at her, "Have you heard the news?"

Imelda looked blank.

"Let me in," Sylvia ordered her imperiously. "I need to speak to Ruth."

"Mrs Rosenkranz isn't dressed yet," Imelda replied sullenly.

Sylvia barged in. "I've no time for procrastination Imelda," she said grandly. "This is a serious emergency."

Imelda followed her down the corridor muttering bad-temperedly.

"Ruth?" Sylvia called loudly. "Ruth?" She had no idea where in the flat Ruth would be but of course she knew the layout like the back of her hand.

She heard Ruth responding faintly from the bedroom and she went straight in, only wondering afterwards if she should have taken more care not to give the old lady a fright.

Ruth was propped up in bed, looking particularly small and frail, the same colour as her ivory pillows.

"Whatever's the matter, my dear?" she asked.

Sylvia sat down, possibly too heavily, on the bed and

clutched Ruth's cold elderly hand. "Something absolutely awful, I'm afraid."

She could still remember how Ruth failed to react with any noticeable shock and horror to the news of the bombings; it was as if life, in her experience of it, had been simply a series of shocking and horrible events and what was so unexpected about news of another?

She listened quietly to Sylvia's breathless account of the latest news reports and shook her head sadly. "At least your little Anand is safe at home," she said soothingly.

Sylvia burst out, "Well, I don't know for sure. I don't know about any of them. And I can't get through on the phone. They're not even answering."

"Of course is Anand is safe at home," Ruth said firmly. "The nanny isn't allowed to take him on the Tube; you told me so yourself."

Sylvia blushed. It was true; only last week, it seemed, she had been complaining to Ruth about yet another of Smita's silly, over-protective rules and now it had turned out to be so wise.

"Your son and your daughter-in-law are almost certainly safe too," Ruth continued. "In such a big city, the chances of being caught up in this slaughter are very small, remember. It is not as if they were being specially selected, targeted."

Sylvia looked at Ruth in blank incomprehension; everyone was being targeted, weren't they?

"You will see," Ruth said. "There will be some sort of hindrance or delay: traffic chaos, phones not working. All will be well."

Sylvia was convulsed by a giant suppressed sob. "What is happening to the world?"

"Nothing new," Ruth replied evenly. "Only different uniforms, that's all."

Sylvia looked at her friend with concern; she was getting on and since her operation she hadn't been the same.

Ruth smiled at Sylvia reassuringly. "Remember, I go back a long way. Now would you mind waiting in the sitting room, dear, while Imelda helps me dress and then we'll have a nice cup of tea and a chat."

That morning, Ruth told Sylvia the story of her life. For a long time, Sylvia practically forgot all about the bombings and her fear for Jeremy and Smita. She discovered that she had not known anything significant about Ruth at all and everything which she had imagined had in fact been wrong.

For a start, Ruth wasn't really German at all, well, not in the sense in which Sylvia's generation meant it; she was Jewish, she had come to this country as a refugee in 1939, fleeing Hitler. She had come alone without her parents, in fact effectively promoted to parenthood herself – at the age of fifteen – because she was in charge of her baby brother who was only four. After their harrowing parting on the platform of the Friedrichsstrasse station in Berlin, her proud and dignified father openly weeping, her gentle, emotional mother turned to stone, Ruth had never seen her parents again and she had from that day on effectively become Siggy's mother.

On arrival in England, they had been sent to stay with

a childless retired couple living in the Oxfordshire countryside. In some respects, they had been luckier than others; sent to working-class Jewish families in poor neighbourhoods, forced to live in cramped conditions with large dirty families who only bathed once a week and shared beds. The house in Oxfordshire was clean and orderly, the Masons – that was their name – were civilised educated people; Mrs Mason played the organ and arranged the flowers in the village church, Dr Mason liked to read histories and biographies. But they were cold, unemotional people, their house was always freezing too and while their act of taking in Ruth and little Siggy was undeniably generous, their behaviour towards them certainly wasn't.

They thought Siggy was over-indulged and spoilt; they set about sternly disciplining him. He was sent at five to the village school where the other children persecuted him because he was German and the teacher hit him across the back of his short chubby legs with her ruler. Ruth had to end her education there and then; she was virtually sixteen and, the Masons said, there was no point continuing. Dependent on them for her board and lodging, she did not dare object although she knew her parents would have been outraged. They had been planning to send her to a finishing school in Switzerland. In any case, the Masons had other plans for Ruth; she was to be their maid and helper, working for nothing in exchange for bed and board and, of course, for their taking care of Siggy.

It was hard to describe the five years which she had spent with the Masons. She thought it was not an exaggeration to say that she had not been fully alive. She had done what she had to; she had worked as a maid and a cook and a cleaner, she had taken care of Siggy and tried to bring him up as their mother would have done. She had improved her English – and tried to carry on her education – by reading the books in Dr Mason's library in her little free time. But she had no friends, no young people around her, no parties or outings, no youth. She had often thought about leaving. She turned seventeen and then eighteen; legally she was free to do as she pleased. But how could she have left Siggy all alone in that cold house with no mother and no father, with Mrs Mason telling him off for his every move and Dr Mason perpetually glaring at him?

Sylvia felt tears cascading down her face but Ruth laughed and said, "Don't cry, it was all a long time ago."

When the war ended, Ruth was twenty. She did not know anymore who she was. She was no longer completely German but she was certainly not English either. In Germany, their family had never been religiously observant, now, with the Masons' encouragement, she went regularly to church. She did not believe in the Masons' church but she thought it could do no harm and, who knew, by a miracle, it might help to bring her parents back. The news coming out of Germany and the Pathé newsreels made her wonder if she would ever see them or her Tante Trude or anybody else again. She did not give up hope though, not for years; she kept searching through the Red Cross and writing to every single person she could think of. Only in 1950, when she was already married and her son was newborn, she had suddenly understood that her parents would never see their first grandchild, *they were never coming back* and she had collapsed and cried for three whole months.

Freedom, when it came, was complicated and at a high price. She had been planning for some time how to leave the Masons; she could not stand another year buried in that little village, trapped in that cold house but the thought of leaving Siggy was of course unbearable. He was all she had left. But she began to calculate that if she found a job, a *real* job with wages, in a city, she could probably support herself and Siggy provided they lived modestly. Secretly, she began answering job advertisements in *The Lady*. Soon enough she was offered a job in the northern city of Sheffield with a family by the familiarly German-sounding name of Rosenkranz. "Yes," Ruth smiled winsomely at Sylvia. "Yes indeed."

Breaking the news to the Masons was extremely difficult but Ruth, although she was barely twenty, felt much older than her years and she already had a strength and determination she believed unusual in one so young because of everything she had lived through. In any case, there was actually nothing the Masons could do; because Ruth and Siggy's parents had not been declared dead – and Ruth absolutely refused to allow that – they couldn't formally adopt Siggy and now Ruth was over eighteen and Siggy's next of kin, she was legally entitled to do what she wanted.

At this point, the Masons had unexpectedly done another remarkably generous thing; they had offered to pay for Siggy, now nearly eleven, to go to boarding school, a very good English boarding school where he would receive an excellent education, far better than what the local school could offer. Ruth had been confronted with a horrible dilemma; did she agree to Siggy being sent away for the sake of his education or was it her duty to keep him with her at all costs? She tried hard to imagine what their parents would have wanted but the circumstances were so unimaginable that it was impossible to come up with an answer. And, in future, what price would the Masons extract for their generosity?

In the end, it was made easier for her by Siggy wanting to go away to boarding school, doubtless imagining it would be like the English boys' adventure stories he loved to read: dormitories and midnight feasts and escapades. So, after a few terrible days of indecision, she thanked the Masons on her parents' behalf and agreed that Siggy should go. So Siggy went away to boarding school and grew up to be a perfect English gentleman. Unlike Ruth, he lost his accent completely and acquired the lifelong nickname of "Posy". Sylvia giggled. Ruth moved to Sheffield and began to work as carer and companion to elderly, disabled Mr Rosenkranz.

The Rosenkranz family was everything the Masons were not: kindly, warm and welcoming. They were also Jewish although not in a way Ruth had encountered before. In Berlin, her family had had a Christmas tree, they had only gone to synagogue for weddings and special occasions. They had been cultured, emancipated people and they had considered Jewish religious practice frankly rather primitive. In this respect, the Rosenkranzes were primitive; they went to their ugly red brick synagogue every Saturday morning, wearing hats. On Friday nights, they would all gather at the house of Mr Rosenkranz's eldest son, Selwyn, for a traditional Sabbath meal. Hebrew blessings were recited and candles lit, Flossie Rosenkranz, his daughter-in-law, covering her face and whirling her hands about as she did so in a way which seemed to Ruth no different from voodoo. The Rosenkranzes included Ruth matter-of-factly in everything as if she were a member of the family and while they seemed to have no understanding at all of what she had lived through, their kindness touched her.

Unlike the Masons, they did however seem to understand that Ruth was not naturally a servant, that she came from a good family and had only been reduced to her present situation by unfortunate circumstances. They made sure that whatever socialising was organised during those austere post-War years for the Jewish young people of Sheffield, Ruth was always included. Her escort was usually Morris Rosenkranz, Selwyn's nephew, who had broken with the family tradition of finance and accounting and was studying to become a doctor in nearby Leeds.

Morris Rosenkranz was a serious, polite young man but Ruth never really considered him as a fiancé. How could she? He might be from the employer's family and Ruth the employee but still she felt herself to be in so many ways superior to the Rosenkranzes. Apart from the ones who had gone abroad to fight during the war, none of them had ever been abroad. Before the war, Ruth had holidayed every year in Switzerland or France or Italy. The Rosenkranzes did not read much either; their leisure pursuits centred around the synagogue, bridge and coffee and cake. Besides, there was the whole religious aspect. How could Ruth conceive of marrying into that primitive ritual and superstition: kissing doorjambs, separate sinks for meat and milk? But in time she came to realise that Morris Rosenkranz was the exception in his family. Not only had he chosen to move away and study medicine, he always had a paperback book in his pocket to read on the train and when he had finished reading it, if it was any good, he passed it on to Ruth.

One evening, he took her out to dinner in a restaurant in Leeds and ordered shrimp. Ruth had been living with the Rosenkranzes for long enough to have learnt that shrimp was a forbidden food. In Germany, her family had eaten everything including pork in all its delicious forms. She must have raised her eyebrows because Morris explained to her that, as a scientific rationalist, he had abandoned religious practice and only kept up appearances at home to preserve the peace. That had been the first revelation for Ruth.

But still it never crossed her mind that she might one day end up marrying Morris. For one thing, she did not see her future in the North of England. Quite where she did see her future was another question. There was obviously no possibility of ever returning to Germany. But she still hoped, hoped desperately for wider horizons than Yorkshire.

In due course, Morris graduated and, to his family's dismay, he took a job in London. Ruth discovered that she missed him and he must have felt similarly because he wrote her letters, beautiful letters which impressed her with his insight and sensitivity. He came home in April for Passover. It was an eight-day holiday and he and Ruth went out walking together every day. Old Mr Rosenkranz was seriously ill by then and needed full-time nursing care which left Ruth with a good deal of free time. On the last day of his holiday, Morris proposed to her, sitting beside her on a bench in one of Sheffield's finest municipal parks.

"In the normal course of events," he said delicately, "of course I would have asked your father first." But in her terribly sad circumstances, he could only hope that she felt her father would have approved of him.

Sylvia was sobbing, with great, wrenching sobs. "Oh Ruth," she repeated, stricken. "Oh Ruth."

Ruth had been so shocked, at first she had not known what to answer. She had asked Morris if she might please think it over and give him her answer the next morning before he caught his train back to London. He had obviously been disappointed – he must have hoped she would fall into his arms – but politely, respectfully he had agreed. Ruth had lain awake all night, debating. Never had she missed her parents so much, nor felt so acutely the absence of anyone to turn to for guidance.

Obviously, it was better to be married than unmarried; that much was simple. But never having thought about marrying Morris, she now found herself, out of the blue, faced with having to make a hugely important decision.

She liked Morris, she liked him a great deal in fact. He was a doctor, an honourable and secure profession. She would be able to move to London: a huge plus. But she was just twenty-one; should she be getting married at all? To the first person to ask? And did she want her life, for ever after, to be tied to the Rosenkranz family and to Sheffield? What would her parents say if they ever miraculously returned and found out they had in-laws who prayed, rocking heel to toe, wrapped in silk prayer shawls?

In the end, she decided to let Siggy, now nearly thirteen and according to the Rosenkranzes' beliefs almost a man, be the arbiter. If he liked Morris, if the two of them hit it off, then she would go ahead. Siggy would have a home, a proper home, to come to in the school holidays. Well, fortunately, Morris and Siggy had got on famously and Siggy had wholeheartedly given his approval. In January 1948, she and Morris had got married in the ugly red brick synagogue with all the hullabaloo the Rosenkranz family expected and Dr and Mrs Mason sitting in the congregation, looking like two fish out of water.

It had all turned out to be utterly unimportant anyway; her worries about social standing and religious practice. She had married Morris because she knew he was the sort of young man her parents would have wanted her to marry and, even though it had not been a match born of great passion but a carefully weighed decision, they had grown to love each other deeply and they had been extremely happy together for forty-seven years.

"Tell me," Sylvia said tentatively, "about your children."

But Ruth put up both her hands in a defensive gesture.

"Not now," she said, sounding terribly tired. "Not now. I think that's quite enough for one day, don't you? Besides, shouldn't you go back up to your flat in case your son is trying to get through to you?"

Sylvia climbed heavily back upstairs, severely shaken by everything which Ruth had told her and by the reminder that someone's life could so easily appear to be one thing on the surface and yet be, shockingly, something entirely different underneath.

As she reached the landing, she could hear her phone ringing inside the flat. It stopped ringing before she could get the door open but started again almost straight away as she came in. She picked it up and it was Jeremy, beside himself.

"Where the *hell* have you been?" he exploded, the minute she panted, "Hello?" "I've been calling you for the past *two hours*. The mobile networks are all down. I had no way of knowing where you were. Why on earth didn't you call me to let me know you were alright?"

"But I did," Sylvia said shakily. "I called your mobile loads of times. And Smita's. I just got your messages."

"I *told* you," Jeremy sounded at the end of his tether. "All the mobile networks are down. Why didn't you try our home number, for Christ's sake?"

"I assumed you were at work," Sylvia said weakly. Even today, of all days, she seemed to be doing everything wrong.

"Well, I'm not," Jeremy retorted angrily. "I've been at home worried stiff about you for the past two hours. Where on earth have you been?"

"I was with Ruth," Sylvia said faintly. "I was frightfully worried about *you*. And Anand and Smita."

"Anand's fine," Jeremy snapped. "You know we never take him on the Tube. And Smita's in New York. I'm quite worried about the nanny though; she hasn't turned up for work and with all the mobiles down, she's probably got no way of contacting us. I just hope she's ok."

Sylvia tried to remember which nanny it was; Galina had left after six months because she and Smita hadn't seen eye to eye. She had been replaced by Eva who had lasted less than a month and Eva had just been succeeded by – was it Anna or Agnes?

Abruptly, she asked, "I didn't know Smita was in New York?"

Jeremy answered briefly. "She had to leave a couple of days early. Something came up."

"Will you be needing *me*?" Sylvia asked eagerly.

She heard Jeremy sigh. "Well, I'm stuck here for now," he said, "unless Agnieszka shows up. But I doubt you can even get here, you know; apparently the whole city's come to a standstill. Only emergency vehicles can get through."

Sylvia imagined herself walking heroically all the way to Belsize Park but thought better of it. She said, "I'll come the minute I can."

But Jeremy said sternly, "No, stay at home until we're absolutely sure this thing's over."

Sylvia asked, horrified, "You mean there might be more bombs?"

"Well," Jeremy said, "have you heard about the bus?"

Of course Sylvia hadn't and when Jeremy told her that

a double-decker bus had been blown up in Tavistock Square, it seemed to Sylvia that her lifelong image of London had been blown sky high too and she had to sit down suddenly as the colours began to drain from everything.

Late that night, as she was finally slipping into an uneasy sleep, her telephone rang and she jolted awake. It was Cynthia.

"So you're still alive," her sister began sarcastically. "Did it not occur to you at any point today that I might be worried about you? Did it not cross your mind at all to ring and let me know you were alright? I suppose you thought I couldn't care less? Is that it? You imagined that if you had been blown to pieces, I wouldn't have batted an eyelid?"

There was something about Cynthia's grating, rancorous voice which had the same effect on Sylvia as chalk being scraped down a blackboard and she cringed under her covers.

"No Cyn, no," she tried to answer but Cynthia was in full spate and wouldn't listen to her stammered self-defence.

"Do you know I saw you on a stretcher on the television?" Cynthia nearly shrieked. "You were dead. You had a grey blanket pulled over your face and you were being carried by two ambulance men. It was ghastly."

"What are you talking about?" Sylvia exclaimed, wide awake now and horrified. "It wasn't me, obviously. Whatever made you think it was?"

"Not wishful thinking," Cynthia retorted. "If that's

what you're implying. It was your feet, if you must know. I saw your feet sticking out from under the blanket. They were blue but I could tell they were yours; I'd recognise them anywhere."

Sylvia curled up her toes instinctively under the covers. "What's so remarkable about my feet?"

Cynthia cackled. "Oh go on, Syl. Don't pretend you don't know; you've always had the most misshapen toes. You used to get teased about them when you were little."

Sylvia wiggled one of her feet out from under the covers and stared at it; were her toes so very misshapen? As she considered her foot unhappily, Cynthia carried on, "That's what sticks in my throat, Syl. *I* can still recognise your feet on television after all these years but I know *you* would never in a million years recognise mine. Or any other part of my body for that matter. Because you've blotted me out, Syl, that's what you've done, you've blotted me out of your life completely."

"We saw each other at Christmas," Sylvia said faintly.

"Oh and I should be grateful for that, I suppose," Cynthia retorted sarcastically. "Lady Bountiful comes down to Lewes at last for Christmas dinner with her sister but just happens to mention that the only reason she has come is because her son and daughter-in-law and darling little grandson are up in Leicester having Christmas with *her* parents and so otherwise she would be all alone in London."

"I never said that was the only reason I had come," Sylvia began.

But Cynthia snapped, "Oh spare me the hypocrisy,

please. You may think I don't care about you anymore but the bottom line is I still do, Syl, I care a great deal but you, *clearly*, couldn't care less about me."

Sylvia blurted out, "Oh stuff and nonsense, Cyn. They weren't my feet anyway. And my toes really *aren't* that misshapen."

Cynthia gave a harsh laugh. "You don't change, do you?" she remarked and she hung up without saying goodbye.

࿐

Ruth's advice about Jeremy's threatened redundancy took Sylvia by surprise. She consulted her the very next time they had tea together, having spent the intervening days fretting over her son's predicament.

Ruth's advice had nothing to do with Jeremy or Smita for that matter either. It had to do with Sylvia herself and she was shocked to realise that she could be at fault here too, even before she had done anything at all.

"You must not become too deeply involved in their lives," Ruth warned. "It is tempting, I know, when one only wants to help and one's own life is sometimes rather – quiet. But it is a mistake, Sylvia dear, maybe even a grave mistake. You must let them solve their problems themselves. Don't go rushing in with unasked for advice and suggestions. They won't thank you for it and they may resent it deeply. Be content with your lovely little golden grandson and leave everything else well alone."

"But if his father loses his job it will have a bad effect on Anand too," Sylvia argued. "And besides, Jeremy and

230

Smita aren't getting on that well already, if you ask me and if Jeremy is going to be unemployed, then surely things will only go from bad to worse."

Ruth looked alarmed. "If there is already conflict between them, how do you think *your* intervention will improve matters? How did you get on with *your* mother-in-law? How would you have liked to have her involved in *your* marital ups and downs?"

Sylvia was aghast at the idea of a comparison between herself and Daphne Garland whom she had loathed with every fibre of her being for twenty-eight years. Roger's mother had thought Sylvia a flighty young woman and when she turned out to be apparently unable to produce grandchildren year after year into the bargain, she had urged Roger to divorce her. She had even turned a blind eye to Roger's indiscretions, believing that Sylvia's shortcomings justified them and maybe even hoping for a welcome little accident along the way.

Mechanically finishing her second slice of coffee and walnut cake in silence, Sylvia considered Ruth's advice.

In the end, she just said lamely, "Maybe you're right."

She poured them both another cup of tea and, as she drank hers, she reflected that if she did nothing, as Ruth advised, then at least neither Smita nor Jeremy could blame her for whatever happened. That in itself would be welcome.

In the end, there was no need for her to intervene anyway because things turned out much better than expected; Jeremy's contract was terminated in the spring of 2006 but, less than two months later, he was offered a new job by another department of the BBC, doing similar work apparently and with a slightly higher salary too.

Relations between Jeremy and Smita were not, Sylvia observed, particularly badly affected. Rather than lording it over her unemployed husband, as Sylvia had feared, Smita was terribly grateful to Jeremy for doing the bulk of the childcare and she joked that he did it so happily he would make a perfect house husband.

Anand's second birthday was celebrated with a big family party. He had a small but intensely noisy tea party on the day itself, Jeremy reported, with a handful of other two year olds. It had been a nightmare apparently, in their stylish apartment, even though Smita had some time back compromised with aesthetics by fixing stair gates on the stairs and putting away most of their valuable breakable things.

Sylvia was not invited to the two year olds' tea party even though she would have loved to come. She had not met any of Anand's playmates and she would have dearly liked to take stock of them; to judge how suitable they were and to observe how Anand interacted with them. But Smita had made it clear that this event was for accompanying mothers and nannies only – and Jeremy of course with the camera – and Sylvia was more than welcome to come along to the family get-together the following weekend.

Sylvia swallowed her disappointment and cheated Smita by organising her own little birthday picnic for

Anand ahead of time in the Sutherland Avenue gardens. There was a pair of two-year-old Chinese twins, rather pleasingly called Ming and Ling, who played regularly in the gardens and Sylvia invited their Australian nanny to bring them over to her big tartan picnic rug and share jelly and cake and join in a ragged rendition of "Happy Birthday". So she got in first with the birthday celebrations and felt secretly smug when Jeremy reported that Anand had not enjoyed the singing of "Happy Birthday" at their tea party and had covered his ears. He had done nothing of the sort at Sylvia's.

The adult party was rather an ordeal for Sylvia and, if it hadn't been for Anand's shining presence, really she would not have enjoyed it at all. For a start, Prem, by far her favourite member of Smita's family, was missing. His absence drew Sylvia into enforced proximity with Naisha who seemed at her most overbearing; she appeared in charge of the proceedings, to an extent which visibly annoyed her daughter and she kept rushing to and fro, loudly issuing instructions to all and sundry.

When she finally sat down in the centre of the big sofa, she insisted on having Anand on her lap – even though you could tell he was reluctant – and feeding him a stream of choice titbits with her perfectly manicured fingers. Jeremy was grumpy – not surprisingly – but of course he was grumpiest of all with his mother.

Worst of all, Anand didn't even seem that interested in Sylvia. Maybe it wasn't all that surprising with so many less familiar people there, all of them vying for Anand's attention and some of them wearing eye-catching shimmering saris and lots of glittering jewellery. But Sylvia still felt jilted and jealous; surely her bond with Anand was special enough for him to single her out in a crowd and show them all that *she* was the favourite grandmother?

Naisha seemed supremely unconcerned when Sylvia enquired after Prem. He hadn't been feeling too well for the past few weeks, she explained casually and hadn't felt up to making the trip to London. The doctor had sent him for a few tests but the results weren't back yet. She made it sound like a big fuss over nothing, as if Prem were just malingering in the time-honoured male way.

So Sylvia was shocked and horrified to hear from Jeremy barely ten days later that poor dear Prem had been diagnosed with cancer, a particularly nasty and very likely fatal form of cancer with a long and complicated name. Smita was devastated apparently although Naisha seemed to be bearing up.

Prem's decline was swift and awful. Although he stepped up his visits to the temple even further and adopted a frankly crackpot raw food regime, the disease continued its cruel progress. By Christmas, the writing was on the wall and when Sylvia travelled up to Leicester in the New Year to see Prem, possibly for the last time, she found him a shadow even of his former grey self. She had hesitated whether or not to go but Ruth said it was the right thing to do and so, one cold and especially unpleasant January morning, she boarded a train at King's Cross, bolstered by a railway cup of tea and a hot bacon sandwich.

Naisha met her effusively at the station, her vigour and

talkativeness apparently undiminished by her husband's illness. She drove Sylvia to their home where Prem was languishing in a reclining chair, attended by a number of relatives who kept popping in and out, bringing Tupperware boxes of home cooked food.

"I haven't had to cook for weeks," Naisha observed happily as she served Sylvia a delicious lunch entirely out of Tupperware boxes. Poor Prem barely ate and barely spoke either although he gave Sylvia a number of sad saintly smiles.

Naisha drove her back to the station in the late afternoon. She thanked Sylvia warmly for making the journey and hugged and kissed her excessively. Sylvia supposed that they were both equally glad to see the back of each other.

On the train, Sylvia grew rather weepy; how lucky Naisha and Prem were to have the chance to say goodbye to each other.

In the last minutes of Sylvia's visit, Naisha announced, "At least we can all be comforted by our children's happiness, isn't that right? And Prem is praying that he will live to see another grandchild."

Sylvia was shocked by this announcement. As far as she was concerned, Anand was utterly perfect and, really, there was no need for another grandchild. Only having had the one child herself, somehow her imagination couldn't go any further. But Naisha, as usual, was one step ahead.

In the final months of poor Prem's life, the issue of the second grandchild became uncomfortably pressing.

Naisha kept repeatedly urging Smita to try and get pregnant again before her father passed away. "Give him the comfort of knowing another grandchild is on the way," she pleaded, apparently sublimely immune to charges of emotional blackmail. Sylvia couldn't help feeling a bit sorry for Smita, in spite of everything; it must be horrid to be put in such a situation especially after the timing of her first pregnancy had been so overshadowed by the death of her father-in-law. Jeremy flatly refused to discuss the issue with Sylvia at all.

But Naisha 's pleading was to no avail and, after six more months of suffering, Prem died in the summer of 2007, leaving a larger silence where his silent presence had been. With hindsight of course, Sylvia realised that what must have been troubling Smita during those months was not producing good news but concealing bad.

After Prem's death, naturally they all saw a good deal more of Naisha. She came down to London more often and Jeremy and Smita made more trips up to Leicester to spend time with her. Sylvia felt sidelined. Even though it was perfectly obvious that Naisha was not as devastated by her husband's death as might have been expected and the optician's was oviously a great distraction, still she now had the status of the newly bereaved widow and, consequently, first call on their attention and on Anand.

During Smita's trips to the US, Naisha sometimes came down to stay, supposedly to help out with Anand although Sylvia suspected that her presence added to Jeremy's burdens. When that happened, of course Sylvia didn't get to see Anand at all and when she did finally see him again after Naisha's departure, he always had a few unfamiliar new words and habits which owed nothing to Sylvia. Naisha's claim that the little boy needed glasses made Sylvia particularly indignant.

The less she saw of her little golden boy, the more she yearned for him. Her flat felt completely empty without him; his bedroom waited silently, his ranks of toys and books lay untouched and whatever the latest extravagance which she had splashed out on – the immense plastic water wheel, the inflatable turtle family for the bath, the trampoline which took up far too much of her sitting-room – it all seemed to mock her, like extravagant decorations put up for a party which had not happened.

What troubled Sylvia most was the fear that Smita had now won. Until her father's death, terribly sad, Prem was such a nice chap, Jeremy had had an edge; his poor mother was recently widowed, allowances had to be made. Now, of course, that advantage was lost and Sylvia knew, knew in her bones that Smita and Naisha were together so ruthless, in the tug of war which was marriage, their side would inevitably win and Anand would become theirs.

Sylvia watched Smita gaining the upper hand and Jeremy, the fool, letting her get away with it. She did her best to right the balance in Jeremy's favour; she lured Anand with all the old songs and nursery rhymes which he loved – Naisha's activities were all educational – she bought him ice creams in Regent's Park and forbidden chocolates and Smarties when they went shopping. One summer's day, she secretly whisked him off to the seaside without consulting anyone. She gave him his first sight of the sea. But nothing made any difference of course; Smita was in control now and Sylvia had to sit and watch as relations between Jeremy and Smita seemed to go from bad to worse. Still nothing led her to expect the shattering announcement which Smita made just before Anand's third birthday.

As her plane took off from Heathrow, Smita's spirits soared. The huge thrust of the engines and the fairground ride pressure which pushed her back in her seat added to her excited feeling of escape. Beneath the grey clouds, her annoyingly clingy little boy and her incredibly irritating husband were beginning another boring day but she, she had got away and ahead of her lay another brilliant week of freedom in New York. Her happiness, only very faintly tinged with guilt, was such that she decided to enjoy absolutely everything, even things which she would normally have scrupulously denied herself. It was rather early in the day for a drink but what the hell? As soon as the cabin crew came along with the trolley, she was going to treat herself. Something mixed with tomato juice or orange juice might feel a bit healthier and anyway it would help her to relax later on.

But first of all she had to go through her notes. The success of the trip – and so the guarantee of a string of future trips – depended on her performance for the US clients. So far, everything had gone really well each time but in this business you were only ever as good as your last presentation. That was especially true in the US where things were even more ruthless and employees even more dispensable than in London; Smita loved it. She found the atmosphere energising and the people she worked with fun and attractive. On the plane, she felt herself changing each time into a more vivid version of herself; brighter, sleeker, more focused. She became in fact the person she could have been if she hadn't saddled herself with a husband and a child before she turned thirty. She had done it for all the right reasons, of course; work-life balance, plus she had wanted to redefine herself, to get right away from the suburban Leicester mode.

Marrying Jeremy had seemed such an obvious thing to do at the time. But she turned out simply to have swapped one version of dull for another; Jeremy wasn't actually who she thought he was. At least, before Anand came along, he had been close. Their first two or three years had been ok. But as soon as she had Anand – why even beforehand – Jeremy had revealed this awful traditional side. He wanted Smita to be a stay-at-home mother or at the very least to work part-time. He never stopped moaning about the harmful effects her lifestyle was supposedly having on Anand – which was bullshit – and you could tell that he thought he was a much better parent than she was with all his touchy-feely nonsense.

Naturally, his nightmare of a mother goaded him on from behind the scenes. It was all Sylvia's fault anyway; if she hadn't been such a *useless* mother herself, then obviously Jeremy wouldn't have such a ridiculous idealised concept of what a mother should be.

But Jeremy had got Smita wrong too. He must have

imagined that once they had a baby, she would turn into a traditional Asian mummy who lived only for her little boy. She was expected to transform somehow into this loving nurturing person who would pop out two or – for God's sake – even three kids and just forget about everything else. Well, no *way*. Her job mattered more than ever now. It was her only way out.

She sipped her Bloody Mary and allowed herself to miss Anand briefly. He really was the cutest little boy ever and she loved it that he was getting more and more like her side of the family all the time. When she came back in five days' time, for all her New York high, she would be desperate to hold him. She would come running up the stairs, with the latest toy from FAO Schwarz and Anand would rush towards her as fast as his chubby two-year-old legs could carry him, calling, "Mum-Mum-Mum-Mum-Mum." She would hug him for at least a minute and that moment would be absolutely perfect. But in the background Jeremy would be standing, looking reproachful. They would greet each other guardedly and then, soon enough, one or other of them would say the wrong thing and set the other one off and the whole miserable business of not getting on would start all over again.

Smita bent down to pull her laptop out of her carry-on bag and opened it on her knees. Enough; time now to focus on the job ahead of her. The vodka hadn't fuddled her yet. She would work for two hours and after lunch she would doze for two hours and then it would be nearly time to land and she could forget about everything but work for five amazing days.

Smita had been coming to New York for just over a year now and this must be her sixth or was it her seventh trip. But the exhilaration she felt on arriving had not got any less. If anything, it had increased because now she knew what was ahead of her and she looked forward to it from one trip to the next.

First of all, there was the momentous sense of arriving somewhere really important which you felt as you waited in the massive queues at Immigration. Even if people grumbled at the wait, there was still this sense that, well, the wait was worth it because you were about to arrive at basically the centre of the world. Wherever you had come from, whatever your profession, New York was the top. The beefy officers in the Immigration booths took their job so seriously too; when they okd you and stamped your passport and welcomed you to New York, Smita always felt this great kick of achievement. God, it was nothing like Heathrow; people shuffled forward towards the passport booths there, depressed and disappointed before they had even entered the country. They could already tell, from the scruffiness and from the other people's faces, that they had arrived somewhere second-rate.

In New York, you came out of the airport and stepped straight into one of those yellow cabs, familiar from every film you had ever seen, with its wild driver from Haiti or Afghanistan – or once even Gujarat – and he sped away with you towards the skyscrapers of Manhattan which rose up spectacularly in the distance. Every time, Smita marvelled that she was there, with her job and her status and her four-star hotel room booked, speeding towards appointments and meetings and colleagues, dinners in the latest restaurants, working breakfasts and all the wonderful heart-racing fun that was New York.

She would think of the important people in her life and imagine that they were sitting there in the taxi with her. She would show them what she had achieved and they would all be incredibly impressed and proud of her. With a lurch, she thought of her father, Prem, now undergoing chemotherapy in Leicester Royal Infirmary. He had never been to New York and maybe now he never would. With all his unworldliness, maybe he wouldn't be that impressed by it. But he would still beam if he saw his daughter stepping out of the taxi, the door held open for her by the uniformed doorman of the Marriott Hotel.

This time, there was something else to look forward to. Gravington Babcock's US associates had recently hired a new partner. Everyone spoke incredibly highly of him; he was really smart, he had been poached from a rival firm for a supposedly huge salary because he had this amazing track record plus he was apparently really fun to work with. Smita was especially curious to meet this new star because he had the good old Gujarati name of Abi Desai.

Her flight landed on time at two o'clock and the luggage came out quickly too. The queues at Immigration were pretty bad but she was still out of the airport by three thirty. In the taxi, she rang London to say goodnight to Anand so she wouldn't have to think about home anymore that day. Anand refused to talk on the phone which sometimes happened. She tried not to feel rejected and gave the nanny a hard time instead over what Anand had

had for supper and whether she had gone over his flashcards with him. As soon as she dropped her phone back in her bag, it beeped with a text message. That was what Smita loved about the US: the energy, the drive, not a moment was wasted. It would be the New York office; they knew she was on the ground and they wanted to get in touch with her. But the message wasn't what she expected: "Call Greg asap" or "Santinelli needs 2 talk". It was from Abi Desai himself inviting Smita for drinks with the team in a bar near the office at six thirty. She texted back "Sure great c u there" and then corrected it to "c u all there". She sat back in her seat and looked out at the dramatic cold grey sweep of the East River. Her trip was off to a brilliant start.

Of course it was a challenge looking her best straight off the plane and when it was already after eleven o'clock at night for her. But concealer worked miracles and she decided to walk the few blocks from her hotel to the bar, which she knew, thinking that the New York winter cold would wake her up. She had underestimated how very cold it actually was. It was mid-November and the store windows were all already decorated for Christmas. The freezing air hit her with a shock as she walked out of the hotel and for a moment she considered ducking into a taxi. But no, the walk would do her good. She drew her coat closer and adjusted her pashmina around her neck. She walked quickly, happy and excited despite the cold and enjoying the feeling of being one with the crowd of fast-walking New Yorkers on their way home. She watched them for signs of the latest craze – things moved so fast here – and was amused to notice that earmuffs seemed to have made a comeback. Well, that was one trend she wouldn't be taking back to London; on a grown woman she thought they looked totally silly.

A vicious wind attacked her at the first intersection, whistling down the deep canyon between the buildings. Her hair was going to be a complete mess by the time she got there and she was already completely chilled. She dashed across the street to get out of the wind the second the sign said "Walk" and she speeded up her pace. But the few blocks she remembered turned out to be nine or ten and by the time she arrived at the bar, she was windswept and absolutely frozen. Still the walk had buoyed her up even more. New York was so wonderful: the brilliantly lit, artistically decorated store windows, the smart busy people hurrying along and all the way there the familiar New York street furniture, the fire hydrants and the steaming subway vents. Smita loved everything.

She darted into the cloakroom to deal with her hair without spotting her colleagues but when she emerged, they were all just arriving and they greeted her warmly. Abi Desai wasn't with them. For a moment, Smita felt terribly disappointed but someone explained that he'd been held back dealing with something and he'd be along right away.

They settled around a big table and someone got drinks. Everyone began filling Smita in on the big make-or-break meeting with the new clients the next day. She was so caught up in listening to what they were saying and laughing at Greg Meyer's anecdotes about all the near disasters which had plagued this project that she didn't see Abi Desai come in. She only noticed him when he was right by their table and making his way round to shake hands with her. She felt caught out because the one thing which no one had thought to mention to her was that he was incredibly good-looking.

They shook hands. Abi had a good strong grip. He drew up another chair and sat down perfectly naturally next to Smita.

As soon as he joined the group, the atmosphere changed noticeably. Even though he appeared so relaxed and friendly and on the level, it was obvious he was in charge. There was no more office gossip or jokes about near disasters. Like the others, Smita felt herself straining to make a good impression. Her second drink was mineral water. Abi asked her politely about her flight, about the weather in London and, showing that he wasn't just making small talk, about the health of a colleague at Gravington Babcock who was recovering from open heart surgery. Nothing personal but nothing about the next day's meeting either; it was clear this was some kind of bonding, team-building time and it was clear too that it was Abi who set the rules here. But he wasn't in the least bullying; he did whatever it was he was doing lightly and apparently effortlessly, teasing one of the guys who had decided to have braces on his teeth at the age of twenty-eight and telling a hilariously funny story against himself about an eccentric old lady in his neighbourhood who had set upon him recently while he was out jogging. Everyone seemed to love him; they roared with laughter at his jokes and vied for his attention.

He didn't stay long. After less than forty-five minutes, he excused himself and as soon as he had gone, the atmosphere relaxed once again and a couple of the guys invited Smita to have dinner with them. She imagined Abi must have a long way to travel home on a suburban commuter train. He doubtless lived in some picture-perfect New York suburb in an ultra-modern architect-designed house which would make the penthouse in Belsize Park seem tiny. There would be a huge state-of-the-art kitchen for his beautiful Gujarati-American wife who spent her days making modern ghee-free versions of Indian meals and raising their two model kids.

The week went really well, the new clients praised Smita's input, the deal was done, everyone in the New York office was on a high – and it was catching. Smita sat in on a series of meetings chaired by Abi and had a chance to observe how he operated. It was so impressive; he always seemed so informal and friendly yet he could apparently make everyone in the room do exactly what he wanted. It was impressive but it was also a bit uncanny. He seemed such a nice guy, he was always smiling and joking but he was obviously incredibly tough underneath.

He didn't pay Smita any particular attention which slightly surprised her. She would have thought that at some point they would have quietly had the Gujarati conversation; so where exactly is *your* family from and when did they leave and do you still have family over there and all that stuff. But maybe in the US people didn't do that, maybe that was just a Leicester thing to do and probably Abi had moved so far away from that whole world that he wouldn't dream of asking those questions. Maybe he didn't want to seem to be favouring Smita either.

In London, Jeremy was having a difficult week and made no effort to spare Smita any of it. He had an awful cold, the washing machine was leaking and he sent her a stream of complaining text messages which irritated her no end. Did he not realise she had to focus on work while she was over here? Did he have to keep distracting her with his irritating petty little whinges? Who cared if the plumber had kept him waiting or if his cold was worse today than yesterday? Smita sent back a series of snappy unsympathetic replies.

On her last afternoon, Abi stopped at her desk and asked if she had plans for the evening.

She said, "Not really" which made him laugh.

"Do you or don't you?" he insisted. "Because I was going to ask you to have dinner with me but if you've got other plans –"

"No," Smita said, flustered. "No, nothing that can't wait."

"Seriously," Abi said, "I don't want to get in the way of any arrangements you have. I know I've left it really late to ask you."

He waited and even though he was being so polite and so considerate, Smita started to feel unaccountably pressured.

"No," she answered quickly. "It's fine, really. I wasn't planning to do anything which can't wait till next time."

"Sure?" Abi asked again, smiling and when Smita nodded and smiled back, he suggested a restaurant and a time and she agreed to that too.

She felt ridiculously apprehensive as she got dressed in her hotel room. She wasn't even sure if she was dressing for a work dinner or a date. Of course, it would have been utterly uncool to blurt out, "You do know I'm married, don't you?" when Abi invited her. The dinner was almost certainly a work thing and she would just have totally embarrassed both of them. Besides wasn't there the beautiful Gujarati-American wife waiting for him in the suburbs? She was just fantasising because she was in New York and he was so good-looking.

The restaurant Abi had selected was miles away. It was in the Meatpacking district, a long taxi ride and, having no idea how long the ride would take or how heavy the traffic would be, Smita ended up arriving twenty-five minutes late.

Abi was waiting for her, on his Blackberry but enjoying a glass of wine.

"I'm so sorry," she exclaimed as she rushed in but Abi couldn't have been nicer.

"It's my fault," he said, "for not having told you how long to allow to get here. You seem so at home here; half the time I forget you're from London."

Smita felt flattered. She handed her coat to a waiter, sat down and ordered a drink. As she sipped it, she regained her composure. It was too late now for any calls or text messages from London to detract from her evening. It was obvious from the way Abi was acting – smooth, polite, slightly formal – that her fears had been misplaced, ridiculous. This was going to be a work dinner and she was going to perform absolutely the best she could.

Things stayed that way for most of the meal; they talked about work, about their strategy for the new clients and some training needs which Abi had identified in the London office. But afterwards, when Abi ordered coffee and Smita mint tea, unexpectedly everything changed.

"So," Abi said – and naturally it would be he who took the lead – "enough about work. Tell me about yourself, Smita" and suddenly she didn't know what to say.

"Well," she began, hating sounding so conventional, "I'm married, I've been married for five years now and I've got a little boy who's just two."

"Two?" Abi said. "Phew, hard work."

So he had children himself, Smita thought. "How about you?" she asked, she hoped casually.

Abi pulled a long face. "I'm divorced, I'm afraid," he answered. "Got married too young, to the wrong girl, the usual story."

Smita said, "I'm sorry" although actually she found the news rather exciting. "Do *you* have any children?"

Abi's face brightened. "I've got a beautiful little girl called Alisha who just turned six. She lives with her mother of course but luckily I get to see her pretty often."

Smita asked, "Does she live in New York?"

Abi nodded. "Just outside. A train ride. It's not a problem." He drank his coffee. "So, what does your husband do?"

"He works for the BBC," Smita said. That bit was easy.

Abi made an impressed sound. "Is he a journalist?"

"No," Smita said, "no, he's a producer."

Abi said, "Uh-huh." He seemed to lose concentration briefly and then he asked, "So tell me about your lives over there. I don't know London that well. Where do you live? What do you like to do for relaxation? What does a cool young British Asian couple get up to on weekends?"

Smita said, "My husband's not Asian by the way." She had always called herself Smita Mehta at work, she had never really got used to being Mrs Garland so, it's true; how would Abi know?

"Oh really?" Abi said. "Neither was my ex-wife."

Smita wanted to ask, "Was that part of why you ended up getting divorced?" but she didn't dare. Instead she asked neutrally, "What was she?"

"She's American," Abi answered. "I was exotic, she was the all-American girl, you know the script."

He looked unhappy for a few moments and Smita wondered desperately what she could safely say.

"Your daughter's got an Indian name," she ventured.

Abi grinned ruefully. "Well, a name which works both ways; if you just heard it, it could be A-l-i-c-i-a. You know what, next time round, *if* there's a next time round, maybe I'll take my mother's advice for a change."

"An arranged marriage?" Smita suggested jokingly.

Abi grinned. "Who *knows*? Anyways, listen, it's getting

late. You're flying tomorrow. We should be on our way, I guess."

He settled the bill, helped Smita on with her coat and saw her into a taxi. There was no physical contact between them, no kiss. Yet, as Smita rode back to the hotel, she felt the evening had ended ambiguously; she still wasn't sure if it had been a work dinner or a date.

But sitting in the airport the next morning, waiting for her flight to be called, she felt unbelievably guilty, guilty out of all proportion to what she had actually done. In the context of a work trip, having dinner with your boss was, after all, a completely normal thing to do. But she knew perfectly well what she had done wrong. It was what Jeremy would no doubt call, in his prissy pompous way, "a sin of *o*mission rather than *co*mmission", repeating one of his mother's silly sayings. When Abi had asked Smita, towards the end of the evening, if she and her English husband were happy together, instead of just snapping, "Yes," she had only shrugged.

The nearer they got to the bus stop, the more of a fuss Anand made. It was true, the long double bus ride back to Jeremy's new flat in Kilburn was a bore, especially for a four year old. But Anand didn't usually make a fuss. He rather liked buses and, even though Sylvia found it quite a challenge nowadays to make it up to the top deck, provided they could sit upstairs, Anand was usually perfectly well-behaved. Something seemed to have got into him today. First he walked slower and slower, dragging his feet infuriatingly, scuffing his shoes. Then he made himself heavier and heavier, hanging from Sylvia's aching arm rather than holding her hand until she was virtually dragging him along. "Oh for goodness sake Anand," she scolded him eventually, "I'm going to end up with one arm much longer than the other if you carry on like this." Finally, he set up the most aggravating repetitive whine, "I don't want to go to Daddy's, I don't want to go to Daddy's, I-don't-want-to-go-to-Daddy's." They were within sight of the bus stop by now. As Sylvia automatically checked the numbers of the buses which stopped there, she happened to notice the number of a bus which went directly to Maida Vale and the perfect solution popped neatly into her head.

"I know what we'll do," she said brightly to Anand. "You don't have nursery tomorrow morning, do you? You can come home with me."

Anand's scowl vanished to be replaced by a look of calculating suspicion which Sylvia didn't like to see on the face of such a small child.

"To sleep over?" he asked warily. "I don't have any pyjamas at your house."

"Actually," Sylvia said smugly, "you do. You just haven't worn them yet."

"What are they like?" Anand asked suspiciously. "They're not flowery like yours, are they?"

"Of course not," Sylvia said indignantly. "What d'you take me for? They've got frogs on them."

"Really?" Anand asked. "Frog pyjamas?"

"Yes," Sylvia said. "Really. And there are frog slippers

to go with them too." Anand considered. "What would I have for my supper?"

Sylvia thought her way quickly round her rather empty fridge. "Soft boiled egg with bread and butter soldiers," she answered, "and one of Grandma's special treats for after."

"And," Anand asked, "would I get a bedtime story?"

Again, Sylvia was indignant. "Of course you'd get a bedtime story, Anand. Don't you always?"

"Not always. Not if Mummy's busy or Daddy's tired. Sometimes I just get a conversation."

"Well," Sylvia said firmly, "at my house, you'd most definitely have a bedtime story, several even."

Anand asked, "How many?"

If the bus hadn't come along so quickly, Sylvia might have got cold feet. What she was doing was, after all, obviously wrong. But the bus to Maida Vale came almost the minute they reached the bus stop. Anand yelped with excitement and Sylvia didn't really have time to think about the consequences of her impulsive act.

They clambered aboard. Anand touched Sylvia's Oyster card to the reader and then ran eagerly upstairs. Sylvia followed him with difficulty; had the steps of the stairs always been this high? When she finally hauled herself up to the top deck and stood there panting, scanning the rows for an empty seat, Anand had completely disappeared. For a second, Sylvia was panic-stricken until she realised that he had found a pair of empty seats near the back of the bus and sat down and promptly become invisible. His small black head bobbed up and he waved and called cheerily, "Here, Grandma, here" and several passengers smiled indulgently. Proudly, Sylvia took her seat next to him. She didn't tell him off for having run ahead because after all, on a bus, it was hardly a risk, was it?

Anand had the seat by the window, Sylvia had the aisle. Secretly, Sylvia hoped that the bus would get so crowded she would have to take Anand on her lap but it didn't happen. They sat companionably side by side, Anand keeping up a steady running commentary on what he could see from the window and Sylvia regaining her breath after the stairs. She would have to call Jeremy and confess what she had done pretty soon after they got back. Jeremy almost always got home by six on the afternoons she spent with Anand so she must make sure to phone him soon after that so he wouldn't worry. She felt apprehensive and guilty. Yet, on the other hand, what had she actually done wrong? A doting grandmother taking her grandson home with her for the night; what could be more natural than that?

Anand seemed perfectly happy as they made their way back along Sutherland Avenue. The front doors all looked exactly the same and he kept asking playfully, "Is *this* one your door Grandma? Is *this* one?"

They let themselves into Sylvia's normally deathly quiet apartment and straight away it became lively and noisy. Even the dull rooms seemed suddenly brighter. Anand was excited to see his frog pyjamas and his frog slippers and then he wanted to have his bath straight away, before supper, so he could put them on. Suddenly, Sylvia noticed it was nearly seven o'clock and she still hadn't got round to ringing Jeremy. Leaving Anand playing happily in the bath with the family of inflatable turtles, she went hunting for her mobile phone to see if Jeremy had left her any messages. Oh blow, she hadn't remembered to switch it on.

Full of dire foreboding, she rang him on her home phone. She couldn't be bothered to switch on the wretched mobile, to tap in her code – which she could never seem to get right – and wait for that silly little electronic fanfare which told you it was ready. Since when had machines started to trumpet the fact that they were ready to work? It was nothing to be proud of; they were *machines*.

Jeremy picked up straight away. He was livid. "Where the *hell* are you? I was worried sick."

"Why on earth should you worry?" Sylvia asked evenly. "You knew Anand was perfectly safe with me."

"I didn't know *anything*," Jeremy answered angrily. "I couldn't get through to you on your phone. I kept ringing and ringing. It was incredibly worrying; anything could have happened."

"Well, all's well that ends well," Sylvia said soothingly. "We're both absolutely hunky-dory. I'm just sorry I forgot to turn my phone on and you got yourself into such a state. Silly me."

"But where *are* you?" Jeremy demanded. "When are you intending to get back?"

"Well," Sylvia said, "actually we're at my flat."

Jeremy nearly shouted. "*What*?"

"There's no need to shout Jeremy," Sylvia said

reprovingly. "We're at my flat. Anand's going to spend the night here, if that's alright with you?"

"Are you *mad*?" Jeremy shouted. "Anand *has* to spend the night here with me. It's in the access arrangements. You can't just ride roughshod over a legal agreement. What's got into you?"

Sylvia couldn't make head or tail of what Jeremy was talking about. Defensively, she said, "I don't understand why you're making such a fuss, Jeremy. Anand *wanted* to come and spend the night here." Meanly, she added, "He kept saying, "I don't *want* to go to Daddy's.""

There was a hurt silence at the other end. Then Jeremy said, with an obvious effort, "It's very hard on him, all this to-ing and fro-ing and compartmentalization: Mummy's place, Daddy's place."

Sylvia wanted to say sharply, "Well, shouldn't you both have thought about that before splitting up?" but she feared the consequences. Instead, she said brightly, "So it's probably the perfect solution for him to come to *me* from time to time. He's certainly having a whale of a time."

"Don't you understand?" Jeremy burst out. "He *can't* stay the night with you. In the access arrangements, he spends one night midweek and every other weekend with *me*. And that's where he *has* to be. Otherwise the whole thing breaks down and it'll have to be renegotiated – which, I hardly need to tell you, will be a nightmare. I'm afraid you're going to have to bring him back."

"But I can't," Sylvia cried out. "He's having such a lovely time Jeremy. I've got new frog pyjamas for him and we've got a special supper planned and then *dozens* of bedtime stories. I can't just bring him back. He'll be devastated."

"Listen," Jeremy said furiously. "If Anand spends the night at your flat and Smita gets to hear about it which she certainly will – we can hardly ask a four year old to keep secrets from his mother – then she will probably go straight to her solicitor and want to change the access arrangements and that will delay the divorce even further and basically you will have screwed everything up for everybody. So please, however much of a fuss he kicks up, you need to bring him back here *now*. You know what, put him on the phone."

"I can't," Sylvia said triumphantly. "He's in the bath."

"In the *bath*?" Jeremy yelled. "For Christ's sake! He's been in the bath the whole time we've been talking and you haven't gone to check on him once? Is he ok? Go and have a look."

"Oh honestly Jeremy," Sylvia tutted. "There's really no need to make such a fuss. He's four, not a tiny baby." Still she called down the corridor, "Everything alright Anand dear?"

There was absolute silence.

"Did he answer?" Jeremy panicked. "Did he answer? Is he alright?"

"For goodness sake Jeremy," Sylvia said condescend- ingly. "Do stop making such a dreadful fuss. I'll go and look in on him if it makes you happy."

She virtually ran down the corridor. Anand was absorbed in an extremely splashy game which involved the smallest turtle swimming at high speed from his Mummy at one end of the bath to his Daddy at the other. The bath had obviously overflowed a number of times already.

She went back to the phone. "He's fine," she reported, hoping Jeremy wouldn't notice the catch in her voice.

"So get him *out* of the bath," Jeremy said tersely, "and bring him back here."

"But Jeremy," Sylvia said reproachfully, "what are you thinking of? Are you seriously suggesting I bring him in his pyjamas on the bus? Or put him back into his dirty clothes after his bath? And what about his supper? It's already late for him to be eating."

"Look," Jeremy said. "I can see you've created a pretty problematic situation – and not for the first time, needless to say. But unless you want to totally mess up everyone's plans for the foreseeable future, you're going to have to stick to the access arrangements which have been agreed with the solicitors just like everybody else. Anand has to spend tonight with me."

The bathroom door was thrown open and Anand emerged, naked, golden and dripping wet.

"Who're you talking to?" he asked suspiciously.

Sylvia mouthed, "Daddy."

Anand stamped his foot and scowled horribly. "I'm not going back to Daddy's," he shouted. "I'm *not!*"

He ran back into the bathroom and slammed the door behind him, hard.

"What was all that about?" Jeremy asked.

Sylvia scarcely hesitated. "I'm afraid he was shouting 'I'm not going back to Daddy's'. *And* he didn't have a towel around him. I have to go Jeremy, otherwise he'll catch cold."

"I hope you realise," Jeremy told his mother, "that you are making my life completely impossible. Now *I'll* have to come and sleep at your place too so that we're at least observing the letter of the law. Then, technically, Anand will still be spending the night with me."

"Oh no," Sylvia exclaimed. "Don't do that."

"For Christ's sake, why ever not?" Jeremy sounded enraged.

"Don't deprive me of my evening with Anand," Sylvia pleaded. "If you must come, at least wait until he's gone to bed. *Please.*"

There was a pause at the other end. Then Jeremy said "Fine" and banged the phone down, just like a petulant child himself.

Anand ate his soft-boiled egg and bread and butter soldiers in Sylvia's kitchen. He leapfrogged exuberantly down the corridor in his new slippers and spent some time croaking and demanding flies for his supper before he would settle down. For afters, Sylvia made him a mug of cocoa with a saucer of mixed biscuits. She was taken aback when he commented with raised eyebrows, "What – no fruit or vegetables?" What was childhood coming to? Would he be demanding prunes or cod liver oil next? She replied, rather frostily, "There are currants in the biscuits Anand."

After he had brushed his teeth, with gusto and without being told to, they settled cosily under a rug on the sofa for his bedtime story marathon. Sylvia had been looking forward to this no end and she was deeply disappointed to realise, only halfway through the second book, that Anand was slumped against her, sound asleep. For a while, she sat there, adoring the feeling of his small warm body snuggled trustingly against her. Then she began to wonder how she would get him to bed. She wasn't quite sure if she could safely carry him all the way to his room. But if she woke him up and made him walk there, he might start crying and then not settle again. If she left him asleep on the sofa, Jeremy might disapprove when he got here. In the end, she scooped Anand up bravely, wrapped in the rug and staggered with him all the way to his bedroom, at one point narrowly missing tripping on the trailing fringes of the rug.

She had just tucked him up successfully when Jeremy rang the bell. He was in a filthy temper. Ever since the Separation, Sylvia had noticed, he had been neglecting his appearance, wearing any old clothes and often going unshaven at the weekends. Once or twice, she had even wondered whether he was washing as often as he should. This evening he looked particularly seedy, standing at her front door glaring at her, with a small overnight bag over one shoulder.

"He's fast asleep," Sylvia said proudly. "We've had a lovely evening together."

"Well I'm glad *you* have," Jeremy answered resentfully, "because you've completely wrecked mine."

He came in and dropped his bag in the middle of the front hall.

"Can I make you some cocoa?" Sylvia offered.

Jeremy snapped, "No." He said, "let me take a look at Anand."

Rather offended, Sylvia led him down the corridor to

260

Anand's bedroom. Nothing to find fault with there surely? Anand lay sound asleep in his irreproachable bed, his arms and legs flung wide, the vivid green brushed cotton of his new pyjamas setting off his lovely golden colour. The whole room was bathed in a gentle apricot glow from the man in the moon night light. Sylvia turned triumphantly to Jeremy and saw that he was crying.

"This is such a bloody mess," he whispered. "Why did it all have to turn out like this?"

Sylvia wanted to hug him but didn't dare. She whispered back, "Come and have a drink dear."

Jeremy poured himself a whisky. He said irritably that Sylvia never made it how he liked. He turned down all other offers of food and drink and sat glowering in silence. Sylvia tried to entertain him with tales of how beautifully Anand had behaved at the aquarium and the hilarious game they had played together, comparing the fish and the sea creatures with people they knew. Jeremy remained unresponsive.

Eventually he heaved a giant sigh and said, "Look, there's no point pretending nothing's wrong and you haven't created the most massive problem by taking it into your head to bring Anand back here because you *have*. And it's not over yet either."

Sylvia quavered, "What do you mean?"

"Smita," Jeremy answered furiously. "She's going to have a field day over this."

Before Sylvia could answer, he stood up abruptly. "Anyway I'm going to bed now. I've got a splitting headache."

Sylvia refrained from pointing out that, in that case, he shouldn't be drinking whisky. She asked where he wanted to sleep.

Jeremy looked surprised. "I'll sleep in Anand's bed of course. We almost always do when he sleeps over."

Sylvia frowned. She didn't like the sound of that one bit but, clearly, there was no point discussing anything with Jeremy when he was in such a shockingly bad mood. She got him another pillow and a fresh towel and wished him sweet dreams. He mumbled something bad-temperedly before closing the door.

In the middle of the night, Sylvia sprang awake. She knew something in the flat was different but she couldn't remember what it was. After a second or two, it came back to her; her son and her grandson were asleep in the other bedroom. Her flat was *inhabited*. She lay there for a little while, excited, savouring the novelty and imagining the two of them sleeping side by side in Anand's small bed. Then she had an irresistible urge to go and look in on them. In a London house at night, it was never completely dark.

She got up silently and padded over to her bedroom door. It opened with the smallest click. There was barely enough light to see in the corridor but once she opened the other bedroom door there would be light from the night light and from the street outside. She hesitated before turning the door knob. Anand would doubtless sleep soundly but Jeremy had always been a troublesome poor sleeper. If he woke, she would murmur, "Just checking" and close the door again immediately. He ought to be touched that she was so vigilant.

The door opened almost without a sound and in the room beyond no one stirred. Sylvia stood in the doorway and waited for her eyes to adjust. Jeremy had switched off the man in the moon night light but through the pastel curtains there was enough light from the street lamps outside for her to see quite clearly the two sleeping figures in the single bed: the tall fair father and the small dark son. Really, when you stopped to think about it, there was almost no physical resemblance between the two of them at all. But they were sleeping in exactly the same position; both lying on their right-hand side, Anand curled within Jeremy's sheltering length, both holding their clenched right fist to their forehead as if deep in troubled thought.

Sylvia watched them, beside herself with delight, before tiptoeing out. How come she had no recollection of ever looking in on Jeremy sleeping when he was a boy? Was it because, infuriating child that he was, he had hardly ever slept? Had she avoided peeping in at his bedroom door for fear of rousing him? Or was it because the ayah had always done that while she herself was off somewhere partying?

Suddenly it struck Sylvia that everything in her life had happened at the wrong time. She had waited ten long years to have a child by which time, frankly, she had rather gone off the idea. When she should have been enjoying being a mother, she was clinging on to the rollercoaster of married life with Roger in his heyday and, if the truth be told, retaliating with a few little flirtations of her own. By the time her marriage had settled down into the cosy companionship of middle age, Jeremy was away at boarding school in England and it was too late to form a proper relationship with him. When she and Roger could finally look forward to a rosy retirement back in England, Roger had promptly dropped dead.

Everything had been topsy-turvy, nothing had gone as it rightly should have. And now, when she was well into her sixties, here she was in the grip of this belated surge of maternal feeling which had taken her completely by surprise and made her do all sorts of things which she should almost certainly not have.

Unable to go back to sleep, she went and sat for a little while in the living room in the dark. All sorts of foolish and improbable scenarios involving herself and her grandson played out in her mind. She told herself sternly to get a grip. Tonight, however delightful it was, was not going to be repeated. Her twin catchphrases of "Buck up" and "Righty ho" seemed to crouch on either side of her like two antiquated firedogs. In the morning, when Jeremy had taken Anand away again, they would be all she had left.

Sylvia knew she would remember the day she heard the news of Jeremy and Smita's Separation for the rest of her life. It happened on a Sunday towards the end of August. The day had begun unpromisingly, with muggy weather and confusion. She had gone to visit Ruth, expecting finally to meet Siggy, the elusive baby brother, only to discover that she had somehow got the Sundays muddled up and he was not due to come until the following weekend. It was the third time they had failed to meet each other and Sylvia had been so sure it would be third time lucky. Not that she harboured any especial expectations about their meeting but it seemed to matter a great deal to Ruth who was obviously not getting any younger.

After Siggy had pulled out of their first Sunday lunch appointment some three years earlier, with that silly excuse about being marooned on the Isle of Wight, Sylvia had felt rather huffy to be honest. Then she had been so taken up with her grandson that when Ruth had suggested another meeting a few months later, she had said rather importantly that she was far too busy.

A fairly long time had gone by and Sylvia was not sure anymore whether it was at Christmas 2005 or Christmas 2006 that Ruth had again tried to introduce Sylvia to her beloved Siggy. The occasion had been a pre-Christmas tea with, Sylvia remembered, warmed mince pies and an iced Christmas cake. Imelda had gone back to the Philippines by then and been replaced by the less forbidding Gloria.

That time, Ruth and Sylvia were already sitting sipping their tea and wondering why Siggy was so late when the telephone rang and Gloria brought in an even more preposterous message; Siggy had been unavoidably delayed on some emergency business for the Magic Circle and was only now setting out from – of all unmagical places – Loughton in Essex. He was most awfully sorry but he would not be there for at least two hours. Ruth had been mortified and Sylvia, who considered herself pretty thick-skinned, felt undeniably hurt. She wondered why on earth Ruth's brother was so reluctant to meet her. At the same time, she could not help concluding that he sounded a frightfully eccentric person.

Ruth, wringing her hands, explained that Siggy had been for years a member of the Magic Circle, a professional association of magicians and he was regularly called out at short notice if a fellow magician was taken ill or was unable to perform at a function. It was a bit like being a doctor, Ruth said; if you were called out, whatever time of the day or night it was, you simply *had* to go.

Sylvia had to leave before Siggy got there; Heather Bailey was expecting her for a pre-Christmas drink – or six, poor Heather – and she couldn't linger. Part of her was glad she had an excuse to hurry away; if someone stood you up twice, then that was only what they deserved, wasn't it? But part of her regretted missing Siggy a second time; she had always loved magic and the idea of meeting a real live magician was intriguing.

So Sylvia was particularly cross with herself for making a mess of the arrangements the third time round especially since, by the time the following Sunday came along, she was in no fit state to contemplate any social occasion. She and Ruth tried to make the most of the mishap. They talked even more than usual and, in the course of the afternoon, Ruth told Sylvia about her difficulties with her daughter. She was called Giselle although a particularly unkind slap in the face was that she had changed her name as an adult to Ganit. Sylvia commiserated; she remembered a trying period during Jeremy's teenage years when he had insisted on being called Jed. Thankfully, it had passed. A troubled young woman, Giselle had in the late Seventies emigrated to Israel, to Ruth's absolute horror: the distance, the instability of the region, the barbaric lack of manners of the people. She had gone to live on a kibbutz and married a man who worked in the fields. In due course, she had three children (all boys) and then, to cap it all, she had developed this highly inconvenient fear of flying so that if Ruth wanted to see her grandchildren – who incidentally had no manners at all – she had to travel all the way to Giselle. Ruth suspected the phobia had an ideological element. Sylvia tutted but she couldn't really understand Ruth's horror. Surely one faraway hot country was pretty much like another, wasn't it? She allowed herself a brief reverie on the bus back to Maida Vale afterwards about a teenage Anand who insisted on being called Ant.

She got back to her flat after her bungled visit in the early evening. She didn't feel like supper, she had as usual eaten a hearty tea at Ruth's and, as was all too often the case these days, she wasn't quite sure what to do with herself.

It was a warm, stuffy evening so she opened all the windows and sat down in the living room, where Anand's multi-coloured building blocks were strewn across the floor. She contemplated the void of her existence and then the telephone rang.

It was Jeremy and he barely said, "Hello."

He said, "I have some really bad news, I'm afraid."

Sylvia's heart stopped.

Gobbling his words so she could hardly follow what he was saying, Jeremy announced, "Smita has told me she wants a divorce."

In the next room, Roger, from whom Sylvia had not heard a sound for more than two years, growled, "Bollocks."

Sylvia struggled to speak.

"Hello?" Jeremy said irritably. "Hello?"

Sylvia gasped, "I'm here."

"Well, why don't you say something then?" Jeremy snapped. "Please don't make this any harder for me than it already is."

Sylvia managed to utter faintly, "Oh my dear."

She couldn't get any further; she felt the sickening vertigo of certainties falling away around her. Forget Jeremy and Smita; who would get to keep Anand? She reached for a chair as her legs gave way beneath her. Smita, the winner, of course Smita would take all.

Jeremy was shouting in one ear, "Look, this is a bloody miserable situation without you as usual making it worse," and Roger was blaspheming in the other. Sylvia couldn't hear herself think.

"Please don't shout," she said faintly, to neither of them in particular.

Jeremy calmed down somewhat but Roger continued to turn the air blue.

Jeremy said, more quietly, "Things haven't been good for a long time. Maybe you've noticed? But I honestly never thought it would come to this."

"Is there any chance," Sylvia asked shakily, "that she might change her mind?"

Jeremy said, "Uh-huh," which Sylvia supposed meant no.

"She's changed so much since we got married," Jeremy went on. "She's become so driven, so *hard*. I thought when Anand was born she might ease up a bit but she seems to have done the exact opposite."

Sylvia forced herself to ask weakly, "What about Anand?"

Even Roger fell silent.

Jeremy answered, "Well, of course, that's the absolute worst of it. The mother always gets custody, doesn't she? I never ever imagined that I would have to live apart from Anand."

Sylvia heard a sound which might have been a sob or maybe just a throat clearing.

"Where?" she asked, pretending she hadn't heard the sound. "Where will you and Smita both live? Where will Anand *be*?"

"Well, for now," Jeremy answered bitterly, "It seems Smita gets to stay in our flat with Anand and *I* have to move out."

Sylvia boiled at the injustice. "What grounds," she asked indignantly, "what *grounds* does she have for wanting a divorce? You've always done what *she* wanted."

"Don't start," Jeremy snapped. "It's really not the time."

"I'm not starting anything," Sylvia said indignantly. "I'm merely pointing out that you've always let her have her own way – which is *true* – and so it really doesn't seem fair that now *she's* the one demanding a divorce and *she* gets to keep everything."

"Fair," Jeremy repeated bitterly. "Whoever said that fairness had anything to do with it? Look," he went on. "I didn't intend this to be a long call. I'm sure you're not enjoying it either. I'm sorry it's come to this; I realise it's not easy for you either. Let's talk again in a day or two, ok? Please only call me on my mobile from now on."

"Wait!" Sylvia cried out. "Wait. When is all this going to happen? Where will you *be*? How will I get to see Anand from now on?"

"I'm going to stay at a friend's place for now," Jeremy said evasively. "Someone you don't know. I suppose I'm going to have to find somewhere. Smita and I are going to have to work out a lot of things. I'm afraid you're just going to have to hang on a bit about seeing Anand until things are a bit more sorted. To be honest, it's not top of the list right now."

Sylvia screamed, "It *is* top of the list! It *should* be top of the list. You can't keep him from me."

"*Mum*!" Jeremy yelled. "For Christ's sake, this is not about *you*! Look, let's talk again when we're both a bit calmer."

Sylvia only registered several days later that Jeremy had called her "Mum". After he rang off, she leapt up in confusion, not at all sure where she was heading but probably to Belsize Park to hang onto Anand for dear life. She turned her ankle badly on a building block and fell awkwardly.

So already Anand was slipping out of her grasp since she spent the next two months with her leg in plaster which of course, on top of everything else, complicated poor Jeremy's life no end.

He camped out at his friend's for a few weeks.

Sometimes, at the weekend, he would grudgingly come and stay over with Sylvia and help her bad-temperedly with all the things she couldn't manage to do with her leg in plaster. He refused to discuss Smita or the divorce and was generally as disagreeable as he could be. He only brought Anand with him once, in spite of Sylvia's pleading.

At first, she was relieved to see that – so far – Anand didn't seem greatly affected by his parents' separation. He had just celebrated his third birthday and was more concerned to tell his grandmother about all his presents. Naisha had given him a toy doctor's case. But when it was time to leave, which it seemed to be awfully quickly, Anand shocked them both by throwing a violent uncharacteristic tantrum. He flung himself on the floor, his entire little body rigid with rage and, drumming his feet furiously on the floor, he screamed, "I don't want to go, let me stay, let me stay, let me stay."

When Jeremy picked him up angrily and told him off, he fought with his father, drumming his fists furiously on Jeremy's chest. "Put me *down*! Put me *down*! You're *hopeless*."

Jeremy looked shaken. He said embarrassedly to his mother, "I don't know what's got into him. He's not usually like this."

Sylvia said, "*I* know." She gave Jeremy a meaningful look. "Poor little mite. His world's been turned upside down."

Jeremy flushed. "Thank you for that. That's really helpful."

Sylvia bridled. "Well, my dear, it's glaringly obvious."

She beckoned to Anand. "Come over here dear and sit on Grandma's lap for a little bit and try and calm down."

Anand trotted over obediently and sat sniffing on Sylvia's lap even though it was rather awkward for both of them with the cast.

"Now, you know it's wrong to shout at Daddy, don't you?" Sylvia said soothingly. "And it's wrong to hit him too. What's happened isn't Daddy's fault."

"Mum!" Jeremy interrupted warningly.

But Sylvia stopped him with a gesture. "Let's talk," she said gently to Anand, "about what we're going to do the next time you come to visit Grandma."

In due course, Jeremy rented a flat in a converted Victorian school in Kilburn. It was not at all suitable for a small child, with immense floor-to-ceiling windows and a perilous railed gallery and although Jeremy claimed it was actually in West Hampstead, Sylvia could tell straight away, when she was finally mobile enough to go and visit, that it was obviously Kilburn.

A nightmarish new period began. Since Jeremy and Smita seemed to be essentially not on speaking terms, all arrangements between them including everything to do with Anand had to be painfully and lengthily negotiated as if by two warring parties. It could take ten days to organise one paltry afternoon with Anand. Arrangements were constantly rescheduled or even worse cancelled. To Sylvia, it seemed as if life, always unpredictable, had suddenly become infinitely much more complicated; the probability of saying or doing the wrong thing, of putting her foot in it was abruptly multiplied tenfold and no one, not even Ruth seemed to have any advice on how to proceed.

One day, out of the blue, Naisha rang her. Sylvia was startled; she had assumed she had heard the last of Naisha. Now the links between their children were severed, what links could there possibly be between them? Besides, Naisha was the winning grandmother and Sylvia bitterly resented that, through no merit of her own, she got to see Anand as often as she liked. But Naisha had taken the initiative yet again and Sylvia felt wrong-footed and unsure how to act.

"Such a shame, isn't it?" Naisha clucked over the phone. "Our generation would just grin and bear it, isn't that right, Sylvia?" She surprised Sylvia with a naughty giggle. "These young people nowadays, I don't know what they want."

Sylvia made a non-committal but she hoped polite noise.

Naisha swept on. "But there is no reason for us to have a separation, is there, Sylvia dear? I think you and I should form a coalition of grandmothers, what do you say?"

Sylvia felt close to choking but she managed to answer gamely, "Why not?"

"Exactly," Naisha continued. "Why not? I feel we should form a united front to make sure that whatever happens is in our grandson's best interests."

Sylvia could not say exactly why she found this pronouncement so alarming. What was going to happen? What did Naisha know which she didn't? She stammered,

"Of course Anand must come first." But even as she said it, she knew, with dreadful certainty, that her view of Anand's best interests and Naisha's could not possibly coincide and that whatever Naisha was lobbying for was most probably not in Sylvia's interests at all.

She fast forwarded a few years and imagined Anand, brought up exclusively by Smita and Naisha, a joyless, bespectacled teenager forced to study monotonously for medicine or pharmacy or dentistry with no leisure pursuits other than vicariously violent computer games. She felt herself suddenly capable of desperate acts for that wasn't what *she* had in mind for Anand at all.

"So we are of one mind," Naisha concluded happily. "I knew that you and I would see eye to eye, Sylvia. One of these days we really must have lunch together, don't you agree?"

"That would be lovely," Sylvia said faintly.

"Lovely," Naisha repeated firmly. "Just as soon as our busy lives will let us, isn't that right?"

That had been over a year ago but they still hadn't had lunch, praise be. Instead, Naisha had gradually taken a greater and greater role in Anand's life and on the rare, rationed afternoons which Sylvia got to spend with him, she noticed increasing signs of Naisha's influence: Anand would arrive dressed in ghastly little brand name tracksuits with matching baseball caps and T-shirts printed with the latest Disney characters. He talked solemnly about going to Kumon maths and the importance of eating certain herbs and spices for good health. Sylvia's blood boiled. She fought back with chocolate eclairs and never-ending stories and games, outings to the puppet theatre and the zoo. But Smita and Naisha had the upper hand now and, frankly, there was very little Sylvia could do.

She plotted. She invented ever more ingenious ways to retain Anand's affection. She stopped short of criticising Smita, obviously, but you could get a long way with implication.

"Your daddy never went to Kumon maths, you know."

"Lucky Daddy. What did he do when he was three and three quarters?"

"We lived in India then. Does your other grandma ever talk to you about India? It's always hot there. He used to play out in the garden a lot."

"I like playing out in your big garden too – so long as it's not too hot – or too cold or too wet or too windy or too *muddy*."

Once Sylvia asked Anand whether his Mummy ever planned to take him to India.

But Anand answered, "No, Mummy doesn't approve of India. She says it's dirty and messy. I think she and my other grandma are planning to take me to Disneyland one day."

Sylvia raged that all the important decisions in Anand's life were being taken without her. He would be starting school next September and the choice of school, a pushy prep school in Hampstead with a nasty coloured uniform, had been made even without her knowledge. She feared she was being edged out. Apart from the loss of Anand which was unthinkable, she could not begin to imagine what her own life would be without him. But there was no point in raising the issue with Jeremy; he was constantly eaten up with anguish about his own exclusion from his son's life.

❧

In the spring, Sylvia had to face up to an obligation which she would have done anything to avoid. For the third time since her return to England, she received a card inviting her to an exhibition of her sister Cynthia's paintings. She didn't like Cynthia's paintings; they were nervous, scratchy sort of canvases on which the branches of trees clawed at the sky in torment and contorted figures battled unseen demons. Of course she liked spending time with Cynthia even less. The first time Cynthia had invited her down to Lewes for one of her shows had been soon after Sylvia's arrival in London and she had said she felt too shaky to make the journey. The second time, she had blessedly had her leg in plaster. This time she could not come up with any more excuses.

Part of the problem, if she was honest, was that she felt out of place amid Cynthia's arty friends. Sylvia would be the first to admit; she didn't have an artistic or creative bone in her body. Cynthia had always been the clever, arty one, pouring scorn on her plodding younger sister. Cynthia had always disapproved of Roger too whom she considered boorish and vulgar. Blessedly, she had never heard what Roger had to say about her. As she got older, Sylvia found Cynthia's condescension ever harder to bear. What was wrong with being *normal*?

It was true that, in recent years, Cynthia was enjoying a certain vogue; her uneasy paintings perhaps chimed with the unsettled times. Sylvia occasionally saw Cynthia written up in the papers. She was apparently well-known for the curious trait that most of her paintings were painted exclusively in the colours of a bruise. Her new exhibition wasn't in Lewes either; it was at quite a well-known gallery in the West End. Sylvia quailed as she imagined Cynthia's friends – Piers and Gavin and that ghastly Mahonia – posing amid the paintings, all being frightfully pretentious and looking down their noses at the plodding sister.

Sylvia considered asking Jeremy to accompany her. Maybe he might even agree to bring Anand along? It was true a private view at a gallery wouldn't be much fun for a four year old. But it would broaden the little boy's horizons. Sylvia doubted if Naisha ever did anything as time-wasting as taking Anand to an art gallery. She acknowledged that having Anand with her would be a most marvellous diversion too. Cynthia had never met her great-nephew, although she had been sent plenty of photographs and she would surely have to be less alarming in the presence of a small child. But Sylvia knew there was no point; Jeremy would refuse to come along himself, she had heard his opinion of Cynthia often enough over the years and he would certainly not let little Anand be subjected to her either. So, in the end, Sylvia had to go on her own, on an incongruously lovely spring evening, dressed in what she hoped were sufficiently arty clothes.

She got to the gallery rather late. There was some sort

of a mix-up with the buses; all the passengers had to get off at Marble Arch and change onto another bus and, as they were in the process of doing so, Sylvia realised that she had forgotten her handbag on the first bus and had to plunge back through the throng of passengers grumpily transferring from one bus to another to retrieve it. She recognised her bag over the shoulder of a rather odd-looking person, neither exactly male nor female who said, when Sylvia hailed him, that he was taking the bag to the lost property office. Sylvia thanked him gratefully. As she settled onto the second bus with her bag safely on her knees, she reflected how true it was that you should never judge a person solely by their appearance.

The gallery looked very full through the huge plate glass window with her sister's name scrawled across it in violet. But Sylvia didn't want to be seen loitering outside as if she didn't dare come in. So she heaved the heavy door open and entered the gallery bravely where a supercilious young woman checked her name on a list. Sylvia looked around and didn't recognise anyone. Even the unutterable Mahonia would at least have been a familiar face. But Cynthia was obviously moving in new circles nowadays. By the look of it, this was a much younger, more fashionable crowd than her friends down in Lewes. The room was full of outlandish haircuts, eye-catching clothes and preposterous spectacles. Sylvia felt an unexpected pang of envy. She liked to think of Cynthia as unworldly, hobnobbing exclusively with ageing artistic folk. But here Cynthia seemed to be surrounded by rather jolly young people and to be the object of their adulation too.

Sylvia wished intensely that she had been able to bring Anand along. Looking around, she acknowledged that he would most probably not have enjoyed himself that much. But she could have compensated him with a sticky treat. Anand would have been her trump card. Paint what you like, wear what you like; none of you has somebody like *this* to hold your hand.

In the distance, she heard Cynthia's carrying voice, identifiable amid dozens. A few moments later, someone in the crowd shifted sufficiently for Sylvia to catch sight of her sister. She was dressed entirely in lurid green, including her tights and shoes. Glimpsed between the shifting groups, she looked almost more plant than person; a tall thin green sheaf sticking up sharply in their midst.

Reluctantly, Sylvia began to make her way towards her, repeating, "Excuse me, oh, excuse me" as she squirmed forward. People turned to look at her and then looked quickly away as if her appearance were embarrassingly eccentric whereas, in fact, her artiest outfit was a plain lilac linen suit which she had livened up with her favourite enamelled hoopoe brooch. Finally, Cynthia saw her and her face fell.

"Oh, you're here," she said, sounding disappointed. "I assumed you weren't coming."

"Why?" Sylvia asked. "I never said I wasn't coming."

"You never said you *were* coming," Cynthia snapped. "You didn't RSVP and you've never bothered to come before."

"I couldn't come before," Sylvia said defensively. "I had

my leg in plaster, if you remember, and the time before that I – wasn't well."

Cynthia shrugged. "You're breathtakingly late," she went on, "even for you."

"I'm sorry," Sylvia began. "There was a problem with the buses."

But Cynthia cut her off with a haughty wave. "Oh Syl," she said, "spare me the tedious details *please*."

The small group of people gathered around Cynthia watched this exchange with faint amusement. As if abruptly aware of her audience, Cynthia turned to them and announced, "My sibling, Sylvia."

Sylvia felt herself beginning to flush. This was simply ghastly; she should never have come. She smiled foolishly at the onlookers – three extremely thin women of varying ages all with extraordinary haircuts and a quite ridiculously effeminate young man – and waited for Cynthia to introduce them but she didn't. She said disdainfully, "Well, take a look at my paintings Syl and let me know what you think of them." She laughed and turned away.

Sylvia plunged towards the back of the gallery where there was a table with drinks. She helped herself to a glass of Buck's Fizz and downed it in one go. Feeling at a loss with nothing in her hands, she took another one and began to move slowly along the walls.

One of the thin women from Cynthia's entourage appeared next to her and introduced herself: "Chloe Butt, *Art Review*."

Sylvia smiled embarrassedly. She took a gulp of her drink to fortify herself against whatever was coming.

The woman smiled back, wolfishly. "May I ask you a few questions?" She peered at Sylvia's glass. "That's looking a bit empty. May I get you a refill?"

Sylvia tried to make her escape while Chloe Butt was at the bar but she pursued Sylvia and caught up with her at the far end of the room, holding out another very full glass of Buck's Fizz. Her expression, Sylvia thought, was like the wicked stranger offering a child a sweet in a story. But that didn't stop Sylvia fortifying herself some more with another almighty gulp.

"So tell me," Chloe Butt began and Sylvia was alarmed to see her taking out some sort of little hand-held computer, "would you say you and your sister were close?"

Sylvia laughed a bit too loudly. "What do *you* think? Did it look like that to you?"

Chloe Butt asked, "Would you say your relationship was conflictual?"

Sylvia laughed again, this time a little wildly. She took another slug of her drink and, as she searched for an adjective artistically to describe her relationship with Cynthia, she realised that she was not tongue-tied anymore; the Buck's Fizz had loosened her tongue and made her in fact extraordinarily eloquent.

Travelling back to Maida Vale on the bus afterwards, she kept giggling naughtily as she remembered Chloe Butt's pretentious questions and her own outspoken answers. She had told Chloe Butt all about their childhood rivalry: the pinches and the hair-pulling, the spit in favourite puddings, the stolen dolls. She had told her about the time Cynthia believed that Sylvia had thrown her first high heels into a pond and then pretended it had been an accident and how Cynthia had virtually set fire to Sylvia's first perm. She had told her about the adder.

The paintings from the exhibition kept careering past her, inducing vertigo with the motion of the bus: dizzy puce and mauve canvases full of torment. Only one stood out. Chloe Butt had pointed it out to her: a wretched-looking, bedraggled lilac bird cupped in a pair of protective but pecked hands – and hadn't that one been called "Sylvia"?

It was only when she got off the bus on the corner of Sutherland Avenue and the cool of the evening revived her a little that Sylvia began to wonder queasily if maybe she had not gone a little too far. Cynthia was her flesh and blood after all and, besides, her revenge would be terrible. She must ring Chloe Butt first thing in the morning, she had her card in her bag, didn't she and tell her not to print a word of it.

She was distracted from this worry by the unexpected message she found on her answering machine. She had feared, when she saw the red message light flashing, that it would be some problem involving Jeremy and Anand. But she didn't recognise the voice on the recording and she had to press "replay" and listen to the message all over again before she realised, in her befuddled state, who the voice must be and why he was calling her.

"Good evening," the voice began politely. "This is a message for Mrs Sylvia Garland." The caller had a cultured, beautifully enunciated male voice. "My name is Siggy Greenborough. I'm calling you on behalf of my sister Ruth who is seriously ill in hospital. Could you please call me as soon as possible on 078 something, something something something zero? Thank you so much. Goodbye."

Sylvia lurched for the replay button to listen to the message again and to take down Siggy's number. But in her haste, she accidentally pressed the wrong button and a few moments later she discovered to her horror that she had erased the message completely.

It was hard not to imagine that she was being punished for her mischief in the gallery. But fortunately, an hour later – by which time, in floods of tears, she had telephoned every London hospital she could think of but not found Ruth – Siggy rang again.

"Good evening," he began, rather formally. "Is that Mrs Garland?" And Sylvia was so hugely relieved, she nearly shrieked, "Yes! Yes it is!"

"This is Siggy Greenborough," he said gravely, as if she hadn't shrieked at all. "So we meet finally on the phone, if not in person."

"Well, yes," said Sylvia.

"My sister is very ill Mrs Garland," Siggy said sorrowfully. "It seems she has had a stroke. She has been taken to St Mary's Hospital. I'm afraid she's only barely conscious. She is in the intensive care unit. She keeps saying your name."

"My name?" Sylvia repeated in astonishment.

"Yes," Siggy answered wonderingly. "Your name: 'Sylvia'. She is partially paralysed but she keeps saying 'Sylvia'."

"Should I come right away?" Sylvia asked. Shamefacedly, she imagined herself unsteady and smelling of drink in the intensive care unit. She imagined the baby brother looking her up and down – blotchy red face, smudged make up – and wondering what on earth his sister saw in her.

"That is extremely kind of you," Siggy answered. "I'm not sure what to suggest. It's terribly late, isn't it? I don't feel I should drag you across town in the middle of the night."

"No," Sylvia said firmly. "If Ruth is asking for me, of course I must come right away." She squinted at her wristwatch. "I'll call a taxi. I should be there within the hour."

She washed her face and made herself a restorative cup of tea while she waited for the taxi. But when she got to the hospital, Siggy wasn't there. The nurse on duty outside the intensive care unit passed on his message; since patients in the ICU were only allowed to have one visitor at a time, Mr Greenborough had just nipped out to get a breath of fresh air.

Although Sylvia stayed at Ruth's bedside for nearly an hour, Siggy didn't come back. Ruth lay with her eyes closed, her face fallen in, hooked up to a frightening collection of tubes and machines. It didn't seem to Sylvia that she was capable of saying anything. When she finally decided to get up and leave, she patted Ruth's cold hand gently and said to her, "So I'm off now dear but I'll be back in the morning. Chin up."

She realised that Siggy's phone call and her visit must

both have been based on a complete misunderstanding because Ruth stirred, one of her eyelids flickered but the name she mouthed was not Sylvia but quite clearly Siggy.

෨

Everything just seemed to go from bad to worse. At the beginning of July, Jeremy told her that the divorce had finally come through. Sylvia imagined that a page would now be turned and the horrid interim period of wrangling over every little thing would come to an end. After all, a divorce was an agreement of sorts, wasn't it? Now they could hopefully each go their separate way and stop fighting over every single second she and Jeremy got to spend with Anand.

What happened instead was worse than Sylvia's worst imaginings. There had been vague discussions of summer holiday plans which she didn't like the sound of at all; it seemed Smita was making good her threat to take Anand to Disneyland. Naisha was coming along too. Sylvia wondered desperately what on earth she could do to counteract such an intense period of exclusive exposure to Smita and Naisha. Obviously many of the experiences Anand would enjoy too: the aeroplane, the rides and roundabouts at Disneyland, the easy infantile aspects of American life. He might turn his nose up at her big garden and the aquarium when he came back. Sylvia worried but she came up with an idea which she thought might do the trick. She went and chose for Anand his own little bright blue wheelie case. It had on it the smiling face of a bottle-nosed dolphin. He would trundle it happily everywhere and it would remind him daily of his other grandma, the main one, waiting faithfully for him in London. Doubtless Smita would disapprove of the dolphin suitcase; it wouldn't go with all her designer luggage. But Anand would cling on to it loyally and refuse to leave it behind and Smita would be stuck with it, gaudy, grinning, a doubtless infuriating daily reminder of her former mother-in-law.

Sylvia took comfort in the suitcase. She had no idea what she herself would do during the long month of August when they would be away. She still visited Ruth from time to time but you couldn't really have a proper conversation with her anymore, poor dear. These days, Heather was often not much better. As for Jeremy, they still couldn't spend more than twenty minutes together without getting on each other's nerves. How had it come about that the only person in the world with whom she really wanted to spend time was less than five years old?

A week before Anand and Smita and Naisha were due to leave for Florida, Jeremy turned up on Sylvia's doorstep one night, unannounced and in the most pitiful state. His hair was a mess, his clothes were scruffy and when he came through the dark hall into the living room, she could see that he had been crying or maybe drinking.

"Smita has just told me the most horrible thing," he burst out. "I don't know, I don't know – "

He sat down heavily on the sofa and covered his face with his hands.

"What?" Sylvia cried out. "What? Tell me. Is Anand alright?"

Jeremy nodded, without taking his hands away from his face. "It's not that."

"What?" Sylvia gibbered. "What?" She longed to say, "For goodness' sake, Jeremy, pull yourself together, sit up straight and spit it out" but he was obviously too far gone for that.

She sat down beside him and, very gingerly, laid her hand on his arm. "What's the matter?" she asked gently. "Tell me dear."

Slowly, Jeremy lifted his head. He looked at her as if she were a ghost. He opened his mouth once and then shut it again before he spoke. "Smita wants to go and live in America," he said.

The room seemed to darken. Sylvia thought she gasped but she couldn't hear anything beyond the ringing in her ears. For a few seconds, she teetered on the edge of a black void until Jeremy yanked her back by putting his hand on her shoulder and saying "Mum? Mum?"

Sylvia summoned all her failing strength. "You have to stop her," she said. But, even as she said it, she knew it was no good; when had Jeremy ever managed to stop Smita doing anything? He would fail this time the way he had failed every single other time. Smita was all-powerful and Smita would get her way.

Exactly as she feared, Jeremy shrugged. "How can I stop her?"

"Well," Sylvia said sternly. "Isn't there something in the divorce, surely?"

"No," Jeremy said. "No, there isn't. She's been very clever. As you would expect. She's managed to keep all this under wraps until the divorce went through. Otherwise I might have been able to do something, stop her taking him out of the country or something. But she kept the whole thing secret until it was too late."

Sylvia asked uneasily, "What thing?"

Jeremy grimaced. "Oh, she's got it all worked out. Apparently, she's been having a thing with this guy in her New York office for the past year or so. Maybe even longer; how would *I* know? Anyway this guy, he's her boss, he's divorced too, he's got a little girl a bit older than Anand. She's got this idea they could be a perfect ready-made family. They have so much in common, she says."

Sylvia tried to control her rising panic. She bitterly regretted her gift of the little blue suitcase with which Anand would trot happily aboard the aeroplane which would carry him away. She quavered, "What if they don't come back from Florida?"

"Oh, there's no danger of that," Jeremy answered. "Smita never does anything which she hasn't thought through thoroughly beforehand. The whole trip's a trial apparently. *He's* coming to Florida with *his* little girl and they're going to see how the children get on together and how they both react to their parent's new partner. That's why Naisha is going along too; she wants to look over her prospective new son-in-law."

Sylvia felt a sharp pang of jealousy; how long had Naisha been in the know?

"Well, I think the whole thing sounds like an absolute nightmare for Anand," she pronounced. "How can Smita think of inflicting such a thing on her own child?"

But even as she asked the question, of course she knew the answer. In Smita's life, Smita came first. Everyone else, her husband, her mother, even her own son could only ever be a close second. If this move was good for Smita, it would go ahead, whatever the cost to poor little Anand. Besides, how often had Sylvia heard Smita praising the US? It was apparently light years ahead of Britain which Smita found increasingly grubby, run down and frankly past it. In her heart of hearts, Sylvia had to admit Smita had a point. Smita doubtless envisaged a better brighter future for Anand as well as for herself in New York. Of course, this person was her boss too; that could only help her on her way.

Since Jeremy seemed incapable of speech, Sylvia declared, "We have to fight this Jeremy. We can't take it lying down."

Jeremy raised an eyebrow. "What do you suggest we do?"

"Well," Sylvia began. "Well. I think first of all you need to speak to your solicitor, don't you, and see what he has to say. There must be some sort of order or injunction, mustn't there, to stop this kind of thing happening. Why, it's practically *kidnapping*."

Jeremy sat looking anguished but didn't answer.

Furiously, Sylvia scolded him. "Jeremy, this isn't a time for hanging back and dithering. We need to act – and quickly."

Jeremy sighed. "You can tell me to do whatever you like. You know perfectly well there's no point; what Smita wants, Smita gets. It's always been that way as long as I've known her."

Sylvia wanted to shake him. As long as she'd known Jeremy, he'd always been the most hopeless, spineless, *useless* individual. And now, when he was faced with the crisis of his life, he was going to fluff it. In that instant Sylvia decided to take the law into her own hands. Jeremy might be a wet blanket but she was not.

⁊

Anand and Smita and Naisha left for Florida as planned at the beginning of August. To Sylvia's surprise, the month didn't drag at all. In fact, she found herself busier than she had been at any point in the past five years. She got up early and went briskly to the library. She read up on divorce and custody and so-called international "tug-of-love" cases. She made three separate appointments at the Citizens' Advice Bureau where a spotty young solicitor called Toby with a disconcertingly frivolous eyebrow piercing advised her on the insubstantial rights of grandparents and cautioned her against taking the law into her own hands. She got in touch with a grandparents' pressure group who were equally wishy-washy and encouraged her to lobby for reform of the law. She was so busy, she barely noticed the month passing nor the glorious August weather. She had no time to sit out in the gardens feeling sorry for herself as she usually did in the summer. For the first time in years, maybe for the first time ever, she had a mission.

She had not expected a postcard from Anand. After all, he was only four and Smita certainly wouldn't spare a moment of her holiday to send a card to Sylvia. But a card came, written in Naisha's extravagant handwriting and signed in outsize letters by Anand. It said only, "Dear Grandma Sylvia, We are having a brilliant time in America. Love Anand" and, rather than giving Sylvia any pleasure, it merely served to turn the knife in the wound. In fact, it was on the day she received the postcard that Sylvia, having come to a dead end with all the official channels she had explored, decided to find a solution of her own to the desperate situation.

When Anand and Smita and Naisha returned, she breathed a little easier. Her little boy was at least back in the country now and she calculated that she had a few months to work out a plan. Anand was starting school in September and Smita would certainly not do anything to disrupt the start of his education. Sylvia guessed that she had at worst until Christmas to achieve what Jeremy could not. At best, she might even have the whole school year ahead of her, assuming Smita would make her move during the long summer holidays.

She got to spend an afternoon with Anand ten days after he came back. He had grown visibly during the month he had been away and it seemed to be a sturdier, less infantile child whom Jeremy delivered proudly to her door. He was browner too.

Sylvia dropped awkwardly to her knees to hug him. "Darling! I've missed you *so* much! Did you have a wonderful time?"

She sensed Anand was a little stiff in her embrace, a little resistant, as if a month was long enough for a four year old to have lost some of that day to day familiarity.

She held him close anyway, relishing the feel and the smell of him. But Anand burst out of her hug, as if she were smothering him and declared, "No, I didn't have a wonderful time. I had a *weird* time."

Sylvia looked up enquiringly at Jeremy who rolled his eyes and drew his forefinger across his throat behind Anand's back.

Anand ran into Sylvia's living room to reacquaint himself with his toys and Sylvia, accepting Jeremy's helping hand, clambered stiffly to her feet to follow him.

"Surely you enjoyed Disneyland?" she asked, falsely cheerfully. "All those whizzing rides?"

"The rides were fun," Anand said solemnly. "But not the people."

He busied himself with his rediscovered belongings and refused to say anything else.

In the kitchen, in an undertone, Jeremy explained. "Smita hasn't said much. But apparently he and the little girl didn't hit it off at all. According to Smita, she's a real little primadonna."

Sylvia raised her eyebrows and Jeremy gave a rare harsh laugh. "I know. It takes one to know one."

"So," Sylvia asked eagerly, "is the whole thing off?"

"If only," Jeremy said. "No, it's very much on apparently. Remember, the little girl lives with her mother so she'd only be with them from time to time. I think Smita is hoping that if she and this guy get married, then his ex-wife will restrict his access to the little girl even more. Which would suit Smita to a T."

"Oh!" Sylvia exclaimed. "How *nasty*."

Jeremy shrugged. "It's a nasty business." He added, "I'll scoot off now. I'll come and get him at six so please make sure he's here and ready. Smita is picking him up from my place at seven."

After Jeremy had left, Sylvia went and sat in the living room with Anand. She didn't want to deluge him with difficult questions but she longed to hear all he had to say. She was a great believer in "out of the mouths of babes and sucklings"; she still remembered the shock and thrill of little Jeremy saying to his father all those years ago: "I saw you playing with Nikki Palmer in the swimming pool. Why was she laughing so much?"

Anand appeared absorbed in his game. He had poured all the plastic animals out of their container and seemed to be sorting them into some kind of categories. Sylvia watched him quietly for a little while and then asked, "So what did you like best about America?"

Anand considered her question. "I liked the ice creams and I liked the sea."

Sylvia was overjoyed; *their* things, he had singled out their things, seaside and ice creams, both of which he had discovered with her. But then she wondered if he was maybe just saying those things in order to console her. "Not Disneyland?" She asked. "Not all those whizzy rides?"

Anand frowned. "Disneyland is hot and smelly," he said scornfully. "There are queues for everything. But we got to the front of the queues because Grandma Naisha felt faint every time she had to stand in one." He grinned cheekily.

Sylvia would have stood it out in the queue of course.

She changed the subject. "Where else did you go darling, apart from Disneyland?"

Anand looked rather vague. "We went to the hotel. We went shopping. We only went to the beach a few times."

Sylvia wondered how to steer the conversation round to the two invisible members of their party whom Anand wasn't mentioning: the bossy little girl and her father. She asked brightly, "Did you meet any nice people in Florida?"

Anand shook his head.

Stumped, Sylvia went into the kitchen to get them some tea. When she came back, Anand had incorporated her oriental metal bird with the bent beak into his game; the animals were grouped in a circle around it and when Sylvia asked him what the bird was doing there, he answered, "The animals are praying to it" and queasily she wondered whether she detected Naisha's influence.

Anand said nothing about Smita's new boyfriend or his daughter the whole afternoon and it upset Sylvia that he was withholding something so significant from her. He was such a thoughtful little chap; maybe he worried it would upset her. But she was frightened to ask anything about it in case it upset him. This was awful; she had to get out of this impasse if she was to get anywhere at all.

At a quarter to six, finally, she tried one more time, "Did your Mummy and Grandma Naisha enjoy America, do you think?"

Anand considered. "Mummy liked it," he said, "but Grandma Naisha was pleased to come home. She said America was too big and too fast for her and she didn't like the food; she said it tasted like cotton wool." He giggled.

Sylvia risked one small step closer. "What did your Mummy like?"

But Anand frowned and caused a diversionary commotion by flapping around the room with a toy owl, hooting and he didn't answer.

When Jeremy came back, Sylvia cornered him again in the kitchen. "He hasn't said a word about the new boyfriend or the little girl," she whispered urgently. "It's not natural. He's bottling it up."

Jeremy said in alarm, "Please don't get involved in all that, Mum. It'll only cause more trouble."

Sylvia bridled. "Why on earth shouldn't I get involved? It's my business too."

Jeremy frowned. "Please," he repeated. "Take my advice and stay well out of it. Everything is terribly, terribly delicate at the moment. I'm doing everything I can, believe me. I just need you to steer clear."

Sylvia bit her tongue. Jeremy was doing his best, was he? Well, that was hardly reassuring. She gave him a hard stare which she hoped made perfectly clear that she had no faith in his best and she went back into the living room and told Anand, maybe slightly too bossily, to tidy his things before he went home.

After Jeremy and Anand had left, she sat down with her new laptop and did some more research. Her computer classes at the library had been a godsend; now she could work on her plan in the comfort of her armchair and in complete secrecy too. She had so much to get ready.

❧

A fortnight later, she saw Anand again. He was full of his new school – Sylvia had bought him his first satchel – and he seemed already to have forgotten all about America. He told Sylvia about his new teacher, Miss Mackerel, and his new friends Baz and Sky (was that possible?) He didn't seem to have done much reading or writing or sums yet but he had learnt a rousing song about a yellow bird high up in a banana tree which he sang lustily for her from beginning to end.

It was only when Sylvia asked him casually whether there had been any word from his mother's friends in America that his face fell and he told her sadly that he and his mother were going back to America again for Thanksgiving.

Sylvia blurted out, "When is Thanksgiving?"

Anand didn't know but he knew it was not long to go. Panic-stricken, Sylvia hurried into the kitchen and looked it up on her calendar; late November. Unsteadily, she came back into the living room and looked at Anand playing on the floor. Thanksgiving was less than two months away. It was a hugely important festival for Americans, she knew that; the sort of occasion on which life-changing decisions might be made public, engagements announced. With mounting horror, Sylvia realised that the crisis was upon her; much sooner than she had anticipated, the moment had arrived when she was going to have to put her highly problematic plan into action. She felt sick. She had imagined comfortably that she had at least until Christmas before she would have to do anything irrevocable. Yet here they were, at the end of September and the moment was now. She felt light-headed and she began to perspire. But she looked fixedly at her grandson and imagined an empty space where he was playing. After that, everything came relatively easily.

Gripping the sides of her armchair with sweating hands, she asked Anand in a bright conversational voice, "Tell me dear, do you have your own passport? Or do you travel on Mummy's?"

Anand answered proudly, "I got my own new passport for going to Florida. Mummy carries it but I give it to the passport man myself."

"Lovely," Sylvia said faintly. "And does it have a nice picture of you inside? Have you got any stamps in it?"

"Yes," Anand said eagerly, "a big American one shaped like an egg in blue and red ink with writing in the middle."

"Ooh," Sylvia said, "I'd love to see your passport." Now she knew she was blushing. "Do you know where it's kept? Do you think you might be able to bring it over here one time to show me?"

Anand nodded. A few moments later, he asked, "Have you got one of Grandma's special surprises for tea today?"

Sylvia said that yes, fortunately she had and, together, they went into the kitchen to get the surprise out. She thought it best not to say anything more about the passport for now. Already, she was consumed with guilt at what she was about to do; beginning with manipulation and deceit, she was going on to lies, outright dishonesty and ultimately cruelty. She reminded herself that it was all for Anand's good. A strange sepia-tinted image came into her mind of Ruth saying goodbye to her parents on the railway station in Berlin in 1939. Sometimes, for the greater good, something terrible had to happen.

After Anand had gone, Sylvia went into his bedroom and took out her suitcase with the transfers of exotic birds from the storage cupboard. Like a woman waiting to give birth but unsure when her labour will begin, she opened the case and started to pack it thoughtfully with all the things she would need.

Later that night, she sprang awake in panic. She was an idiot; of course Anand would tell Smita about the passport and Smita would see through her ruse straight away. She had wrecked everything, she had fallen at the first hurdle.

After a wretched day, she rang Anand at four o'clock, the time when he came home from school with his nanny. He sounded happy to hear her voice, poor mite, alone with that stony-faced Wanda, after a long day at school.

Sylvia listened to his detailed account of his day, the highlight of which seemed to have been sausages and mash for lunch. Then, she hoped casually, she said, "By the way dear, don't tell Mummy anything about showing me your passport, will you? Nor Daddy either. Promise me? It'll just be our little secret, alright?"

Abruptly, Anand said, "Bye" and hung up.

Sylvia was left wondering helplessly whether he would follow her instructions. She doubted it; he was barely five, and yet recently, since the divorce, he had shown a disturbing readiness to compartmentalise.

October was a rotten month; firstly Anand fell ill with chickenpox and Sylvia couldn't see him for a fortnight. Jeremy reported that Smita was complaining that since Anand started school, it had been a non-stop succession of bugs. Sylvia worried all day, every day that Anand wouldn't keep the secret, that he would innocently mention her sudden interest in his passport to Smita and Smita would instantly see through it. Sylvia would be branded a danger. Maybe she wouldn't be allowed to see Anand anymore. She worried herself sick. Most unusually, she even stopped eating.

To distract herself and to try and make up for the wrong she was about to do, she telephoned Cynthia. Cynthia had still not forgiven her for the terrible article which had appeared in *Art Review* soon after Sylvia had blabbered to the young woman at the gallery. But when Cynthia heard her voice, she put the phone down. She went to visit Ruth, a sad duty nowadays since Ruth's speech was so severely affected by her stroke. Sylvia tried to entertain her with stories of this and that but, without mentioning the only important topic in her life, she did not have anything of much interest to say. As the weather grew cooler, she prepared her hot weather clothes.

At the beginning of the October half term, she got to spend a whole day with Anand, the first time she had seen him for a month. It had been supposed to be Jeremy's day with him but Jeremy had unexpected work commitments. He brought Anand over to Sylvia unusually early, for breakfast and left in a great hurry, warning her that he would not be back until late. Sylvia could not have been happier. She made Anand a splendid breakfast with bacon and eggs and milk in his hippo mug. She decided not to say anything at all about the passport until it was time for Anand to go home. Then she would remind him, firmly.

It was really too cold to play out in the gardens and Anand wasn't in the mood for the zoo or the aquarium so they decided to spend the morning quietly at home and go to a film in the afternoon.

It was only towards lunchtime when they were finishing a rather bothersome jigsaw puzzle that Anand fished in his little rucksack and said, "Oh, I forgot. Look, I brought you my passport to show you."

"Oh glory," said Sylvia. She stood stock still and gaped at the passport.

"Don't you want to see it?" Anand asked, thrusting it at her.

"Oh," Sylvia said. "Yes. Of course I do."

She took the passport in suddenly shaking hands and leafed through it, pretending to be absorbed in its pages.

Anand came and stood next to her. "Look, that's the American stamp and that's my photo. And here, in the back, these are the names of the two important people to telephone in an em-er-gency: Mummy and Daddy."

He looked up at her. "Why are you shivering?"

Sylvia put her arm around him. "Because I'm cold. Warm me up."

Anand snuggled obligingly against her. Holding him close and doing her best to subdue her trembling, Sylvia said, "You know, I've had a wonderful idea where we can go this afternoon. Much more fun than the cinema."

Anand had not taken much persuading. Of course, a taxi, an airport, a plane; what self-respecting little boy would pass up on all that in favour of a cartoon? He seemed less enthusiastic about their destination so Sylvia played that down. She concentrated on the attractions of the airport and the ride out to it. She had to make a number of urgent phone calls of course – to the airline, to the minicab company – so, even though she disapproved of too much television, she sat Anand down in front of it while she rushed around, her teeth chattering, her heart hammering alarmingly, trying to remember everything she was meant to do.

She had not imagined their departure like this. Over the slow hot weeks of the summer, when she had hatched her plan, she had imagined a long buildup, careful preparations, not this bolt from the blue followed by a helter-skelter rush. But Sylvia was old enough to know that in life everything happens willy-nilly, regardless of the best laid plans and all you could do was simply blunder along and make the best of unpredictable circumstances. Sylvia blundered; she blundered into Anand's bedroom and lugged out the heavy suitcase, she blundered into her own bedroom and got herself ready. There was no time to tidy the flat or prepare it for a long period of absence; too bad.

Just when the minicab was due to arrive, Anand announced that he wanted lunch.

"No time," Sylvia snapped. But Anand scowled and whimpered and complained that he was hungry so Sylvia marched him into the kitchen and gave him a zoo biscuit and a glass of milk.

Anand scowled even more and said, "That's not *lunch*."

Sylvia spoke to him, she feared, rather haughtily. "You can't always manage a proper lunch Anand," she declared, "when you're having an adventure."

The minicab driver rang the bell just then which distracted Anand. He raced ahead of Sylvia down the stairs, his small rucksack bouncing on his back. Sylvia followed laboriously with both their coats, her handbag and the heavy case.

The driver, a jovial middle-aged Indian, loaded everything into the boot and when he heard they were going to Heathrow, asked officiously, "Do you have your passports?"

Anand answered proudly, "Yes" but Sylvia, on checking, realised in dismay that she had forgotten hers upstairs. How *could* she have? Hastily, she left Anand in the back of the taxi and rushed up to her flat to retrieve it. Only on the way back down did it occur to her that the minicab driver might have driven away with Anand, one abduction within another. But the cab was still waiting, with the meter running and Anand and the driver were ignoring each other. The driver had switched on a loud Indian music station and Anand was staring rather disapprovingly out of the window.

Sylvia flopped into her seat beside him and squeezed his hand. "Alright dear?" Anand nodded seriously, without smiling.

The whole way out to the airport, they barely spoke.

Sylvia was beside herself; she simply could not believe the speed with which this was happening. One moment, it seemed, she had been struggling to sort out the pieces of a tedious farmyard scene, the next she was hurtling towards an improbable destination. She was terrified too; what would Smita *do* when she found out what Sylvia had done? Jeremy would – ultimately – forgive her; of that she was certain. He would get very angry, he would go extremely red in the face, she would no doubt have to listen to a whole long lecture but he would understand her motives and he would forgive her. Of course what Sylvia was doing was in Jeremy's best interests too. But Smita's revenge would be terrible. Well, Sylvia thought, well – and she sat up straighter – let Smita reflect on why her child had been taken away from her. Despite the rising tide of guilt which threatened to overwhelm her, Sylvia reminded herself that what she was doing was for the best.

Anand looked solemnly out of the window. Sylvia wasn't sure if he was just watching the other cars or if he was feeling scared. She remembered suddenly how frightfully irritating Jeremy had always been as a child on car journeys, forever being sick. Anand didn't get car sick, thank goodness. Sylvia looked down at him fondly and mouthed, "Everything ok?" Anand nodded again, tautly, without a word.

Sylvia worried he was getting cold feet. She would reassure him at the airport; she would buy him a decent lunch and get some more books and games for the long flight. Even if they had both been in the mood for talking, the jolly raucous music blaring from the driver's radio would have made it impossible anyway.

They had told her over the phone that there were still four seats left on the six o'clock flight to Delhi, seats they held back specially in case of family emergencies such as hers. As soon as they had got their things out of the taxi, Sylvia headed briskly for the check-in desks. Anand cheered up considerably at being allowed to steer the trolley. There was virtually no queue so far ahead of the check-in time. In fact the girl at the counter told Sylvia rather bossily that it was still too early to check in for the Delhi flight and she only agreed to let Sylvia and Anand do so on account of their respective ages. She expressed surprise and slight disapproval that they had only decided to make such a major journey that very morning and Sylvia had to repeat the story she had told the airline staff over the phone; that they were flying out in a hurry because of a family emergency. Fortunately, Anand was absorbed in the workings of the scale which weighed the suitcases and didn't contradict her. Finally, after endless checking and eyebrow raising, the girl handed Sylvia their tickets and passports. Slightly superciliously, she wished them a pleasant flight.

"Now," Sylvia said to Anand. "Our adventure begins."

They got through passport control without any problem, Anand proudly handing his passport to the official himself. Sylvia took him straight to the nearest restaurant to have lunch. She could barely manage a mouthful herself but never let it be said that she didn't feed her grandchild properly. Anand cheered up visibly as he ate: battered pieces of chicken in the shape of aeroplanes, a pile of chips and lurid peas. He ate it all with great relish and chose an ice cream sundae for dessert. When it came, he was too full to eat it. Normally, Sylvia would have told him off for that sort of wastefulness but today she decided to make allowances. She scooped up a little of the bright pink ice cream herself.

After lunch, they moved to an out of the way corner of the departure lounge and settled down to wait. Their flight was not due to be called for another three hours and Sylvia worried that Anand would get bored and restless. It was a long time since she had travelled together with a small child. But at first he seemed quite content to sit and let his lunch go down and play with some frightful electronic game he always had in his rucksack. Sylvia decided to keep her store of new books and pastimes up her sleeve. It was only in mid-afternoon that Anand stopped twiddling the knobs on his little console and looked up and asked her, "Do Mummy and Daddy know what we're doing?"

"What do you mean dear?" Sylvia asked carefully.

"This," Anand said indignantly. "This *trip*. Do they *know* where we're going?"

"No," Sylvia said reluctantly. "No they don't. It'll be a surprise for them."

She could lie to everyone else, she discovered; she could not lie to Anand. She had been planning to say, "Oh yes of course they do, dear" but the words stuck in her throat.

Anand looked terribly worried. "Will I be home in time for bed?"

Sylvia exclaimed, "Anand! How could you possibly be? Think of your holiday in America; how could you fly all the way to Florida and be home in time for bed? India's even further."

Anand threatened to start crying. "I don't want to go such a long way away Grandma. When will we come home?"

Sylvia said soothingly, "It'll be a little half term holiday dear. Like when you went skiing." She told herself this wasn't a lie; she was creeping up on the truth one step at a time, like Grandmother's Footsteps.

Anand still frowned. "*When* will we tell them? They'll think we've got lost."

Sylvia reassured him. "I've left a message. Don't worry darling." The message was in an envelope on her kitchen table; Jeremy would only find it when he arrived to collect Anand some time after eight. By which time of course she and Anand would be somewhere over the Eastern Mediterranean, enjoying an airline meal with all the little compartments and heading East. She did feel distinctly uncomfortable when she imagined Jeremy ringing the bell and getting no answer. At first, he would be angry; he had had a long day and the least his mother could have done was to be at home and ready when he arrived to fetch Anand. He would let himself in crossly with his key and then he would find her note. Or maybe he would telephone her first on his way to her flat. He often did that; an impatient reminder that he was on his way, that he expected Anand to be dressed and ready, he had to be returned to his mother by such and such a time. 'Well,' Sylvia thought triumphantly, 'not tonight.'

She imagined Jeremy trying first her home phone and then her mobile and when neither answered, beginning to worry. She consoled herself; his worry would be short-lived. He would let himself in and call out, "Mum? Mum?" in case they were there but for some reason not answering the phone. Even in these undeniably dubious circumstances, Sylvia felt great pleasure as she imagined Jeremy calling out "Mum." He had gone so many years without ever calling her that. Jeremy would find the note and his worry would give way to something worse. He would tear it open and read her heartfelt handwritten five page letter and he would swear abominably. With his heart in his boots, he would have to telephone Smita.

To assuage her guilt, Sylvia put her arm around Anand and gave him a consoling smile. "Really, everything will be fine."

Anand still looked worried.

The long afternoon wore on. They made three trips to the toilets and one to a coffee shop. Sylvia read Anand two story books and unwrapped the first of the new games.

At one point, Anand looked her straight in the eye and said, "Mummy will be cross, you know."

"Oh," Sylvia said. "Do you think so?"

Nervously, she looked around the departure lounge. Even though there was realistically no possibility such a thing could happen, she half expected Smita to come charging across the lounge, calling her every name under the sun and scooping Anand up and carrying him away.

She cuddled him closer. "I think she'll understand," she said. "Eventually."

A little while later, Anand said, "I want to telephone Mummy."

Sylvia became alarmed; he wasn't going to make a scene and attract attention in the middle of the airport, was he? "I haven't got my mobile," she said – which was true. "I didn't think to bring it with me."

Anand said, reaching into his bag, "I've got mine."

"What?" Sylvia exclaimed in horror. "You have your *own* mobile phone Anand? I didn't know that."

Anand smirked. "Mummy said it was a good idea to have it for em-er-gencies. Is this an em-er-gency?"

"Certainly not," Sylvia said crisply. She refrained from criticising Smita to Anand's face but said instead, "You can't possibly telephone her now dear. She's at work and I'm sure she won't want to be disturbed there, will she? She might be in some important meeting or something. You wouldn't want her to get cross, would you?"

Anand sat glowering and fiddling with his phone.

"I know what," Sylvia said briskly. "You can telephone her to say we've arrived safely as soon as we get to Delhi."

Reluctantly, Anand put his phone back in his bag and said that he needed the toilet again.

At long last, coming up to half past five, their flight was called. Praise be, it seemed to be on time. Sylvia stood up stiffly and began to gather their scattered belongings. Taking Anand firmly by the hand, she set off on the interminable trek to their departure gate.

Joining the long queue of passengers lining up to have their boarding passes checked, Sylvia's heart leapt up; here she was, on her way back to India, after all these years. Around her, passengers in saris and chappal sandals, passengers with sleekly oiled hair and dark liquid eyes, passengers with enormous amounts of hand luggage (surely forbidden?) were shuffling forward happily, excited at the prospect of their destination. She sneaked a look down at Anand's frowning face. Oh, he would come round to it.

Ahead of them, she could see there was heavy security at the gate, hardly surprising in these sorry times. Two men and a woman in dark blue uniform, like policemen but not quite policemen, were standing next to the airline staff who were checking the boarding passes. They were watching the queue of passengers with grave expressions. Really, Sylvia thought, what good did that do? They weren't checking bags or searching passengers; they were simply standing there looking sternly up and down the line. Well, she supposed it might just possibly deter some opportunist.

The queue inched forward terribly slowly. She worried that Anand was going to demand to go to the toilet yet again and they would lose their place in the queue.

Finally, they reached the gate. Sylvia fished for their boarding passes in her handbag and, after a moment's sheer terror, retrieved them and handed them over.

"Mrs Garland," said one of the men in dark blue uniform, "would you and your grandson please come with us for a few moments?"

"Why?" Sylvia exclaimed. "We don't want to miss our flight."

The three uniformed officials seemed to be surrounding her. The woman was concentrating on Anand, smiling down at him with a business-like smile and saying, "Come along now, little fella."

Sylvia was proud to see Anand smartly put both his hands behind his back so the lady couldn't take hold of one of them.

"We just need to ask you a few quick questions," the pseudo-policeman said blandly. "It'll only take a few minutes, that's all."

They led Sylvia and Anand some way back down the long corridor they had walked to the departure gate, through a pair of swing doors marked Staff Only and into a small windowless white room where Jeremy and Smita were sitting waiting, not speaking and both deathly pale.

Anand gave a great cry of joy and, letting go of Sylvia's hand which he had pointedly taken in preference to the uniformed woman's, rushed towards them.

Sylvia stopped dead in the doorway. She could not begin to understand how this calamity had come about but she knew the game was up and that, for her, everything was over.

❧

Smita was at her desk, googling Thanksgiving traditions when her mobile rang. She and Anand were going to spend Thanksgiving with Abi's parents, the first time she would meet them. Even though she knew it would be

Thanksgiving with a Gujarati twist, she still wanted to be well up on things, not to appear unsophisticated or out of her depth. At first, she wasn't concentrating properly, she thought the call was a wrong number. A woman was ringing her from Air India; what on earth? Her mind was too full of her future to focus seriously on anything else. It had been that way for weeks now, for months.

Ever since they had come back from Florida in the summer, Smita had been totally taken up with this amazing second chance which life had given her: a new life in New York with an unbelievably wonderful new husband, a perfect job and a brilliant future for Anand too. The small blemishes in the big picture – the annoying little diva who would be her stepdaughter, her mother's ridiculous reluctance to leave Leicester for long periods of time – could all be dealt with. Now, at last, she had a real happy ending in her sights and nothing was going to get in her way.

The woman from Air India had the most irritating officious manner. "Would you please confirm," she was repeating bossily, "that you are Mrs Smita Mehta?"

Smita snapped, "I'm at work. Why are you calling me?"

But then, in sheer horror, she understood that the woman was telling her something completely inconceivable: a Mrs Sylvia Garland, she was saying in her bossy little voice, had just checked in for the eighteen hundred hours flight to New Delhi together with her son Anand and, she wanted to know, did this woman have Smita's permission to take the child out of the country?

Smita was aware she screamed. Cara, her PA, who was

eating sushi at her desk, nearly jumped out of her skin and all across the room, heads bobbed up from screens and conversations stopped dead.

"No!" Smita yelled, "No, she doesn't. You must stop her. She's completely mad."

The woman was saying something bureaucratic in her automaton's voice, something about security procedures and rules for detaining people who were not bona fide passengers but Smita screamed over her, "Stop her! Do you hear me? You've absolutely *got* to stop her. She's a danger to the child." And then she screamed, for good measure, "She may be a danger to the aircraft too."

Still shouting into her phone, she leapt up and grabbed her coat and bag. Before running out of the office, some remainder of her usual self made her stop and close the Thanksgiving article on the screen.

"Cara," she panted at her gaping PA, "I'm sorry but I have to run somewhere. There's a major major emergency."

She ran out of the office. She knew people were staring and wondering. They would pump Cara, who was a chatterbox at the best of times, for a full account of what Smita had screamed down the phone. To her surprise, Smita couldn't care less.

She stood on the pavement outside the Gravington Babcock building and nothing in the world mattered anymore apart from Anand. Her phone had cut out in the stairwell and when she tried to call the Air India woman back, it turned out she was ringing from a withheld number. Terror took hold of Smita. Her head was spinning. She could hardly think. How had this *happened*? Anand was spending the day with *Jeremy*, it had been agreed. Nothing had been said about Anand seeing Sylvia. Was this a conspiracy? The Air India clerk had not said anything about it but was Jeremy at the airport too?

Smita tried to call Jeremy but his phone went straight to voicemail. Why was she ringing him? She was wasting valuable time; she had to get to the airport as quickly as possible. She checked her watch; it was quarter to three and the flight would leave at six. There was still time. She mustn't totally panic and lose her head. A taxi would get her to the airport by four, worst case scenario by four thirty, before the rush hour traffic anyway. She would run straight to the Air India check-in desks, she would make the biggest scene of her life. They were responsible of course; they had let Sylvia and Anand check in for the flight. If they had suspicions, why hadn't they called her *first*? Now Sylvia and Anand were through passport control and of course Smita didn't have her passport with her. Would she even be able to go after them? Should she go home and get her passport quickly first – just in case? No, that would only lose valuable time; it was in completely the wrong direction. She had to get to the airport as quickly as she could and, once she was there, she would solve things somehow. She would involve the police if need be. This was a kidnapping after all, a *crime*. Sylvia should end up in prison. She would never ever be allowed to see her grandson again.

Shaking with fear and fury, on the verge of tears, Smita

stepped out into the street to hail a taxi. Fortunately, there were always loads of them round here.

She said to the driver, "I need to get to Heathrow as quickly as possible please."

He appeared unconcerned – as if distraught women with no luggage asked him to get them to Heathrow as quickly as possible every day of the week. "Which terminal?" he asked.

Smita panicked. Of course she had no idea. "Air India," she said. "The Delhi flight. Which one would that be?"

The driver shrugged. "Not a clue, love. There's hundreds of flights. We can't possibly keep track of them all. Check your ticket."

"I haven't got a ticket," Smita snapped. "I'm going to meet someone."

She leant forward. In an instant, she was her usual self again. She pointed at his radio. "Ask your controller."

The driver checked his rear view mirror and leant forward and said, "Air India. Delhi. Someone tell me which terminal?"

A babble of voices responded, "Three."

The driver said to Smita, "You'll know for next time."

She sat back in her seat and looked out of the window and ignored him. For a moment, she considered telling him what was happening to her; how her little five-year-old son was being kidnapped and, if he didn't get her to the airport in time, her little boy would be whisked away to India, of all places, by his lunatic grandmother. But she was embarrassed; it was a horrible humiliating feeling to be at the centre of a soap opera. Feeling even more embarrassed, she thought of Abi. She was sure nothing so luridly out of control had ever happened to him. Everything in Abi's life seemed so beautifully organised; his divorce had been smooth and amicable, his ex-wife was apparently reasonable, she conveniently already had a new partner herself and she had agreed with no fuss to Alisha coming to Florida with her father to meet Smita. There was no crazy ex-mother-in-law waiting in the wings to wreak havoc.

Smita had a sudden flashback to Alisha sitting crouched at the edge of the swimming pool, whining about Anand and Smita to her mother on her pink mobile phone. Of course; Anand had a mobile now too. Smita had given it to him as a security thing when he started school. But because she was worried about the health implications, she had forbidden him ever to use it except in an emergency. He had actually never called her on it although she had once or twice, for fun, called him. Fumbling in her agitation, she called Anand's number but it rang and rang with no answer. She knew it was charged and switched on because she had thought to check it before sending him off with Jeremy in the morning. So why didn't the child answer? Had Sylvia, who disapproved of mobiles, confiscated his phone? Or was there some other sinister reason why he couldn't talk to her?

Desperately, Smita called Jeremy's number again. Of course this nightmare was all *his* fault. He had tricked her; he had told her *he* would be spending the day with Anand, he had never said a word about his mother. Smita knew that somehow or other Anand still saw a good deal of his other grandmother, on days when he was supposed to be with his father but his father was too busy. When she was in the US, she knew that Anand sometimes spent whole days with Sylvia which she resented intensely but arguing with Jeremy about it was so unbelievably aggravating that sometimes she just couldn't be bothered.

Smita believed Jeremy had a blind spot where his mother was concerned. It was perfectly obvious to anyone who had spent as much time with the two of them as Smita had that Sylvia did not have natural maternal feelings for her son. Smita had realised that much long ago. It was doubtless part of the reason Sylvia so ridiculously over-compensated with Anand. Not that she could ever make up for the wrong she had done to Jeremy. But Jeremy had some sort of deep-seated hang-up about his mother. Despite all the self-pitying stories he had told Smita over the years about his lonely childhood and his distant party-going mother, in some inexplicable stubborn way, he still had her on a pedestal. When he and Smita argued about Sylvia, he would always defend her. It was sick, Smita had often thought angrily, it was simply sick to be so loyal to someone who had treated you so badly.

Two things had made it incredibly much worse of course: Roger's death and the arrival of Anand. Once Sylvia became a widow, Jeremy's sense of duty knew no bounds. Whatever Sylvia wanted, Sylvia got, whatever the cost to Smita, to Jeremy and, ultimately, to their marriage. Smita had raged about it often enough but got nowhere; Jeremy would dig his heels in, go all quiet and long-suffering and do exactly what Sylvia demanded. And then

Anand had become the battleground. To Smita's disgust, Jeremy seemed to share Sylvia's delusion that she could make up for her past failings as a mother by becoming a wonderful grandmother. Well, that was bullshit. On this Smita and her mother agreed absolutely; Sylvia's child-rearing methods were simply crazy. And now, sitting in the taxi, on the verge of throwing up from sheer nervous tension, Smita had this one small satisfaction; they had been right.

She checked her watch for the hundredth time. Should she call her mother? Would she have, through her vast network of Gujarati connections, some contact at Air India, somebody at Heathrow who might be able to help? No, she didn't want her drama broadcast to the entire extended family. Besides her mother might have a heart attack, her mother who loved Anand selflessly, who would never ever in a million years do what Sylvia had done.

Smita suddenly remembered the day Anand was born, the glow of happiness briefly darkened by Sylvia's visit with her bizarre gift: that weird, unsafe mobile with all the dancing Indian figures. It was like the moment in the fairy tale when the wicked fairy appears at the cradle with her poisonous blessing. It had been a clue to all the wickedness which was to follow, all the wickedness which had come to such a hideous climax today.

The taxi plunged into the nasty orange Heathrow approach tunnel and Smita checked her watch again: ten past four. She had almost two hours ahead of her to rescue Anand. Please, please let it be enough. She gripped the armrest and leant forward, getting ready to race from the taxi the minute it stopped. She was in such a state she could hardly get the fare out of her wallet. It cost a bomb but she didn't care.

Before the taxi had even come to a halt, she had her seatbelt off and was pushing at the door handle, urging the driver to release it. She leapt out and thrust her wad of ten pound notes at him through the window. Thank God she had happened to go to a cashpoint that very morning.

Inside the terminal, she frantically scanned the indicator boards near the entrance; Air India seemed to have dozens of check-in desks. She noted the range of numbers and began to run towards them.

Of course there were massive queues at the check-in desks, massive chaotic queues with ridiculous amounts of luggage. Smita pushed forward through them, repeating mechanically, "Excuse me, emergency, emergency, excuse me." People meekly let her through, no-one objected and she reached a desk where a sulky-looking girl was checking in an elderly couple with enough luggage for a huge family. Smita interrupted them. "Sorry. Sorry. My name's Smita Mehta. I'm here about my *son*. I don't know who I need to talk to?"

The girl's sulky face lit up. She stood up and called out, "She's here. The mum's here."

All up and down the row of check-in desks, the counter staff raised their heads and looked eagerly at Smita. Hot with embarrassment, Smita understood that she was the excitement of the day; the mother of the would-be kidnapping victim.

"I'll call my supervisor," the check-in girl said busily to Smita and, to the elderly couple, "Wait just a moment."

The supervisor came over briskly, a short plump woman squeezed into a too-tight uniform. She turned out to be the owner of the officious voice on the phone and she said bossily to Smita, "Please come with me quickly."

"I came as fast as I could," Smita said defensively, annoyed that she seemed to be somehow at fault here.

The woman threw her a sideways look as she led her away from the crowds at the check-in counter. Smita knew that look; it said, "Bad Mother" and it made her livid.

Showing a staff pass, the woman led her through some anonymous double doors into a drab part of the airport which was obviously not open to the public.

"Your ex-husband is already here," she announced smugly. "He came by Tube."

Smita exclaimed. "How come?"

"We called him," the woman answered coolly. "Both numbers were in the child's passport and, to be on the safe side, my colleague and I called both."

Smita calculated quickly: Jeremy had been summoned, so he hadn't been here all along, he wasn't part of the conspiracy. But that didn't excuse him; *he* had been supposed to be spending the day with Anand, not palming him off on his mother behind her back. If he had done what he was meant to, none of this would have happened. This time she was literally going to kill him. And how *typical*, how absolutely bloody typical of him – even in the direst emergency – to take the Tube. He was so *mean* and always accusing *her* of extravagance too. He had wanted to send Anand to the local state primary. He said it would be good for him to mix with a range of different children. Well, she didn't *want* him to mix with a range of different children, thank you very much. She had heard the horror stories. If Anand's father was too mean to pay for him to go to a good school, she could perfectly well do it herself, thank God, out of her own pocket.

Abruptly she asked the woman, "How come my ex-mother-in-law even *has* my son's passport?"

The woman shrugged.

Struggling to control her anger so as not to lose face, Smita asked the woman, "Where are they now?"

To her horror, the woman answered, "We don't know exactly. They are somewhere airside, waiting for their flight to be called."

"But someone needs to stop them," Smita exclaimed. "I'm telling you; that woman is dangerous."

"There is a procedure," the woman replied, incredibly patronisingly, Smita thought. She surprised herself by thinking sharply, 'I suppose you say that to your husband in bed, do you?'

"We know from experience," the woman went on, "that if people become alerted to the fact that we are after them while they are still at large in the airport, there is a risk that they will flee. We normally intercept them at the departure gate."

Smita felt the urge to hold Anand in her arms so powerfully that she was ready to cry. "So where are we going?" she asked desperately. "Where are you taking me?"

"Aviation Security," the woman answered smartly. "Your ex-husband is waiting there."

That was enough for Smita to pull herself together; she had to be on top of this.

The woman led her to an unmarked white door in an unmarked white corridor, somewhere – it seemed to Smita – in the middle of a labyrinth. She knocked officiously and waited for the door to be opened. A woman in uniform, something like a policewoman but not quite a policewoman, answered the door. When she saw Smita, she said, "Oh good" but in a neutral business-like way, without smiling. She opened the door for Smita to come in and thanked the Air India woman. Smita knew she should thank her too – the woman was standing waiting for Smita's thanks, she was the important person who had averted disaster – but Smita decided to snub her and went straight inside without saying anything.

Jeremy was sitting there, looking sick. When he saw Smita, he flushed deep red and she saw him stiffen for the onslaught. There would have been an onslaught too, worse than anything she had ever put him through before, but of course with the policewoman standing there and a policeman – or someone like a policeman – sitting at a desk in front of Jeremy, Smita had to control herself and make do with throwing Jeremy the nastiest look she could manage. She was pleased to see him flinch.

"We need to ask you a few questions Mrs Garland," the policeman said.

Smita snapped, "My name is Mehta, Smita Mehta. I'm

not Mrs Garland." She didn't look at Jeremy but she thought she sensed him cringing.

The policeman seemed unconcerned by his mistake. He continued monotonously, "First of all, would you please confirm your relationship to Anand Garland?"

"For God's sake!" Smita exploded. "I'm his *mother*."

Unruffled by Smita's reaction, the policeman continued, "Do you have any ID?"

Smita nearly erupted again and it didn't help that Jeremy said in a low voice, "I had to go through the same thing" as if Smita was being irrational and hysterical.

She threw him another vicious look, took her wallet out of her handbag and smacked it down on the desk in front of the policeman. "Take a look. Everything's in there."

He went through her wallet calmly, took down the details of her driving licence and handed the wallet back to her. "Would you please confirm your relationship to Mrs Sylvia Garland?"

Smita burst out, "I don't *have* a relationship with Sylvia Garland. She used to be my mother-in-law."

"So," the policeman said doggedly. "She is Anand's grandmother?"

Smita snapped, "Obviously."

It seemed to Smita the policeman and the policewoman, who was standing next to Smita, exchanged glances.

"Listen," Smita said desperately. "The flight leaves in less than an hour and a half. Why are you wasting time asking me all these pointless questions instead of going after them and rescuing my little boy?"

"We'll intercept them at the departure gate," the policeman said woodenly. "Don't worry. We just need to make sure we have things absolutely straight first."

"But you *have*," Smita implored him. "You have. There's no grey area here; she's kidnapping him."

"So my next question is this," the policeman said calmly. "Do you want to press charges?"

Smita said, "Yes."

Jeremy, surprisingly loudly and firmly, said, "No."

They looked at each other.

"No," Jeremy repeated loudly. Smita could see he was perspiring.

Smita turned away from him. "*I* will certainly want to press charges," she said, "so can we please keep that option open?"

From beside her, the policewoman spoke up unexpectedly. "Will we be arresting Mrs Garland at the gate or just bringing her quietly back here together with your little boy?"

Jeremy said furiously, "You are not to arrest my mother." And then, "Smita, please, why are you doing this? Think of the effect on Anand."

"Think of the effect on Anand of what your mother's done already," Smita snapped. She sat back in her chair. "Fine. Just bring them back here first and then we can decide. When I see what sort of a state Anand is in."

After a few more infuriating questions, the police pair went out and Smita and Jeremy were left on their own.

Jeremy said, "Look Smi, I'm sorry."

Smita rounded on him. "I bet you're bloody sorry. But

not as sorry as you're going to be by the time I'm through with this. How *dare* you dump him at your mother's without telling me? I know you've done it before, probably loads of times, thinking you could get away with it. Well, not any more. Neither of you is ever going to be allowed anywhere near Anand again."

Jeremy said, "You can't do that."

"Watch me," Smita snapped. She turned her back on Jeremy and glared at the wall.

After a couple of minutes, Jeremy said, "I think she did this because she's so upset about your taking him to America. She thinks she won't ever get to see him again."

"Well, she won't ever get to see him again *now*," Smita answered "and whose fault is that?"

"America!" She went on furiously. "She's upset about *America*? What about taking a five-year-old child to *India*? He hasn't had any vaccinations, has he, she probably hasn't got malaria tablets either, she's *endangering* him. I don't care what pathetic excuses you come up with; the minute I get him back, I'm calling my solicitor and I'm going to make bloody sure neither of you can get anywhere near him ever again."

"I will fight you," Jeremy said solemnly, "every step of the way."

They waited in painful silence for about forty minutes until, without warning or any sound of approaching footsteps, the door opened and Anand appeared in the doorway.

With a great cry of joy, he ran forward and Smita and her child hurled themselves into each other's arms.

She had not registered anyone else in the doorway. But once she held Anand, once she could see he was himself and fine, she looked up at Sylvia who was standing turned to stone in the doorway, surrounded by policemen and hissed at her, "You're *mad*. What were you *thinking* of?"

Jeremy stepped forward. Oh, of course, he was going to take his mother's side now too, was he?

Smita snapped at him, "I don't want to hear a word from you."

She hugged Anand closer. "I'll work out how I'm going to deal with this," she said softly to Sylvia, keeping her voice low so as not to upset Anand. "But I hope we never see you again."

Anand cried out shrilly, "No, no!" He wriggled out of Smita's arms and dashed over to his grandmother. Clutching her round her broad stripy skirt, he pleaded, "*I* want to see Grandma again. It was only a little half term holiday. *I* want to see Grandma again."

Jeremy spoke up. He doubtless meant to diffuse the situation. "Hey Anand, what about a hug for me?"

But Anand, overwhelmed by all the conflicting demands on him, let go of his grandmother and began to scream. Flailing his arms and drumming desperately with his feet, he spun round and round, screaming hysterically.

The policewoman, who was still standing in the doorway, surveyed the mess they had made of Anand's childhood and commented censoriously, "Poor little mite."

ও

After the fiasco at the airport, Sylvia didn't get out of bed for two or three days. She had no reason to and, if she had, she would have had to confront the contents of her flat, the little hidey-hole she had created for Anand away from his unsatisfactory parents. She would have had to face the unbearable fact that Anand was, most probably, never coming back there. So she stayed in bed, weeping and vaguely contemplated suicide. When she absolutely had to, she tottered to the bathroom, drank from her tooth mug and averted her eyes from the plastic turtles round the edge of the bath.

No-one telephoned. She knew there was no possibility of Smita phoning; her revenge would be served cold, long distance and Sylvia dreaded it. But she half expected Jeremy to call; to tell her off some more, to berate her yet again for all her multiple shortcomings and, funnily enough, she would have welcomed it.

She lay and in the distance heard the gloomy inhabitants of Sutherland Avenue going about their gloomy business. She understood that the colossal mistake which she had made was just the latest in a lengthy catalogue of mistakes. What had come to an end a couple of days ago at the airport had begun thirty-five years ago in a nursing home in New Delhi.

She had not clutched onto Anand and tried to take him for herself just because she had lost her husband and little Anand had obligingly come along to replace him. The truth which faced her now from her bedroom ceiling was deeper and darker and more shameful than that. She writhed as she remembered it.

Roger was of course largely to blame. Even though, in the five years since Roger's death, Sylvia had done her best to remember only their happiness, the long stretches of their marriage when everything was going swimmingly, she supposed it was inevitable that the bad times would sooner or later return to trouble her. You were not meant to speak ill of the dead. So she hadn't; she had pretended that their marriage had consisted only of its jolly, well-intentioned beginnings and then the long calm period of companionship which had finally come upon them – perhaps from exhaustion – in middle age. Everything which had come in between she refused to remember.

Now though – for why should *she* bear the blame for what had gone wrong alone? – she let herself consider Roger's part. She cried as she lay and let herself remember what had stopped her from being a good mother to her own son. The tears ran round the back of her neck and reminded her of sweat and suffering in hot countries.

There must have been others before PeeJay Clarke, must have. Not that Sylvia had ever found any evidence of them but, after the move to Hong Kong, they were so often apart, she and Roger. He was forever travelling for the firm, visiting their construction sites all over South East Asia and she was stuck on her own in Hong Kong week after week. Then, a few years down the line, there had been all her trips to London for the fertility treatment which wasn't yet available in Hong Kong. What had Roger got up to on his own in the heat and humidity all that time Sylvia was away, with her legs up in stirrups in Harley Street?

She had found out about PeeJay Clarke in the most

shocking way while she was expecting Jeremy. The treatment in London, which had cost an arm and a leg, had paid off and, after ten years of waiting, she had, rather disconcertingly, fallen pregnant. It had taken so long that, by the time what she thought were her wishes came true, she wasn't really sure anymore if she wanted a child after all. She had got used to her leisurely life, she rather liked her freedom. The period when she had envied her friends their adorable babies and toddlers was over; they weren't babies and toddlers anymore but far less appealing ten- and twelve-year-olds with shrill voices, grubby habits and non-stop demands. Some of them had already been sent away to boarding school. There was Sylvia, rather taken aback, with her big tummy, preparing a nursery.

Because of her age, the doctors told her to take it easy: no swimming and no tennis. Although nowadays 32 seemed to be a perfectly normal age to have a first baby, then it was considered rather elderly. In fact that was what the doctors had called her: "an elderly prima gravida". "An elderly prima ballerina", she and Roger had joked as she waddled around in the heat in her tent dress on swollen legs. Not allowed to exert herself in any way, she had no choice but to sit around the house all day, getting bored and fat. The move to India when she was four or five months pregnant hadn't helped of course; leaving her jolly circle of Hong Kong friends, starting afresh with all the Delhi coffee mornings had made her rather moody.

The last straw must have been the troubles she developed in the later stages: panicky little false starts to labour which meant she had to keep being rushed into hospital and then kept in there for a week or two at a time. Marital relations, as dear old Dr Daruwallah so quaintly put it, were strictly forbidden.

It was after one of those hospital stays that she found out about PeeJay Clarke. The doctors had told her one lunchtime that she was free to go home and, rather than get Roger from work yet again, Sylvia decided simply to call a taxi and make her own way home.

She was a bit surprised to find the front door unlocked but the maid was sometimes careless. She went into the kitchen to get a glass of cold water and spotted in the middle of the floor something small, bright pink and shimmery. When she bent with difficulty to pick it up, she saw it was a pair of silky knickers. She considered them for a moment, still thinking that they had something to do with the maid, when from the verandah beyond the kitchen she heard the most peculiar noise. It was half way between a laugh and a gasp. Very quietly, Sylvia walked over to the glass doors which led onto the verandah, imagining that she was about to catch the maid up to some sort of mischief. But what she saw, waving in the air from the sun lounger, were the fleshy pink legs of PeeJay Clarke and jigging away between them Roger's familiar backside.

The shock nearly felled her. She had to hold onto the door frame as a giant spasm gripped her belly and she let out the most ear-splitting wail.

Was it any surprise if after that Sylvia had blamed the baby? If it hadn't been for her pregnancy and all the problems it had caused, Roger might never have strayed.

When Jeremy was born, less than a week later, Sylvia had a shameful urge to ask the midwife to take him away. Even though Roger was contrite, swore he would never do such a filthy thing again and Peejay was already on a flight back to London.

Sylvia hadn't forgiven Roger, not for years and she hadn't really forgiven Jeremy either. When Roger brought her and the baby back from the nursing home and she found herself stuck with a small uninteresting creature who did nothing but scream and soil its nappy, her resentment grew. Everyone else was out partying, including Roger; only she was stuck at home.

In due course obviously, Jeremy grew. He developed into a delightful though clingy toddler and then a well-behaved little boy. But there was something about him which always got on Sylvia's nerves somehow, however hard the poor boy tried. It was no excuse that Roger found Jeremy aggravating too; the little boy was such a sissy, always frightened, always shy, not at all the sort of son Roger had anticipated.

With her grandson, Sylvia imagined that life had given her a second chance but she had bungled it.

When her phone finally rang, on the morning of her third day under the covers, it was the last person in the world she expected to hear from: Naisha.

"Sylvia!" She exclaimed purposefully. For an unrealistic moment, Sylvia hoped that Naisha was simply ringing by chance, that she knew nothing at all about the shameful episode at the airport. That was, of course, ridiculously implausible.

"I am very cross with you," Naisha began solemnly as if she were addressing a small child. "When Smita told me what you had done, I couldn't believe it. Couldn't *believe* it! How could you *do* such a thing? Try to take our little boy away to India?" And, her voice rising shrilly, "What were you *thinking* of?"

Sylvia drew a laboured breath. Wearily, she said, "I meant well."

"*Meant* well?" Naisha repeated indignantly. "*Meant* well? What on earth do you mean?"

Sylvia pondered; what did she mean? "I meant him no harm," she said very softly so that Naisha, whose hearing wasn't what it once was, had to order her, "Speak up! I can't hear you."

Sylvia repeated weakly, "I meant no harm."

"You *meant* no harm," Naisha chastised her, "but you might very well have *done* him a great deal of harm. Do you realise that Sylvia? If you had taken such a young child to India with no medical precautions?"

Sylvia's heart lurched. It was true; she hadn't given a thought to vaccinations and so on. What a terrible person she was. Suddenly she recalled Jeremy spluttering and protesting as she made him take his bitter-tasting malaria tablets. Well, of course, she thought foggily, she could have taken Anand to dear old Dr Daruwalla as soon as they got to Delhi. He would have given the boy his vaccinations.

Before Sylvia could answer, Naisha carried on, "Smita is beside herself, you must understand that. She is talking of all sorts of extreme measures. But I hope she will calm down eventually and not do what she is threatening to. As

331

a grandmother myself, I'm not comfortable with the idea of the other grandmother being *banned* from seeing her only grandchild. Also, from time to time, a boy must see his father."

Sylvia listened intently. Of course it was no surprise that Naisha had seized the moral high ground or that she had appointed herself the major grandmother and Sylvia the minor one. But was it possible that, from her high and mighty position, Naisha might show benevolence?

"Prem always had a soft spot for you," Naisha said unexpectedly. "Whatever anyone else said, he always insisted you were a good person. And, for his sake, I am going to try and make sure you can still see Anand from time to time. But first you must promise me, promise me Sylvia, that you will never *ever* try to do such a thing again."

Sylvia said weakly, "I won't."

"Good," Naisha said firmly. "Good. Well, in that case, I hope that in due course my daughter will come round. Of course, you will only be able to see Anand together with me, you understand that, I'm sure?"

"Of course," Sylvia said faintly.

"So let us hope," Naisha said briskly, "that before too long, once poor Smita has recovered from this dreadful shock, something can be worked out." She gave an artificial cry. "My goodness me! Is that the time? I must rush."

Sylvia cleared her throat. "Thank you Naisha," she said just as Naisha rang off.

Naisha's phone call gave Sylvia the strength to get up. In the distant future, albeit in humiliating circumstances, she would see Anand again. She washed and dressed and ate a meal although what meal it was she couldn't say. She tidied away Anand's toys and the farmyard jigsaw puzzle which was still lying where they had abandoned it, it seemed months ago. Then she sat in her armchair and for the second time since Roger's death, wondered how on earth she would make a life for herself now. She had done it once; she supposed, if she could only summon the energy, she could do it again. But, apart from Anand, what in life was worthwhile? Should she take up some hobby perhaps, something soothing and creative, pottery maybe or painting on silk? No, why would she compete with Cynthia?

Of course Anand would not stay a five-year-old child for ever. He would grow up and when he was older, he would make up his own mind; no one would be able to stop him coming to see his favourite grandmother. When he was ten or twelve, he might come by himself. That left her five to seven years to wait.

Sadly, she considered the remnants of her life in London: poor dear Ruth, now bed-ridden and barely able to communicate, Heather Bailey, her life unexpectedly taken over by an absolute invasion of grandchildren. Her daughter's marriage had come undone and, without warning, she had arrived on her mother's doorstep in London with her three impossibly noisy and badly behaved children who had looked so yearningly sweet far away in their photographs but proceeded to wreck Heather's flat and life. The daughter made Heather attend AA meetings. From time to time, Heather would escape to Sylvia's flat for a few forbidden drinks. Sylvia used to feel sorry for Heather. It must be hard to go from a famine to a surfeit of grandchildren overnight. She had thought, rather smugly, that her illicit afternoons with Anand were pretty near perfect. But now the thought of having to listen to Heather's complaints infuriated her; how dare Heather complain when she had her grandchildren with her round the clock? What wouldn't Sylvia give right now for just one hour with Anand?

Sylvia wondered how long it would be until she could make up with Cynthia. Since that terrible article had appeared in *Art Review*, Cynthia had refused to speak to her. She had retaliated via her paintings. A new series of canvases called "Two Sisters" had featured sentimentally in magazines and Sunday supplements over the summer. Painted in Cynthia's trademark palette of purples, blues and greens, the pictures depicted Sylvia as a scowling child, cradled and protected by a loving caring Cynthia. Sylvia's feet, grotesquely misshapen, seemed to be in the foreground of every painting: bleeding and being bandaged by Cynthia, impaled on a bent and rusty nail which Cynthia's thin fingers were delicately extracting. Sylvia shuddered; she supposed she would have to buy one and hang it on her wall before Cynthia would forgive her.

When the telephone rang again, she assumed it was Naisha. Her heart leapt up at the imagined prospect of some progress; Naisha had told Smita about their conversation and Smita had relented. Sylvia could see Anand next week.

At first, she didn't recognise the voice at the other end;

it was a man and he was speaking very softly. It was only after a moment or two that she recognized the cultured voice of Siggy Greenborough and wondered why on earth he was speaking so quietly.

"I'm afraid my sister has taken a turn for the worse," he was saying softly. "If you want to say goodbye to her, you should come now."

Sylvia cried out. She was losing everybody all at once. "Where is she?" she asked, already standing up, wondering groggily where her coat and handbag might be.

"She's here at home," Siggy answered softly. "Where she wanted to be."

Sylvia staggered slightly but regained control of herself with a mammoth effort. "I'm coming," she said gently and she was pleased that, despite the state she was in, she managed to sound consoling.

After her days in bed, she felt weakened, like someone recovering from an illness herself. It took her a ridiculously long time to get ready; to smarten herself up and find her coat and shoes and handbag. The minicab company told her for some reason they were too busy to send a cab so she had to take the Tube which, with the changing, seemed to take forever. On the way, she wondered whether Jeremy and Smita had had her blacklisted by the cab company.

By the time she finally got to Overmore Gardens, it seemed to her that several hours had passed since Siggy's phone call although probably it was only one or two. She rang Ruth's bell and the street door clicked open but no one spoke to her through the intercom.

As she entered the familiar hallway, the reality of what

she was about to encounter made her suddenly falter. All the way there, the shock of being in a crowded, noisy Tube carriage after spending the past three days alone in bed had distracted her. In any case, compared with the prospect of losing Anand, the prospect of losing Ruth seemed deeply sad but in the natural order of things; swings and roundabouts. Still, even in the case of a ninety-year-old woman whose life was restricted to her own four walls, death was not for the faint-hearted and Sylvia had to pause and tell herself to buck up before she rang the bell outside Ruth's flat.

The door was opened by a stranger, a short, dapper rather rotund stranger whose appearance, despite the sorrowful expression on his face, made Sylvia feel inexplicably cheerful. She must really have been at sixes and sevens because it was only when he greeted her, "Sylvia!" that she understood who he was and responded, "Siggy!"

He gestured to her to come in and closed the front door softly behind her. He offered to take her coat. Perfect manners, Sylvia noted, even in such circumstances.

"How is she?" she asked quietly. Siggy's quietness was catching.

He turned away to hang her coat and when he turned back, he answered, "I'm afraid she's gone."

Sylvia blurted out, "Oh, I'm so sorry." She didn't know whether she was expressing her condolences or apologising for having got there too late.

"The only member of my family," Siggy said softly. "Gone."

After a pause, he gestured towards the end of the hallway and asked, "Would you like to see her?" and Sylvia knew she had to say yes.

Ruth was lying in bed, it seemed to Sylvia, already stiffening. Her face was a faintly blueish colour and, without any expression, it looked uncharacteristically severe.

"Goodbye my dear," Sylvia murmured, choked.

When she turned away from the bed, Siggy was standing in the doorway, dabbing at his eyes with a perfectly pressed handkerchief.

Sylvia said, "Let me make you a cup of tea. Is Gloria here?"

Siggy shook his head. "She left after the doctor had been."

"Well, I know my way around the kitchen," Sylvia said. "Why don't you go and sit down in the living room and I'll make us both a cup of tea."

She hoped she wasn't being too bossy but Siggy looked faintly relieved and went docilely into the living room.

Sylvia made a pot of tea and took it in on a tray together with two of the usual cups and saucers and a plate of suitably plain biscuits. There was a deliciously moist-looking ginger cake in the tin but even though Sylvia was peckish, she felt it was inappropriate to eat cake at this juncture.

Siggy seemed to have composed himself. He took his tea appreciatively, declined a biscuit and they sat sipping for some moments in silence.

Eventually, Sylvia asked, "Did it happen quickly?"

337

Siggy nodded. "Gloria noticed she was breathing in a strange way this morning and called me and the doctor and by noon she was gone."

"She didn't suffer for long then."

Siggy shook his head.

There was another silence.

Sylvia had so many questions, it felt as if her mouth was full of wriggling things. But most of them she didn't dare ask: why has it taken this long for you and me to meet? Why did you run away every time we were supposed to be introduced? That story about being marooned on the Isle of Wight; how on earth could you expect me to believe that? And the emergency callout for the Magic Circle; was that an excuse too? Why were you so elusive? What did you have against me? What did you think I would be like? And, now you've met me, am I as awful as you imagined?

Instead she asked, "Have you phoned her children? Are they on their way?"

Siggy frowned. "Simon and his wife are coming on the night flight tonight. Giselle – " he paused, "Giselle has not yet made up her mind whether she is coming."

Sylvia tutted. She remembered Ruth's difficulties with her daughter.

"She had better hurry up," Siggy added irritably. "We need to hold the funeral as soon as possible."

"Oh surely she'll come," Sylvia said soothingly. Then she remembered that Ruth's daughter had a morbid fear of flying, on top of everything else. Oh, how complicated life could be. Sylvia wondered whether Smita would allow Anand to come to her funeral.

Siggy cleared his throat. "May I ask you a favour?"

"Of course," Sylvia said eagerly. She leant forward.

Siggy hesitated. "As I'm sure you know, Ruth and I lost our religion along the way, together with everything else. But there is one tradition which I would like to keep. I think Ruth would have wanted it. After someone dies," his voice quavered, "and has been buried, the family and friends sit together for seven days to mourn them. In this case, there is no family to speak of and only very few friends left but would you be willing to come and sit with me to mourn my sister?"

Sylvia gulped. "For seven days?"

Siggy gave an almost mischievous smile. "Well, I wouldn't expect you to stay all day every day, obviously. But if you could perhaps drop in from time to time, it would be a great comfort to me."

"Of course," Sylvia agreed. "Oh, of course."

Only then a terrible thing occurred to her; Jeremy and Smita and Naisha might come looking for her and she wouldn't be at home. They would interpret her unexplained absence as another sign of instability and she would be doomed. The tiny possibility of forgiveness offered by Naisha's phone call would be snatched away. Anand would be gone forever.

She clasped her hands. "There is just one thing," she said slowly.

Siggy waited.

Sylvia said, "I'm in terrible trouble. I've done something absolutely awful."

Siggy smiled. "I can't imagine you've really done

339

anything absolutely awful, Sylvia. I'm sure it's not that bad."

Sylvia answered. "Oh yes it is." She drew a shuddering breath. "I tried to kidnap my grandson."

Siggy's eyebrows shot up. "Why on earth – ?"

Sylvia said, "It's a long story. But I'm not a wicked person. Believe me, I had my reasons."

"I'm sure you did," Siggy said. "I'm sure you did." He looked grave but Sylvia had the peculiar impression that he was struggling to restrain laughter. "How serious is it?" he asked. "Are the police involved?"

"No," Sylvia said. "At least, I don't think so."

"Because," Siggy said, with a straight face, "if you need to disappear, I'm sure I can help you. I'm a magician, remember. I'm good at disappearing tricks."

He couldn't restrain himself any longer. He burst into great peals of laughter which went on for so long and became so infectious that Sylvia helplessly joined in and they sat there, hooting away, until the tears ran down their faces.

Simultaneously, they stopped. Mopping his tears, Siggy said, "I don't mean to make light of your troubles" and Sylvia added, "I'm far too large to fit into a top hat anyway."

"Oh," Siggy said, "there are plenty of other ways of making a person vanish. If that's what's called for."

"Well," Sylvia said. "Well, actually, on balance, I think it's probably better if I don't vanish. It's true, I really am in terrible trouble with my son and my former daughter-in-law. But I think I should still be around in case they try to get in touch with me."

"Of course," Siggy said. "Of course. And I wouldn't want to impose. But if you could maybe see your way to joining me for a couple of afternoons, it would mean a great deal to me, you know."

"Will you be here?" Sylvia asked. Wearily, she imagined herself criss-crossing London on the Tube day after day.

Siggy said, "No. I think I will do it at my home in Northwood. That will be more convenient for the few people who're still around." He hesitated. "Really, there are only two or three of them. And they will just drop in. I'm sure Ruth's son will have to fly back to New York after the funeral. He won't be able to stay on for another week. To be honest, Sylvia, most of the time it will only be you and me."

Sylvia paused. Out of habit, she listened for Roger's reaction but there was none. Only after a moment or two, she fancied that she heard a distant guffaw. Although she worried afterwards that the words she had used were all wrong, she surprised herself by answering simply, "Of course I'll come. That would be lovely."